BAD FOR BUSINESS

FOR THE LOVE OF CRIME
BOOK 1

ANNA GRACE

BUG'S BOOKS

BAD for BUSINESS

To Nana and Papa, who never stopped asking,
"Where's your next book?"

Here it is.
I love you guys more than words can say.

PLAYLIST

♡ Bad for Business | Sabrina Carpenter
　♡ Supercut | Lorde
　♡ I Wish You Would (Taylor's Version) | Taylor Swift
　♡ In All Honesty | Chloe Ament
　♡ Amelie | Gracie Abrams
　♡ Since We're Alone | Niall Horan
　♡ Man! I Feel Like A Woman | Shania Twain
　♡ Nobody | Hozier
　♡ The Bottom | Gracie Abrams
　♡ Cross Your Mind | Niall Horan
　♡ Better Than I Know Myself | Del Water Gap
　♡ Sweet Talk | Saint Motel
　♡ imgonnagetyouback | Taylor Swift
　♡ About You | The 1975
　♡ Full machine | Gracie Abrams
　♡ Still The One | One Direction
　♡ Magnolia | Laufey
　♡ Linger | The Cranberries
　♡ I should hate you | Gracie Abrams
　♡ Every Single Time | Jonas Brothers
　♡ This Town | Niall Horan

♡ Complicated | Avril Lavigne
♡ Daphne Blue | The Band Camino
♡ I Hate Boston | Reneé Rapp
♡ Cool | Gwen Stefani
♡ Lover Of Mine | 5 Seconds of Summer
♡ Are You Satisfied? | Marina
♡ Rearview | Brenn!
♡ Suburban Legends | Taylor Swift

1

———

AMELIE

In a rare moment of stupidity, I've chosen my prettiest dress to scope out a rather expensive painting.

You'd think I'd be able to better curate my outfits after twenty-two years on this Earth, but I haven't found that to be the case. Yes, I know to always choose something neutral. I know I shouldn't draw attention to myself, but that isn't *fun*! Sometimes I just want to wear a puffy pink dress, regardless of how many people will see me.

Today, however, the goal is *no one*. Hence why I attempted to cover up, at least a little.

It killed me to grab a coat on the way out of my apartment. Some dingy leather jacket that Jensen keeps on our coat rack. I'd rather leave the house naked than wear black, but I didn't have time to find a better option.

The art gallery that I'm headed to—so creatively named *The Gallery*—is only three blocks away. I've got about ten minutes before these heels start blistering my feet, so I pick up the pace.

My plan is very simple: I get in, snap a photo of the piece, and get out.

It'll make our work tomorrow go much smoother.

I pop my gum as I turn the corner. The line to the museum

appears in my field of vision, and I sigh through my nose. For a Tuesday, it's a strange level of crowded. Don't people have jobs on Tuesdays? Normal jobs, anyways. Not something like I do.

Whatever. It's easier to stay hidden this way.

I wait patiently in line, fiddling with the rings on my fingers. A kid in front of me is tugging on the hem of his mom's shirt, asking for a toy out of her purse, but she keeps waving him off until they reach the front. They pay the fee and enter, and I dig a bill out of my purse to do the same. The man near the door gives me a stiff nod as I hand him the cash and walk inside.

This building is one of my most hated places on earth.

It looks so sterile in here. Canvases line every wall—which I get, because it's an art museum, but it lacks a look of chaos. The pieces are in straight, perfect rows, and they're more classical than abstract. Most are painted with brown or white acrylic; or, if you're lucky, you can spot the lightest shade of indigo.

My face is trained into what I hope is an amazed expression. I try to appear somewhat awestruck, like I'm observing this place for the first time. Like being surrounded by art is the most surreal experience of my life, something I'd pay to do again on my own free will. In reality, I'm staring numbly at these pieces. I've seen them too many times.

Only one in this building elicits any sort of positive emotion from me, and it hangs to my left.

I've never looked at this piece for anything other than enjoyment. It's off-limits to me—I'd never take an offer on it. It's the best one here, the only *good* one in my eyes, and I will not remove it from this wall.

It's simple, yet not.

A flower. That's all it is. But the closer you look, you can see that the petals and stem and leaves are made of words. *Names.* The letters are jumbled, tangled in each other and practically unreadable.

I've only been able to see *my* name amongst the others. Right in the center of the stem.

And for that reason, I've never looked at the plaque beside it.

Never looked at the piece's name or who painted it. I know that when I do, it'll be ruined, and I don't need to put a name to its creator and confirm my suspicions. I need to live in oblivion and have a sliver of joy in this place, *thank you.*

To my right is my *least* favorite painting, only because it's so bland in comparison. I am nothing if not a maximalist. Singular blotches of color are my nemesis, and this piece is made entirely of different shades of beige. *Beige!* It physically hurts to look at it. I don't even allow beige furniture in my apartment, much to my roommate's dismay. Jensen and I fought for weeks over a jade green couch—he said it was too much, I said it wasn't enough.

I won, by the way. The couch is my most prized possession.

Semi-reluctantly, I make my way toward the back where a particular painting waits for me. I move slowly, still trying to give the illusion that I care about this place, but I don't. I've memorized every corner in here, every canvas on these walls. I see them in my dreams, and I mean that in a derogatory manner.

It takes me a moment to navigate through the mass of people —seriously, who comes to an art museum at this time of day?— but I finally reach the piece.

This one? It's pretty new. Been here for a couple of weeks. We got an offer for it on the day of its reveal, so it's much past time for it to go. Personally, I couldn't be more eager to get it out of here.

I hate the look of the piece. I hate the person who painted it. I want it all *gone.*

At the base of the canvas is a stone path. Gravel. Nothing laid by hand. It's too chaotic to be intentional. The rock leads into an ocean, or maybe just a very large pond. Some body of water none-theless.

But what's unsettling, what startles me when I look at it, is the gaping black hole that seems to hide behind the water.

The part of the canvas where the sky *should* be is just...black. Jet black, like the artist thought *regular* black paint wasn't scary enough. The water seems to tunnel into the darkness until it disappears. I step closer than I've dared to before and notice a body swimming toward the void. Nearing the edge.

The air conditioning kicks on somewhere above me, and I shiver.

"A lovely painting," I mumble to myself, letting sarcasm seep into my voice. Expelling what disdain I have for this piece isn't a crime. Ripping it off the wall will be, I guess, but that's a technicality. And anyways, talking to no one in particular is fun. It's interesting to see who will listen.

In this case, a split second too late, I notice someone standing near me. He's staring at the same canvas I am, head tilted to the side. I can't make out his features, probably because I'm only viewing him through my peripheral vision. "I think so too," he says.

And that voice, low and reverent, sends goosebumps over my skin.

If he knew who he was talking to, he wouldn't be talking so freely. He would probably be escorting me out of here in handcuffs.

I don't take my eyes off what's in front of me, but I do make it a point to keep talking.

"Come around here often?" I ask stiffly, then mentally kick myself for asking that question. Are we at a *saloon*? Am I about to draw my handgun and ask for ten paces? Ridiculous!

The man takes a step forward, and I fight the urge to turn toward him. To turn away. To run directly up the wall in front of me and claw my way out through the ceiling.

"More often than I'd like," he says, and it sounds like an admission for something I don't understand. "Though it's quite nice. Atmospherically, anyways."

I bite down on my lip, fully aware that I'm ruining my lipstick. I've got to turn around. It would be a bit odd if I didn't, and the door is behind me. If I want to leave, *ever*, I literally have to turn around.

What if I just back away slowly and keep my head down? Maybe he won't find it odd.

I take a breath through my nose, the air suddenly stale.

No. I'm not going to do that. I'm going to woman up and face the man behind me.

"It is nice," I say, allowing myself a full look over my shoulder.

And when I do, when his eyes meet mine, his entire face drops.

"You," he breathes, his voice slightly strained.

I plaster on the sweetest, most patronizing grin I can muster up. "Me."

I never thought the day would come.

Henry Arlington is staring at me, completely speechless. I can't tell if he's just taking in the sight of me or if he's truly stunned. I give him a look over, only because I'm curious, and I'm absolutely aggravated at what I find.

He looks the same as he did four years ago. Classy outfit—as in, *beige* trench coat and wire-rimmed glasses. It's like looking at our high school English teacher, if Mr. Beal were younger and his life hadn't gone down the drain.

Cut jaw. Dark hair. Glassy blue eyes, hidden behind those glasses I pretend not to like. Crooked smile, if he *would* smile, which I'm not expecting whatsoever.

He's devastating.

Abhorrent.

Everything I want and everything I hate all at once.

"I don't want to talk to you," I say simply, popping my gum to tick him off. I know it's a pet peeve of his, but he shows no signs that he cares. "At all."

Henry swallows hard. "That's not—"

"It was nice seeing you."

It wasn't, but that's alright. I don't care much to tell the truth, especially not to him.

I pull my phone out of my purse and take a photo of the canvas, getting enough of the location in the gallery that Meg will get me an easy in tomorrow evening.

Even more than a few moments ago, I cannot *wait* to rip this piece off the wall.

My stomach is in knots when I lower my phone. Henry's eyes

are still on me, lips parted like he wants to say something. I don't think he will, though. Words left us long ago.

I take a deep breath and turn around, my palms sweating an embarrassing amount as I step away.

"No," Henry says suddenly, moving toward me. "Ames, let me—"

"No," I say in return, not looking over my shoulder as I basically bolt from the premises.

I'm two blocks away before realizing that he used my old nickname.

2

HENRY

Amelie Benoit is five feet ahead of me on the sidewalk.

I don't think she's aware of it. If she were, she'd probably run down an alley or spin around and question me. *Why are you following me? Have I done something to re-capture this attention of yours? Have you considered stepping in front of a taxi?*

Or maybe she'd stay silent. Brush me off like she did in the museum. I have no idea anymore.

It's taking a lot of willpower to stay where I am. To not approach her and attempt a conversation. I want to figure out what happened, *why* it happened, then promptly kiss her into oblivion like I've wanted to do since I last saw her.

Yeah. Definitely not going near that one.

Saying that Amelie and I have a past is...an understatement. It's something I try not to think about, but if I'm honest, it invades my mind every day. No matter what I do to clear my mind, I fail.

I can go to parties and events galore, and at the end of the day, I'm still curious what she's doing. If she's okay. And it's been that way for *four years*.

I used to know everything about her. Now I know exactly two things: she's an art thief, and she wants my painting. The very one we met over today. Technically, I have no proof to back that assumption, but it was almost obvious. She stared at it like it was the most loathsome thing she's ever beheld.

And with what I know about her, she's going to get it.

Amelie is unaware that I know any of this. Honestly, I'm not sure I want that to change. By the look on her face, she didn't even know I was back from school. It makes no sense—I got back a month ago, and since then, I've gotten my exhibit. It isn't fully completed, but it must be enough that she noticed my name on advertisements for The Gallery.

She probably hoped it was a *different* Henry Arlington. She seemed quite disappointed to find out that it wasn't.

Amelie turns the corner ahead of me, going to the left. Good. My penthouse is still a few blocks down, and I don't want to look like I'm following her. I'm not. I'm *aware* of her, sure. But that's only because she's been terrorizing this city—and my mind—for years.

I try to shake all thoughts of her away as I walk into my building. The doorman gives me a quick nod, one that implies he knows me and doesn't need my identification. This building is quite secure; upon entering, most people are requested to show their apartment key. If they haven't got one, they're asked to intercom their connection in the building. If *that* can't happen, they're escorted outside. It's a level of thoroughness I've come to appreciate, especially when working on something confidential.

I stick my key into the top button in the elevator. The thing takes ages to start moving, and I'm not sure why I'm counting seconds like they matter. Something about that run-in has me extremely restless.

When the doors open, I go straight to my apartment and unlock the door. I'm not shocked to see my sister sitting on my couch, but I *am* shocked to find my dad beside her.

"Hen!" Lizzy says, waving me over to the coffee table. She's been in my game closet, I guess, because she's got a 500-piece-puzzle of a tree spread out in front of her. "Come inside. Dad has been waiting for you, so we're puzzling."

"*She* is puzzling," Dad corrects, "though I'm sure she could be editing her articles right now?"

Lizzy shrugs. "Could. Won't."

I fight the grin that I know would get me scolded. Liz, unlike me, takes a certain pride in getting under our dad's skin. She's three years younger than me and an absolute firecracker. I try to stay on Dad's good side, only because he's my employer.

Him and I have a good thing going. We rarely speak outside of business anymore; he owns The Gallery, and I paint pieces for him to display. Our relationship is not so much father-son as boss-employee. It's been that way for years, and truthfully, I have no urge to change it.

Plus, he's more apt to disown me than he is to say a cross word about Lizzy. She sort of won the favorite child spot at a young age.

"If this is about the latest piece," I tell him, "I'm almost done. I'll have it by the end of the week."

"Good." He nods, verifying that it is, in fact, about the latest piece. "I've got an auction quickly approaching. We can display that one."

"Have you gotten any offers for me recently?" I ask, though I know he won't tell me. My dad declines all other offers I get—he wants my art in *his* museum. Personally, I wouldn't mind branching out. More publicity wouldn't be the worst thing in the world. Getting away from my dad *certainly* isn't the worst thing.

As expected, he shakes his head. "No. I assume they'll contact you, rather than me."

"Have they ever before?" Lizzy asks, looking up at Dad innocently. "I recall you saying—"

"That'll be enough, Elizabeth," he says. Liz goes back to her puzzle, giving me a quick glare before she does so. "Can I see the piece, Henry?"

I blink. "You haven't taken a look?"

"Didn't want to overstep."

"You're in my living room with a bottle of my wine."

"And I own the building."

Fair.

"Follow me," I say, removing my coat and tossing it over the back of my couch. I expect Lizzy to follow, but she starts talking to Betty, my cat, so I assume she's preoccupied.

My studio is just another room in the penthouse, and it's my most crammed. There's hardly an empty space, save for the wall made entirely of windows. It's a prize at sunset, but in the early mornings, it's blinding.

I start to fish my key out of my pocket when I realize that the studio's lock is broken.

It's been chipped away. The metal is dented and scratched around the bolt, and the door is slightly open.

"What?" I mutter, opening the door with a single push.

My heart drops when I get a look inside.

Paint is spilled all over the floor. In corners. On walls, some on the window. Brushes and pallets are strewn across the floor, and my easel is the only thing that's right where I left it.

My painting isn't.

My painting is gone.

"What *happened*?" Dad's voice rises with annoyance. I hear footsteps run into the hallway, followed by Liz's signature gasp. "I thought you kept this locked up!"

"You saw the same exact lock I did," I say, dragging my hands roughly through my hair. How did this happen?

"This is unacceptable." Dad crosses his arms. "When was the last time you worked on the painting?"

"Last night. Sometimes, I put it in the closet, but I left it out to dry. It's almost completed."

His face is drawn with aggravation. "Find it."

"I will." I have no idea how to do that.

"I need it before my event, Henry." Dad huffs. "You need it back immediately. I'm not losing out on this."

"I know. I'll go to the police tomorrow."

As soon as the words leave my mouth, I know they're a mistake.

"No," Dad says immediately. "You will not go to the police."

"What else is he supposed to do?" Liz asks, moving into the room. She steps in a puddle of spilled paint, but she doesn't seem to realize it. "It's not like he had a tracker on it."

"He will find it himself," he says, instead of offering any further guidance. "The police will be no help."

Liz scoffs. "We *both* know—"

"He will be much more efficient on his own, Elizabeth," Dad finishes, his voice final.

Neither of us decide to argue this time.

Dad mumbles something that I don't catch before leaving. I hold my breath until I hear the front door close, signifying that he's gone.

"Well, it wasn't me," Lizzy says, looking around the room. "I swear, obviously. I wasn't even here for that long before you showed up. It was only—"

"Give me a second, Liz," I say, sighing as I look around the room. The canvases in the corner are untouched, even the ones that have been painted. Only a few are fully completed, but whoever did this knew what they wanted. They didn't look through their options; they ransacked the place for show.

I sit on the floor and grimace when I land in paint. Betty trots through the door, looking wary of each paint splatter. She steps in one, meows at me like it's my fault, then curls up in my lap, leaving blue paw prints over my pants.

Liz lets out a dramatic sigh and sits down, managing to land directly in a glob of purple acrylic. "Check the footage, I guess."

I scoff. "Yes, like he'd have the cameras on."

Our father—the self-made man who has never once been satisfied—flat out refuses to leave the security cameras on in this building. He won't tell us why, but I have a good guess that it has to do with his past. It's no secret that he's had a few run-ins with the police for...a couple of financial crimes. I presume he'd like to keep himself, as well as his children, out of any further misunderstandings. Anything shady that goes on in this building will not be tied to him. If he can be oblivious, maybe he can avoid the blame.

"What's there to do besides file a report?" I ask incredulously. That was my initial *logical* response. Of course, who knows what that would really do. I have a feeling that a report for a missing painting wouldn't get high priority.

But that's my only option.

Unless...

"Lizzy," I start, my brain spinning in dangerous circles. "How mad do you think Dad would be—"

"Mad," she says instantly. "Very, judging by the look on your face. But whatever it is, I say do it."

I laugh dryly. The idea is horrible, absolutely pathetic, but I can't overlook it. It's the only thing sticking in my mind.

Amelie might know.

Amelie might help me find it.

I blink, forcing that idea away. *No. What?* She might have *stolen* it, for goodness sake. Even if I somehow got in contact with her, she wouldn't help me. There's no way.

"No," I say aloud. "I don't think I should."

But what else do I have?

Lizzy sighs and stands, still completely unaware of the paint on her legs. Or maybe she just doesn't care. At this point, I don't see how she could ignore it. "I've got to finish an article for work tomorrow. Tell me what you decide to do, Hen. I'll help you if I can."

"Thanks, Liz."

She waves over her shoulder and leaves.

I stay on the floor for a good while, Betty asleep on my lap. The ideas coursing through my mind are horrible. Absolutely awful. Not a single one would work, and they all keep circling back to Amelie.

She would know.

Fine. Maybe she would. It's impossible that she'd know the exact whereabouts, but she might have *some* knowledge, right? More than I do, surely. She has to know patterns. How these things usually go. Perhaps she'd enlighten me if I asked nicely.

She'd also hang you if she had the chance.

Yeah. There's no way this will work.

And still...I can't get the idea to leave my mind. Not completely. But then again, thoughts revolving around her never do.

3

———

AMELIE

I walk home in a complete daze.

The effect that encounter had on me is dehumanizing. I wish I could say that I'm unbothered; that seeing Henry did nothing to me, and I'll never replay our exchange in my mind again.

But that would be a lie. And while I'm not against the action, I don't feel like putting in the effort. Lying to oneself is a different feat than lying to another.

I trudge up to my apartment, taking the stairs rather than the elevator just to torture myself. I have hope that it will calm me down. Wear me out a bit. I even stopped at my favorite bakery down the street to try and quell my energy, but it didn't work.

I reach my apartment and shove my hand in my purse for my key, only to find that it isn't there. The only things I have are my wallet, a tube of lipstick, and a rollerball perfume.

And the perfume is *leaking*! Of all days.

"Come *on*!" I sigh, tapping my foot on the base of my door. Jensen is going to give me so much grief for this. "Hello? Let me in. I'm distressed."

Distressed is a loose term for my current state. I'm jittering like a madman who just snorted three lines of cocaine and downed a RedBull. Jensen is going to ask me what's going on, and I'll have to tell the truth, because if I don't, he'll manage to come up with something even worse.

What's wrong, Ames?

Oh, nothing, you know.

So you got chased by the police on the way here, tied them up in the elevator, and left them for dead?

Yeah, Jensen has the worrisome mindset between the two of us. It either makes him levelheaded or gives him gas. But I got him a cinnamon roll to make up for the added stress, so he'll be fine.

When the door swings open, I practically fall through it. Jensen takes a step back, looking at me with a deep frown. "You can't use your key?"

"Forgot it," I say, locking the door behind me. I give him the paper bag in my hand and watch his eyes light up. "Cinnamon roll."

He snatches it from me and practically tears the bag to shreds. "What did you do wrong?"

Oh, Jenny. Let me tell you something.

"I didn't do anything wrong," I say, and that's the truth. "But... something odd happened today."

"Something bad, I'm guessing."

"Eh." I exhale. "You've heard me mention Henry Arlington, right? In passing?"

He chews aggressively as he tries to register the name. It only takes him a moment to place it, I guess, because he finally says, "From high school?"

I nod.

"Vaguely."

"Okay. Well, the piece we're nabbing tomorrow is his."

Jensen gracefully chokes on his mouthful of food.

While he's attempting to breathe again, I step into the kitchen and dig a tea bag out of the cabinet, then put a pot of water on the stove. He stops hacking by the time I'm choosing my mug.

"Sorry," he says breathlessly. "Food down my throat. Anyways, I should've connected the dots. I read the file this morning, the one Meg sent over. Like, how many 'Henry Arlington's do you know?"

I know exactly one. And I wish I didn't even know *that* many.

"Yeah," I say. "It's just...it was weird."

Jensen just shrugs as he devours the last of his cinnamon roll. "It really doesn't affect us. Guess you should get in touch with Meg, though. See if she wants to make any changes."

He's right, but I really don't want to. Meg and I are friends—close enough that working this job hasn't ruined us yet. Her and Jensen, on the other hand... They've been 'on-and-off' for a few months, and any time they speak, it ends in catty arguments.

"I'll call her tomorrow," I tell him. "Has she found the floor plan yet? I got a photo of the location for her."

He gives another shrug as he wipes his sticky hands on his pants, and I cringe. Stickiness is not something I tolerate. I'd really rather tear my arms off my body than be sticky. "I'm not sure. She said she'd be by tomorrow afternoon beforehand to talk things through with me."

I narrow my eyes at him, at the wording of that statement. "With you..."

"Yeah, so, she's mad at me." He pinches the bridge of his nose and sighs. "Who's shocked? Respectfully, you women are confusing."

"No, you *men* just assume you know us."

Jensen pulls my teapot off the burner and loosens the lid. I grab a mug out of the cabinet—my favorite, with the *Breakfast at Tiffany's* movie poster on it—and make my tea while he goes on.

"I just thought it would be over by now. The arguing. Like, how back and forth can it be? We've like, *admitted* things already. Shouldn't that sort of seal the deal?"

I shake my head. "Not particularly. It can be back and forth for a long time. A very *ridiculous* time, in fact."

He rolls his eyes. Since I'm a nuisance, I pat his arm, then press my knuckles extra hard into the spot under his neck. He smacks my hand away, and I act all innocent, though I know he's sore from all the working out he does. That was his stipulation for the jade couch—I got that, and he got to turn the dining room into a home gym.

It was fine until our place started smelling like sweat. I took care of it with a few bottles of Clorox and a hazmat suit. And no, I'm not exaggerating—I still have the thing in our closet.

"Clear it up by tomorrow," I tell him, aware that isn't what he wants to hear. "Really. We can't work together when there's a rift."

Last time we tried to ignore a conflict, Meg slugged Jensen for tripping an alarm. I'm not saying what they have going on is healthy, but for some reason, they won't let it go. I consider the two of them my horribly dysfunctional, sometimes-divorced parents.

"Just talk it out," I press when he doesn't answer me. "You're both adults. Why don't you tell me what happened, and I'll help you work on your approach?"

He snorts, and I'm rightfully offended. "Yeah, no. Thanks though."

"I'm a great problem solver!" I take a sip of my tea and burn my tongue, so I abandon it on a coaster. "Come on, Jenny. Let it out."

"I don't even *know*. I think the whole 'actual feeling admission' thing screwed with us, and now…"

"Now you're two confused little angels."

"You're irritating me, but yes. I think we're just confused and angry."

I take a deep breath. This isn't what I wanted to come home to, and I *certainly* don't need it to carry into tomorrow, but I haven't got time to mend things. I'm a fixer—bordering on a control freak, per Meg. But clearly she isn't the wisest, given that she's involved with Jensen. So who can say?

"You'll figure it out," I say, more so a command than encouragement. "Just get it done by tomorrow."

He groans. "Amelie—"

"No. I'm not arguing, Jen. Call Meg, take her out for coffee, and either figure it out or put it on hold until next week. I want left out of it, but it has to be resolved."

Reluctantly, Jensen saunters off to the bedroom. There's only one *real* bedroom in this place, and he's been so gentlemanly as to let me have it. He takes three quarters of my drawer space in return, but that's fair. My clothes are hanger clothes, anyway.

I duck behind the dressing screen in the middle of our space and take off my dress, then slip into my pajamas from this morning. Once I'm clothed, I collapse onto the sofa and grab my laptop off the coffee table. I flip it open and plug it into the charger so I can research our painting for tomorrow.

Not to snoop on Henry. This is for work, obviously.

I open my inbox and click the newest email from Meg. The subject line is *Nautical Abyss,* which I assume is the name of the piece. It's a bit on the nose, really, but I suppose it could be worse.

There are three files attached to the email. The first is the museum's floor plan—apparently, she *did* complete it—and the next is a basic biography of the piece, the museum, and Henry's new exhibit. I skim it briefly before clicking on the last one.

When the image clears on my screen, I clench my jaw so hard I'm frightened for my teeth.

It's just a photo of Henry. But he's standing near his painting, and he's smiling, and it's...

Nothing. It's nothing.

I swallow and click out of that tab, tempted to chuck my laptop across the room.

"Did you see the file Meg sent?" Jensen calls from the hallway, making me jolt. His voice is so *loud.* Why does his voice carry at full volume? Is that a man thing?

"Just got it," I croak. "We're all good."

He nods and reenters the living room, now donned in what *he* classifies as dressy clothing. He's wearing jeans—they're nice ones, I'll give him that—and a sweatshirt. It was once white, but I accidentally washed it with my red one, and, well...we all know how that goes.

"You going to talk to her?" I ask, taking another drink of my now-lukewarm tea.

"Hopefully," Jensen says, grabbing his keys. "If I make things worse, then I'm blaming you, and we'll reschedule the job."

"Oh, no, we won't." I look at him pointedly. "We will *not,* Jensen Velasco. Do not test me."

He scratches his stubbly jaw. "You don't scare me. I'm more worried about what Meg is going to say when I show up at her door. It's a toss-up."

"It's Russian roulette," I correct.

He shrugs and walks out the door.

I burrow deeper into the couch and continue drinking my cold tea while scrolling through emails. I've got offers on offers on offers, all which I need to decline but don't have the guts to.

Used to, the three of us only took one or two jobs a month. It's how we stay under the radar so well—you can't trace a pattern when there isn't one. But lately...I've taken more jobs. Neither Meg or Jen like it, but I call the shots. On *their* terms, no less. They don't want to be in charge, lest it come crumbling down.

I like the responsibility. I've learned to bask in the constant adrenaline, learned to crave it.

Right now, though, I think these emails are just tempting because of how out-of-control I feel. My chest is tight, and I'm thankful this tea isn't caffeinated. I think my heart would implode if it were.

I drain the mug and set it aside. Clear out a few emails, just so I don't click one and get us into a slew of trouble. My team wouldn't even be mad—just annoyed. But I'm trying to keep the peace right now, so I can't be adding problems.

With a heavy sigh, I set my laptop on the table and grab the TV remote, then wrap the knit blanket tighter around my body. Meg's apartment is a fair distance, so even if all goes well, Jen won't be back until later tonight.

So, like the lazy bump-on-a-log that I am, I watch *Friends* until I can't think anymore.

4
____

AMELIE

I wake up with the remote pressed to my cheek and a blanket wrapped around my neck.

It's morning, I think. The TV is still on and a phone is ringing somewhere. I had no intentions of falling asleep on the couch, but after housing half of a pizza and an extra-large Dr. Pepper, it was inevitable.

I sit up and paw around the table for my phone, but all I manage to do is knock my mug onto the ground and crack the rim.

"Come *on*!" I huff, picking the thing up. Now I'm annoyed, which is not a good start to my day. It's only ten in the morning. That leaves me a lot more hours to get *more* annoyed.

I find my phone wedged between the couch cushions, and Jensen's name is flashing on the screen when I answer. "What do you want?"

"Hello. That's mean."

"I said—"

"Just thought I'd see if you were awake. It's pretty late in the day."

"It's ten o'clock," I say, but then I look around the apartment. Now that my brain is registering things, I'm realizing that he isn't *here.* I never heard him come inside last night, either. "Did you stay with Meg?"

"No, I came home," he says, just as I'm looking for him under the kitchen table. "I'm out getting groceries."

I frown. "That means you slept in my bed."

"I did. Did you get new sheets?"

"TELL ME YOU DIDN'T."

"I did," he says again. "And I rolled *alllll* over them."

I gag and set my mug in the sink. "You're horrible!"

"You took the couch. What choice did I have?"

"The *floor*?" I sigh. "Whatever. Did everything go well last night?"

"Yeah, we're good. Tonight will be fine."

"Good." His tone isn't convincing, but I know not to question it. If anyone can start something back up, it's me. Some would consider it a talent. "When are you coming back? I'm bored."

"Soon enough. Do something in the meantime."

"Like?"

Jensen gives his signature sigh of annoyance. "Wash your mountain of laundry, cook something, clean the apartment. I don't know."

"How very progressive of you."

He laughs. "I'm hanging up."

"Thank goodness."

"Love ya."

"Mhm."

The line goes dead, and I check my other notifications. There's a call and a few texts from my parents, but I don't open them right now. If I do, I'll have to respond, and I'm not ready to be social yet, even if just over the phone.

I toss my phone onto the couch and look around the apartment, hands on my hips. Much as I hate to admit it, Jensen is right —I need to do my laundry and eat something, and we have *maybe* three clean forks. Washing dishes wouldn't hurt.

But instead of doing any of that, I bake a cake, because baking cakes is the only way to avoid responsibilities.

The kitchen is clean enough that I can navigate because we aren't pigs. Dirty dishes are set aside on the counter, so I wash them while the cake bakes. I'm scrubbing an old blue plate when a heavy knock comes to the front door.

A mischievous grin curls on my lips. It appears that Jensen forgot his key after giving me grief about losing mine. I could have fun with this, really. Open the door and slam it back. Get his hand caught near the lock. The possibilities are endless.

"Coming!" I sing, peeling my dish gloves off. I'm still in my pajamas, and my hair is bunched up on top of my head, but I don't care. I fling the door wide open, because it's *Jensen*. The poor guy has seen me looking much worse than I do right now.

Except...it's not Jensen.

It's Henry Arlington.

I make an inhuman squealing noise and duck behind the door. First of all, he doesn't need to see me like this, and second, I don't *want* to see him! How did he even find me? What is going on?

"I'm not here!" I squeak, yanking my hair down from its knot. I drag my fingers through the tangled mess, trying to look presentable, though I have no intention of opening this door again. I will die here, and they will say that I died with dignity.

"Amelie," Henry says, and just the sound of his voice sends chills over my arms. "Please open the door."

My heart is racing so fast that I'm shocked I can hear him over the blood pumping in my ears. "No. I said, I don't want to talk to you."

"Okay. *I* want to talk to you."

I wish that didn't pique my curiosity. I wish that I was stronger, that I had more resistance. But I'm not, so I open the door wider and look at him.

And that is my first mistake.

I should've kept talking to him through the door, because looking at him makes this ten times worse. I'm focusing on things that are *not* of utmost importance, as in, his entire face.

"How did you find my apartment?" I ask, incredulous. "How..."

He clears his throat. Works his jaw. "I just...I had to see you."

"That doesn't answer—"

"I think I need your help."

My jaw drops.

The correct response is to decline, obviously. To laugh in his face and close the door. But instead, I'm frozen, because that wasn't what I expected. What *did* I expect? An apology? An explanation?

I think I need your help.

Well, that's not happening.

"No, I don't think so." I cross my arms, suddenly aware of the state that I'm in. My pajama shorts are twisted, and I didn't take my makeup off last night, so I probably look like a raccoon. "I don't even...what do you want?"

"Your help," he says again, as if that's an answer.

I nod once. "Yeah, I got that. What do you want help *with*?"

Henry looks over his shoulder once, the motion frantic. He's nervous, and it's painfully obvious, so much that it starts rubbing off on me. The back of my neck stings with sweat, and I fist my hands at my sides to keep them from shaking. My heart is doing very irregular things as I study his actions, trying to determine what on Earth he's checking for.

Finally, once he's decided he's not being hunted, he steps inside my apartment uninvited. The doorway is extremely narrow, and Henry is not a small man, so he bumps into my shoulder in the process. It's brief, so faint that I shouldn't notice it. But I do. And all at once, my focus shifts from the floor to the scent of his cologne surrounding me.

I should want to bash his head against the wall. I *do* want to bash his head against the wall. Yet something is stopping me from doing so, whether morals or curiosity, I'm unsure.

"I had a piece stolen recently," Henry starts, wringing his hands in front of him. "Yesterday. It was taken from my apartment, and I'd like you to help me find it."

Warning signals start flashing in my brain.

No.

No.

No.

If he thinks—if he's even *asking* for my help—then he knows.

He knows what I do. There's not even any point in lying.

I was never able to lie to him, anyways.

"What makes you think I could do that?" I ask, hoping I can at least evade the question. "Why would I have anything—"

"Come on, Amelie. I know. You know that I do."

Well, that's just great.

I bite my lip, keeping my arms crossed over my chest. Henry glances around my apartment, eyes landing anywhere but me. What do I even say? If he knows, why hasn't he gone to the police? Why hasn't he gotten me caught?

Unless...maybe he doesn't have *proof*.

"I'm not helping you," I tell him again. "I'm not a detective."

"You're the closest thing I've got, Ames."

"Okay, one, don't call me that." Knowing it's a mistake, I meet his eyes. "And two, I'm saying *no*. Why would I help you?"

Henry sighs and pockets his hand, and for just a moment, I imagine that I've won. That he's going to leave in defeat. I'll spend the next week trying to forget this conversation, and then *BAM!* He'll be caught in a money laundering scandal. It'll be all over the news. His face will be on wanted posters, like they have in old western movies, and I'll draw mustaches on it.

But Henry doesn't start toward the door. He doesn't even flinch as he pulls his hand out of his pocket, holding a tiny black chip.

My heart drops to my feet.

"A *memory card*?" I ask, voice pathetically weak. Those things are my nemesis, as one would expect. Why is he holding one?

"I have proof of your job." Henry clears his throat. "On this card. It's the only copy of the footage."

I gape at him. "Are you trying to *blackmail* me?"

He has the decency to look embarrassed. "Not...in so many words?"

The timer for my cake rings as he finishes his sentence, and we both jump. I look into the kitchen and contemplate my current options. Honestly, I don't have many, but I have enough that it's reasonable to think through them.

1. I help Henry find his piece, then leave the country.

2. I wrestle him to the ground and snatch that SD card.

3. I jump out my window and pray that I don't break any bones.

But no, the last two would never work. He's stronger than me, and I would definitely break my bones. I live on the sixteenth floor and I despise milk.

"You'll destroy that if I help you," I say, nodding to the chip. "Actually, no. You'll give it to me."

"I'll give it to you," he says. "Promise."

I shouldn't believe him, but I don't have a choice. There's no other way out of this. He's the one dragging me into this situation, and he's the only way out.

Ironic, isn't it?

"Give me ten minutes," I mumble. "We'll go to the bakery on the corner and talk."

He gives me a stiff smile. His pity smile. It makes me want to break something. "Perfect."

"Go wait in the hallway."

He does, without question.

Once he closes the door behind him, I let out a breath and yank at my hair. Embarrassment turns my face hot when I realize my ponytail holder was tangled in the ends through that entire conversation.

This can't be happening. I am not truly getting blackmailed by my ex-boyfriend.

Maybe I'm believing all this too easily. That could be an empty memory card, and he could be doing this to get a rise out of me. But ultimately, that just...doesn't add up. Him bluffing is somehow less believable than this whole thing. No matter how much I'd deny it, I do know Henry. Used to, anyways, though it doesn't seem like he's changed all that much.

He wouldn't threaten something he couldn't follow through with.

Sighing, I take the cake out of the oven and put it on a cooling rack. I turn the oven off, then triple check it, because I don't trust myself at all. Then I bolt to my room and fling open the closet. My blue sweater is the first one to catch my eye, but I really want something with a bit more lace. It's cold today, though, so I reluctantly tug it over my head. I find a white mini skirt and pair it with some sheer tights and boots.

I brush my teeth—I cannot believe I hadn't done that yet—then dab a little makeup on before opening the front door.

Henry is leaned against the wall with a book between his palms. He doesn't look at me for a considerable amount of time, but when he does, he swallows hard. "Are you ready?"

"Why not."

With a nod, he shoves the book in his coat pocket. "Okay. I walked, so—"

"We'll walk," I say stiffly, stepping behind him. I reach into his other pocket and yank the wallet out with ease. He turns around, brows drawn together, and I wave it in his face. "You're paying."

"How did you—"

"A true gentleman." I grin—though it would be more accurately classified as baring my teeth—and walk to the elevator.

Henry just sighs and follows.

5
______

HENRY

I'm going to be very honest. I have no idea what I'm doing.

Amelie is currently dragging me to a bakery I've never heard of. I'm shocked that I even got this far; I sort of expected her to slam my arm in the door, but that wasn't the case. She took my wallet, led me out of her building, and hasn't said a word since.

I guess I should take it as a positive that she hasn't yelled at me, but honestly, I'd rather her do *that* than keep giving me cold glances.

We're coming up on a building that looks worn. The lettering on the window reads *Parlon's Patisserie.* I try to get the door for Amelie, but she steps in front of me and opens it herself. She even goes so far as to pull it closed behind her. I wordlessly open it back up and follow, aware that this is probably going to be the least fun morning of my life.

And I deserve that. I *am* technically blackmailing her.

"*Dave!*" Amelie sings into the empty café. She does a little spin in the middle of the floor, then leans against the counter. "I've brought you a victim."

I tense up involuntarily. She notices, and the corner of her mouth lifts at my discomfort. I can't tell if I'm irritated or enjoying this. Maybe a bit of both. The mix of anxiety coursing through me, along with being in Amelie's presence again, is bound to be confusing.

A short man, who I assume is Dave, walks out from behind the counter. His graying hair and generally round stature aren't threatening in the slightest, but maybe that's the goal.

"Hiya," Dave says to Amelie before sliding his eyes to me. "Who are you?"

"He's my friend," she says before I can answer.

I expect some sort of question or elaboration, but neither are necessary. Dave just says, "Ah. Hello, friend."

"Hello," I say warily. "Who are you?"

I understand that he's Dave. But I have no idea who Dave is.

"He's my hero," Amelie deadpans, motioning to him. "He makes the best coffee in the city."

"So she says," Dave sighs, but his eyes wrinkle at the corners. He's smiling without fully doing so. "What can I get you started with?"

I tap my foot as I read over the menu. Nothing stands out—nothing that won't give me a cavity within seconds, anyway. I don't understand people who dump a pound of sugar in their coffee. I don't even like to flavor it.

"I'll take a black coffee," I say.

In 3...2...

"You're *still* addicted to black coffee?" Amelie scoffs. She looks more disgusted than she did when I showed up at her door, and that's saying a lot. "Try a macchiato, for goodness sake."

"I don't want a macchiato."

"But there are so many flavors!"

"I don't like any of them."

She frowns. "Have you *ever* considered removing the broomstick that's shoved up your—"

"Is that all?" Dave interrupts, cutting Amelie off with a smile.

She grins back, erasing all the venom in her stare. "My usual?"

"I've already got it." He holds up a brown paper bag and a large to-go cup.

"That'll be it, then," she says, handing over a twenty she snagged from my wallet.

I take the coffee that Dave gives me and lift the cup to my mouth, aware that Amelie is watching my every move. Her eyes are glued to mine as I tip it back. She's either trying to gauge my reaction to the drink or make me nervous, the latter of which works too well.

The scalding hot coffee burns my throat on the way down, but I keep my expression neutral. "Hm. This is good."

"Thank ya." Dave gives me a solid nod. He slides the change to Amelie, and she slides it right back to him. With a sigh, he puts it in the register, mumbling something incoherent under his breath. I'm guessing that Amelie frequents this coffee shop, and that this is a fight they have every time. He knows not to argue with her. He knows that she'll win.

Before I can bid the man goodbye, Amelie grabs my wrist and drags me outside.

"You're in a rush," I note.

She hums. "Well."

"Well, what?"

"No," she says, shaking her head. "Don't do this right now."

So I don't.

There are a few fold-up tables outside the patisserie. I have no doubt that the wind is strong enough to knock them over today, but no one seems to pay that any mind. Amelie takes a seat under an umbrella and starts picking at the fruit tart she just purchased. I sit across from her, taking the liberty of studying her face, of noting what's different about her and what stayed the same.

She is the same, at least outwardly.

Her hair hasn't changed—it's still light brown, wavy when she hasn't bothered to style it. She's got a ribbon tied in the back, which is new, but it suits her. Red polish covers her nails. The shade matches her lipstick perfectly, which I know was purposeful. She still wears the same silver necklace her mom gave her in middle school, the same earrings that complete the set.

I make the mistake of looking at her eyes, which are burning a hole right through my forehead.

"I'm not sure why you're staring at me as though I've sprouted antennae," she says, annoyance bleeding into her voice. "Let's get this over with."

I exhale. "Alright. Let's recap."

"We don't need to recap. You spoke fifteen minutes ago."

"Alright," I say again. "I need your help tracking down a painting."

"Yeah, I'm aware of that." She takes a long drink of her coffee, slams it back down on the table. "What do you want from me? And I swear, if you say *your help*, I will take that coffee and dump it down the neck of your shirt."

The corner of my mouth ticks up, threatening to give me away. "I want your resources."

Her jaw tightens, and I know I've successfully gotten under her skin. I shouldn't try to—especially not right now. But her having a reaction to me, *any* reaction, is too tempting a thing to let get away.

Besides, it's not like she's innocent in this whole thing.

"That's just what every girl wants to hear, if you're curious." Amelie leans back in her chair, letting it tip back just slightly. "But the thing is, I don't *have* the resources. That's not my department. If you seriously want my help, I have two rules."

"Which are?"

"One." She puts a finger up. "You won't be working with *just* me. I'm not a one-woman circus. I can't help you without my team, so they'll have to be in on the details."

"I have no opposition to that," I say truthfully.

"Good. Two." She leans forward. "This will not get out. And I mean that, Henry. You think you're smug, threatening me with that piece of plastic, but that's preferable to what could happen otherwise."

Her face is completely unreadable. She gives nothing away as to what those happenings might be, and for a second, I wonder if she's lying. If she's finally perfected the act. But there's a certain desperation in her voice, one that's so intent, I know she isn't. Her face may be emotionless, but her voice tells all.

The strangest sense of worry comes over me as I wonder what could possibly be so threatening. What is she really involved in? What comes with this job she has?

Why do you care, and can you make it stop?

"Okay," I say, attempting to keep those thoughts at bay. "I can work with that."

"Good. Now, what are we looking for? What's your plan?"

"I don't know," I admit sheepishly. "I was kind of hoping you'd just...know where to look."

She blinks once. Twice. "You think I have a radar in my brain?"

"I just thought you'd have some ideas. You do this stuff frequently, right? You know the patterns?"

"I don't keep up with all the Heist Drama, if that's what you're asking." She crosses her arms. "Where did the piece get stolen from? Was it displayed?"

"No. It was in my studio."

She turns that information over in her mind. "When was it taken?"

"Yesterday. When I got home in the afternoon, it was gone. The lock on my door was broken."

Amelie narrows her eyes. "Is this a roundabout way of saying you suspect me? Is that what this is?"

"No," I say quickly. "No, not at all."

I shouldn't sound so confident in that answer, but for some reason, I just *know* it wasn't her. Maybe it's wishful thinking; maybe I'm naïve. But she doesn't know where I live, and she didn't seem to know I was in the city, so I'm sort of counting on it to be true.

"Hm." Amelie leans forward more, enough that we're elbow to elbow now. "What if we make a decoy for you to put in your studio? Then you can nab the thief there."

I shake my head. "No. I mean, yes, that would help, but it isn't enough. I need the original back, unharmed and *quick*."

"Can't you just try to replicate it?"

I bark a laugh, and she rolls her eyes. "*Replicate it?*"

"Oh, here we go."

"I can't just replicate it. It's art."

"Okay!" Amelie holds up her hands in an innocent gesture. "Geez. What did the thing even look like?"

I exhale. "You know *Ophelia*? By Friedrich Heyser?"

She gives a weak shrug. "Yeah, I know it. Were you ripping it off?"

"No," I say coolly. "But it's a rendition of that piece. I'm meant to have it in a week, and I've only just begun the final touches."

"Sounds like a procrastination issue."

If I weren't so worried she's going to turn me down, I'd laugh.

"Please, Amelie," I say, hoping my voice is sincere. "Can we work together or not?"

She licks her lips. "I'll have to ask my team first."

"Okay." I nod. "We can meet up later this week and discuss a plan."

Wordlessly, Amelie stands and hands me her cell phone. "Put your number in."

I look up at her. "That isn't necessary."

"What, you have carrier pigeons?"

A laugh almost escapes me, but I do my best to stifle it. "I meant, we can just make an arrangement now, rather than discussing it later."

And I still have your number saved.

It's a ridiculous thought to have, really. Surely her number has changed in four years, but I can't bring myself to delete it.

"That won't work," Amelie says. "I'm a busy woman."

"Yes, I'm sure your kleptomaniac hobby is grueling."

She frowns. "I'm offended you don't think I can make it full time."

I just sigh and take her phone. A part of me is tempted to look for my number, see if she still has *mine*, but I don't. She's watching me like a hawk, and I know she's suspicious enough.

I quickly punch in my number, then ring myself once so I have hers. The chances of her contacting me are slim, which is probably why she wanted *my* information, not vice versa. She wants the upper hand.

"Let me know soon, please," I say. "I'm on a deadline."

"I'll do whatever I can to make your life easier," she says dryly, shoving her phone into her pocket and walking away. The tension in my body seems to melt away the further she gets, but once she's about three feet away, she spins back around and walks toward the table with a glint in her eye. Unintentionally, I hold my breath as she approaches, and I don't release it until she's right in front of me.

"You never told me," Amelie says, head tipped to the side, "how you know what I do."

I blink. That isn't what I expected her to say. I mean, it's not as though I had much time to think up options, but that wouldn't have been one of them.

"I've seen you myself," I say quietly.

I've caught her once, and I'm certain I'm the only one to ever do so.

That's what's on the SD card in my pocket. I've had the footage of her strolling around the museum for a few weeks. Recorded it on my phone camera out of a panicked instinct. I'm glad I did, because the security cameras were cut that night. I'm sure that was the work of her *team*.

I happened to be in the museum that night, trying to find a bill that my dad had left in his office. He often sends me on petty errands, so I thought nothing of it. I unlocked the maintenance door and got in.

Amelie got in too. Right behind me, I think. I didn't know it at first.

She was quiet, clearly. No shattering things or whispering curses under her breath. It was completely silent—the thing that gave her away wasn't noise. There were no whispers, or footsteps, or heightened breaths.

You know what it was?

It was her *perfume.*

The reality of the situation is nearly impossible. I don't know how she walked past the office door without noticing it was open, or how I managed to be close enough to breathe in the scent. But she did, and I was, and that godforsaken perfume...

Regardless, I should've turned it in by now. I *know* this. But when I confirmed that it was her after watching the footage, I just couldn't.

I haven't let the SD card be more than two feet away from my person since then. My intentions of actually turning it in are *zero*. I'm aware that it's morally unsound to keep it hidden, but quite frankly, I don't care.

"Okay," Amelie says finally, after staring at me for what feels like years. "That's all I wanted to know."

She leaves again, and this time, she disappears around the corner.

I stay at the table for a moment, waiting until she's gone to breathe. Something about her—now, more than in the past—absolutely unarms me. Her composure, maybe. The way she carries herself in this insane situation I just threw us into. It's different. New. Inexplicably tempting.

But I've still got questions.

My main one being, why isn't she the *slightest* bit suspicious of why I went to her and not the police?

I'm shocked she didn't ask. That's the one question I would've answered with no hesitation. It would've been simple, would've rolled right off the tongue.

My dad is crazy and won't let me get real help, and somehow, I think you're my only hope.

Amelie never met my father. I was able to keep her away from that mess; therefore, I've got no idea if she'd believe it. What kind of man wouldn't go to the police for something like this?

I shake my head and stand, tossing my coffee cup into the trash. It's fine. It's irrelevant. If all goes to plan, I'll have my piece back within the week, and Amelie and I can part ways. She'll hate me doubly, I'll be even more confused, and we'll never cross paths again.

Simple.

6
___

AMELIE

"You're bluffing."

"In your dreams." I fan my cards out and hope that Olive can't see them. I'm not really sure she *can* see—I think she's legally blind. Her lenses are as thick as my cell phone. "I think Jerry is, though."

"Don't you dare turn it on me," Jerry mutters, pushing a stack of chips toward the center. "I'll raise ya thirty."

"Mhm," Olive hums, matching his stack. "Mimi'll match you, too."

"Don't push me, Ol," Mimi grumbles, staring at Olive over her purple rims. The cigarette in her mouth has long gone out, but she doesn't seem to notice. "But sure. I'll match the old bag."

I grin. Every Wednesday, I find myself in my building's activity room, playing poker with a bunch of eighty-year-olds. It's nostalgic. Reminds me of weekends with my parents. Poker was—and still is—a family game, and I've known how to play since I could differentiate the suits of cards. Jensen normally plays too, but I didn't make it up to the apartment to ask him. Olive nabbed me before I could get on the elevator.

It's a great distraction from my everyday life. Today, it's helping me get away from whatever just happened at Parlon's. Why *me*? Why does Henry—of *all* people—have to know? I guess it's better him than law enforcement, but I don't care. I can still be in a mood about it.

Ronald, our dealer for time's sake, pulls me back to the present. "I think you all need a slap upside the head."

"You don't get input as the dealer," I remind him, flashing a smile. "And anyways, we're almost done. Jerry is about to fold."

"I am *not* about to fold." Jerry pushes another stack of chips to the center. "Who wants some of *that*?"

Olive swears. "I ought to wring your neck, boy. I'm out."

"I'm out, too," Mimi sighs, slamming her cards on the table. She had a two and a nine, both different suits. Poor gal. Her poker luck is as good as my getting-out-of-being-blackmailed luck.

Jerry grins and looks at me. "Whatcha got, girly?"

I've got a six and an ace, but I'm not about to tell him that.

"Better than yours," I say, raising my bet. Both Olive and Mimi make *oooh*ing sounds. Ronald just chuckles.

"I'm not sure I buy it," Jerry says slowly.

I click my tongue. "You're gonna want to be sure."

He narrows his eyes. Lays his cards down. Two kings, which go nicely with the two queens on the table. "Beat that."

"Dang it," I mutter, setting my poor hand down. "Fine."

Jerry is practically beaming as he gathers his chips. "You can't lie to an old man."

"Then why do we even try?" Olive huffs. "Someday we're going to ban you, Jerry."

I shrug. "It'd be no fun without him."

"I'm certain it can't be any worse." Ronald slides the cards in front of me. "Another round?"

I nod and split the deck. Technically, this is a weekly thing, but today, I'm using it to avoid talking to Jensen. I have no real interest in telling him what just happened, because he'll flip out and tell Meg, and then *Meg* will flip out, and then I have to deal with it all even though I didn't ask to be in this position.

And I really want to nap.

"I'm out of this one," Mimi mumbles, pushing her chair back. "Out of patience and out of chips."

"Same here," Jerry says. "I mean, I'm winning, but *Jeopardy!* is on."

"Ooh!" Olive stands quickly, grabbing Ronald's shoulder for support. He grunts as she digs her bony fingers into his skin, but she doesn't notice. "Thanks for saying so."

"Bye, Ol," I say, giving her a backwards wave as she walks to the elevator. I stand to help Ronald out of his chair. Just as he puts the cards in his shirt pocket, the door to the stairwell swings open and Jensen appears.

I gape. Ronald gapes. Perhaps at Jensen's apparent urgency, or the fact that he's sweating through his shirt.

"Hello," I say. "Did you just run down the stairs?"

"You guys played without me?"

"I lost, if it makes you feel better."

Jensen doesn't respond before going back up the stairs. I've got no idea why on earth we're walking up sixteen flights of stairs when the elevator is in perfect condition, but I follow regardless and try to think while it's quiet. Well, not *quiet*—Jensen is stomping, and he's doing it loudly. I wonder if something has ticked him off or if he's just his usual irritated self.

"I have something to tell you," I say when we reach our floor.

"No," Jensen says.

"No?"

"I wouldn't."

He opens the door to our apartment and trots inside, and I understand why.

Meg is sitting on my couch, a teacup in one hand and her phone in the other.

"Thank God," I say, closing the door with my heel. "Now I can be your stand-in couple's therapist."

"That is *not* why I'm here," Meg says, attempting to toss her blonde hair over her shoulder. She mostly fails, given that it's no longer than her collarbone. "I'm here because we work tonight."

I squint at her. She must've been here for a pretty good while, because I never saw her come through the lobby. I don't bother questioning her on it, though—the teacup in her hand is getting all my attention.

"What?" She wrinkles her nose. "Stop staring at me."

"You're drinking my good tea."

"Jensen made it for me."

I spin toward him. "*You used my good tea?!*"

He sighs. "Tea is tea, Amelie."

"TEA IS *NOT* TEA."

"Then I'll buy you more."

"Good." I turn back to Meg. "Continue."

She sets the teacup on the side table. It's too close to the edge, but I keep my mouth shut. "Okay. I've made a couple marks on the floor plan, but nothing that's like, detrimental. I also saw some advertisements for the museum yesterday. Photo must've been taken while you were there, because you're in it."

My ears turn hot, and suddenly, I couldn't care less about the teacup. "What do you mean?"

She taps on her phone screen before handing it over. I'm unsure of what I'm looking at for a moment, but I realize it's the museum's website. The homepage.

And Henry's exhibit is now being promoted with a photo of us looking at his piece. The one I'm stealing tonight.

"Gotta love that," I mutter, clicking on the image to make it bigger.

Unless you know what the back of me looks like, you'd never guess that it's me in the photo. I'm wearing my favorite bow, but lots of people probably wear bows. It's a fabulous accessory.

I'm not mad, honestly. My calves look exquisite.

"Do you want me to take it down?" Meg asks, but I don't answer right away. I finally let my gaze wander to Henry, and instantly, I wish I hadn't.

While I'm looking at the painting in front of us, hands wrung behind my back, he's looking at me.

"Don't worry about it," I say, handing her phone back. "It isn't obvious. It could've been worse."

"Much," she agrees. I flop down beside her, curling my legs up under my thighs. I grab my laptop off the table and open it up, clicking the file she sent yesterday.

Meg, alongside being Jensen's favorite nuisance, does all the techy things that need to be done. She gets us the museum floor plans, kills the lights and cameras, and gets us around security. I met her a few months after I graduated high school, and we stayed in touch, and eventually, this all just...happened.

Jensen came next. We were roommates when this whole thing kicked off—which, you can see, hasn't changed—and I had to tell him. It was impossible to keep it a secret, especially when a friend of mine was constantly over here, discussing how we were going to tie up security guards.

He offered to help. Literally just...offered. Out of the blue. I don't think he knew what he was getting into. I think he just had a crush on Meg.

Jensen walks into the living room with a bowl of cereal. He sits down on the coffee table and sighs. "Now that that's all over, can we—"

"Actually, I have a question for both of you." My voice is a little too loud, and I know it's because I'm nervous. Now is probably not the time to bring up Henry's proposition, but I don't think there's ever going to be a *good time*. I can ease into it, though. "Have you heard anything about recently stolen pieces? Anything through the grapevine?"

Meg hears a lot of gossip. She knows almost everything that goes on in our line of work, so I'm shocked when she shakes her head. "No, nothing I've seen. Why?"

"Just curious," I mumble, gnawing on my cheek. Maybe the piece hasn't been listed yet, or maybe it's a private sale. "If you get anything, let me know. And have the new floor plans sent to me by this evening."

She ties her hair up, oblivious to the pieces that fall back down around her neck. "Whatever you say, boss."

I roll my eyes. Despite being in charge of this whole charade, I detest being called 'boss'. It makes me feel like the bad guy. Or some weird mafia dude. I know I technically have the felonies and everything, but I'm not *bad*.

I'm simply doing what I've learned to do best.

"Are you staying until tonight?" I ask.

Meg shakes her head. "No. I've got work to do, and I won't focus here."

"Wonder why," Jensen says under his breath, staring at her.

She clenches her jaw. "You need to stop."

"You need to leave, apparently."

"You both need to get a grip." I pull a pillow into my lap. "I thought you two were fine now."

"Don't try to understand it," Meg says, so I don't.

I open a new tab on my laptop and start researching Henry's paintings. Despite the urge I had a few weeks ago, when I saw his face plastered everywhere regarding The Gallery, I haven't stalked him. I think I deserve a medal for it, because I've wanted to. *Badly*.

The first piece I see is *Nautical Abyss*. No shock, obviously. I'm very aware that I'll be ripping it off the wall tonight.

But the second one, that's what catches me off guard.

I'm staring at a photo of my favorite piece in the gallery. The flower made of words. I can still see my name, even on my tiny, grainy screen.

It's called *Fleur of Words*.

Created by Henry Arlington.

I'm going to break my computer.

"Bye guys," Meg says suddenly, already headed for the door. "Be back tonight."

I mumble a goodbye as I continue clicking links regarding Henry, trying to find more about him. Things I don't already know. All I learn is that he does commissioned work, more often than actually displaying in museums. The pieces in his exhibit are favorites. They draw a crowd. Every article I see is raving, practically worshiping him for his work, and my stomach churns as I read over the words.

Because I wanted him to make it. And something inside of me —albeit buried by aggravation—is glad he got what he wanted.

I just don't want to hear about it.

"Whatcha doin?" Jensen asks, plopping down beside me on the couch.

I lower the laptop screen so he can't see. I want to explain before he further deems me a stalker. "I have something to ask you."

He raises a brow. "Is there a reason you waited for Meg to leave?"

"Probably because she's feisty and wants your head on a stick right now."

"Fair," he murmurs, sitting up. "What is it?"

I chew on my lip, dig my nails into my palm. "I'm afraid I'm... being blackmailed."

He blinks. "I'm sorry?"

"Remember Henry Arlington? I spoke of him yesterday."

"Yes, my memory goes that far back."

I huff and open my screen up a little, not that it really matters. "Well. He found me this morning while you were gone. He wants me to help find a stolen painting."

"That's the stupidest thing I've ever heard."

"I know."

"What if it's one we stole?"

I shake my head. "It's not. It was taken yesterday from his studio."

Jensen sighs. "Why do we have to do this?"

"Because, *again,* he's blackmailing me. He has footage of me in the museum. I think it was the night we stole *Last Goodbye.*"

"Why do you assume it was then?"

"The door was unlocked that night, remember?" I shrug. "He must've been the one inside."

Jensen groans. He's always hated me for being so careless, and I used to say he was being paranoid, but now he's got reason. That night, I just went in an open door. I was on my period—more argumentative than usual—and I didn't feel like going along with Meg's plan. It worked, until *apparently,* it didn't.

"Why would *he* be there, though?" Jensen asks.

"I don't know."

"Well, why didn't he just go to the police?"

"You're asking a lot of questions," I say, "and I don't have answers. I don't *know*."

There's a heavy pause, followed by an eye roll. "I guess we're going to do it?"

"I really don't think we have a choice," I admit. "But it'll be easy, right? We're smart. We can help him out, then drop it for good."

My tone is confident, but I know that won't be the case. You can't do something like this and never cross paths again. Something will always be tangled up, whether it be evidence, contact, or a shot at working together in the future. What if he gets another piece stolen and comes to us for help? I can't commit to something like that. It's not what I do.

But the fixer part of my brain, it wants to do this, because it knows that I can. It probably won't be all that difficult.

Jensen finally shrugs, and I take that as his response. "Meg is the deciding factor here. She's got the resources."

"I know. That's what I told him. I said it would be all of us, not just me."

"You'll do the communications." Jensen pats my shoulder. "I don't want to talk to him."

"What makes you think I do?" I ask, wondering if I've somehow given something away. I don't want to give anything away. I *have* nothing to give away!

"You probably don't," he says, "but you're the one who went through that door."

And I'll never regret anything more.

"I dated him," I say quietly. "Henry. I dated him in high school."

"I know," he says.

I blink. "How? I never told you."

"I'm very good at drawing conclusions," he says, and that's true. He is. I've probably talked about Henry more than I realize, which makes me feel a little embarrassed. I don't want Jensen thinking I'm doing this because of that. Any positive emotion I had for Henry left when he did.

"Also," Jen says, "I've gathered that you hate him. Just a little."

I bark a laugh. "More than a little."

And I mean it. Henry is my nemesis, whether he knows it or not. I hate him for leaving. I hate him for leaving *me*. I hate that I ever missed him, and I hate him more for showing back up and looking like *that*.

Jensen takes the laptop from me and starts scrolling through my tabs. I turn on the TV and kick my feet up on the coffee table, thankful that I can direct my attention toward something else. I don't like thinking about Henry. That's not where my focus should be right now.

"Hey," Jensen says suddenly, turning the laptop toward me. "Look at this."

I squint. He's got a multitude of windows open, so it takes me a second to realize what I'm looking at, but when I do, my face drops.

It's right there on the screen. The headline is in bold letters.

HENRY ARLINGTON, SON OF ROMAN ARLINGTON, IS NEW FEATURED ARTIST AT <u>THE GALLERY</u>

"Roman Arlington owns the gallery," Jensen explains. "This article is dated about a month back."

I raise my brows. I pay very little attention to the men in charge of these things, but this...this is gold.

"That's how Henry caught me," I say. "Because his dad owns the place."

Jensen frowns. "You didn't know?"

"We never talked much about our parents." An understatement. "Does that mean you're in?"

He sighs before bookmarking the tab. "Sure. But we'll have to get Meg on board."

"I know," I say, aware that getting her to agree will be harder than most of this.

But it *could* be easy, this charade. Maybe it won't be so horrid. We could be off the hook within the week, and Henry will have his piece, and I'll never have to see his stupid pretty face again.

As long as Meg agrees.

$$7$$

HENRY

Amelie may be helping me—*may* being the key word there—but that doesn't mean I'll have my painting in time for the auction. Since I have no display-worthy pieces to choose from in my home studio, I'm on my way to my *back up* studio at the museum.

My dad, though he owns the place, is hardly ever there. The main office is often empty, so I dragged my paints there one night when I wanted a change of scenery. I've got three or four pieces stashed away, and I'm hoping one will be good enough to pacify him.

"Hi hi!" Someone says to my left. I glance over to find Liz walking in step beside me, headphones covering her ears. She's got a large bag on her shoulder and a pink smoothie in her hand, seeming almost oblivious to her surroundings. "Lovely seeing you here."

"Mmm." I nod. "How did you find me?"

"I saw you when you walked past the smoothie bar. I assumed you were going home, and I don't like walking by myself, so I was like, '*Oh, I'm gonna walk home with Henry.*' It's spooky alone and I have no one to talk to."

"And a moment of silence would kill you?"

"Stone cold dead," she says, nodding. "Where are you going?"

"The museum."

"Ew. Why?"

"Because I need a painting for Dad, and my search isn't going... as smoothly as I'd hoped."

"Oh?" Liz removes her headphones and leaves them around her neck. "What are you doing to find it?"

"Just...asking around," I mutter.

Telling Liz the truth is absolutely not an option. She and Amelie were friends, and Liz had to hear more about the whole thing than anyone else. I will not be telling her *anything* if I can help it. "It'll turn up eventually, right?"

"Unlikely, but I admire your faith in society." Liz elbows me in the side. "You want company?"

"If you want to watch me rifle through a stack of canvases for an hour."

She shrugs. "Can I play music?"

"I suppose."

"Then yes." She claps her hands in front of her, picking up the pace as we cross the street to the museum. People are still filing through the front doors, and they won't stop for a few hours. Liz and I walk inside, moving past the ticket collector and all the people with ease. They're used to us at this point.

About a month ago, I couldn't be here without people talking to me. Questioning me. Sometimes it was reporters, and other times, just people who were curious about me and what I did. I'm thankful for the interest, given that it's what supplies me with work, but I was glad when it died down. I don't exactly enjoy speaking.

Liz and I head up to the second floor. Sculptures litter the area, and Lizzy is so preoccupied with sucking the last bit of her smoothie out of the cup that she nearly bumps into one. She looks stunned as she maneuvers around it, as if this inanimate object has inconvenienced her. "I don't like that one."

"Why?" I ask, looking at the piece. It's a snake wrapped around a body, so I guess I understand. Nobody likes snakes. Even more so when they're harming someone.

"Because it's gross! Imagine you get killed, and then when people tell your story, they're like, '*Oh, poor guy! He got killed by a snake*'. That's so dehumanizing."

"That's rude to anyone who has ever died via snake."

Lizzy waves a hand at me and walks ahead.

When we reach the office, I unlock the door and step inside. This place is nearly as bare as my apartment. It's furnished with a desk, a file cabinet, and two chairs, one of which belongs to the desk. Bills are stacked high on the file cabinet, but I don't look at them. I always have the urge to, but I've refrained so far.

Liz tosses her bag onto the desk, and it makes a loud thunking noise. I'd guess she came from work, which means her laptop is in there. I don't know how it isn't broken yet. "Okay," she starts, throwing her smoothie cup away. "Show me what we're working with."

I go to the closet where I keep my supplies and dig out the first canvas. It's a piece I hate—a basic landscape, one that I did months ago out of sheer boredom. The same painting exists in every single home décor store I've ever stepped foot in.

"I hate it," I say plainly. "Dad will, too."

"He will," Lizzy agrees, unwrapping a Twix bar she found in the desk. "Next."

I lean the canvas against the wall and go back for another. We go through three of them, each one worse than the last. Dull. Bland. There's no passion behind a single one of these.

By the fourth, Liz gives an exasperated sigh. "Is that all?"

"Yes," I admit. "That's all. But surely I could rework one of them?"

She gives a shrug. "You *could*, Hen, but do you really want to?"

"No." I fall into the desk chair with a huff. "I'd rather start fresh than rework anything."

"Then do that."

"I don't have time. A piece that I'm proud of could take weeks. Dad's auction is, what, next weekend?"

Liz nods. "Yeah, but...does it have to be something you're proud of? I think it just has to be done."

"No. I'm not going to put an awful piece out."

"It's just for an auction, Hen."

"I don't care." I sit up straighter. "It's going to be under my name. I'm going to be proud of it."

Maybe it's ridiculous of me to care so much. Lizzy is technically right—it's just an auction. Someone will buy the piece and I'll never see it again. But I hate to think of someone owning a painting I don't like. That I put no emotion into.

It's *art*. It's not supposed to be numb.

The only problem with that is, I'm feeling more uninspired than I have in months. It may have something to do with staring my past inspiration in the eyes earlier today, but that's none of my business.

"I get it, Hen," Lizzy tells me. "Really. If I had to publish an article I wasn't proud of, I'd be heartbroken. I'm just reminding you that Dad doesn't understand."

I forget that she knows what it's like to have a job like this. To have people constantly looking at what you do, judging what you create.

Lizzy writes for a fashion magazine. Started as soon as she got out of high school. I'm honestly convinced that she hates it, but she's never said anything about changing paths. I let her complain about her boss, and she lets me complain about our dad. It's a win-win.

Suddenly, Liz stands and dusts the chocolate off her lap. She grabs her headphones and places them on her head, then hikes her bag up her shoulder. "I should go. I need to finish up whatever I'm supposed to have done before nine tomorrow."

I give a laugh. "You haven't started it?"

"Nope. See you tomorrow."

She leaves before I return the sentiment.

With a sigh, I stand from the desk and remove my coat. I'm wearing a button down under it, so I remove that, too, which leaves me in a white tank that I couldn't care less about. It's looking like my only option is to paint, or at least clean up one of these pieces, and I'd rather not ruin my nice clothes.

Revamping a piece that I hate is out of the question. I'll end up annoyed, drained, and probably on the verge of snapping in hours. Working on something new, though? That sounds even worse. I feel like every creative bone in my body has been broken.

And still, I don't have time to think up a different solution.

I crack open a can of paint, wash a brush, then drag out a new canvas.

8

AMELIE

"No." Meg slams a stack of papers onto my kitchen table. "We cannot do that. Are you guys insane? Like, I'm seriously asking."

"We're optimistic," Jensen corrects. "And come on. This guy has proof. He could get us in trouble."

She shrugs. "I look good in orange."

"*Nobody* looks good in orange!" I sigh. "Meg, please."

"It won't end well."

I roll my eyes. She isn't *wrong*, but we don't have time to argue. We've got about an hour until the sun goes down, which leaves us even less time to go over these floor plans and get to the museum. I was sort of hoping that it would be an open and shut thing, as in, Meg would blindly agree with us, but that didn't happen. I've never seen her so against something. Except for when Jensen got frosted tips last summer—we were all against that.

"We don't have much of a choice, Meg." I pick up the stack of papers and start sorting them into piles. "I'll do the back-and-forth. The dirty work. I just need you to *find* the thing, then tell me where it is."

She huffs. "Can we worry about this later? Like, I don't think it's our main focus right now."

"Our focus is staying out of jail, but sure! Sure, Meg." Jensen flicks her forehead. She elbows him square in the chest.

I set the last of the papers down and grab a red pen. "Okay. Pay attention. We're going in through..." I squint at a mark Meg has already drawn. "The maintenance closet *window*? Why does a closet have a window?"

"Don't question it, just be grateful." Jensen leans against the table and takes the pen from me, drawing a big *X* over the painting's location. "You know exactly where this is?"

I nod. "Without a doubt. It'll be easy."

"And Meg's driving?"

"As always, yes," she responds. "I'll be out back. The painting won't fit through the maintenance closet, so you'll have to break a different window. There's one near the alley. We'll be out of there before anyone shows."

I drum my hands on the table, skin tingling with something like excitement. "What about the cameras?"

"Disabled them before I came over here," she says with a nod.

"Good. So we're ready?"

"I'm ready," Jen says. "Your uniform is on the bed."

"Perfect," I mutter, twisting my hair into a bun.

Yesterday, when Jen was out for groceries, he *also* snagged two janitor's uniforms for us to wear over our clothes. We've used this tactic before, but this time, the uniforms don't smell like rotting garbage. I slide the jumpsuit over my leggings and bra, buttoning all but the top one at my neck. I put on a pair of sneakers that aren't obnoxiously loud and tuck a pair of nylon gloves into my pocket. The uniforms come with hats, but I don't want lice, so I veto it.

We're out the door and in the van by seven.

Our little vehicle is maybe the least discreet thing I can imagine. The outside is rusted orange, with 70s flowers painted all over it. Even the inside has retro seat covers and dash décor. It's basically equivalent to the Mystery Machine. I think the only reason we haven't gotten caught in the thing is because Meg drives like a madwoman away from the scene.

"How big is this painting?" Jen asks, pulling his gloves on.

Meg hums. "At least seventy inches wide, if I remember correctly."

"You're gonna have to have the van doors open."

"I've never failed that task before," she snaps, turning sharply onto the road.

I hold my breath as The Gallery comes into view. Meg drives close to the sidewalk, stopping a few blocks away from the building. "I'll circle around," she says. "Back in a few. Remember: window in the maintenance closet. It opens. Do *not* break that one."

"Got it," I say, tugging my gloves on as I exit the vehicle. Jen is on my heels, closing the van door as quietly as he can.

We reach the museum and find the correct window with ease. It's small—small enough that I'm actually worried we won't fit through it. Jen wrenches it open with the file in his pocket and lifts me up, pushing me through head-first. I bite back a scream as I land, my hands breaking my fall as I balance into a poorly formed handstand. When I'm on my feet again, I help guide Jensen through the window. His entry isn't as smooth as mine, but it's quiet.

We're surrounded by vacuums and cleaning products. Bottles of floor cleaner are lined up on a shelf, and nasty, oil-ridden rags lay on the ground. Jensen nearly knocks a jar off the shelf, but I grab his arm and yank him away before it can clatter to the ground.

"Let's not cause any unnecessary damage," I mutter, opening the closet door. I let my eyes adjust to the darkness before peeking down the hall. It's completely empty, save for a flickering dome light. The rest of the place is lit solely by the moon.

"To the left," Jensen says, and I nod. We walk quietly, our shoes all but squeaking on the waxed tile. I keep my eyes forward and hang close to the wall.

"I see it," I whisper, pointing ahead. *Nautical Abyss* is a few feet away, hung right under an AC vent. I squint to read the information plaque beneath it once we're close enough. My eyes practically magnetize to Henry's name, and something bitter starts clawing its way up my throat.

I blink. Good lord, is that guilt? That won't work.

"That's horrifying," Jen states, staring at the painting.

I laugh. "That's exactly what I said."

"Have you considered that your blackmailer-slash-ex might be crazy? Why would he paint someone that is so obviously going to *die*?"

"He was always a little moody," I admit.

"Odd." Jensen pulls his file back out and begins working on the edges of the painting. One thing we learned early on is that paintings aren't simply *hung*—most are stuck to the wall all the way around the perimeter. I don't know why, I just know that it's a pain.

Using my file, I start at the opposite edge. The hardest part about this is trying not to chip the paint on the wall. It's obviously clear that the painting is *gone*, but it's best to leave no further damage. I wedge my file behind the canvas and start slicing upward, hoping this one will be light work.

"Do you think Meg'll come around?" I ask Jen, hoping if we talk, we'll work quicker. "About Henry."

He grunts. "Maybe. You act like we don't have a choice, so I'm sure she won't defy you."

"You make me sound like a dictator."

He snorts, and I hear a loud *pop*. His edge is freed.

"Come help me," I say, nodding toward the painting. "This side won't come loose."

"You're just weak," he grumbles.

I raise my brows. Pocket my file. "Just for that, you can do it yourself."

"Fine. I do it better, anyways."

"Mhm." I pull out my phone and snap a photo of Jen. He freezes when the flash goes off, looking eerily similar to a deer in headlights. "I'll send these to Meg for you."

"Do my arms look good?"

"They look like arms."

"Do they look like *good* arms?"

"THEY LOOK LIKE ARMS, JENSEN," I whisper-hiss. "I don't know what a good arm is! That makes no sense."

"Never mind," he sighs. I hear another loud *pop,* and he tugs his file out from behind the canvas. "Help me get the top off."

I dig my fingers behind the frame. It chips the paint as it leaves the wall, so we make quick work of the bottom. My fingers are tingling when it's finally loose, and Jensen grabs his edge before it drops to the ground.

"Let's hurry," he says, and he says something after that but I don't catch it.

I hear something. There's noise coming from somewhere in this building.

"Jenny," I say, trying to shut him up.

"Like, honestly, if Meg ever ran a red light, we'd be—"

"*Jensen.*"

He quiets down and suddenly, the noise is louder.

Footsteps.

All my nerve endings light on fire, because my first thought is, Henry is going to catch me *again.* I don't think it's him, though. There are multiple pairs of feet coming toward us—it isn't just one person.

"Move, Amelie," Jensen urges, nodding toward the hallway. "Come on."

But I don't know which way to go. Meg said the back, but I think the noise is coming from that direction and I don't want to go toward it. That seems incredibly foolish.

"*Ames,*" Jensen says firmly. "We have to go."

"You take it," I say numbly, looking back over my shoulder. "Can you lift the whole thing?"

"I can, but—"

"I'm going to lead them somewhere else. Find the back door."

"Amelie—"

"Find it," I repeat, letting go of the painting. Jensen grunts as he takes its full weight, and I, against my better judgment, barrel straight toward the lobby.

9

———

AMELIE

This isn't how I saw the night going.

Currently, footsteps are running toward *me*. I understand that this was the plan, but now that it's happening, I don't like it. I run up the next flight of stairs I can find, praying that it won't lead me toward security guards.

The Gallery has three separate floors: the base floor is for paintings, the second is for sculptures, and the third is for random abstract constructions. We've never taken anything from the second or third floor—we deal solely in paintings.

So of course, I nearly slam right into a statue when I hit the top of the stairs.

I jump back when I feel cool marble and bolt into a corner. The sound escalates, feet slapping comically against the floor, and I see flashlights shining on the wall opposite of me.

"Come out," a weak voice says. "Make it easy on us."

I bite my tongue. Literally. It hurts, but the spike of pain reminds me to stay quiet. I hold my breath and keep my back against the wall, hoping that some miraculous thing will lead them away from me. A car chase. A car *crash,* even, one that involves—

An alarm.

An alarm starts blaring.

"Jensen." I say it like a swear word. The alarm is earsplitting, rolling through every square inch of this building. Flashlights start in a frenzy on the wall, looking for me even though I didn't trip it.

Carefully, I turn and run down the hall, hoping that I can find the control panel even while knowing how unlikely it is. The thing won't be out in the open, but I'm just desperate enough to hope otherwise.

"She went this way," a different, booming voice says, just as the lights turn the corner.

I run.

I don't know what I'm running toward, but I keep on anyway.

After a few seconds that feel like centuries, I spot a door at the end of the hall. There's no chance that it's unlocked. I'm *really* wishing I had snagged a key out of Henry's pocket yesterday, but you live, you learn.

I throw myself against the door handle, expecting to bash my face against the wood.

So you can imagine my surprise when it falls open.

Screaming—and I mean *screaming*—I fall on my stomach. Right there on the floor. The air gets knocked out of my lungs, but I manage to stand, coughing as I do so. Given the abundance of noise I just made, I lock the door behind me. I close my eyes and lean back against the wall, hand on my chest as I try to catch my breath.

What do I do now? A solution hasn't crossed my mind. I can't get out of here without equipment; it's only two stories, yeah, but I don't really feel like breaking my ribs. Again—weak bones.

Maybe they'll leave me alone. Maybe they'll assume I ran out of the building. If I were smart, I'd have led them up here, locked them in this room, then run downstairs. But I don't hear sirens yet. I'm still in control, if I could just *think*—

"You have got to be kidding me."

My eyes pop open, and I feel dizzy.

Henry Arlington is standing in front of me, looking like a whole different person than I met with today.

He's ditched his glasses—I hate that he looks good both ways —and the general lot of his clothing. He's wearing khakis and a *tank top*? Here? In a museum? Where's the class!

But whatever. I'm wearing a janitor's uniform.

"What are you doing here?" I croak.

He laughs dryly, and I feel the sound in my chest. "I'd like to redirect that question toward you."

"Uhm." I lick my lips. "No, thank you. How do I get out of here?"

"You think I'm going to help you escape when you likely just robbed me?"

"Does it *look* like I'm hiding a canvas in my bra?"

He doesn't retort. Instead, he reaches behind my head and flips a switch, which makes the shrieking alarms go quiet. I blow out a breath of relief, but the feeling is short lived. Police sirens slowly pollute the silence, causing my heart to beat even faster.

I've been close to being caught. Never this close.

Henry-2. Amelie-0.

"I didn't expect to see you tonight," Henry says, eyes on mine. His hand is still beside my head, and I have the urge to bite his wrist to make him move, but I also haven't been this close to him in a very long time. It's distracting, despite how much I wish it weren't.

"Same to you," I say, because what are the odds of him catching me twice?

Better question, what are the odds of him *letting me go* twice?

Very slim. Not great at all.

"I don't know what to do with you," he mumbles, and I can tell by his tone that he means it. He doesn't know whether to turn me in or let me go just to get my help. The fact that it's even a decision for him speaks volumes.

Quickly, I weigh my options. I really *could* bite him. Then I'll knock him out and jump from the window, regardless of the broken bones I'll acquire. Meg and Jensen are probably back at the apartment already, so I'll have to run, but I won't make it far.

It's cold outside. Maybe I can take up residence in a ditch until someone finds me and takes pity upon me.

But no, I hate pity. And ditches. There are spiders in ditches.

My only option is to give him what he wants and hope that it's enough.

"I'll do it," I bite out. "I'll help you."

His brows shoot up. "They agreed?"

They will after this. "Yeah. They agreed."

"Hm." He relaxes his arm until it bends, which brings him a little closer to me. I hold my breath, unsure of where to look. I don't want him to think he's making me nervous, because *he* isn't. The sirens are. "That's surprising."

"It is," I agree. "But, just a little tidbit. If you don't help me stay away from the cops, I can't help you."

"I'll help you," he says, and he sounds sincere. "Don't worry about that."

"Good. Now please step away from me."

Henry starts to grin. I can understand why he's so amused by this—from *his* perspective, it's probably hilarious. He's caught me twice. *Me.* The girl who has gone under the radar for years, somehow.

I don't know what luck this man has gained since I last saw him, but there's apparently a great deal of it.

Henry finally moves away from me, and when he does, his fingers catch in my hair. My ponytail must've fallen out while I was running, because the slight movement is enough to send it loose down my back. He says nothing as he steps out into the hall.

I swallow when the door closes, completely shocked.

Did he just...touch my hair?

Did he do that on purpose?

Whatever. It doesn't matter; there's no time to think. No time to figure out why my face feels warm.

I keep my feet planted on the ground instead of trying to eavesdrop. I could—easily. It wouldn't be hard to tiptoe over to the door and push my ear up against the wood, but my heart is pounding so hard in my chest, I'm not sure I'd hear anything.

Seconds of silence pass. I count to the number forty-seven before Henry comes back into the room, hands in his pockets and bottom lip between his teeth. He moves closer to me, and I take an involuntary step back. I'm starting to hate the way he towers over me. I used to like it, but now it's aggravating.

"They're leaving," he says, tilting his head.

I take a breath. "Thank you. Can I leave now?"

He nods once. "I'd give it a second to clear out, but yes."

I nearly laugh in his face. Only minutes ago, he was taunting me for assuming he'd let me go, and now he's doing exactly that.

Doesn't he understand how *strange* this is?

I can't move past it. Him helping me out of this only further proves my theory that something is up. Something he doesn't want the police to know. He has multiple accounts on me, multiple ways to get me in trouble, and he's choosing to ignore them. Truthfully, I don't think my help is worth all that much.

But he can't be doing it because of our past. That option flew right off the table the second he showed me that SD card.

We wait in a standstill for a couple of minutes, though it's not as intense as it should be. He's just looking at me, and I'm just looking at him, and I have the urge to question him *and* rip his hair out, but I'm more than a little focused on his biceps.

And look. I've seen the man's arms before. It's not as though this is some scandal, like a woman lifting her hem in the 1800s. *By George! She's got ankles!*

They're just...different now. As in, I suddenly understand what Jensen means by *good arms.*

I'm just a woman.

Henry chuckles, clearly seeing straight through me. "My eyes are up here."

"And my ability to care is not in this room." I actually do meet his eyes out of spite. "I'll be leaving now."

"You can head out that broken window if you don't want to trip the alarms again."

I blink. "How do you know about that?"

"Securities told me."

He must know that I know his father owns this place. I think it's the only reason he hasn't told me flat out.

Swallowing against my still-hammering heart, I walk to the door, taking good care not to bump his arm or get too close. "Night, Henry. I pray the bedbugs eat you alive."

"Night, Ames," he says softly. Condescendingly. "Get home safely."

What a git.

I'm cautious as I descend the stairs. I'm not sure if the guards left, or just the police, but I don't have time to worry about it. If they find me, I'll make up some lie about how I'm Henry's secret lover. His family hates me—*he's betrothed to another!*—so we're forced to see each other in seclusion. We madly embrace every night in the museum for six seconds before I bust a window and leave.

The glass that Jensen shattered is easy to find. The break isn't clean at all—I step over multiple shards just to reach the frame, and even then, the leg of my jumpsuit snags on the base. A jagged piece cuts my hand, but I don't bother to look at it. I just lick the blood off my palm and *run*.

10

———

HENRY

It took me about twenty minutes to get everything back to normal in the museum. I attempted to clear the alarm history without invoking my dad's help, and the security guards helped me cover the shattered windows for the time being. That one will have to be explained, though I haven't decided what I'll say yet.

If he finds out that I've let Amelie go *twice,* that'll be the end of me.

Not that he's even caught her once.

I tried to reason with myself on the walk home. Figure out what's going on in my brain, why I've let her go twice. A valid answer still hasn't presented itself, and the choices that *have* are terrible.

Because I need her help, so she can't go to jail yet.

That's my most viable option.

Because I, myself, wanted to.

And that...that is the other.

A knock on my door drags me out of this swirl of thoughts. I look down at my attire, which has been pajamas since I returned home, and reluctantly go to the door.

I don't know who I'm expecting to see, but it isn't my dad.

"There was a security breach at the museum," he says.

It isn't a question.

"Yes," I say. Apparently, my attempts to keep him out of it failed miserably.

He steps inside without an invitation and takes his shoes off, then sits on my couch. I refrain from asking him to leave and take a seat across from him. "What's the matter?"

"There was a security breach, and you were there."

I nod slowly. "Yes. That's what I just said."

"Did you see them? Catch their face by chance?"

I swallow. Can I lie to him? Will he know? *Why am I willing to lie for her?*

"Hardly," I say, rapidly digging my own grave. "I was in your office, trying to mess with the panel. I assume the security guards dealt with it."

This is bad. Horrible. I told the guards to let *me* deal with it. If he asks them, that's what they'll say. Then we'll be right back here, and I'll have to explain why I not only let Amelie go, but why I also lied about it.

You've really done it this time! Great job.

"I'll ask them about it eventually," he mumbles, and I pinch the bridge of my nose. "Tomorrow."

"Wait, just—Don't bother." I take a breath, aware that I have to tell him. Backtracking now is better than being caught in a lie tomorrow. "I think...it may have been Amelie Benoit."

The room falls dead silent. It stays that way until Betty falls off her cat tower and hisses at my shoes.

"What?" Dad says, voice raising slightly. "The same—"

"Yes."

He turns his face toward the ceiling, eyes closed, and I know.

He's thinking of every possible way to get her caught.

My dad has always known of Amelie, back before she began her slight reign of terror over artists in the city. Back when she was just *Henry's girlfriend,* brought up during meals and short car rides. They never met—Dad rarely let us have friends over—but that didn't stop him from disliking her. Though he never tried to keep us from each other, I know he was happy when we fell off.

Dad runs a hand down his face and exhales. I'm thankful that he's focused on this piece of information, rather than the fact that I just lied to him. "So she's begun thieving, hm?"

"Yes," I say, hoping I can leave it at that.

"Do we have proof?"

I swallow. Lie through my teeth. "No. It'd be her word against ours."

He stands and begins pacing, back and forth without a word. I've got no idea what he's thinking. What he's planning. Despite him looking just like me, I've never been able to read an emotion on his face.

"I'll catch her," he says, and the determination in his voice is firm. "I will."

"It's not our top priority. Not right now," I try to remind him. "Finding my piece is."

He looks up, brows arched. "Have you started looking for it?"

"Yes."

"And how's that going?"

"It's...going." I shrug. "I've not found anything yet, but I'm sure I will soon."

He just nods, like this is normal. Like asking me to conduct a search on my own while he tries to get my ex-girlfriend booked is an everyday task. Maybe this will be our new thing. I'll stop painting and start finding ones that are stolen, and he'll do the legal work. My trench coats will work perfectly for the part. I've even got a tobacco pipe somewhere that my granddad gave me.

"Have you run into her?" Dad asks suddenly, bringing us back to the subject I'd like to avoid. "Amelie. In the city."

"No," I say, hoping this is a lie he can't catch me in. The questions he's asking are too close to what's happened, and I worry he knows more than he's letting on. I don't *think* that's the case, though. He's not one for tact. If he knew something, he'd make me come out and say it.

Instead of questioning me further, he just keeps pacing. "That's fine. You work on finding the piece, and I'll work on catching her."

So basically, the nightmare of a partnership I just conjured up.

"And Henry?"

I look up. "Hm?"

Dad stops walking to look me in the eyes. "If you do run into that girl, you will not fall for her tricks again."

I release a tight breath. "Yeah. No, I won't."

He gives a stiff nod and steps away.

I've never understood his dislike for Amelie. She never hurt anyone, not back then. Granted, it's a little different *now*, but he wouldn't have known that.

"I've got something to take care of," Dad says, opening the door. "Find that piece, Henry. I mean it."

So, *so* many words come to mind, yet the ones I say are, "I will."

He gives me one final glare before leaving.

I exhale sharply when I hear the elevator ding outside. My breathing always comes easier when he's gone, and it's an odd sensation to behold. Something about his presence is incredibly suffocating.

Frustrated, I stand from my couch. *Why* do I get into these situations? Someday I'll learn how to say *'no'*. Liz is very intent on teaching me, but I'm not there yet. I'd really like to have another job lined up before I destroy Dad and I's 'partnership'.

At least he doesn't know I'm working with Amelie. I'll have to keep that one hidden extra well.

I go to my room and grab my laptop, then sit on the end of my bed and open it. Betty jumps up next to me with a disgruntled *mrrp*, walking across the keyboard before I gently set her aside. Once she curls up on my pillow and falls asleep, I get to work.

I click open a browser and search for reports of missing art. I'm not really expecting *Nautical Abyss* listed here, given that I watched it be stolen less than an hour ago, but I still give the page a once over. Maybe it'll help me locate my *Ophelia*, or, at the very least, give me something else to focus on.

But it doesn't. Each of the reports are dated back a few weeks, and none of them are even from The Gallery. They're sparse and mostly reports of busts or vases. Only two are paintings, both abstract pieces that I can't decipher.

I close the laptop and lay back on my bed, hands over my eyes. Betty swats at the curls of my hair, but I pay her no mind.

You will not fall for her tricks again.

What tricks? Amelie has tricks now, but I don't think she did in high school.

Maybe everything she told me was a lie. What if this was all some long play at getting what she wanted? What if this was always her plan? She knew what *my* plans were—exactly this. Painting. Having my work displayed, making a living off my art. Granted, I thought I'd be away from my dad by now, but things don't always go according to plan.

I just need to ask her everything. Questions have littered my mind since I saw her yesterday. Since I realized *she* was the one staring at my piece. Judging it. Hating it.

I need answers.

Are you doing this because of me? Why does my dad hate you? Was it all fake? Was this always your plan? How long did it take for you to start hating me?

Sighing, I press my fingers into my eyes.

I need to sleep. I need to tell Liz all of this so she can keep my head level. I *need* to clean up the paint in my studio, because I just remembered it's there and it's a mess, but I don't do any of that.

With Betty still pawing at my hair, I let myself think on one more question. The question I should've asked myself *before* getting into any of this.

What if she's playing me for a complete fool?

She could be. She'd drive a knife into my back while wearing that beautiful smile.

And still, that knowledge doesn't tempt me to change a thing.

11

AMELIE

"Okay. Everyone in this apartment is getting their head shaved."

Meg and Jensen spring up from the couch. They're bundled up and warm, cups of hot cocoa in their hands. The TV is playing some rom-com, but they've muted it.

Good. I'm mad. And cold.

It started *snowing* on my run home.

"Meg," I start coolly, grabbing my inhaler and taking a puff. Being asthmatic is my one and only downfall in this life. "What was *that*? Where did those guys come from?"

"I'm so sorry," she says. "I did a body scan before, I swear. Nobody was in there when I checked. They must've *just* arrived."

I brush a pile of snowflakes off my shoulder. "It's fine."

"How did you even get out?" Jensen asks, handing me a mug of cocoa. He attempted to make a smiley face with marshmallows, probably to humor me. It doesn't work, but I still take a sip.

"Well," I start, "while you two were here canoodling—"

"We were worried about you!"

"*I* was forced to make a deal with Henry Arlington."

They gasp in unison.

"Yeah," I say. "We're basically indebted to him now. I reckon we'll meet with him tomorrow or the next day to discuss...things."

"NO!" Meg groans. "Come on, Amelie. We aren't getting in *more* trouble with this man."

"Too late for that. He got the security guards and police to let me go, so we don't really have a choice."

Her eyes widen. "They didn't see your face?"

"Not once."

"Wow," she mutters, looking at Jensen. "He's desperate."

"Very," he confirms with a nod. "Something is up."

"And we'll figure out what it is," I say. "I promise you that."

Meg sighs and sits back down on the couch. I take the cushion next to her, intent on splitting her and Jensen up, just because I'm a bother. He isn't discreet with his annoyance, but he sits down beside me anyways. I grab my laptop off the table and set it in my lap.

"The missing piece resembles this," I say when I've got a picture of Heyser's *Ophelia* pulled up. "He wants it back fast. I'd guess it's worth a hefty amount of money, given how intent he seems on finding the thing."

Meg hums and takes out her phone. "I've been looking at new trade-offs, but I haven't seen anything. Is that all he told you?"

"That, and it wasn't displayed. I don't think it's completed, either, which is strange. Why would anyone want an incomplete piece?"

"Maybe to finish and sell? To change it up, just enough that it looks different?" Jensen shrugs. "I don't know. Why do we do what *we* do?"

"Because it's what we're good at," I say simply. "Maybe it's the same for them."

But Meg shakes her head, clearly not agreeing with my observation. "No. This isn't the result of a job like ours. When have we ever taken an incomplete?"

"Never," Jen and I say simultaneously.

"Exactly. So maybe it was personal."

I hadn't come to that conclusion yet, but it isn't an impossibility.

"If that *is* the case," I say slowly, "what are the odds of it being out in the open?"

Meg sighs. "Slim to none. You've got us in an impossible position, Ames."

"No such thing," I argue, closing my laptop a little too forcefully. "We'll just tell Henry that we think it's personal. Maybe there's someone he suspects. I'm working out some plans in my mind; surely one will be good enough by tomorrow."

She raises her brows. "Please share with the class."

I take a sip of my cocoa. "Not until they're good."

Jensen sighs, and I can tell he's wary. Which is fair. My plans are a sight to behold, even more once they're put into action. I consider anyone who has been at the hands of one a *very* lucky human.

Currently, I've got three ideas.

The first is simple: to get Henry out in the open. To tempt the thief with something new and shiny. I wasn't just throwing words around when I suggested a decoy—I think it's smart. Basic, maybe, but it's the one Henry is most likely to agree to.

The second is a little worse: we get an actual detective involved. That would lead us *slightly* closer to the police route, though not too close. I bet we could swing it if we tried hard enough, but I don't know Henry's opinion on that, and I won't be asking.

The third is to leave the country and take my business to France where Henry can never find me again. It's the most fun and also the most ridiculous. But I could never bear to leave Dave or my parents, so really, it's void.

Ugh. My parents. I need to call and let them know that we'll be working through them tomorrow, all with minimal details. They own a concert hall downtown; Grand Arts Hall. It's their pride and joy, second only to raising a family, I assume. We run our business through there, which includes cashing our earnings to them so it can be legally dealt. They mark up enough tickets to get us a 'paycheck', no money is lost, and it all looks good enough. We often drop the piece off, make sure it's covered, then let our client know when and where to pick it up. The hall has a couple separate loading docks, so it works well.

Now, I can imagine what questions this is drawing.

Your parents know you're a felon? My goodness! Why don't they turn you in?!

And that's the funny thing.

Before hosting ballets was their job, they did exactly what I do. Art trading was basically their life, but I guess they wanted something more normal when they started a family. I don't think they really intended for me to pick it up, to follow in their footsteps, but we can't help what we're drawn to.

They don't scrutinize me for it. Honestly, I think they're still a little drawn to it, and that's why they let us work through the hall.

Suddenly, my mind shifts from all this to the fact that I still haven't seen the painting we got tonight. Did it even make it back here? Why are Jensen and Meg just *sitting* here?!

"WHERE IS IT?" I basically shout, sitting upright. "Where's the piece?"

"In the van," Jensen says calmly.

I am not calm. "You left it in the van? Are you stupid?"

"We wanted to make sure you were okay before we sent it to trade," Meg says, sounding more than a little sympathetic. "Forgive us for having souls."

"I have a soul, and it is anxiety-ridden. Let's get it over with before someone catches sight of the thing."

She shakes her head. "We're fine. I tucked it away, and the van is covered. It can wait until morning. We've had enough excitement for one day."

I close my eyes and lean further into the cushions. I don't *want* to wait until morning. Leaving something unfinished makes me nervous. I need an abundant amount of sleep to deal with all this, and that won't happen if I'm worrying.

"Fine," I mutter, despite my reluctance. "But *early* morning. Earlier than either of you prefer."

"That's fine," Meg says. "I'll stay the night."

"You can sleep in bed with me."

"No, you snore."

I gape. "I do *not*."

"Oh my gosh, do you seriously not think you snore?" Jensen's brows raise. "You're like a chainsaw, Ames. It's bad."

"YOU KNOW I HAVE ALLERGIES!"

"That doesn't mean we should suffer," Meg says.

"Well then." I stand and down the rest of my cocoa, then rinse the mug out in the sink. "Opposite ends of the couch."

"Oh, good grief, Amelie," Jen mutters.

"I mean it, too." I make a show of walking backwards and watching them until I close my bedroom door. Once it latches behind me, I change out of my still-wet clothes and turn the lights off before climbing into bed. Jensen absolutely destroyed the state of my room—the sheets are on the floor and the pillows are flattened beyond belief. I fix the blankets and fluff the pillows before doing my best to drift off.

I'm halfway asleep when my phone buzzes on my nightstand.

The screen manages to light nearly my entire room. I paw at the nightstand until the phone is in my palm and squint to read the message.

It's Henry, which is not at all what I expected to see.

ARLINGTON

Hello.

If you wouldn't mind, I'd appreciate you and your 'team' meeting me tomorrow morning. The cafe you chose today will be fine. 10:00.

I all but snort at my phone screen. *This* is what I wake up for? For him to demand I meet him at the patisserie tomorrow?

Okay, that's a little unfair. He didn't demand in the slightest. He's actually being overly polite. Who texts like this? And why are we completely glazing over what happened just hours ago?

Whatever. *I'm* not going to be the one to bring it up.

fine

> and why did you put your name in my phone as arlington. what if i didn't know that was you. what if i sat here confused for an hour, wondering who you were. imagine me scared. curious. TERRIFIED.

I set my phone back down, assuming he won't say anything to that mess, but he replies seconds later.

ARLINGTON

> I did it for old time's sake.

Oh. I don't like that.

He's not *wrong*, I guess. I used to call him Arlington, back before I wanted to strangle him with his intestines. It's just a snazzy word, you know? Like those names in old time-y dramas that everyone likes. I find it *classy*. It suits him very well.

But I absolutely won't stand for that right now.

> no. we won't be doing that.

ARLINGTON

> Oh, what? Reminiscing?

> LET ME GO TO SLEEP

I can practically hear his laugh as I read his next message.

ARLINGTON

> Whatever you want, Ames. Goodnight.

It takes a good portion of my willpower to put my phone down and close my eyes.

When I get to the patisserie, I see three people already waiting for me. Amelie stares me down as I walk toward the counter, a slight smirk on her lips. The other two stare at me like I'm the most horrid thing they've ever seen, and I can't really blame them. There's no telling what Amelie has said about me.

We order our drinks and sit at a covered table outside, each of us shivering like crazy. It's forty degrees out here, but we can't very well sit *inside*. I've got a feeling this conversation isn't going to lean on legality.

"We can make this quick," Amelie says as soon as we're seated. She's taken the chair closest to me, though I don't think much of it. "In fact, let's do exactly that."

"Okay." I turn to her friends. They look like they're trying to set me on fire with their eyes. "Amelie said you have the resources to find my piece?"

"Uh, no, I didn't." Amelie tilts her head to the side. "You *assumed* that."

"You did nothing to correct me."

"So? That's not my fault."

I sigh. "Just give me a starting point, and we—"

"A starting point? *Seriously?*" She gives a dry laugh, and I cannot for the life of me figure out what is so comical about this situation. "I can't just keep telling you—"

"Can you two *shut up*?"

Amelie and I slowly turn our heads toward the blonde girl across from me. She's pulled out a laptop now, glaring at us over the top of it.

"Yes, Meg, we can shut up." Amelie takes a sip of her coffee. "My apologies. You know how I am."

"I do." The girl, who I assume is Meg, nods. "Now, Henry, I just need a few details about your piece. Quickly, please. Canvas size?"

"30 by 50," I say.

"Medium?"

"...Paint?"

"Just verifying," she says. "Amelie said it was inspired by a classic?"

"Heyser's *Ophelia*." I nod. "The color palette was different; a deeper, more blatant choice, but—"

"I don't need to know all that."

I snap my mouth shut. Amelie stifles a laugh.

Meg lets out a heavy sigh and keeps typing. Her face gives away nothing, but Amelie's forehead is wrinkled in concentration, so I'm guessing she can read the girl's expression much better than I can.

"I'm not getting anything," Meg says finally. "I'm seeing talk of a *reimagined classic*, but no specifics."

I tip my head to the side, suddenly amused. How do they just *find* these things? Is there some page that has all the up-and-coming thievery news? Amelie heavily suggested that there wasn't, but she isn't above lying to me. The concept is *just* ridiculous enough that she wouldn't want to tell me.

"Oh, what are you smirking at, Henry?" Amelie asks.

"I'm only curious," I say. "Do you guys have like...a thievery gossip site?"

"I have friends," Meg says flatly.

"Ah," I hum. "Friends, felons..."

"Do you want help or not?" Amelie smacks my arm. "She's not scared of prison. You can't threaten her."

"You can't threaten me," Meg confirms, dabbing her mouth with the ends of her scarf. "And anyways, I'll keep an eye out. Don't worry about it. I get updates frequently; if something new shows up, I'm on it."

"Thank you," I say.

She gives me a nod. I look over at Amelie, whose expression is blank. It seems to startle her when I meet her eyes, and she clears her throat, straightens up in her seat. "Okay. Well, I have a plan that we can use in the meantime. One that would be more direct."

I raise a brow. "Okay?"

"I think we should make you more public."

I blink. "I'm not sure I understand. I'm public already."

"Yes, I'm aware, Henry. We've seen your pretty face on those banners." She pats my cheek, and I know the action is condescending, but the feeling of her skin against mine is embarrassingly distracting. "But we need to make you a *target*."

The word sobers me up pretty quickly. "That...sounds like a very stupid idea."

"Not like you're thinking." She shakes her head. "We need to make your process more public. To make it all about your paintings, and the fact that you're about to start a new one. If you're his only target, it's guaranteed to catch his eye."

"But I'm not about to start a new piece."

She sighs. "Mmm, but you are."

"No, I'm...not."

"I literally just said you are. You have to!"

"No," I repeat. "This sounds like a great way to get further tangled up in a situation that I have no interest in. This wasn't the deal, Amelie. I don't care if we *catch* the guy. I just want my piece back."

She pinches the bridge of her nose, annoyance coloring her features. I know that this is an argument I'll lose, but I can't stop myself from pushing back. I don't want this to be an intricate thing. I don't have *time* for it.

"Okay," Amelie says slowly, "but this is sort of a twofer thing. *We* want him caught. I don't know if you know this, but anyone that steals art is kind of in this...how do I put it..."

"Unspoken competition?" The man, who has not talked this entire time, supplies.

Amelie snaps her fingers. "That's it. We're in an unspoken competition. Because the more work they get, the less we get. It's technically ethics."

"There is nothing ethical about that."

She shrugs. "I said *technically.*"

I close my eyes and wonder, just for a moment, if this is a nightmare.

I decide that it's not when a voice pulls me out of my reverie.

"Listen, Hector, I think you should do it." Meg is staring at me once again, and before I can ask if she's truly forgotten my name, she keeps on. "Seriously. Ames is smart. She knows how to get things done. Besides, this route buys us some time away from you."

"Ah, Meg." Amelie flashes a bright smile. "Always the poet."

Her friend grins back patronizingly.

I sigh and remove my glasses, cleaning the lenses against my shirt. I *know* that Amelie is smart. Whatever she suggests will probably work. But the difference between us is, I don't have the luxury of breaking the law. I have to be careful with this. Nobody can find out, and I can't be stirring up trouble.

"Alright," I say against my better judgment. "But I'm not getting another piece stolen. This will be a *decoy.* And if *you* manage to steal it—"

"I won't," Amelie says, meeting my eyes. "Promise."

"I caught you stealing a piece of mine last night."

She toys with her bottom lip. "Well, I mean, no one would want two of those things."

The man to my left barks a laugh, and the sound is as grating as it is dehumanizing.

"Alright," I start, standing from my seat. "I'll start on a decoy."

Amelie jumps up, and I think she's about to tell me *no, not yet,* but instead she says. "I'll help."

All eyes go to her, including mine, and there's a simultaneous *HUH* from the three of us.

"What?" She says, face painted with false innocence. "You clearly don't want to work on it. I assume you're lacking inspiration, so I'm going to help you. And besides, we should really catch up. We've got a lot to talk about, don't you think?"

I really *don't* think, for my sake.

Being in Amelie's presence for too long could be disastrous. It's something I should be thoroughly against, and I'm *not,* which is a problem. Even last night, those few minutes around her made my head spin. I shouldn't have touched her, shouldn't have gotten too close, but I did. She clouds my judgment and she always has. But in the past, it wasn't wrong. The decisions I made over her weren't illicit.

Though that isn't to say I wouldn't have done anything she asked of me.

No. No. I can't do this.

You will not fall for her tricks again.

He's right. I won't.

"What do you get out of this?" I ask, voice lowered so only she can hear.

Amelie looks up at me with wide eyes. "Nothing. Really. I just… it was my idea, so I'll help you out. Not that you need help, but you know. I'll give you some company."

"You know I don't like company when I paint."

"Well, that's too bad, because I think this is important."

"In what sense?"

"All!" She sighs. "We need to have a good foundation for our new blackmailer-blackmailee relationship."

My brain snags on that last word a bit too long for my liking.

I seriously need to get a grip. What is my problem? Did seeing her *steal from me* last night trip some wire in my brain? Is this what I've come to?

"You can join," I say tersely. "But if you give away the location of my studio, I —"

"I won't," she says. "You have my word."

"That means very little to me now."

She gives a brief shrug before looking at her friends. "I'll see you two later. Meg, check in with the clients from today, okay?"

Clients from today.

Perhaps over the piece she took last night.

I file that away for later, though I can't figure out what good it'll do me.

"Gotcha," Meg mutters, back on her laptop already. "I'll let you know if I find something on Herbert's painting."

Ah. So she *is* screwing with me.

Amelie grins widely at the incorrect name, and I wish the sight didn't fill me with warmth. "Thank you very much, Meg." She grabs her coffee cup and turns back to me, head tilted as she says, "Lead the way, hm?"

I do, of course. I always do.

13

———

AMELIE

I should've expected Henry's apartment building to look like something out of a movie.

It's ridiculous. A downtown skyrise with a ridiculous number of floors. Every time I passed this building on a walk, I imagined snooty businessmen with unhappy wives were living here. *Now* I know it's inhabited by annoying artists with strange coping tactics.

If I'd really cared to dig back into the past, it wouldn't have been much of a shock. Henry's family had the nicest house of anyone I knew. That, too, looked like a movie set, albeit more cluttered. There was no shortage of photos and newspapers on any flat surface.

It's always been strange to me that I so vividly remember his home. That I can clearly recall the pictures of his and Lizzy's first days of school, or the childhood dog whose frame rests on their mantle. I only visited there once or twice, both times because his parents were gone. He said that he and his sister weren't allowed to have friends over. I never cared enough to question it, though now, I realize how odd it is.

I shouldn't be thinking back on that, especially not while I'm next to him. But I'm brave enough to admit that, no matter how much I've hated Henry through the years, I've missed him and his sister.

Liz was one of my best friends, though I didn't have many to pick from back then. She was an angel sent to grace this horrible planet. I can think of multiple times she helped me out, whether it was getting me ready for my prom or lending me jewelry and a pair of shoes for a night out.

I grimace at the memory. It's too fond. Too tender. I wish that I hadn't lost her when I lost Henry, though I guess it couldn't be helped.

I shake my head, trying to forget all of that. What happened, happened. My preferred outcome may have been something different, but I can't change the past.

"You know," I say to Henry as he opens the building's door for me. "I was picturing a studio. Like a *studio*. Because you *said* it was a studio."

This is not a studio. This, again, is a high rise, and I'm quite sure he's taking me to the penthouse. They've got a doorman, for goodness sakes, and *he* has a snazzy hat with gold detailing.

Henry sighs as we get in the elevator, then sticks his key into the top button. As I figured. "Repeating the word over and over again doesn't alter the meaning."

"Mmm, yeah it does."

"This *is* my studio."

"No, it's a penthouse."

"Same thing."

"Uh, no, *misinformation*."

He glares at me from the corner of his eye. I stare back, if only to try and read his expression, but I'm realizing that I can't do that anymore. Used to, I could read him like a book, and now, he's guarded toward me.

I don't know why that makes me feel a little down.

"This is my apartment," he says once the elevator stops. "My studio is a separate room *in* said apartment. Locked."

"So they know where you live."

He shrugs. "Or they got lucky."

"I don't believe in luck."

"I once didn't believe in gravity," he says, "but then I fell down a flight of stairs."

"You're just full of personality today."

He starts to grin, and from him, that's as good as a full-blown fit of laughter.

Henry finds a key on his lanyard and unlocks a white door, and I nearly gasp when I catch a glimpse of the room behind it. It's *massive*. That's the best way to explain it. There's an entire glass wall that looks out over the city. The furniture looks untouched. A nearly full bookcase rests against the far wall, and I have the urge to go see what titles fill the shelves.

It's gorgeous. Absolutely stunning.

I genuinely cannot believe I'm standing here.

Simply *getting* here was a total shock. I put the offer out just to annoy Henry. I didn't expect him to take me up on it, and if he did, I wasn't planning on coming. But when I *really* thought about it...

I'm nosey, okay? Extremely nosey. Part of it is because I think he's hiding a body or something weird, and the other part is because I want to see what his house looks like. Sue me.

"Home sweet home," Henry says flatly, closing the door behind us. He taps my right shoulder and tugs at the back of my collar, so I shrug my coat off for him to take. It's a reflex, almost second nature, and I don't even catch how strange it is until he's got the thing off me.

Why did I do that? If anyone else came up behind me and started pulling at my coat, I'd elbow them in the sternum. Why didn't I take the shot at him?

He used to do that, I remember, going rigid at the memory. *All the time.*

He did. I'd completely forgotten about that.

Any time I was wearing a coat, Henry would do exactly what he just did. He'd flick my shoulder and hook a finger in my collar, tugging gently until I took it off. In the time that we dated, I don't think I ever once dealt with my own coat. No matter if it was at a party, or restaurant, or school event, he'd take it from me, only to put it back on before we left.

I frown, suddenly wishing I'd just stayed with Meg and Jensen. I've been alone with Henry for about twenty minutes, and I've already had too many memories stirred up.

"You can look around," Henry says, hanging my coat next to his.

I hum. "I'm shocked you trust me here."

"I don't think you're going to steal my kitchen counter, if that's what you mean."

"No, I'm just saying." I cross my arms and glance around. The room, while fully furnished, feels very empty. It's like no one has actually *lived* here. I have the urge to bring over some throw blankets and jump on the cushions just to dent them. "Where's the studio?"

"Down this hall."

I hear rather than see him walking away, so I turn and follow, peeking into random opened doors as I do. To the left lies an untouched bedroom and bathroom, which I assume is the guest room. To the right is what looks like a storage closet, though I know better than to ask. We stop at the end of the hall, right in front of a cracked door. Henry pushes it open with a heavy sigh. "I kindly ask you to never discuss what you see here."

"Is there a corpse," I deadpan.

He doesn't respond, nor does he enter the room. His stance is almost nervous, the way he's turned away from me, hands fidgeting with the buttons on his coat. I quickly get tired of waiting and just go around him.

It looks exactly as I expected.

The entire thing is packed full of canvases and easels and paints. Colors are smeared on the wall and spilled on the floor, and it smells like acrylic. It's as comforting as it is aggravating, and yet, I don't have the urge to leave.

I figured the living room wasn't lived in, and I was right. I think Henry lives in his studio more than anything else.

"Wow," I breathe. "You're still messy."

He laughs. "Yeah."

"Do you have any finished pieces?" It's a square room, and I only see one other door. I don't think he can have much hidden, especially with how big his paintings seem to be, but I feel like I have to ask.

"Not here," Henry says. "I do a lot of commissioned work. When they're done, I either sell or display them."

"Huh," I say, then accidentally step on a paintbrush. The handle splinters underneath my foot, but he doesn't comment on it. To be fair, he shouldn't have left it on the floor.

"I would say 'take a seat', but I'm not sure I have real chairs in here," Henry says, almost shyly. "I'm never really sitting."

"I know," I say, hating the response even though it's true. "You never were."

He opens his mouth like he's going to respond, but he doesn't end up saying a thing.

I find a wooden crate and plant my butt on it. Henry lifts a fresh canvas onto an easel and tears the plastic covering off, letting it fall to the ground.

"What are you thinking?" He asks, sketching lightly on the canvas with a paint covered pencil. "What should I do?"

I blink, caught off guard. "I don't mess with painting anymore."

"No, you do, just in a different way. Don't you know what thieves look for?"

"No. We go by request. I don't curate a catalog for buyers to flip through."

"Ah," he says, and it feels a little condescending, though I'm probably just overthinking it. "Well, then."

"Well, then," I repeat, leaning forward on my uncomfy crate.

Henry exhales, eyes glued to the canvas. "I'm sure you've figured out that my dad owns the museum?"

Huh. We're getting right into this, then. Do I want him to know that I know? Lying seems pointless; it's clear that he already knows, or else he wouldn't ask. I must've mentioned it. Given it away somehow. Or he's become a psychic since I saw him last.

"Yes," I say cautiously. "He bought this place for you, I assume?"

A shake of his head. "He owns the building."

I file that away for later. His father must know the tenants, then, and Henry's painting was likely taken by someone who knows their way around this place. Anyone mildly observant could see which floor he goes to. This isn't as black-and-white as I expected it to be, and it's already getting on my nerves.

"Do you suspect anyone?" I ask. "Any mortal enemies, occupational competitors, salty exes..."

He laughs, and I close my eyes against the sound. That last question is a cheap shot—he knows it, I know it. But I don't even care. I'm not above petty questions. So what if I want to know if he's had a few girlfriends? It's been four years. I'm sure he has, and at least one must have a vendetta against him. He's quite aggravating.

"No," Henry says, squinting at the floor. "I try to keep as few salty exes as possible. They tend to make my life difficult."

He glances over at me, a not-so-subtle grin on his face, and I look away.

"It makes it easier if you have suspects," I say. "You should at least have a guess on who took it."

He shakes his head. "I don't. If I *had* a guess, I wouldn't have asked for your help."

I hum and lean forward. "But you never suspected me."

A pause. "No."

"That's very foolish of you."

"I know."

He goes back to sketching, and I go back to praying I don't get a splinter in my thigh.

"What do you like to paint now?" I ask.

Henry pins me with a blank expression. I think he wants me to be quiet—he doesn't like company while he paints, but I'm not going to shut up. This situation is making me chattier than usual. "You know what I like to paint."

I shake my head. "I said *now*. I know what you painted four years ago."

"The same."

"The *same*?"

"Yes."

I blink. "You haven't evolved at all."

"No," he says. "I'm the same."

"That seems unrealistic."

"Why? I've always painted the same things. The things I care about. Things I want to preserve." He shrugs. "You're the one who's changed."

Instead of arguing, as I so naturally want to do, I stand and walk toward him. Whatever he's drawing looks like nothing more than random squiggles, though I'm sure there's meaning to him. He says this piece won't be personal, but I know that's not the truth. He's never been able to separate himself from his art.

Henry sighs. "You're evaluating."

"I'm just curious."

"Hm." He crosses his arms. "You ever paint anymore?"

And this is where he strikes a nerve.

"No," I say flatly. "I don't."

I feel his eyes on me as he asks, "Not at all?"

"New topic."

"I just—"

"New. Topic."

He turns away. "Alright. What do you think of this sketch?"

"I don't know. I don't see anything but lines." I squint. "And a duck. Why did you draw a duck."

Henry frowns as he looks back at the canvas. "What are you talking about?"

"There's a duck." I motion to the center of the sketch. "Right here."

"That's not a duck."

"Well it *looks* like a duck, and you—"

I shut my mouth when I hear a scratching noise at the door.

My entire body freezes, and my heart starts trying to beat its way out of my chest.

A trap.

This is a trap, one that I walked right into. One that I set in motion by inviting myself over here. How can I possibly be this much of a failure? I should've just gone home.

Maybe in the future I won't be so nosey. But also, I'll be in jail. So.

The cops are outside the door by now, I'm sure. Handcuffs open and ready to slide onto my wrists. I can practically hear their voices as they read me my rights, which probably won't come in that handy, but—

"Betty!" Henry's words carry his smile, and I nearly choke at his change of composure.

"I'm *sorry?*"

"That's Betty." He opens the door, and I *actually* choke this time from how hard I gasp.

A small black cat trots through the room, meowing every so often in my direction. Probably because I'm hacking on my own spit.

"I LOVE HER!" I croak through my blocked airways. Betty meows at me again, so I drop to my knees and pet her. She rubs against my hip before plopping down on my thighs.

"That's Betty," Henry says again. "She's my cat."

I look up at him with wide eyes. "You hate cats."

He nods. "Detest them. Yes."

"So why would you get a cat?"

"Because Betty isn't a cat. Betty is Betty. She's a *good* cat."

"She's a perfect angel," I correct, scratching her behind the ears. She purrs even louder, and I start calculating how much I can spend on a cat that isn't mine before it gets concerning. She needs a wardrobe. A collar with a little bell, or a *bow,* or even a flower! The possibilities are endless.

"You're planning to buy her an outfit," Henry says knowingly.

I sit up a little straighter. "No. Absolutely not."

"I can practically see the gears turning in your mind."

"Irrelevant."

He chuckles, and the sound startles me so much that I make it my mission to never hear it again.

I set the cat down and get back on my feet. In the short time I was distracted, Henry slathered half the canvas with a deep blue paint, some of it dripping down onto the floor.

"That's why this place is so messy, then," I say.

He nods. "Pretty much."

"Have you turned into one of those crazy artists yet? The ones on the brink of insanity with every passing day? Please let me know so I can take Betty home with me and spoil her silly."

Henry stifles a laugh. "No. I don't think so, anyways."

"Good."

"Though it's never impossible. Will we ever be aware that we're on the brink of insanity? Or will it just overtake us on a random day?"

I snort. "Don't start. Not today."

"If not now, then when?"

"You need to stop."

"I need to focus, actually." He grabs a smaller brush and starts cleaning up the base. "I want this done quickly."

Before I can respond, my phone starts buzzing in my pocket. I whip it out to find half a dozen messages littered across my screen, and my eyes dart over the words at lightning speed.

MEGAN

Found the listing for Harvey's piece

No location

Call me

Like now please

My eyes hurt from staring at this screen

I vow to teach her how to text a full paragraph later, then dial her number. When she picks up, the first thing I say is, "What's wrong?"

"No location," she repeats, just as I get another message from her. I put the call on speaker and click the link she sent, which ends up being a photo of Henry's piece. It's simply the canvas and a brief size description. Nothing else. "There's no contact, no name, nothing. It's just a picture."

"I don't understand," I mumble. "It's never *just* this. There's always a way to find it. Maybe it's cryptic?"

"I've done all I can to *un*-cryptify it," Meg tells me. "I think it's just a dead end."

Just as I'm contemplating throwing my phone out the window, Henry steps closer and stares at the screen over my shoulder. "That's my piece. You're saying we can't find it?"

"'Fraid not," Meg says. "Not right now, at least. I'll dig until I get it uncovered, but for now, keep working on the decoy."

"Henry's got it started, so I'll come home now, I guess." I pinch the bridge of my nose. "I'll see you guys soon." I hang up my phone and turn to Henry, huffing so hard my hair blows away from my face. "Well, you heard her. Your painting is being held hostage in a shed, probably owned by a creepy old man."

"It'll be okay," he says, and I have the sudden urge to smack him. He should be angrier about this than I am. "That's the point of the decoy, right? To buy us some time. It's not going to be easy."

It was *supposed* to be easy. I thought once we found the listing, we'd be fine. Set up a fake meeting, get the guy to leave it, and give him a hefty amount of cash, per Henry's pocket. But if we can't even track the guy down, we have nothing. The photo is basically him dangling a carrot in front of our noses and forcing us to follow.

"I guess," I mumble, instead of saying all that.

"Regardless, I had a productive day." Henry motions to the canvas in front of him. He added more, just in the short time I was distracted. It's only a mix of colors, but I swear I can see bodies and faces taking shape already. Or maybe I'm just being imaginative. "Might've gotten more done if you and Betty hadn't been so loud, but y'know."

"The angel and I did nothing." I scoop the cat off the ground and hold her against my chest, fully aware that she's *not* enjoying it. She's purring, but it's getting quieter and she's swatting at the ends of my hair. I set her down before she makes me bleed, then turn to her owner. "I suppose you'll need something else before long?"

"Possibly," he says. "I'll send a carrier pigeon if I need to reach you."

I allow myself a singular, dry laugh.

Henry holds a paint covered hand out, and I stare at it blankly. "I feel like we've got to shake on it," he explains.

I shake my head. "I don't think we do."

"Is this because I have paint on my hands?"

"Sort of," I admit. And what about it? My sweater is pink. Do you understand how vividly indigo paint is going to show up on a pink sweater? I got this last week, half price. You couldn't pry the thing away from me.

I wonder if I should explain this to Henry because he isn't moving his hand away.

"For old time's sake," he says, and with that look on his face, I know he's doing it to rattle me.

I won't give him the satisfaction.

Sighing, I roll up my sleeve and grab his hand, giving it a firm shake. The feeling of his rough skin against mine is strange, distant, and I hate it. I wait for him to drop my hand, but he doesn't, so I drop his instead. I find the rag he dried his brushes with and wipe the paint off my palm, then walk out the door without a word.

"Don't forget your coat on the way out," Henry calls as I leave.

And I'll never admit it, but if he hadn't said that, I would've forgotten.

14

____

AMELIE

Meg attacks me with a lint roller the second I step foot in the living room.

"NO NO NO NO!" She screeches, rolling the thing down my side. "I will not have cat hair all over this place. You played with his *cat*?"

"You don't even live here! You don't get a say in how much cat hair I drag in." I huff. "But yes, I did. Her name is Betty and I love her."

She huffs, sounding equally as exhausted as I. "I'm thrilled you got to spend the day with a cat. Really. But did you, oh, I don't know, find out why Harry wants our help?"

"You're smashing my new bra!" I yank the lint roller out of her hand and chuck it at the couch. It hits Jensen's shoulder, but he's smart enough to keep quiet. "And no, I still haven't figured that out. Jen and I did learn that his dad—Roman Arlington, if you aren't caught up—owns his apartment building."

"I don't care if his daddy pays his rent."

"I didn't say he pays his rent." I cross my arms. "He owns the *building.* If he wanted to, couldn't he just get the security footage? Henry has the penthouse. It's not like someone can get in there without being seen. He even had a key to the elevator. It was a whole thing."

I'm vaguely aware that his dad might find out *I* was there, but hopefully he wouldn't think anything of it. Old friends, right? Nothing fishy. Just two kids catching up. I've never met Roman, but he has no reason to be overly suspicious of me.

I mean, he *totally* has reason, but not that he knows about.

Jensen stands. "I think something is going on."

"We could be overreacting," Meg offers, but I don't think we are. Henry shouldn't be so willing to go through with all of this. The whole thing is off.

"I just don't like it." I shake my head, bite my lips together. "Something is unfolding right in front of us, and we're going to figure out what."

Meg takes Jensen's seat and pulls a blanket into her lap. For someone that doesn't live here, she certainly *thinks* she does. "We'll get it, Ames. Promise. You've got him already, right? You know more than he wants."

"No." I shake my head. "I don't think he even *cares* what I know, and that's what's bothering me."

Logically, his only reason for not going to the police would be some issue of legality. Perhaps he's got his own thing going for him —maybe he steals cake pans for sport or something. But I didn't find anything like that today. There was *nothing* suspicious about him, and it's killing me. I'd almost rather him have told me upfront.

"I've murdered four people this week," he'd say, to which I'd respond, *"Great! I understand now. Your perfect disposition is a facade. Let's deal with that before moving on."*

But no. I think he's seriously just desperate.

Panic seeps through me when a knock comes to my door. The last time someone knocked on our door, it was Henry, carrying a pocketful of blackmail with him. We don't get a lot of company, and I'd like to keep it that way.

"Peephole," I say to Jensen.

He scoffs. "*What* did you just call me?"

"No, you dunce. Go check the peephole."

"Oh." Jensen crosses the room and puts his eye up to the lens on the door. I hold my breath as he tilts his head to get a better view, but he unlocks the deadbolt seconds later. "It's your parents."

I blink and walk to the entryway. "What?"

"Pumpkin!" My dad is beaming as he walks through the door, and Mom isn't far behind him. It's almost sickening what a picture-perfect couple my parents are, especially on workdays. Their outfits *match;* today, they don identical sweaters. "Surprise!"

"What for?" I ask, returning the hug they both wrap me in.

My dad laughs. To this day, his voice is one of those comforting sounds I'll never tire of. "Well, it's more of a surprise on *our* part, I guess. We got a call this morning...were you doing some business at the hall?"

I wince. This morning, before meeting with Henry, we dropped the piece off at Grand Arts. I was so preoccupied with *him* that telling my parents slipped my mind.

"Yes," I say, hoping I didn't cause any unnecessary trouble. "Jensen locked back up. Unless he messed up, which is possible."

He crosses his arms. "I did *not*."

"He did not," Mom confirms, patting him on the shoulder. Her and Jen have a whole alliance; he's basically the son she never had, and she's the mom he wanted. It works for them. Me, on the other hand, I'm not pleased when they gang up on me. Mom acts as Jensen's metaphorical shield in all our arguments.

"We're actually here because of two things," Dad says, drawing the attention back to him. "First off, has the painting been picked up yet?"

"Not sure," Meg says before I can respond. "I called them and they didn't pick up. I'll try again later."

"What's the other thing?" I ask.

Dad sighs. "Well, your mom—"

"Don't you know what today is, Amelie?" Mom asks, and I instantly begin to panic, because I have no idea. It could be an anniversary, or a national holiday, and I wouldn't have a clue. I don't even know whether it's morning or night right now.

"No," I say slowly. "I've got no idea."

"It's the third."

"And your point is...?"

"It's February third."

February. *February.*

Oh, no.

"Mom—" I try, but there's no use.

"Two weeks, Ames," she says. "Yours and Margot's birthday is in two weeks! I refuse for us to be split up this year."

I'm still shaking my head. "Mom, I don't think—"

"It's about time my girls are together again," she argues pointedly. "It's been too long, and this is the perfect excuse. I've got everything figured out."

"You do?" I croak.

She nods. "I do. And I know I shouldn't have without your permission, but I don't care. I'm pulling the *mom card.*"

"She can do that," Jensen tells me. "She can do anything with the mom card."

I squeeze my eyes shut. Take a breath. "And Margot agreed?"

"That's the thing..." Mom looks at Dad, and he gives a shrug. "Margot agreed because she has a showing for the week I've got planned. The exhibit is near our cabin, so..."

"You want us all to stay in the cabin," I finish, wringing my hands together. "You want us to have a birthday vacation, go to Marg's showing, and have a jolly time."

"Exactly," she says, nodding proudly. "It'll be the best thing we've done in a while, Ames."

I do not feel as though it would be the best thing. In fact, it sounds like a very bad thing to me.

Margot, my twin sister, is sort of a sore subject. Not to Mom and Dad, but to me. Mom isn't being dramatic when she says it's been too long. The two of us haven't talked in...well, it's probably been four years since I've seen her in person. Not since she left for art school. I haven't thought about our birthday once since then. Jen simply buys me a cake, Meg gets me a new pajama set, and we move on. By noontime, it's just another day.

Four years. Four years since I've seen her, since our family has all been together.

I abandoned a lot of things that year. Sometimes I wonder if it was too much.

"Okay," I say quietly. "Maybe. But I've got things lined up, Mom. I do this stuff months in advance. It's hard to just drop it all."

"The cabin is only a couple hours away," Dad says. "Couldn't you just come back and deal with it all next weekend? We're only planning a week-long stay."

"A *week?!*" That's like a year! "When is this all going down?"

"We'd get there on the tenth," Mom says. "Marg's exhibit is on the sixteenth."

I pull out my phone and find the calendar. It's the third, or so everyone is telling me (I hadn't even realized we left January!). That gives me a week to tie up loose ends here.

"I don't know," I say, staring at the little dated boxes on my screen. "It's not that I don't want to, but I'm *busy*. I have things to keep up with."

Dad winces. "Well, pumpkin, we rented out the hall for that week, so you can't work through there."

Hmm. That puts a dent in things. Nothing that I can't solve, but a dent nonetheless.

"Okay," I mumble, adding this to my mental list. It's right next to *deal with blackmail scheme* and *fix broken mug*. "I'll let you know by the end of the week."

"Thank you, Amelie," Mom says, giving me a soft smile. Her genuine look of happiness makes guilt sink into my stomach, given how reluctant I feel right now. It isn't that I don't want to spend time with *them;* my parents are some of my favorite people, and they're right. Despite me running business through their workplace, we haven't *really* seen each other in a while.

I just don't want to see my sister.

Mom suddenly grabs my wrist, instantly dragging me into the hall. It's not really a hallway—it's more like a square foot of space next to the bathroom, but it's close enough. The boys are already preoccupied with something on Dad's phone, but Meg is listening.

She's eyeing me like she knows something, even though she can't possibly.

"Honey, you know our neighbor?"

I blink. "That's so vague."

"You know, the Bridges."

I shake my head. I do not know the Bridges.

Mom waves a hand. "Well, anyways, their son is going to be at the lodge when we are. I've been in contact with his mom—Courtney, remember? The one who owns the winery?" She's grinning now. "We think you guys should meet up this time around."

I close my eyes. "Absolutely not—"

"Oh, why not? You're young and beautiful."

"I know."

She ignores me. "You should be going out and having fun, not being obsessed with your work. One date wouldn't hurt, right?"

I groan. I thought I had escaped my mom setting me up on dates, though I know her intentions are pure. My parents, despite *their* history of thievery as well, don't have a single bad bone in their body. Mom just wants me to find love. Probably would rather me settle down with a man with a stable job than continue what I've got going. I think I'm the reason her hair is graying.

But no.

"I can't, Mom," I say, shaking my head. "Maybe next time." *There will be no next time.*

"Really, why not, Amelie?" Her eyes are bright. "He's a handsome boy!"

"She can't because she has a boyfriend."

The words come out of Meg's mouth, but I can't understand why.

Immediately, my gaze connects with hers. I probably look like the personification of terror right now—my eyes feel like they're bulging out of my face, and my teeth are pressed together so hard, I'm concerned I'll need dental work after this is all said and done.

"What?" My mom says ecstatically.

"Yeah, *what*?" I say, less discreetly than I'd planned.

"That's right. Our favorite girl has a boyfriend." Meg stands and folds the blanket back up—something she's never done—before joining our little hallway gathering. "Am I wrong, Ames? Haven't you been seeing someone?"

I have two options here. I tell my mom that Meg is a filthy liar and go on a date with what's-his-face, or I lie.

I'm very good at lying.

"Yes," I say, looking at my mom. "I've been seeing someone lately. We've only gone out a few times, but I quite like him. I couldn't go on a date with Jacob—"

"Jack!"

Close enough. "—while knowing how much I like this boy. It wouldn't be right."

Mom sighs, and I think I'm free. I think this will never be spoken of again, at least not right now. But then her face lights up. Her eyes widen and she smiles and I just *know* I'm in trouble.

"Bring him to the cabin!" Mom says. "That would be fun! Arnie, wouldn't that be fun?"

"Huh?" Dad says from the living room. He and Jensen have parked themselves on the couch, now locked in on a football rerun.

"Couldn't Amelie bring the boy she's dating to the cabin?"

"She's dating?" Dad asks, looking mildly appalled. "I guess so. I'd like to meet the chap."

This is going downhill so much quicker than expected. "Guys, no. I just started seeing him. It's only been, like, a month—"

"Your father and I were married by then." She waves a hand around like that's normal. "And it isn't a big deal. Just think of it as a vacation for the both of you. No one minds getting away from work, and you *need* a break. Let us all celebrate you and Margot for a bit, okay? Just ask him."

I squeeze my eyes shut. The second I get ahold of Meg, it is *over*. I'm finding Jensen's hair clippers and ending her. She'll look nice with a buzzcut. She's got the head shape for it.

"I'll decide everything by this weekend," I tell her, starting to move toward the door so she'll follow. Dad notes my tactic and complies, but Mom keeps her feet planted in the living room. "And if I can make it work...I'll see what he says."

"Yay!" Mom gives me a quick, suffocating hug. "Thank you, honey. You won't regret coming. It'll be so great, and maybe, you and Margot can—"

"Maybe," I interrupt so she won't finish the sentence.

Mom's mouth turns to a thin line, like she knows how intent I am on *not* breaching that subject. Relief sweeps over me when she just nods, keeping her words to herself.

Dad sighs and puts a hand on Mom's back, then grabs the door handle with the other. *Thank you.* "We oughta get back to the hall. Orchestral performance tonight. You guys comin'?"

Jensen stands. "You know—"

"I think we're good," I say, leaning against the wall in the entryway. I close out of my calendar app and shut my phone off, slipping it into my front pocket. "Maybe next time."

Dad nods and gives me a side hug. "See ya, pumpkin. Give us a call tomorrow."

"I will." I wave to them as I close and lock the door. When I spin back around, Jensen is staring at Meg, shaking his head.

"You are in *hot* water, darling," he says.

"I'm so sorry," Meg starts, and I'm shocked to find her tone sincere. "Genuinely, Ames, I thought I was helping. I thought she'd just leave it. I didn't realize—"

"It's fine," I tell her, because I believe her. She hasn't been around my mom as much as Jensen; therefore, she doesn't know that she's never let anything go, *ever.* "You're just a little insane."

"We already knew that."

I groan. "But what do I do?"

"You don't have to do anything," Jen says pointedly. "Just say you asked, but he couldn't make it."

"That won't work, and you know it." I'd have to give her a name, but it wouldn't stop there. Details—albeit fake ones—would be drawn out of me before I even notice it. It's like sorcery.

Jensen shrugs. "Just ask a friend of yours to go as your date. A week at a lodge sounds nice."

I sigh. I don't *have* any other friends, let alone guy friends. There's seriously no out here, not unless…

I turn to Jensen. "You could do it."

"Ew!" He scoffs. "Ames, we're like *siblings*. That's disgusting!"

"I'm sorry!" I huff. "I'm desperate.'"

"You could bribe Henry," Meg suggests.

I gape at her. "You're kidding. Henry Arlington? You want me to ask my *ex-boyfriend* to pretend he's dating me for a week? I'd rather gouge my eyes out with fire pokers."

"Just a suggestion." She shrugs and crosses her arms. "Regardless, I'm going to help you figure it out. Promise. It's my fault, so I'll think of something."

I groan and flop down onto the couch. "Okay, well, this is going to have to wait. I need to call our client and see if they ever picked up the piece."

"I'll pull up their number," Meg says, sitting down beside me.

I get out my phone and frown. The screen is on, but I don't remember *leaving* it on. Henry's and my text messages are on the screen, and I see one that I didn't send.

A voice text box.

"No," I say aloud, holding the phone up to my eyes. It's too close to see, but it's perfect for dramatic effect.

The tiny numbers in the corner send my heart into a fit.

Three minutes.

I just sent Henry three minutes of conversation about needing someone to be my fake boyfriend. One of those *someone*'s being him.

"What's wrong?" Jen asks.

"I just sent a voice recording to Henry."

"Of *that* conversation?"

"The one we just had, yes."

"Oh, Ames." Meg winces.

"Can you delete it? Please? You're techy."

She shakes her head. "Once it's sent, you can't delete it."

"You're *lying*." I hope she's lying. If not, I'm going to take the fire poker route.

"I'm sorry," she says again, right before going back to her laptop.

I chew my lip raw and try to delete the message. Meg is right—there's no way. I consider sending a follow up, something like, *please don't listen to this, I'm so sorry it was a joke,* but that would just tempt him further.

I exhale and rub my eyes. "Just forward me the number. Please."

"Working on it."

I unlock my phone again, ready to click the contact, but that's not what I see.

No, my first notification is a text from Henry.

ARLINGTON

I'm going to assume that wasn't for me.

My face heats as I read the message over and over again. Why couldn't he have dropped his phone down a sewer grate or something?

you're so smart wow! please leave me alone. as you can see i am clearly in distress right now. let's just never bring it up again ok THANK YOU

ARLINGTON

Eh, I can't promise that.

you git.

ARLINGTON

You wound me, Ames.

I'm going to throat punch him if he keeps calling me that. And not because I hate it. More so because I don't.

haven't you tormented me enough for one day?

ARLINGTON

No. I'm afraid I could never tire of that.

On an unrelated note, please meet me at the café tomorrow, same time. I'd appreciate it. We have more things to cover.

My client's number comes through just as I read Henry's final message. I start to click it and make the call, thankful for a distraction from *him*, but I decide against it. Instead, I just shut my phone off and vow to call tomorrow.

For now, I've got to cook up some excuse to feed Henry.

15

HENRY

"What are you looking at?" Lizzy asks, flicking me with the end of her scarf.

I shove my phone in my pocket and flick her back, though *my* scarf does little damage. Hers has got those weird tassel things on the end. "Nothing."

I can't tell her. Lizzy nearly knocked my lights out when I told her Amelie and I were done. She doesn't know the reason, though —I never told her.

Mainly because *I* still don't know the reason.

Liz sighs. "Well, you ought to relish in it, because your fun won't last long."

She's not wrong. Every Thursday night, our parents—who despise each other, if that's any shock—make us come to dinner at their house. It's possibly the worst night of my week, and though I can't escape it, I always try. I've only gotten out of it once, and that was because I had pneumonia. So, not often.

"I still want to know what you were looking at," Lizzy says, dodging someone who nearly knocks into her. "It's not like you to be smiling at your phone. Who's on the other side of it?"

"It was a cat video," I deadpan. "The one you sent me last night."

She gasps. "Of the cat on the horse? How do they *do* that? He's just a cat! He doesn't have a butt to sit on."

"I have no idea," I say. I did not *watch* said video, but I'm not about to say I'm texting—and setting up another meeting with—the girl who is currently tormenting me. That's actually the last thing I'd admit to. There are a hundred different lies I'd go through first.

But that voice message...it's been on my mind since I heard it. And no, I haven't played it more than once. That would be weird. I definitely have not done that.

"What color was the cat?" Liz asks.

I blink. Look over at her. "What?"

"What color was the cat in the video?"

Great.

"Orange," I say nonchalantly. That's a cat color. That could totally be the correct one.

"Hm," she says. "And the horse?"

"...White?"

"Saddle color?"

"Brown."

"*AHA!*" She points an accusing finger at me. "There was no saddle. You didn't even watch the video. You never watch them."

"I do," I say, which is true. I just didn't watch this one. "They give me a good laugh."

"Don't try to change the subject. *What* were you grinning at?"

I keep walking. "Nothing."

"Hen."

"Really, Liz. Nothing. Just a stupid text from a friend."

She huffs, and I know she isn't buying a word. I text my acquaintances about as frequently as she listens to our dad, but she shockingly doesn't press for an answer.

We inevitably make it to our parent's house, and I almost consider faking some illness to get out of this. Liz can sense my ideas, though. She grabs my arm and drags me to the porch, ringing the doorbell with her free hand. "You're not ditching me tonight."

"I just assumed you'd join."

She shakes her head. "No. I miss Mom, and between you and me, I think she might gift me something tonight. She's been asking me if I prefer gold or silver."

I laugh. Mom doesn't favor Lizzy over me, not the same way Dad does, but she certainly loves spoiling her. I think it's because Liz accepts it. I don't like gifts, but Lizzy? She'd give anything to be showered by presents twenty-four seven.

The door opens, and Mom stands before us, a pristine apron tied around her waist. She smiles and hugs Liz and I at the same time, pulling one of us into each arm.

"My babies," she says wistfully, taking one of each of our hands. "Come inside."

"You have to move over," Liz says.

"Oh!" Mom says as if she forgot. She steps aside, still holding my hand as we walk through the door.

It's warm in this house. Much *too* warm, which means Mom has had the oven on all day. The air smells like chicken and spices, so I'm guessing she's made the soup we like. I spot a loaf of home-made bread on the table and know I'm correct.

Mom squeezes my hand once before dropping it. "Your dad is upstairs, Henry. I think he wants to see you. Says he has something to tell you."

I stiffen up. "Do you know what it is?"

She shakes her head, causing grayed hair to fall into her eyes. Mine does that, too—anytime I move my head, a piece of my hair falls right between my eyebrows. It's the most irritating thing in the world, but I like sharing something with her. "Not a clue," she says. "Go deal with it before dinner, please. I've got something for Elizabeth that I want to show her in the meantime."

Liz squeals and follows Mom to her bedroom. She throws a glance over her shoulder and mouths 'told you' before disappearing around the corner.

I'd rather saw my hand off than find my Dad right now.

Slowly, I climb the stairs, hoping that if I wait long enough, the oven timer will go off. Or maybe a stampede of elephants will take me out. Anything to keep distance between me and him.

The house itself does little to ease my anxiety. Most people seem to find their childhood home comforting, but I find it the opposite. It's not as though I had a bad childhood—in fact, I'm quite grateful for my parents and how they raised Lizzy and me. But that doesn't mean I have to like this house. Doesn't mean I have to trust my dad, or who he's turned into since I left my place under this roof.

I pass my old bedroom and hold my breath as I open my dad's office door. He's writing furiously in a checking register, glasses on his head rather than his face. The daylight is long gone, and the only light in here is a nearly burnt-out lamp.

"Henry," he says, voice formal as ever. "Sit down."

"Dinner is almost ready." I have no idea if that's true. "Will this take long? I have a feeling that Mom and Liz—"

"Your mom and Elizabeth will be fine." He motions to the chair in front of his desk. Even his home office is set up for business affairs. "Sit."

I take a seat and kick at the carpet. I'm sure I know what this is about—he's realized my piece is gone by now, that Amelie took it. I'm stunned it's taken him this long, but I almost wish it had taken him *longer*. What do I even say?

He doesn't give me time to think about it. Dad caps his pen and sighs, then looks at me over his glasses. "I'm pushing the date of the auction back."

A breath of relief escapes me before I can catch it. "That's *great*—"

"But." He leans back in his seat. Looks at the ceiling. "That doesn't mean you are off the hook on looking for the thing. I've got an idea, and I think you'll take a chance on it."

Translation: I'm going to hate this, but I'll end up doing it anyway.

"Okay," I say numbly. "What is it?"

"I think you need to find Amelie." He expels a breath. "You

need to make her trust you again, then use that closeness to get proof of her work."

My mouth falls open. "What do you mean? I don't have time for that."

"You don't have time to catch a criminal?" He laughs dryly. "Henry, looking for your piece can't be taking up your time, especially since you haven't found it."

Yes, well, I'm getting help from the girl you want me to narc on, so it sounds like a bad idea.

"I'm doing what I can," I say, my voice a little firmer than intended. "You gave me *very* little to work with. I'm using what I have."

"You're doing fine," he says, contrasting what he implied just moments ago. "It'll be fine. But you need to hear me out on this."

I won't. But I *will* listen and find out what he wants, only because I'm curious.

"What could I possibly help you with?"

Dad leans even further back in his chair and takes a deep breath, making his tie strain around his neck. "Bring her with you to the auction."

No. *No.* Why did I let him talk? I should've just left. He wouldn't have made a scene with mom in the house; I could've bolted downstairs and joined them at the dinner table.

"I don't understand," I say coolly, "but I'm not doing that."

"Make her trust you again. It'll be easy." He's not listening to me anymore. I don't think he ever was. "By the time the auction rolls around, you'll have enough proof to get her caught. This could *work*, Henry, and it could work well. You just have to help me."

I gnaw on the inside of my cheek, stare at the wall. I can't do it. I *should* be able to, though it's obvious that I'm not the most logical when it comes to Amelie. But making her trust me, then turning her in? That would involve getting close to her. *Betraying* her. I don't care what happened to us—I don't care if she brings me and my career to the ground.

I won't do it.

"You don't have a very solid plan," I say warily. "Even if that worked, why would she tell me everything? People trust on different levels."

"She already *knows* you," he says, and it makes me feel sick, him being the one to say it. "And it's not about what she tells you; it's about what you can find. Get in her apartment. Find evidence. Proof."

Proof. Like the SD card in my pocket.

I swallow. "I'm not doing that."

Dad's eyes flare. "Henry—"

"*No.* Please." I look away, because that is not a word my dad and I use often. It's a clear show that I'm desperate, and I hope he doesn't think any further into it. He can't know what I'm doing. I can't have him holding this against me. "I don't want to do that."

He presses his hands into his eyes, looking discouraged when he pulls them away. "I'm not having this argument tonight. Make a wise decision and don't cause me any problems."

I nod, hating the guilt that twists in my chest. I shouldn't feel bad for defying him. He's using me—that's all he does. He uses my work for profit and gives me no control over my distribution. He gives me things and holds them over my head when I accept them. I haven't been fully in charge of myself in *years,* all because I'm too scared to say no to him.

But I don't know how to change it.

"Regardless of that," Dad continues, "you'll have a piece on display at the auction. Yes?"

"Yes," I force out. "I'll have something."

"You'll have the *Ophelia.*"

I take a breath, aware that I'm putting all my trust in Amelie. "I'll have it."

"Good." Dad stands and shoves the checking register in his desk. I note the stack of torn envelopes in the corner, but as usual, I don't mention them. "Let's go eat, then."

I follow him out of the office, hands shoved in my pockets. Mom and Liz are already at the kitchen table, poring over a box of rings. They clear the surface and set the dishware down. Mom brings the food to the table, and we pass the dishes around, word-lessly making our plates.

The meal isn't awkward. It's normal. Mom and Dad argue, Liz cracks jokes, and I sit quietly, wondering how to dig myself out of this situation.

I'm not even *in* it, not really. But I will be if my dad has his way.

And the memory card in my pocket will be the least of my problems.

16

———

AMELIE

The Boyfriend Debacle has taken over my life.

It's all I can think about. The second I woke up, when the sunlight hit my face and dragged me out of my restless sleep, questions flooded my mind. *What do I say to Mom? How do I tell her it's a lie? Should I keep it up? Should I find a way to make it happen?*

Bottom line—I don't know.

I'm meeting Henry in an hour, and I've just begun getting ready. My hair is in rollers and my face is bare. I derive the most pleasure in life by simply getting ready. It's something I've found a routine in, which is nice, since my job revolves around chaos.

I take a sip of my tea and open a tube of concealer, letting my mind wander as I get ready. When I told my parents that I'd make a decision by this weekend, I didn't realize that *this weekend* is actually *tomorrow.* I've got twenty-four hours to decide. If I end up saying yes, then I've got an additional week to find a fake boyfriend. Someone willing to put up with me for seven days, and someone that *I* can tolerate for that amount of time.

It's a very bad idea. If I bring someone I've just met, my work will get mentioned in passing, and I'll get caught. Mom and Dad will assume they know about my job, and Margot will try to convince said boyfriend that he's too good for me.

She hates what I do. I hate what she does. And until Mom forces conversation out of us, I'll leave it at that.

I finish off my makeup with a muted red lip and take my rollers out. I tie a ribbon in the back of my hair and admire the way it turned out in the mirror. With rollers, you simply never know if you're going to look like a runway model or George Washington.

It's freezing today, as it has been for the past two months, so I change into pants and a thick sweater. I throw a heavy jacket on top and pull my hair out of my collar, mortified with the amount of static I'm creating. My head feels like a satellite dish.

I slip my feet into a pair of chunky heels and step into the living room. A gasp escapes me when I notice Meg on the couch, laptop balanced up on her knees. She left last night after the... incident, so I'm not sure how she got back in.

"Morning," she says, sipping my *good tea* out of a mug. "I've got something for you."

"Oh?" I shuffle over to the sink and set my teacup in it. "Tell."

"Well, I've tried and tried to get a read on the background of this photo, but I've failed. It's literally a blank wall, so it's not my fault. But I *did* find a different listing with an altered background. And guess what?"

I raise a brow. "Just tell me."

"*That* one has the location."

"Ooh!" I clap my hands once. "Where?"

"Bondi's. On 28th."

"I thought that was a nightclub?"

"It is. Opens at nine this evening. You can go tonight, surely." She turns the laptop around, and on the screen, I see an unfamiliar canvas propped up against the wall. "I think it's a back room. Not the kitchen—maybe a storage room, or a walk-in freezer or something. There's a Bondi's logo on the wall and a stack of milk crates in the corner, see?"

I hum in acknowledgement. "So I need to get in there."

"It would be preferable."

Fine. I can do that. That's probably the easiest task on my to-do list. The others aren't very fun, and they don't involve me getting to wear fancy clothes.

Call our client and make sure they don't want to sue me.

Meet up with Henry. Avoid all questions about voice message.

Bust into Bondi's and find the Ophelia.

"I'll get it done," I tell her. "Henry can help. Cause a diversion or something. It's his painting, after all. He shouldn't be opposed."

"I don't trust him," Meg says, a hint of warning in her voice.

I give a shrug and hope it's casual. "Neither do I, but he can't do much damage."

"Be careful, Ames."

"What do you mean?"

"Nothing." Meg shakes her head, but I don't buy it. Solely from her tone of voice, I have no doubt that Jen told her about Henry's and my past. But that's fine. It's not a secret. "Just be careful."

"You know I will." I stuff my wallet and a few extra bills in my purse. "I'll see you later. Where's Jen?"

"He's out."

"Hmm. How'd you get in here, anyways?"

"I have a key."

"Who gave you a key?"

"Santa Claus." Meg pins me with an unimpressed stare. "Who do you think?"

"I don't understand *why* Jen would give you a key, but I guess that's the answer."

"If you want to believe that, that's up to you."

I sigh and turn the door handle. "You're ridiculous."

"Says the girl plotting with the enemy."

"I am *networking*," I say, right before closing the door.

The second I'm out on the sidewalk, I whip my burner phone out of my purse and dial our client from yesterday. Usually, we call them the day of, but we've never had one *not* answer. I'm starting to worry that something went wrong since they never responded, but maybe they're just busy.

Whoever is on the line picks up after two rings.

"Hello," I start, using my practiced work voice. "I'm calling on behalf—"

"Are you the one we got in contact with a few weeks ago?"

I blink. "I'm sorry?"

"About the painting." It's a man, and he sounds quite annoyed with me. "The ocean one. We were supposed to pick it up at Grand Arts Hall."

"Oh. Yes, that's me. Did everything go well? Was the painting what you wanted?"

"We wouldn't know," the man says flatly, "because when we got there, it was gone."

I stop in the middle of the sidewalk. "*What*?"

"We did exactly what you said. Met with a manager, got in the back. It wasn't there."

"I don't understand. We left it there yesterday morning."

My voice stays steady, though the one in my head is thoroughly reminding me that I've failed. Failed myself, failed my team. *Failed,* period.

"Well, it was gone when we arrived." His voice is clipped. "We already paid you, and when we pay, we expect the other end of the deal to be held up."

"I understand," I say sweetly. "I'm not sure what happened, but I promise I'll get it taken care of."

The man practically snorts. "You'd better. And if you can't, I'll expect the deposit back next week. Get in touch with my secretary."

"I will," I assure him, though I've got no clue who his secretary is. Thankfully, I won't have to find out. I'm going to find that painting and deliver it to whoever is on the other end of this line.

The man grumbles something I don't catch and hangs up the phone.

I slip mine back into my purse, head spinning as I try to figure out what just happened. No one saw us enter the hall, and everyone that my dad hires is safe. Someone must've gotten in after us.

Briefly, my mind flashes to Henry.

But that can't be possible, right? He doesn't know how we operate. Just because he has proof of me in his museum doesn't mean he's connected me to Grand Arts. There are a million other ways for me to go about my work. Conspiring with my parents seems like the *least* logical approach, at least on normal standards.

No. It isn't him.

The problem is going to be finding out who.

Henry is standing outside of Parlon's with a cup in each hand. He wordlessly gives me one, and I eye him warily as I lift it to my mouth. "I don't trust this."

"I don't trust *you* when you haven't had caffeine. Drink it."

Without protesting, I tip the cup back. I nearly jump when I get a taste of the drink, and I think Henry notices, because he grins just slightly. "You know my order?"

"Yes," he says, as if it's obvious. "You get the same thing you always have."

I don't acknowledge the fact that he remembered because I don't care.

"I still think you tampered with it," I say, just to argue. "Put a laxative in it or something."

He laughs and starts walking down the sidewalk. I assume we're going to his penthouse, but he doesn't give me any clues, so I'm just following aimlessly. "I didn't. But if you don't believe me, then I'll take it back."

Henry reaches for the cup, and I hold it all the way out to my side. A low laugh slips out of him at my glare. "Thought so."

"*Thought so,*" I mock, pocketing my free hand. "Why did you ask me here?"

"Well, we've got a few things to discuss."

My heart jumps into my throat.

If he brings up the message, I'll push him into oncoming traffic.

"What?" I ask slowly.

He exhales. "The painting, obviously. That's the most important one."

"Yes. Absolutely." Of course he doesn't care about the message. It's ridiculous. He probably hasn't given it a second thought, and why would he? No one wants to hear me complain about men. I mean, *I* quite enjoy the task, but that's me.

"Oh, *and*," Henry starts, looking down at me. "I think—for pure entertainment value—"

"No."

He chuckles. "Come on, Ames."

"*No.*" I turn around and walk backward so I can keep looking at him. It's probably a foolish thing, given that we're walking the streets and I could step in front of a taxi, but I don't care. "Henry, we will not be discussing this. I'm serious. I've got to figure something out, and I don't need you making fun of me."

"I wasn't going to make fun of you."

"What were you going to do, then? Offer suggestions?"

Henry opens his mouth to respond, then rolls his eyes and closes it. He appears at my side, and I tense up when he puts a hand on my lower back, spinning me around so I'm facing forward again. Seconds later, a car speeds past the sidewalk that I was about to step off. I blow out a breath before noting Henry's hand flat against my stomach, holding me back from *literally* killing myself.

"Please," he says, right into my ear, "do not walk in front of a car. I have no idea how you've stayed alive this long."

I nod stiffly as he removes his hand from my body. He keeps walking, seemingly unbothered, though I have to force my legs to work again. There's a strange absence of warmth where his hand was just seconds ago, and I've got no clue why. It *should* irritate me that he did that. If I want to step in front of a car, that is my prerogative.

"I can take care of myself," I say, catching up to him. "And can you slow down? I have something to tell you. We need to check out a place on 28th later."

He stops short. Turns around and looks down at me, making a

stray piece of hair fall into his eyes. Used to, I would've reached up and brushed it away from his glasses, but I don't do that right now. Obviously. He'd probably swat my hand away or something.

"Why didn't you *say* that?" He asks, sounding exasperated. "28ᵗʰ is the other way."

"*Later*," I enunciate. "We need to get into a back room, and I'll need a distraction. That'll require some work on your part."

Henry raises his eyebrows. "You need me to knock out the bouncer or something?"

"No, nothing so grotesque."

"I'm shocked this isn't just a normal day for you."

I frown. "I'm not so bad, Arlington. I've got a job and so do you."

The name slips out before I can catch it. I've not referred to him that way since we were eighteen, but I try not to show my discomfort at doing it so casually.

"Not the same thing," Henry quips, clearly not caring. "But tell me your plan."

"Well, it's the weekend, so we won't need *too* much of a diversion. People are going to be focused on themselves anyways; no need to cause a scene. I just want you to keep watch and make sure no staff is slinking around. Meg found another photo, and it looks like the painting is placed in a storage room. I'll need to get back there and get it."

"Okay, that's great, except what will you do with the painting?"

I hadn't thought of that part.

"Uhm," I say. "Okay, better plan. You do the same thing, and I... I'll just bust a window or something. Toss the painting out. You can grab it from the outside, and then I'll deal with the people from the inside. Talking my way out of things is my greatest talent."

"Somehow, I don't believe that."

"I've charmed *you* out of handing me to the cops multiple times."

Henry eyes me, and I get the urge to look away. "If I really wanted you behind bars, you'd be there."

"I know," I say, my voice too quiet. "That's what unsettles me."

Henry doesn't respond to my comment, but he clears his throat before speaking. "Alright. We can try that, I guess. But I think it's a bad idea."

"You'd think all my ideas are bad."

"No. Some of them are probably okay."

I roll my eyes. "If you have something better, suggest it. We've still got hours before we have to commit to a plan."

"I'll try anything, as long as it ends with that painting back at my loft. Which—" He turns to walk backwards now, and I'm annoyed that *he* doesn't almost step in front of a car. "—still isn't adding up in my mind. You're going to carry that thing up to my apartment?"

"Don't be ridiculous. I have a team for a reason, Henry. I wasn't meant to carry heavy things. That's how you strain muscles."

I haven't *technically* mentioned this plan to Meg and Jen, but I'm hoping they'll agree to it. They're used to my last-minute ideas; I'm sure this won't be any different.

"What if..." Henry takes a breath, sounding less hesitant than I'd expect right now. "What if this goes badly, Ames? Seriously."

"It very well might."

"And we're *good* with that?"

"*You* were good with dragging me into this." I look up at him, though there's no point. His face is blank. "Now, you've got to be good with my plans."

I'm waiting for the push-back. The argument. But instead of that, Henry says, "Fine."

And that's that.

17

————

HENRY

Amelie scoops Betty off the ground the second we walk into my penthouse. The cat swats at the strands of hair around Amelie's face, but she doesn't seem to mind. I'm not sure she'd care if the animal made her bleed.

"Have you gotten any further on the piece?" She asks me.

I shake my head. I've hardly made progress since she last saw me. This piece has been like pulling teeth. Being forced to create never ends well. I can feel myself growing tired, more uninspired, and yet, I don't have the choice of stopping. Especially not with Amelie watching my every move.

"Very little," I say, rather than stating all of that. "What I *have* done, I've hated and scrapped."

"It doesn't have to be a Van Gogh," Amelie says, absolutely not helping this situation whatsoever. I know that I don't have a right to be frustrated—after all, this is something *I* dragged her into. But that doesn't make it any easier. "It's a decoy. If all goes well, no one will see the thing again."

I give a shrug as I unlock my studio. "I don't really care who sees it. If I create something, I want it to be good no matter what. It's the principle of the thing."

"Ah, yes. The principle of..."

I glare at her, and she only grins. "It's a personal thing. I hold my work to a certain standard. I don't care what it's for. I want my art to be good, just like you want your plans to be accurately carried out. They're both art forms. There's nothing wrong with wanting merit."

"Of course there's nothing wrong with it, especially when I'm involved." Amelie sits on the floor and lets Betty climb onto her lap. The cat is asleep in seconds, and I'm honestly stunned. I knew Betty liked her, but it's strange.

"She doesn't like new people," I say aloud.

Amelie shrugs and scratches Betty's ears. "She's a good judge of character."

I chuckle dryly as I drag an easel out of the closet. "Okay."

"Really, Henry, I think we're past this. Surely you can admit that I'm not an absolute torment to be around."

"Never said you were," I tell her. "But I'm not going to say otherwise."

"You're incorrigible."

"I'm honest."

I'm not. Time spent around her has gone straight to my head, just like I knew it would. It's getting harder to separate the Amelie I knew years ago from *this* Amelie, who is right in front of me and a *felon*. But she's tangible. She's real.

She's someone I used to love, despite the criminal record. And I'd be lying if I said I weren't a little intrigued by her.

This is why you shouldn't be allowed to make your own decisions.

"I'm going to give you a compliment," Amelie says, leaning back on the palms of her hands. Betty hisses when she does so. "I'll give you one, then you give me one. It's a bonding exercise."

"We do *not* need to bond," I say flatly.

She ignores me. "I personally love your cat. I think your apartment is lovely, and I like those glasses of yours. But you knew that part."

I *did* know that. It's embarrassing how often that fact pops into my mind.

"Now it's your turn," she says when I don't respond. "You say something nice about me."

I chew on my lip. I could say a lot of things, none of which she needs to hear. Amelie's ego is solid enough without my words, though she loves to be doted on. But what can I say without crossing any lines? Metaphorical ones, I guess. We have no bounds here.

You're incredibly smart for not getting caught before I caught you.

Maybe not that.

I'm starting to think you may be crazy.

She'd take that as a real compliment.

You're achingly beautiful, maybe now more than ever, and I can't ignore it, despite how hard I've tried. I haven't been able to forget it. Ever.

Absolutely not that.

"Your ribbons," I blurt, more suddenly than I mean to. "I like the ribbons you wear in your hair."

Amelie's cheeks flush, and I can almost see the gears turning in her mind. She's trying to figure out when she's worn a bow around me. When I've paid any attention to her. It makes me grin, and I'm thankful for the canvas to hide my face.

"Did you start wearing those recently?" I ask, just to bother her more. "Or was it something I never noticed?"

Unlikely. I'm confident that I notice everything about her.

"They're new," she says, her voice quieter than it was a moment ago. "And I like my ribbons, too. See? We're much closer now. I know that you have good taste in accessories, and you know that I love your cat."

"Everyone loves my cat."

"And everyone loves hair ribbons," she counters. "But it's important to be informed."

I laugh and retrieve another bucket of paint, setting it on the small table near my easel. "Is it my turn to ask questions now?"

"I guess."

The response stuns me. I was expecting a very emphatic *no,* but now that I have this opportunity, I won't waste it.

"What, exactly, did you mean by that voice message?"

"UGH!" Amelie groans. "I knew you were going to bring that up."

"I think it's fair."

"It is *not*." She twists her hair around a finger. "But it was just a joke. My mom wants to set me up with someone, so my friend swooped in and said I had a boyfriend. She was trying to help, but Mom told me to bring him along, and now…"

"You're caught in a lie that only a fake boyfriend can get you out of."

"Not…exactly?" Amelie shrugs. "I could tell her the truth. She wouldn't even be mad—you know she wouldn't. But I don't want to. I've got enough to deal with there, and an added date with some guy I don't know sounds horrible."

"What else do you have to deal with?"

She looks over at me, eyes narrowed. I ask the question carelessly, and I think we're both a little stunned that it left my mouth, but I'm curious. I've wondered about her family more than I care to admit. Oftentimes, they were more a family to me than my own.

"Margot," she says, and I look up from my work, intrigued. "We don't talk anymore, and Mom is intent on putting us back together for our birthdays. I don't see it going well, and I'm not thrilled to be trapped in a cabin with her for a week. Plus, I've got to tie up all my loose work ends by next Saturday, and it's not going to be fun. My clients are mad at me, and I—" She stops. Blinks twice. "No. Why am I telling you this?"

I shrug. "Don't know. I assumed you needed to talk, so I'm letting you."

"I do, but not to you." Amelie sets Betty aside before walking over to me. She appears at my side and stares at the painting, and I track the movement of her eyes, trying my hardest to gauge her reaction. It's pretty apparent that she has no idea what she's looking at. Which is fair—I don't either. I've been sketching random shapes, coloring them in, and calling it a piece of art. "What is it?"

"Not sure yet."

Amelie nods and moves closer to the canvas, which only draws her nearer to me. My breath hitches when I register the warmth of her body, the scent of her perfume. She must be aware of me too, at least somewhat, because she takes a stiff step away and crosses her arms.

"Well, I like it. I think you're on the right track."

"It's boring," I admit. "I don't like it."

She exhales sharply. "Henry, it doesn't really matter if you like it. Didn't you hear? I have a week to tie up loose ends. *You*," she pokes me in the chest, "are a loose end. Whatever you need to do, get it done by then."

I grab her hand and put it back at her side. "I don't know if I can do that."

"You will."

"That's not how this works. You left us *one week* to finish this, set a trap, and catch the guy. That's on you. The timeline is insane."

"That timeline is preferable," she counters.

I drag a hand through my hair and sigh. This should've been something I factored in—the unpredictability. But I hadn't realized we had multiple deadlines, either: hers *and* my dad's.

Regardless. I don't think I can swing it.

"I'll try," I say quietly. "But I—"

"HENRY?!" The word is shouted through my living room by a familiar female voice.

Liz.

If she sees Amelie, I will never live this down.

"That's Lizzy," she says, voice filled with awe. "Isn't it? Isn't that Liz?"

"Get in the closet."

"I'm *sorry*?"

"In the closet." I put my hands on her waist and steer her toward my storage closet. She opens her mouth to protest, but before she can, I close the door. I'm aware that this isn't the *best* way to buy her silence, but I don't have another choice. I walk to the studio door and open it, praying Liz doesn't say anything we need to keep under wraps.

"Hen!" Liz sings, strolling in. Today, she's decked out in a very 70's-esque outfit. Bright pink bell bottoms and a psychedelic neon shirt. Her outfits are often eccentric, but I have to say, this is a new level. "You didn't tell me there was a breach at the museum the other day!"

I can almost see Amelie laughing to herself.

"I handled it," I tell her. "I didn't want to stress you out."

"Oh, *I* couldn't care less. But did Dad tell you he moved the auction?"

My jaw tightens. That's *another* thing Amelie doesn't need to hear. "Yes. I'm not sure the exact date, though. Did he tell you?"

"No." She drops her bag off her shoulder and gives Betty a quick pat before looking at the canvas in front of us. "What are you painting?"

"I'm not sure."

A laugh. "You always say that, and then you paint something incredible."

"That doesn't mean I know what I'm doing."

Liz shakes her head. "I think you *do* know. You just don't want to tell anyone in case it doesn't live up to their imagination."

I stare at the canvas, hating that she's right. Rarely do I tell someone what I'm planning to paint. I did that once—told my Dad about an idea, and he loved it. Wanted to display it. But when I started working, it was all wrong. The proportions. The colors. It looked nothing like what I'd envisioned, and it felt like a failed reflection of myself.

Since then, I don't talk about my plans. I just paint.

"I think you had one too many espresso shots this morning, Liz," I say after a pause.

She lets out another laugh. "I did. Five too many, actually. But that's not important. And anyways, I love it so far. I think you're doing great. Is this the replacement for the auction?"

No, I want to say. I want to tell her that this is a fake. That Amelie and I are trying to get my original piece back. But then I'd have to explain a *whole* lot of things that I'm not ready to discuss, and I don't want to drag Liz into my trouble. She doesn't need that from me.

"Yes," I say instead. "Though it's taking longer than I'd like."

She sighs. "Well, you've gotta kick it into gear. He won't be happy if it's late."

I swallow. "I know."

Lizzy walks over to her bag and picks it back up. "I guess I'll get going, since you seem to be in the *zone*."

"You don't have to. Just take a seat somewhere if you want."

A horrible offer, really, given that there's an art thief in my closet.

Thankfully, Lizzy shakes her head. "I've got work to do. My editor wants a new article by Monday, and I've hardly started the research."

"What's it about?"

"*Fashions of the seventies.*" She spins to show me her outfit, which, as I guessed, is heavily inspired by the era. "And why we shouldn't let them come back. Do you know how embarrassing it was when I walked into work, and he handed me the assignment? I didn't even *want* it! I love bell bottoms and bright colors. He's sick."

"He's a fashion editor."

"Still demented," she mutters.

I hold back a laugh. "But you're still going to write the article."

"Of course I am. I'll write the best article he's ever read on how Penny Lane coats should be burned."

"You'll do great."

"I will. And you will, too." Her heels click loudly as she walks to the door. "See you Sunday, Hen. Bring a bottle of wine."

I look up from my canvas. "What's Sunday?"

"I don't know, but you're always over on Sunday."

"Okay, but you don't like wine."

She sighs. "I need it to cook."

"But you don't *cook*."

"I know!"

And with that, she leaves.

"Can I come out now?" A soft voice says from the closet.

Sighing, I walk over and lean against the opposite wall. "Yes."

Amelie opens the door and steps out. She looks up at me curiously, and I wait for a lecture about shoving her in a closet, but it doesn't come. It's almost like she's waiting for *me* to say something.

"What?" She asks finally. "Why are you looking at me like that?"

I shrug. "Just curious why you stayed in there. I sort of assumed you'd claw your way out and kick me in the shins."

She crosses her arms to mirror my stance. "Walking out seemed like a good way to get caught, and I don't really want Liz to know what I've been up to."

"Liz wouldn't care," I say honestly. "She'd probably kiss you for terrorizing our dad, then drag you downstairs for manicures."

Amelie sighs fondly. "It's fine. The closet was lovely, anyways. I had lots of friends there. Dust bunnies. Spiders. I think there was even a shadow monster."

I fake a gasp. "Maybe *he* took my painting."

The corners of her mouth lift, and I get the most ridiculous urge to trace the shape with my thumb. "Maybe he did."

She doesn't say anything more than that, so I don't either. After a few moments of silence, Amelie steps around me and goes to the window, staring out over the city. I'm tempted to go up beside her, to ask what she's thinking, but I keep my feet planted on the ground.

"Tonight," Amelie says suddenly. "We're getting your piece tonight, Henry. Nine o'clock. Wear your best clubbing outfit."

I practically snort. "What?"

"Your piece is at Bondi's. The nightclub, you know." She looks over her shoulder, brows furrowed. "Did I not tell you?"

I shake my head. "No, but this doesn't seem smart. Won't it be crowded?"

"Like I said: more people to hide amongst."

This is a horrible idea.

"I'll be at your apartment at a quarter 'til."

Amelie turns around, a full smile on her lips. "Such a gentleman. First, he blackmails me, then he escorts me to clubs."

I exhale. "You're intolerable today."

"Ah!" She points a finger in my face. "Say one nice thing. Let's keep it going."

"No."

Amelie makes a *tsk*ing noise. "You used to be so *kind*."

"I still am."

"No, you're a nuisance now."

"Such a sweet talker," I murmur, taking a step closer.

Amelie's eyes widen, and her gaze dips below mine before she says, "No. Stop that."

"Stop what?"

"Just—stop talking." She looks over her shoulder, then back at me, her eyes now dull. "I'll see you tonight. Don't aggravate me."

"I might."

"Keep your mouth shut, then."

"And let your night be boring?"

"Arlington," she warns, but it's not so threatening when she says it like that. "Don't test me."

"Wouldn't dream of it," I say, opening the door for her. "Bring a coat tonight."

She says nothing as she leaves my apartment.

18

AMELIE

"Jensen," I yell once I unlock the apartment door. "Living room, please. Now."

I hear a groan as I throw my purse onto the table, hard enough that my wallet slips out. Jensen emerges from his makeshift gym, looking positively disgusting. Sweat glistens over his arms, and I refrain from telling him to go shower. I have to talk to him, but that's going to be difficult when he looks like he just dunked himself in movie popcorn butter.

"What?" He asks, grabbing a towel and wiping himself off. Thank God. "Where were you?"

"I don't want to talk about it right now. We have a bigger problem."

"Oh, joy," he mumbles, plopping down onto my couch. My *jade* couch. Whilst looking like a wet ham. "Go."

I slip my heels off and sit down on the opposite end, holding my breath so I don't smell him. "I called our client. *Nautical Abyss* wasn't at Grand Arts. They got in the back and never even saw the thing."

He gapes. "How? We covered it. We locked back up. Everything was right."

"I have no idea." I lean back into the cushions and close my eyes. "Maybe...maybe we're just close, Jen."

"To what?"

"Being caught." My voice drops off at that, because I don't want to admit these things. I don't want to voice that I've been messy lately. It's never intentional, but I'd be kidding myself to think there isn't something we could do better.

That night in the museum, when Henry caught me a *second* time, I really thought that was it. I thought we were done. And whatever fear that was, whatever coursed through my body when those alarms went off, that doesn't need to happen again. It shouldn't have happened in the first place.

My parents always managed to fly under the radar. They were never caught, likely because they kept to themselves. Minded their business. They weren't foolish enough to tangle up with someone who had cold, hard proof of their work. I can only imagine the disappointment they'd feel if they knew what I've been up to.

That's why I can't screw this up. I don't get to blow the cover they've given my team by 'hiring' us at Grand Arts. I don't get to uproot everyone's lives because of one bad decision.

I won't fail.

"Do you..." Jen trails off as he grabs the TV remote. "Do you think it's The Dealer?"

I stiffen up. "What makes you think that?"

He shrugs. "It's similar, right? It's just like last time."

He's right, and I wish he weren't.

The Dealer is the most generic name for someone who isn't so basic. A year back, we *did* have something like this happen. Someone took a couple of paintings right out from under our noses. It was only two, and we found them back a week later, but The Dealer baited us. They put them in a remote place, got word out, then switched it up. The only reason we got them back was because we noted a pattern.

They'd leave playing cards at the scene. Aces. *Every time.*

I don't know if there was an ace at Grand Arts, but I'm not going to check. I won't even *have* to. If this is The Dealer, they'll make it clear. They'll have us chasing them until they get what they want. I've got no idea what that would be, and really, I'm hoping this whole thing is just some random, down-low art thief that needs cash.

"Call Meg, please," I tell Jen, slipping my jacket off. "Let her know that the piece is gone and ask what she can do. I'd search for it myself, but she's password protected every one of her internet personas, and I haven't guessed a single one correctly."

Jen snorts. "Sounds about right."

He goes to the bedroom and rings Meg. I hear him mention the painting, and I wait a few minutes for him to return to the living room, but I guess they start talking about something else because I hear laughter shortly after.

Sighing, I stand from the couch. I flip on the TV and find a channel playing old black-and-white movies, then drag my sewing machine out from the corner.

Aside from work, I have few hobbies, but my main one is sewing. Many of my dresses are ones that I've made. It's perfect, really, because I need a new shirt for tonight. Yes, *need*. My shirt supply is dangerously low, and I've got no blue ones. I'll probably end up in leather pants tonight—though they're incredibly impractical—so I need a shirt to match. A blue, long-sleeve top will do the trick nicely.

I measure myself and start tracing a loose pattern onto some cobalt blue fabric when Jensen finally returns to the living room. He's sporting a poorly hidden smile, and I can't help but assume that he and Meg are on good terms today.

"You two made up for now?" I ask.

"Ha, ha," he mocks. "What are you doing?"

I hold up the fabric and scissors in my hands. "I'm making a shirt. We're going to the club tonight, Jenny."

He blinks. "I can't tell if you're kidding."

"I'm not. Didn't Meg tell you?" He shakes his head, so I keep on. "She found a listing for Henry's piece at Bondi's. Him and I are going tonight; we made plans earlier. But if you and Meg could be there, too, that'll be better. We'll need the van."

"We'll be there," he says. "Any details I need to know?"

"None that I can think of."

He flops down on the couch beside me. "Alright. What time?"

"Nine. I'll head over with Henry. Let me know when you guys get there, then we'll put the plan into motion."

He nods. "And the plan is...?"

"Whatever presents itself in the moment."

"Oh, *lord*—"

"Not now," I say firmly. "Not while I'm sewing. Let me relax for a moment."

Shockingly, Jensen moves to another topic. "Has he asked you about the message?"

"This isn't relaxing," I mutter. "But yes, he has."

"And?"

"I told him to drop it, much like I'm going to tell you to do the same."

"I was only asking. It was quite an ordeal yesterday."

I stay silent as I thread the needle. Jensen, thank goodness, seems to pick up on my unwillingness to talk and keeps his mouth shut.

Honestly, I shouldn't care so much. I think that's what bothers me. I should just tell my parents the truth, explain that Meg thought she was helping, and be free of all this.

But I don't want Margot to find out. I haven't seen her in years, and I don't want the first thing she thinks about me to be, *You're a liar.* Granted, I'd be lying by bringing a boy to the cabin, but somehow, that's preferable. Margot wouldn't know. Nobody would ever find out, and even if they did, they wouldn't dare ruin our birthday by making it a big deal.

It's sad that I'm more apt to find a fake boyfriend than own up to the lie, but whatever.

"You're thinking too far into it," Jensen says, as if that's helpful. "I don't think anyone would give it a second thought."

"Drop it."

"I just—"

"Drop. It."

He huffs. "Fine. But I'm not helping you find a fake boyfriend to torment."

"How would you even help me? You don't have any friends, either."

"I do too. Mimi from poker has a grandson that she's always jabbering about, and he's your age. I'm sure I could get something worked out."

I hold the scissors up in a sword-like manner. "Do it. I dare you."

Jensen doesn't budge. "I will. I'll even tell her that you like men who wear houndstooth."

I shudder. Houndstooth plagues my nightmares, and yes, I mean that literally. This is a very sick threat. There's simply no equal return toward Jensen. *However...*

"Drop this conversation and I'll do the dishes for the next week."

He gives a smug grin, one that tells me this was his plan all along. "Dropped."

***

Someone knocks on my door at eight forty-five sharp.

"DON'T LET HIM IN!" I screech from my bedroom. I'm not opposed to Henry coming in, but I'm not ready yet. My hair is not cooperating, and my lipstick is smudged. I won't be seen like this. I just *won't.*

"What do you want me to do?" Jensen calls back. "Tell him to stay out there?"

"YES!"

A heavy sigh follows, as well as the opening of a door. I assume he goes out to relay this message to Henry, but I don't really care. I'm more worried about the lipstick currently staining my skin.

The mark is stubborn, and it takes a few seconds of scrubbing to get it off. After that, I haphazardly tie a black bow in my hair and glare at the girl in the mirror. She isn't to her highest standard, but she'll do for tonight.

I step into a pair of blue heels—the exact color of my shirt—and grab Jensen's old leather jacket. It's a stark contrast to my *new* leather pants, but it's cohesive enough.

With my lockpick in tow, I leave the apartment and find Jensen standing across from Henry in the hall. Neither seem quite as perturbed as when they met at the café—I've never seen Jensen look so annoyed with someone, which says a lot. People aren't generally his favorite.

I'm shoving a piece of gum in my mouth when I look over at Henry, and my jaw threatens to unhinge itself.

This...is not Henry Arlington. I have seen multiple versions of this man in my life, but I've never seen this one.

He's wearing all black. Black pants, black button down—with the top two buttons undone, no less. Sleeves rolled to his elbows. Newly shined shoes. A coat over his arm, but not his normal beige one. It's just a plain black coat.

And he looks *good*.

"You look ridiculous," I say, pressing the elevator button. "Like a Johnny Cash wannabe."

He clicks his tongue. "Is that what was going through your mind? Wouldn't have guessed."

I roll my eyes and try to keep them away from him. "See you at Bondi's, Jen. Don't be late, and don't call when you get there. Just text."

"Gotcha," he says, pushing off the wall to stand straight up. "Be there in half an hour."

"Thank you."

The elevator doors open, so Henry and I get in. I press the ground floor button and lean against the wall, coat folded over my arms. I don't want to put it on until I'm outside, mainly because my shirt turned out better than I could've imagined. Only I care, but that's okay. I'm my target audience.

"It's cold outside," Henry says, looking at the ceiling. "Spitting snow."

I clear my throat. "Thank you."

"You look pretty."

"I'm fully aware."

His face gives away nothing, and again, I'm reminded that I don't know him anymore. Maybe he stopped wearing his emotions on his face, or maybe, he never truly did; maybe I just knew how to read him. It was a luxury, knowing his tells. The loss makes me feel shockingly dejected.

The elevator stops, and we step out together. Mimi and Olive are sitting in the lobby, each with a fan of cards in their hand. All these women do is play cards, and honestly, I admire it. I hope my future looks exactly like this.

"Amelie, join us!" Olive says, her voice rough. "Mimi wanted to get Ronald and Jerry to play bridge, but I told her no. So we settled for Go Fish."

I grin. "I'd love to, but I can't tonight. Maybe tomorrow? I'll get Jen to play bridge with us."

Olive sniffs. "Fine. I like that boy."

"A real gem," Mimi agrees, putting her glasses back on. She blinks a few times before her eyes slide to Henry, and her barely-there brows raise up into her hairline. Unsurprising, I guess. Much like I can admit talent when I see it, I can admit aesthetic value.

And Henry is, indeed...aesthetic.

Sure. Let's use that word.

"Well, Amelie, who's this?" Mimi asks. I swear Olive bats her eyelashes, and I suppress the laugh that threatens to bubble out of me. They're worse than my mother. "I've never seen him before. It's been so long since you've brought a man around."

She's not wrong. I haven't brought a man around in...ever, actually, so I'm not sure who Mimi is imagining. But why should I be ashamed? It's not as though I don't receive offers. It's simply that I detest most of them. And besides, if I *were* to go on a date, it's not like I could keep it up. Once a prospect learns what I do, he'll run to the police. That's why Henry is such a bump in the road.

I hate that he knows. I hate that this is a whole thing between us now. I'd be lying if I said it hasn't crossed my mind—that he's the only man I could ever trust, simply because he knows and he hasn't told. But that's not true. He's getting something out of his silence. It's a trade. A business deal.

It's *fake*. Regardless of our past, the trust we share is fake.

"This is Henry," I say casually, pushing those thoughts out of my mind. "He's a friend of mine. We're going out for the evening."

Olive whistles. "Where to? That top won't hold for dancing, Amelie. Once, me and my husband—"

"Just out to dinner," I say, cutting her off. I don't need to hear about Olive's nip-slip thirty years ago. "We won't be long. If you can stay awake past ten, I'll even play you a round of Go Fish. He'll join." I elbow Henry. "He's good at Go Fish."

"It's true," Henry says, not at all thrown by these women. "I'm great. The best, even. None of you would stand a chance."

Mimi *tsks*. "Cocky one, isn't he? I won't make it past nine-thirty though, girly. Maybe next time."

I give her a solemn nod, though I'm hoping the ladies will be asleep well before then. If they're still here when I return, they *will* rope me into a game. Mimi can only be denied so much before she starts playing dirty.

She likes bribing me with butterscotch candies. Olive too. And it works, because I *cannot* figure out where they're buying them.

After a few moments of weird silence, Henry bids the ladies goodbye. He puts his hand on my back and guides me toward the door. The placement isn't low enough for me to elbow him in the ribs, but his hands are large enough to cover a decent portion of my waist without trying. "Before they start talking again," he says, quiet enough that only I can hear.

I suppress a shiver and let him lead me outside.

19

HENRY

Amelie looks like a distraction tonight.

She pries my hand off her back once we get outside, then starts shivering moments later. The term *spitting snow* is too light for what's actually going on out here. There's a heavy dusting on the sidewalk, the roads, and the trees. In half an hour, I reckon it'll be covered. More reason for us to get this over with.

"Put on your jacket," I tell her.

She scoffs. "Thank you, *Mom*."

"You're obviously freezing."

"How would you know?" She asks, though she's rubbing the backs of her arms with embarrassing vigor. "Maybe I'm toasty. Maybe I'm sweating real bad."

"Your nose is red, your teeth are chattering, and it looks like you're trying to start a fire. Put it on."

With a glare she relents, slipping her arms through the sleeves. The leather is wet from the snow that's fallen on it, but she doesn't seem to mind. I put my jacket on as we continue down the sidewalk, then shake the snow from my hair. I was hoping it would lighten up, not fall harder, though clearly, it was wishful thinking.

I'm really hoping that Bondi's will be empty, but the chances of that are low. Despite the weather, that place has never had an off day.

Neither of us speak as we walk. Amelie's focus seems to lie on *not* slipping, given that the ice is nearly forming under our feet, but I'm fixated on making sure tonight goes smoothly. It may be our only chance to find my *Ophelia* before Amelie leaves, and if *this* doesn't work, my dad will take things into his own hands.

And his solutions have always been a little rocky, to say the least.

We reach Bondi's and get in line. It's not a slow night—not one at all. We're wrapped around the corner, about twenty places from the front. This many people cannot be good for whatever Amelie has planned, but perhaps someone will be more suspicious than us.

"So," Amelie says, clearly sick of the silence. "Liz is a fashion writer?"

I raise my brows, shocked that she even remembered that detail. The conversation was minimal to me, so I figured it was to her, too. Though I know she's the type of person to remember everything that happens in a room.

"Random, but yes," I say. "She writes for *High Fashion*. Personally, I believe she hates it, but it's her choice."

Amelie hums. Crosses her arms and burrows a little deeper into that oversized leather jacket. I think it's her roommate's, because I don't see why she'd purchase it herself. It's two sizes too big. "I wanted to be a fashion writer," she says flippantly. "When the academy didn't work out, I considered that."

My mouth goes dry. The sole mention of the academy is breaching a dangerous topic, much more than anything we've discussed prior. But I can't stop myself from questioning her further, because even though I shouldn't, I crave more. More answers. Details. The sound of her voice.

More of her in general. Which is bad.

"Why'd you give up on that?" I ask, deciding to keep my curiosity at bay.

"Because I still can't spell worth anything."

I laugh, and she does the same. "Valid reason."

The corner of her mouth twitches. "Maybe."

"How did you go from wanting to do that, to doing what you do now?"

Amelie shakes her head, and I know I've crossed a line. "No. Off limits."

"We have off-limit topics?"

"Ninety percent of what we've discussed is off limits," she mumbles. "I just don't find you to be any harm. *Yet.*"

Her emphasis on that word drags me back to my dad's words. His request for me to gain Amelie's trust, then inevitably lose that gift.

"I should take that as an honor," I say, looking over my shoulder.

"You should," she agrees. "Don't you?"

I do, I think, but even that answer feels wrong. I'm too paranoid to think straight. For some reason, I'm almost convinced that my dad is somehow aware of this partnership. That he knows we're here right now. But it's ridiculous—it's not like he's omnipotent. He's at home, probably in his office, sifting through bills and checks.

Yet even through that logic, I can't shake the feeling that he *knows.*

"I do," I say aloud, "but not without a dose of fear."

Her face breaks into a smile. A genuine one that makes my stomach drop. "Good."

When we finally reach the door, I step up first. The bouncer nods when I flash him my ID. I start to walk inside, expecting Amelie to follow, but when I check over my shoulder, she's frozen.

And then I realize that she probably doesn't carry her ID. Because why would she? She's a thief. That cannot be a good idea.

She pokes me in the side, looking up at me with wide eyes, and I know she's waiting for me to vouch for her.

"I'll need your ID," the bouncer says.

Amelie's expression changes in a second. She puts on a sweet, innocent smile and takes hold of my arm. "I left my purse at your place, Hen."

I hold my breath and pray she can't tell how distracted I am by her touching me. At the way she's looking up at me through her lashes. "You did?"

"I did." She turns toward the bouncer. "Can we just call it even for the night? His apartment is far, and I don't enjoy walking in these shoes."

The bouncer looks unimpressed. "I can't let you in without an ID."

"She's fine," I say coolly. "She's older than me, actually."

"I'm fine," Amelie repeats. "Really. Do I look like someone who would lie?"

The man's face implies that, yes, she looks like someone who would lie.

I take a step closer, hoping the man can hear me over the horrendous noise coming from inside. Some techno-pop song is blaring, and it's nearly deafening. "Look. We're here on business for Roman Arlington. Just let us inside. We won't drink, won't cause any trouble. And we *are* both legal."

"I can't let her in without an ID," he says flatly, voice louder than mine.

I look over at Amelie and find her staring at me intensely. She's counting on me to get us in here, but I'm not sure it's going to work. I have to try, though. Leaving without an attempt isn't an option.

Sighing, I grab my wallet from my pocket and fish out a one-hundred dollar bill. The bouncer is watching, eyes squinted as I unfold it. I doubt he gets bribed that often, and when he does, it probably isn't with any more than twenty dollars. Nobody is *that* desperate to get into a nightclub.

"From Roman," I say, handing him the bill. "Don't let it get back to him."

The man has zero qualms about being bribed. He pockets the bill and waves us through, bidding us a goodnight as he does so. I thank him and put my hand on Amelie's back as we walk inside, hoping that we won't get separated by the horde of people.

And when I say horde, I do mean *horde.*

It's atrocious. So bad that I'm wondering *why* I let Amelie talk me into this. We should've waited until tomorrow. I could've talked our way in here much easier during the day. So why didn't I suggest that?

Why am I blindly going along with *everything* Amelie says?

"This is bad," she says simply, looking up at me.

"I think we'll be fine." I do not, in any way, shape, or form, think that. "Do you want to sneak into the back now, or...?"

Amelie checks the time on her phone. "No," she yells over the noise. "Let's give it a sec. Get drinks or something."

I really don't want to give it a *sec,* but fine.

Without thinking, I tug Amelie's jacket off her shoulders, tossing it over my arm with my own. "You think we need drinks?"

She huffs and pats a ten-dollar bill into my palm. "Shut your mouth and get me a cola."

I do, unsurprisingly. I walk to the counter, nervously popping the bill between my hands. When I get to the bar, every seat is taken. I squeeze between two sweaty men screaming at a game on TV and order our drinks, settling on water for myself. I look over my shoulder and attempt to locate Amelie, if only to make sure she hasn't run off to handle things on her own, but I find her laughing with some guy in a green polo shirt.

Something tugs low in my stomach at the sight, and it aggravates me. What right do I have to feel jealous at Amelie laughing with someone? *None.* I have no right. I'm annoyed at myself for even giving them a second glance, though it's not as though I can help it. Nothing I've felt lately is in my control.

The bartender gets my attention and hands me two glasses. I thank him and slide over the money, then find my way back to Amelie. She's standing in the center of the floor, alone once again, her face still bright with laughter. For a moment, I let myself imagine that I was the one who made her laugh. That I caused that smile on her face.

And then her eyes land on me, and the glow in them dulls.

"I hate this song," she says loudly. I hand her the glass of cola, but she stares at my water like it's poison. "You went for straight vodka?"

I rattle the glass. "Water. I'm not going to be tipsy on one of your 'thought-out' operations."

She hums. "*Thought-out* is an extremely relative term. In the grand scheme of things, what is thought out? How long does one have to think—"

"We don't need to do this right now."

Amelie grins and lifts her drink to her mouth. I take a step forward, trying to make space for a server behind me, but the gesture fails miserably as someone slams into my shoulder. It's enough of an impact that I spill my drink right down the front of my shirt. I close my eyes and exhale, setting the glass on a tray to my right. Amelie is trying to hold in a laugh, but I can hear her giggling against her palm, failing to stifle the sound.

"I'm sorry," she says.

"You're laughing."

"I'm not."

I grab a napkin to dry myself off, but it's useless. The papery fabric pills against my shirt, leaving tiny white specks in its wake. I give up wholly when Amelie turns on her phone and stares at the screen with a furrowed brow.

"What?" I ask.

"They're here. Meg and Jensen."

My heart speeds. "Okay. What do we do?"

"I'll be in the back." She starts walking away. "Meet you outside in fifteen."

"Be careful, Ames," I call over the music. "Please."

She gives me a wave over her shoulder.

I have a sneaking suspicion that *careful* is the last thing she's going to be.

20

AMELIE

My shoes are sticking to the floor, and it's almost enough for me to call this whole thing off.

I don't, though, because I'm a professional. I set my drink on the bar near a pretty blonde girl and sneak to the back. There's no one here—not even a line for the bathroom, which is shocking. I'm sure it's because it's still early. In five minutes, the stalls will be more crowded than the dance floor.

A back room is very little to go off of when doing something like this. The kitchen is to my left, and the restrooms are to my right, but I don't see another door aside from the kitchen. Employees are *packed* in there—I hear voices and spatulas scraping on pans, accompanied by dishware clinking against itself. My stomach tightens with nerves.

I'm going to smell like grease after this. But I suppose it's a sacrifice I'll have to make.

The first step when talking your way into a room is to be calm. Confident. To act like you're supposed to be there. No one in this kitchen will think I'm *supposed* to be here, but hopefully, I can act relaxed enough that they won't throw me out.

The clanging dishes get louder when I open the door. Words are tossed around, all varieties of drinks and foods to be made.

One of the men is yelling about mayonnaise, and another is tossing around a knife. And yes—he is actually tossing it. In the air.

I no longer feel calm, nor confident.

"You can't be back here," says the chef, finally noticing me. I'm suddenly more worried about the fact that he's not wearing a hairnet over his long hair *or* his beard, but I'm not here to critique. I wouldn't eat this food if I were paid to.

"There was a spill out front." I stand a little straighter. *Don't slouch.* "A bad one. It's a hazard, and no one else is taking care of it."

If the painting isn't in a janitor's closet, I'm going to lose my everloving mind.

Another one of the men looks at me curiously. He crosses his arms and squints in my direction, trying to decide whether or not I'm lying. He'll never figure it out—my face is trained so well, I might as well have Botox.

"Down that staircase. Hang a right, should be a closet," he says, giving me a toothy smile. It makes me want to scratch my skin off. "Be back in a second, or I'll come back there and find you."

Oh. Ew. Okay.

"It'll take no time at all," I say, voice perky. I can practically feel every pair of eyes on me as I cross the room, and I shudder.

The 'staircase' is small. Four steps. I go right, which puts me in the mouth of a very small alcove. Three separate doors greet me, and they're all identical.

Because *of course* they won't make this easy for me.

"Why don't you tell me which door?" I say, forcing my tone to stay light.

A low laugh follows my question. "One on the left. Should be unlocked."

I don't try that one because I don't trust him. Instead, I go for the middle. The squeaky handle turns, and I step in cautiously, hoping the men can't see me.

I find myself inside a walk-in freezer. There are multiple stacks of frozen foods; fries and meats and milk crates filled with onions. They're the same items from the photo, but I see no painting.

Maybe it's the wrong room. Maybe this isn't over.

I take a breath and try the door that the man said. It opens as well, and I force myself inside. For being a janitor's closet, it is *disgusting*. Puddles of liquid pool on the floor, and I have absolutely no desire to know what it is.

My heart stops when I glance around the room.

Against one wall rests a mop.

Against the opposite, milk crates and a painting.

But it isn't Henry's *Ophelia*.

No, it's *Nautical Abyss*. The painting taken from me just days ago.

"What?" I whisper to myself, stepping closer to the piece. It's real. It's *Nautical Abyss*. Henry's pristine signature is at the base, and my eyes single in on the person in the ocean, swimming toward their doom.

It's here. Right in front of me.

And *Ophelia* is nowhere to be found.

"Did you find the mop?" Asks a deep voice from outside the room. I can't tell if they've come any closer, but I don't have time to worry about it.

"Got it," I say, frantically looking around for a window. "Just... trying to find a bucket."

"I can help you with that," the man drawls.

I grab the mop, for a weapon if nothing else. "No! No, I've got it. Just give me a moment. I need to collect myself."

"...Over a bucket?"

"*Yes!*" I cry, hoping it's dramatic enough to deter him.

There's a window near the ceiling, but it looks too small for the painting to fit through. I should've measured from the outside, but I didn't, because I knew the *Ophelia* would fit. That thing is half the size of this one.

A deep chuckle floods my ears, and I roll my eyes. "You've got about ten seconds, sugar, before I come find it myself."

Ugh. I hope he spills hot oil on himself.

Instead of responding, I brace myself against the painting and hold it up to the window. It fits—*barely*. The edges will no doubt be scraped against the window frame, but that's not so big of a deal. It'll have to be okay.

"I'm coming!" I squeak, right before I close the door and wedge a serving cart under the handle. It looks weak—like a single push will move it. There's a damaged wine cooler in the corner, so I push it next to the cart. I even jam my lockpick between the latch and the doorframe, though I know it won't do anything. None of this will keep those men out of here for long.

So I grab the mop, and I shove it through the window.

Glass falls everywhere. The men must hear it because they come running into the hall. They're shouting and banging on the door, and I'm just trying to sweep the jagged shards away from the window frame so I don't bleed out in the van.

"*HELLO*?!" I scream out into the night. In seconds, Jensen appears outside, crouched down by the opening. I'm glad he and Meg figured out where this room was, because I'd be totally screwed otherwise.

Without a word, Jen takes the painting from me and guides it through the window, managing to load it in the van before I can catch my breath. Meanwhile, I'm trying to stack some milk crates so I can just climb out instead of facing the angry men.

Jensen reaches in to help me, but he shrinks back when the glass cuts into his forearms. He grunts and removes his left shoe, using the sole to clear more glass. It's mostly pointless. The shards fall in random directions, raining around me, so I take a step back and peek at my barricade.

The serving cart has moved, I notice. Probably from the pounding on the door. I'm shocked that the wine cooler is actually helping me out—I think it's the only reason the men haven't gotten in and murdered me yet.

"Amelie, I can't get you through here," Jen says quietly, frantically. "You'll get sliced up."

"It's fine."

"It's not. I'm not pulling you through there."

I ignore him and stand on three wobbly milk crates. There's nothing for me to grab onto, so I try to get some traction on the concrete outside, but that makes it worse. The glass digs into my arm, and I bite back the scream that claws at my throat. Fire shoots through my wrists as I shake them out, trying to free the loose shards embedded in my flesh.

But I try again, because I don't know what else to do.

And again, of course, my fingers slip, causing more glass to dig into my skin.

"Stop it," Jensen yells. "*Stop.*"

"Jen, please." I shake my head, hair falling into my eyes. "Those men are going to kill me back here, or worse. Let me try."

"*No.* I'll come inside." He stands up. "I'll get them away. Just give me—"

He stops talking. I stop listening. Because someone outside either throws themselves against the door, or they fall against it. The shouting stops, and faint words are passed back and forth.

And then I hear what sounds like a fist hitting something.

Not the wall. More like a person.

"Jen," I say quietly, my eyes stinging. "I don't like this."

"I'll come around," he says again. "Just tell me what to—"

Another loud *thud* echoes from the hall. This time, I drop my arms from the window and close my eyes. They're going to get in. The wine cooler is knocked away from the door now—only a few inches, but enough that they could move it the rest of the way. There's no use in cutting my arms up worse. It's—

"*Ames.*"

Henry.

It's him. Henry is outside.

"Amelie, it's me," he says breathlessly, tugging at the door handle. "*Let me in.*"

I nearly topple off the milk crates and run toward his voice. My hands are trembling as I retrieve my lockpick and shove everything away from the door. Henry opens it the rest of the way and steps inside, and his eyes go directly to the storm of glass behind me. He lets out a humorless laugh, one that's sealed by the blank look in his eyes. "I thought this was going to go smoothly."

"That was *your* assumption," I say, noting how shaky my voice is. I swallow hard, trying to stop my adrenaline from literally exploding my heart, but that becomes my last concern when I see Henry's hand.

"Oh," I mumble, taking his fingers and lifting them up to see. His knuckles are all messed up—bloody and torn, already beginning to bruise. "I'm so sorry."

He doesn't respond. At first, I think he's angry with me, but then I realize where his gaze is.

It's on my arms. On the blood that's soaked through my torn sleeves. He grabs my wrist and flips my arm over, pulling the sleeve of my shirt up the slightest bit. I gasp when his finger brushes one of the cuts, and I swear his eyes narrow further. "Did they do this?"

"No," I say, pulling my arm away. "It's fine. I'm fine."

He doesn't agree in the slightest, but he knows not to argue. Not here, anyways. "Come on. We're leaving."

I look up at him. "What did you do with them?"

"They aren't dead, if that's what you're asking." He stops by the door, waiting for me to leave, but I glance once more at the broken window. There's no sign of Jensen—I'd bet that he left the second Henry entered the room, satisfied that I was safe enough with him. I don't know how to feel about that, and I don't know why it's what I'm focusing on right now, especially when I can feel my heartbeat behind my eyeballs.

"Amelie," Henry says firmly, drawing my attention back to him. "We need to go."

I nod and step out into the awkward hallway. Henry is on my heels as we bolt toward the exit, and I notice that the men are nowhere in sight.

It takes us a while to get outside because of how many people there are. Someone steps on my foot, and someone else manages to drive their elbow into my back, but I keep a quick pace. Henry is basically racing toward the exit, but it still doesn't feel fast enough.

Cold air hits my arms as soon as we step outside, and I yank my jacket away from Henry. It stings, the leather against the cuts, but I don't care. Nothing is more important to me right now than getting home.

"What was that?" He finally asks, completely out of breath. "Are you okay?"

No. "I'm fine."

He sniffs. "Did we get it, then? The piece? Or was it all for nothing?"

I clench my jaw. A very large, very petty part of me wants to be annoyed that he's even asking right now, but I know he's doing it for me. He knows I don't want to explain what happened. What went wrong. How I ended up with blood on me.

So what do I tell him? It wasn't technically for nothing, but there's no benefit to him. All we found is something that will help *me,* and it feels wrong. I feel *so* wrong about selling his painting now. He did just keep me from getting potentially murdered, after all.

But also, why did he let me go that night in the museum? Why didn't he just snag the piece then? I can't stop thinking about it. Henry knew exactly what I was doing, and he didn't stop me. He didn't even seem to care.

I hate it. I hate all of this. I just want to sleep.

"Ames?"

I swallow, suddenly aware that I haven't spoken for quite some time. "Hm?"

"Did we, or did we not get the piece?"

"Oh," I mutter. "Um, no, we didn't get that one."

He blinks. "You got another?"

"One I've been looking for, yeah."

"They lied and swapped them out?"

I bite my lip. "Something like that."

"So my piece is just...gone."

"It's not gone," I tell him. "You're being messed with, Henry. *We're* being messed with, but I'll figure it out. Promise."

He sighs, pockets his hands. I have the urge to free the right one and see if the bruising is worse, but I don't. "We're running low on time," he says.

I nod. "I know. I'm doing my best."

"I know you are," he returns. "But it isn't enough."

I don't let that go to my conscience. Not like it wants to.

Neither Henry nor I say another word until we reach my apartment. He bids me a bland goodbye on the sidewalk and leaves. I don't bother saying anything back.

Jen and Meg, despite having the vehicle, aren't home yet. I assume they're unloading the piece, or at least hiding the van, but it's fine. I'm glad to be alone right now. I go to my bathroom and try to clean my arms, which ends up being a feat. Apparently, there are tiny shards of glass residing in my arms, so I try to remove them with a pair of tweezers. It hurts, bad—I pinch my skin a million times, and the cold metal does nothing to help, but eventually, I decide the cuts are clean enough.

I turn the shower on full heat and take my clothes off. I feel disgusting. I *smell* disgusting. I want this water to burn me until I feel clean. The steam stings my skin, but I ease myself under the literal stream of fire and stand there for a good while. I don't even move. I just think.

Henry saved me tonight. Whether or not it was a big deal to him, it was to me. I didn't have a good way out of that situation, and I was *terrified.* No close call has compared to that...ever.

But he didn't know that. He didn't know what was going on, only that something was wrong. And I don't know why he cares. I don't know why he's still working with me or why he won't just hand me over to the police and put us both out of our misery.

I do know one thing, though.

After I get rid of *Nautical Abyss,* I am never taking another piece of his art again.

21

HENRY

My head is spinning when I leave Amelie's apartment. What on *earth* happened tonight? How did we get from point A to point B?

I don't know, but I know how *I* got involved. I was standing as close to that alcove as I could without looking suspicious. Her voice somehow managed to get through the noise, and I just... panicked. And then I got closer, and I heard the men shouting at her, and I didn't know what else to do.

I could've taken a photo. Could've gathered the evidence my dad wants and ended this 'partnership' altogether.

Instead, I punched the guy closest to me and bribed the others to keep quiet.

I've lost 300 dollars and some dignity tonight, but I can't find it in myself to care.

Snow is still falling as I walk home. I'm shaking, whether from the wind or the adrenaline coursing through me, I've not decided. It's extremely unpleasant—my entire body is in some mode of panic, and it's all because of Amelie. Because I was *worried* about Amelie.

My phone buzzes in my pocket, and I grab it embarrassingly quickly, assuming it's her.

It's not.

ROMAN ARLINGTON

Where are you? Elizabeth said you aren't home.

I stop near a lamppost, kicking myself for even checking the notification. *Not* answering is an option, yes, but giving him reason to assume something is up would be worse.

I've been out for the evening. Where are you?

The second I hit send, I rethink the message. I don't think I've ever asked my dad where he is, and it's an odd time to start. But I want to know if he's got the slightest clue what I'm up to.

He wouldn't tell me by any means, but maybe he'd give it away accidentally.

ROMAN ARLINGTON

I've been holed up in my office. Any luck on finding the piece?

Not yet.

ROMAN ARLINGTON

Hurry.

Thank you. Very helpful.

"Henry?" Someone calls, and I turn around slowly. Amelie's friends are walking toward me hand in hand. They're both bundled up in a ridiculous amount of clothes, which honestly sounds preferable to the wet shirt I'm still wearing.

"What?" I ask, wary as they approach me. "Weren't you guys just—"

"Did Ames get home?" Meg asks.

I crack my knuckles, just to do something with my hands. "Yeah, I'm on my way home. Why? Is she okay?"

The amount of worry in my voice is pathetic.

"We haven't talked to her," Jensen says, nearly frowning. "Figured she'd want some alone time."

I blow out a breath. "What *happened* back there?"

"I think the men heard her break the window, and it just spiraled." He shrugs. "It was horrible to watch. I've never seen her that scared, not on a job. But it never should have gotten to that point. I *knew* we shouldn't have—"

"Don't be like that right now," Meg says, pulling her gloved hand away from his bare one. He rolls his eyes and drops his arm, and I notice that he's got a tattoo across the back of his hand. "Amelie will be okay, Henry. She's probably cozied up on the couch, drinking hot tea and simmering. Or watching *Breakfast at Tiffany's*. Either one works as a coping mechanism for her."

The thought of Amelie safe in her apartment is enough to loosen the knot in my chest. I *need* her to be okay. Not knowing if she was—and thinking that she wasn't—was one of the worst things I've ever felt.

I hate myself for not doing more. For not cleaning the cuts on her arms and making sure she stopped bleeding, though I know she wouldn't have allowed me that close. There's a likelihood that she wouldn't have even let me walk her to her door, but I should have *asked*.

She's driving me out of my mind. I assumed that would go away after four years, but it's only getting worse.

"Hey," I say slowly, remembering a question that Amelie couldn't answer. "What...what piece did you guys get?"

The two of them swap a glance, confirming a suspicion that I already had.

It's one of mine.

"I don't even care," I add on. "I just want to know what's going on. Please."

Meg looks at Jensen, and he's shaking his head subtly. All that does is further solidify my guess, but I keep my mouth shut. It doesn't matter. If they have it, I won't be getting it back, regardless of the answer.

"It was yours," Meg finally says. "*Nautical Abyss*. It got taken from us. Karma and whatever, probably. But Ames wasn't lying about your *Ophelia* being there. I have a photo if you don't believe me."

She starts to get her phone out, but I wave a hand. "I believe you. Thank you. That's all I was wondering."

They give me the most miniscule smiles before leaving. Jensen throws his arm around Meg, but she elbows him before they turn the corner. I pocket my hands and wait until they're out of sight to keep walking.

So. Amelie still has *Nautical Abyss.* I assumed that was dead and gone by now—off to trade, never to be seen again. Should I even care at this point? Do I try and snag that one back, alongside my auction piece? I'd like the thing back, but my dad would kill me for focusing on it. *Nautical Abyss* is not of utmost priority. It isn't a favorite, therefore, it means nothing to him.

I don't think it would matter anyways. Every plan we've made so far has worked against us.

Well, that's dramatic. We've only put one into action, (Bondi's, which I hated anyways) and the other (the decoy) hasn't seen the light of day. I've got to finish it soon, but even then, what are the odds of it working? What if it doesn't accomplish our goal?

I have too many questions, and no one has answers. This charade isn't solid. Everything has multiple outcomes, and I hate it.

I give the doorman a brief wave as I step on the elevator. I make sure to keep my right hand hidden from him, lest it raise suspicion—or actual spoken questions. I've never punched anyone before. I didn't expect it to batter up my knuckles, but my middle finger landed right on the man's nose. It doesn't *hurt,* it just looks bad.

Which might be worse, because now Lizzy and Dad will see it, and neither of them are very reserved with their questions.

I shrug off my coat once I'm inside my apartment. It's nearly ten now, I think, and I'm exhausted. Adrenaline rushes aren't for me—I don't like the low that comes afterward. But for some reason, instead of going to my bedroom, I skip right past it and go to my studio.

I roll up my sleeves and drag out a box full of acrylics. My brushes are all caked with paint, so I find the most usable one and start working on the decoy. This piece still hasn't presented itself to me. It's ridiculous to say I've got no idea what I'm painting, but it's the truth. A vague picture in my mind is all I have. Will the subjects end up happy, or sad? Will the piece have an edge of anger or regret? I never know for sure. Not until the very end.

Time is ticking by. I'm aware of it as I stack layers of color onto each other, waiting for a perfect image to appear before my eyes. The paint on my pallet is dwindling down to nothing, and the shades are all smeared together in the middle. It's a mess—the piece, my now paint-covered clothes, all of it. It's horrible.

And when I take a step back and stare at the canvas, I wonder what Amelie will see when she looks at this piece.

I've never cared what someone thinks of my art, not directly. I care if it's mildly desirable, because if it weren't, I'd be out of a job. But I paint what I want. No one can sway me from my instinct, from creating what I feel.

Amelie could, though.

She was the only person I've ever asked for feedback. Back in high school, the two of us would often share pieces and critique the other's work. If she told me the perspective looked off, or the shading could be better, I'd work on it, and the next day I'd ask her again. I trusted her to guide me in the right direction. And she *did.* Everything she ever suggested was good. She made my art better. She made *me* better.

She was good for me. So, *so* good.

But now, it seems as though she hates my paintings, and I don't know what changed. What shifted her love for art. I don't know if it's my work, or how she views me as a person, or another thing altogether. But I want her to tell me. I'm willing to beg for an answer.

You're ridiculous, I tell myself, slathering on another coat of paint. *Utterly.*

It's hours before I'm content with the piece. Before I see the image in my mind presented on the canvas. Faces stare back at me, a mix of good and bad and emotions I can't quite identify. I couldn't be happier with it.

With a heavy sigh, I carry my brushes to the sink and wash them. I set them on a drying towel, then turn my easel toward the wall, not the window. No need for someone *else* to get a glimpse of it.

Amelie said I may not see this piece again, but I'm sort of counting on that not to happen. If this whole operation doesn't go to plan, then this will be my auction piece. I don't have another option.

And if my dad has a problem with it...

He will. But I'm slowly losing my will to care.

22

———

AMELIE

The next morning at dawn, I call our client and agree to meet them in person with *Nautical Abyss.*

I rarely—if ever—meet clients in person. It takes the anonymity away from it, and the risk multiplies an insane amount. If I'd been thinking last night, I would've just left the piece at Bondi's and told our client to get it from there, but I'm not taking any chances.

Instead, we're meeting our client at Grand Arts before the doors open. It's not far from the apartment—ten, fifteen minutes on a bad day, but it seems much longer this morning. Meg has been listening to some 2000's band the whole drive, but neither Jen nor I have asked her to lower the volume.

"What did you tell Henry last night?" Jensen asks me under his breath.

I look over at him. "What do you mean?"

He snorts. "He punched through a few chefs to find you and *still* didn't get the piece he wanted. Surely he had questions."

"I just told him it wasn't there," I murmur. "I told him that someone is screwing with us. He didn't seem all that shocked."

"Why would he be?" Meg says. "He probably thinks you've got a plethora of enemies up your sleeve."

"After last night, I do. Put Bondi's on the *DO NOT ENTER* list."

Jensen chuckles, but I really don't find it that funny. It's not like I haven't been in sticky situations before. In fact, I sort of thrive in them. They give me something to do. Something to think about, a solution to plot. But last night threw me completely off kilter. It has me anxious. *Who* is doing all of this? Am I being dramatic about it? Is it all a coincidence?

I don't think so. I don't believe in coincidences, not with things like this.

"Meg and I ran into Henry last night," Jensen says casually, as if he's discussing tax rates or something. "He asked what piece we got."

"Did you *tell* him?"

"He already knew, Ames," Meg says, eyeing me through the rearview. "It was obvious. Besides, do you really want him to think we lied about his *Ophelia*? That sounds like a good way for him to end this scheme by getting us booked."

I sigh. "Doesn't mean I have to like it."

Meg suddenly slams on the brakes and throws me into a window. I yelp and grab onto Jen, who does little to steady me. The two of us nearly end up on the floor.

"Please learn to drive," I say through my teeth.

She sighs. "You drive, then."

"I'm too busy actually taking the paintings, thank you."

She mumbles something I don't catch as she pulls into the parking lot.

I hold my breath while we drive around Grand Arts. There's a limousine parked by the dumpster, complete with blacked out plates and tinted windows. It's got to be our guy, though I can never be too sure. Not after last night.

"Who wants to go out?" Meg asks, turning to look at Jen and me.

I stand. "I'll do it."

"No, I will," Jen says, standing as much as he can under the roof of the van. "I don't want a repeat of last night."

"I *can* hold my own, Jen," I tell him.

He nods. "Okay, yeah, but I don't want you to. Good enough?"

"No."

"Perfect." Jen opens the side door and steps out before I can.

Obviously, I follow him. He sighs when he notices me but doesn't make a scene. He won't overreact in front of a client, and I'm taking advantage of that.

We open the back doors on the van, and as we do, a tall man steps out of the limousine's driver side. He's decked out in a three-piece suit, dark glasses on his eyes. He looks like he should be in *Mission Impossible* rather than my dad's parking lot.

"That him?" Jen whispers.

I shrug. "I don't know. Keep it hidden."

He drags the painting further out of the hatch, keeping all but the corner out of sight. I don't know the correct way to go about this, but I know not to offer it up at first pass. What if this man is here for *legal* business at the hall? Giving up my cover would be the most amateur move I could make.

"Hey there," I say, leaning my hip against the van. I cross my arms and flash the man a smile, hoping to lighten the mood. The expression on his face tells me that I've failed. He looks constipated. "You wanna tell me what you're here for?"

"I'll ask you the same," the man says, and I fight back an eye roll. His voice is similar to the one I heard over the phone, but it's unlikely that the actual buyer would even leave his house. Most of them have lackeys to do this part of the job.

"Just say the words, and I'll leave you alone," I tell him.

His jaw clenches, and I can see the wariness in his body language. He's careful—that's why he won't just come out and say it. But I'm careful, too, at least today.

Jensen steps forward and leans against one of the open doors, letting more of the painting show. It's enough to let him know what we're here for, but not enough that we couldn't backtrack if needed.

The man pulls out his phone and begins swiping at the screen. I bite my lip, starting to get antsy, but he finally says, *"Nautical Abyss."*

I let out a breath. "Give me the number."

He rattles off my burner phone number like he's memorized it, and Jensen nods. "We have a winner."

Letting loose a sigh of relief, I move to the left and let Jensen unload the painting with the unneeded help of Mystery Man. I watch like a hawk as they carry it to the limousine, and right when they settle it in the back, I notice something. It's hard to see with the sun shining directly onto it, but my mouth drops open when I get a glimpse.

It's a playing card.

An ace of hearts, tucked neatly against the canvas's frame.

My parents are in my living room when we get back from the hall.

I let out a huff as I hang up my purse, pulling my sleeves over my palms so they don't see the scrapes. Giving my mom a key when I moved in was a foolish move in general, but I never expected her to show up at seven thirty in the morning.

Now isn't the time. Actually, now is the one time I really *don't* need this.

"What is it?" I say, forcing an ounce of humor into my tone so they don't think I'm angry. I *am,* but not at them. This is botching my nap time. I'm exhausted—I was up until two last night, trying to sort through all the happenings. Trying to find any sort of pattern in what's going on. I failed miserably and ate seven chocolate chip cookies before falling asleep.

And now, I know exactly what's going on.

It's the Dealer. Of course it is.

But *why*? What did I do to get their attention?

Mom stands and walks up to me, an adorable smile on her face. Her and my dad are matching today, as they often are. His sweater has Rudolph on it, and my mom's has Clarice. They sent me photos on Christmas when they received them as a gift. Apparently, they're going to be wearing them year-round.

"Honey, we aren't here to pressure you into a decision," Mom says slowly, and I am acutely aware that that is exactly what she's going to do. "But...Margot is asking for a final answer today."

"I'm trying, Mom," I tell her, letting guilt settle into my stomach. "Really. I'm trying my hardest to get everything finished up. I just don't know..." I let my voice trail off as I plan my next words. I need to give her a solid reason and answer: no. I can't. Why? I don't know yet, but I'm going to figure it out.

"Please, Amelie," Mom says, her voice softer than usual. "It would mean the world to me. I just want us all to be together again. It's been years."

She's right. It has been years.

And for some reason, her saying it makes it all the more real. For the first time, I'm realizing that the no-contact didn't just go for Margot and me. It affected Mom and Dad, too.

"I'll be there," I hear myself say, even though the words feel wrong. "Promise. I'll figure things out."

"Really?" Dad says, his voice bright.

"Really." I nod. "I may have to skip out early, but I'll be there."

"Will you still bring your boyfriend?"

I grit my teeth. Now's the time to back out. Now's my chance, and *yet*—

"Yes. He said he'd come." My smile is so tight that my eyes water. What am I doing? Seriously? I should've had this talk over the phone. I can't look my parents in the eyes and disappoint them, but I can over a phone call. I've done it many times. "We'll drive up together that morning."

Mom claps her hands and literally cheers. "I can't wait! Packs lots of warm clothes, honey, and make sure he does, too. What's his name?"

What's his name? What's his *name?* I don't know his name! HE DOESN'T EXIST.

"You forget the boy's name, pumpkin?" Dad laughs when I don't answer right away.

"What? Come on now." I force a laugh. "I didn't forget. His name is—"

"Henry," Jensen says, throwing a heavy arm over my shoulder. "Name's Henry. I've met him a few times. Seems like a great guy."

I am going to slit Jensen's throat in his sleep. He won't even see it coming.

Mom's eyes widen, and she looks at Dad before looking back at me. "Henry? The same Henry—"

"The same one!" Jensen gives me a clap on the back. "They're reunited, Ames tells me."

He must've had his brain probed while I was at the bar last night, because there's no way he's seriously doing this.

"Where did you meet him?" Mom says frantically. "I've seen his name everywhere, of course, but I didn't think—"

"Saw him at the museum," I say, my throat tightening. "Happened like in the movies."

I deserve to be shot for that line, honestly.

"This is so perfect!" Mom says, giving me a tight hug. Dad joins, and I stand there like a statue, completely speechless. Their lack of questions is astounding and, quite frankly, ridiculous. "Did you two work everything out? Does he know what you're doing now? How's it all working out? Margot is going to be so shocked!"

Margot isn't going to believe a thing.

"I'll explain it all at the cabin," I say numbly, stepping out of her grasp. Her and Dad slowly start toward the door, and I thank whatever divine power is listening for the escape. "Love you guys."

"Love you too," they call back, closing my front door behind them. I lock it and lean my forehead against the frame, trying to lessen the weight in my chest with deep breaths. It doesn't work.

Jensen starts cackling, and it makes my blood pressure shoot up.

"You'd better start running," I say, turning to face him, "if you favor any *particular* body parts of yours."

He holds up his hands. "Listen to me. I was helping you out."

"That was not helping! In what world was that *helping*?"

"Listen," he says again. "I'm not saying you're going to enjoy it. But you need to ask the real Henry."

"No."

"Yes." Jensen stares at me with an odd intensity. "He cares about you, Ames. Last night, he was asking about you like you were all that mattered. He'd do it in a heartbeat if you asked him. And offered loads of money."

I ignore all his other comments because one sticks out like a sore thumb.

He cares about you.

He doesn't. The man who stopped speaking to me when I needed him most does *not* care about me.

But if that doesn't pique my curiosity...

"What do you mean by that?" I toy with my nails as I talk, hoping my tone is nonchalant. "That he cares? He was probably just making sure I was home and not out causing trouble."

"No, Amelie, not everyone is convinced you're going off the rails." Jen leans against the kitchen counter with a sigh. "He asked if you were okay. Plain and simple. It was clear from his voice that he was worried about you."

I drop into a chair at the kitchen table and frown too dramatically. Pouting isn't my thing; normally, I just go straight to revenge, if it's needed. But it's unnecessary in this case, which brings me to the truth: this *sucks,* and there's nothing I can do about it.

"You needed a name," Jensen says. "And you weren't thinking fast. I'm sorry if I got you into deeper trouble, but just like Meg, I *was* trying to help you."

"I don't know what to do," I mumble, leaning my forehead on my arms. "I should've just told them."

He gives me a rough, dad-adjacent pat on the arm. "I don't think it's about them. It's about Margot."

I wince, because he might be slightly correct.

I want to have something to show for the years I've been gone. Margot will come back with her stories of success, of all the things she did, and I have nothing to show for my career—nothing that she needs to know, anyways. If I show up alone...I don't know. It's not bad. There's nothing wrong with it. I just don't want to.

But this is *not* any better.

"Just remember," Jensen says, forcing me to look over at him, "that this is all Meg's fault."

That wrenches a laugh out of me. "It'll be fine. I'll see Henry in a few days, get everything dealt with, and *then* worry about the boyfriend thing. I'll be okay."

"You will," he says. "And think about it. If worst comes to worst, you can say he got hit by a bus and he couldn't make it to the lodge."

I shake my head. "You underestimate my mom. She'd drive to the hospital with flowers and balloons."

"Melinda is a good woman," he says solemnly.

"She is," I agree. "All the more reason that I'm literally the devil for lying to her."

He sighs. "You panicked. And technically, Meg dug you into this."

"I can hear you guys," Meg calls from my bedroom. "And I already apologized."

"She did," I tell Jensen. "So let it go."

"I'll let it go if you find a solution in five days."

He gives me a sideways glance, one that lets me know exactly which solution he advises.

I hate it more than most of the things that have been going on. And yet, I don't hate it enough to push it completely out of my mind.

23

AMELIE

I double check my phone as I leave the Chinese place down the block. He said it right there—I can show up whenever I want. Open arrival times have my heart. If I want to get there at six or nine, it's fully up to me. It's beautiful.

Speaking of *open times,* I'm being tormented by the exact opposite at this moment. It's been four days since I promised my mom I'm coming to the cabin, and I've spent that time tying up loose ends. All my clients are aware that I'm on leave. We delivered a piece two nights ago. Our money was deposited through the hall's pay system just yesterday. Everything has lined up perfectly.

Except that I'm still going solo to the cabin. But that's a later problem, given that I'm on my way to Henry's with a bag of food. I've already decided that I'm not asking him, which is good. It leaves us more time to focus on work. He's ready to take the next step and make his piece public. It should help speed up this process, but I'm not sure how much.

He's waiting for me in the lobby when I arrive. I swear his face lights up when he catches sight of the bag on my arm. Good for me, honestly—he'll be much more open to my antics if I've fed him.

"You're a darling," he says solemnly, and I nearly trip over my feet. Because of my shoes, obviously—they're slick on the bottoms! "Though I won't repeat it."

I snort as the elevator opens. "Yeah, I'll be expecting payment for the curry chicken later."

He eyes me. "Curry chicken?"

"Mhm. And egg rolls, and rice. Surely you can find something you like."

"You know I like all of that," he mumbles, taking the bag from me. "And why would I reimburse you? You stole my wallet and bought your breakfast a week ago, if I can remind you of that."

"Okay, and then I paid for my own drink at the bar. A lady should never do that. So basically we're even."

He sighs, but I think he's biting back a smile. I look at the ground as the elevator hits floor eighteen, willing it to go faster. Why does being in enclosed spaces with him feel so tense? I think I'm about to start sweating, and if I do that, I *will* scream.

The shiny doors open, and right before I step forward, Henry pats something into my palm. I look down in shock at the twenty-dollar bill resting in my hand, then glance back up at him. "What are you—"

"Thank you for dinner," he says casually, stepping out of the elevator.

My jaw is fully agape. I hadn't *actually* expected that. I don't even want the money. I just wanted to be a nuisance! An argument was the most I thought I'd get from him, and that was enough to satisfy me.

Keys start rattling around, and I realize the elevator is about to close again. I run to catch Henry as he unlocks his apartment, and when we walk inside, he takes the food to his living room. He sets the bag on the coffee table and carefully lowers himself to the floor, kneeling onto the rug before sitting on the ground completely. I assumed we'd just go to his studio, since that's basically the only place I've been here, but he motions for me to join him.

"Come eat first," he says. "This stuff is awful when it gets cold."

I don't have to be told twice. I take my heels off by the door and join him, cautious as I pop open the container of chicken. Henry goes for the egg rolls, and the first thing he says is, "Why do you look more tense than normal?"

I blink, caught off guard. "Huh?"

"You just look...stressed." He unwraps a pair of chopsticks, snaps them apart, and hands them to me. "Your eyes look crazy, and your jaw is clenched. Grinding your teeth is bad for you."

"I know." I did not know that was a thing. "And anyways, it's the whole family situation."

"Ah. The fake boyfriend thing?"

"That," I confirm, stuffing a piece of chicken into my mouth. "I doubled down on it yesterday, and I've never regretted anything more. And *then*, Jensen—you remember Jensen, right? I feel like you need to picture him before I tell you this."

"I recall," he says. "Keep on."

I exhale. "Actually, I don't think I should even tell you this." I'm going to, though, because I have nothing to lose. He'll probably get a kick out of it, and I'll get to tell a story. Win-win. "But my mom was hounding me for my boyfriend's name, and Jensen said 'Henry'." I roll my eyes and pray it looks nonchalant. "So now she thinks you're coming with me tomorrow."

Henry is silent as he chews his food. A good quality, really—this is something I've always given him credit for. If I can hear you chewing your food, you are immediately an enemy. I believe that with my whole heart and I'll never change.

"I'm going to say something," he says, "and I don't want you to cut me off. I want you to let me finish."

"Okay."

"I'll make a big deal online about a new piece, right? I've got a decent audience, so it'll get some word out. I can even tell my dad to put it in the flyers. Subtly, I can hint that it's here, in my studio."

"Okay," I say again, growing more wary.

"Then we'll leave that up to fate, and I'll go with you to your parent's cabin."

Gracefully, I start choking on my chicken.

"You're *kidding*," I say, grasping my water glass. "You're lying."

"No," he says plainly.

"You haven't—Henry, you haven't seen my family in years!" I'm practically stuttering now. "And you and I don't even get along. This wouldn't work."

He shrugs. "I don't know. I have a pretty fun time with you."

NO. "What about Betty? She can't stay here all alone. She's a baby."

His eyes are a little too heavy on me. "Lizzy can feed Betty when she gets home from work."

I bite down on my lip. Take another sip of water to get the burning out of my throat. What if...what if this isn't horrible?

No. No, it's definitely horrible, and it wouldn't work. We are *not* about to go back to the past. Pretending to date him wouldn't end well for either of us. I know this.

But it *is* an easy solution, kind of. And a marvelous way to irritate him.

"You don't have anything to gain from this," I say.

Henry shrugs. "Maybe not."

"And you wouldn't be able to stand me for a week straight," I continue. "I mean, even *way back when,* I was still on good behavior. You know, like early relationship behavior? Where I don't eat in front of you and all that?"

A crease appears between his eyebrows. "You ate a rack of ribs in front of me after our prom."

"Yes, and I ate them *daintily*."

He snorts. "Yeah. Okay."

I huff, still intent on convincing him this is a poor idea. "Are you seriously up for this? Was seven months not enough torture for you? Because it was for me."

"We must define torture differently, Amelie."

I gape, waiting for him to say more. He just goes back to eating.

Am I really considering this? Surely not. I can't be! My mom is insane. She'll lure Henry into a false sense of security with muffins and then start talking about grandkids. Dad will make him watch football for hours on end. The poor guy's eyes are going to be bleeding by the time we make it back here.

But also...it'd be nice to have a focus other than Margot. I'd prefer that it's not Henry, but beggars can't be choosers.

"Pack warm clothes," I mumble, regretting all of this already. "And something nice. Margot's got a showing at a local museum."

I wait for his questions about that last part, but they don't come. Good. He can probably sense my hostility, which isn't a shock whatsoever. I stopped putting on a front for him a while ago.

"Okay," he says.

"My family is insane," I remind. "You remember that, no?"

Amusement lights his eyes. "I remember."

"And my mother is insistent on grandchildren."

"I'm pretty sure all moms are."

"We don't need to do this." I say that one more to myself.

Henry takes a breath. "But we're going to, aren't we?"

Yes. I'm afraid that we are.

"We'll leave tomorrow morning," I say. "Do you have a car?"

"Yes."

"Perfect. Pick me up at six in the morning."

"Mm-hmm." He takes a long drink of water. "Anything else?"

I pretend to be deep in thought, tapping my nails on the table-top. "Donuts in the morning?"

"Well, that was a given."

We finish eating in silence. When we're done, I dump both our cups of water in the sink, and he throws the boxes away. There was very little leftover, but if we'd had more, I would've taken it.

Once everything is cleaned up, Henry leads me to his studio and uncovers the painting. "It's all done," he says, sounding oddly nervous. "Should I upload a photo of the thing? Or just mention that I've completed something new?"

I don't respond, mainly because my eyes feel magnetized to the canvas. I know Henry's staring at me, trying to figure out what I'm thinking, but I couldn't care less about him watching.

Two children. A boy and a girl, running through a field. They have the same exact faces, so I do well to assume they're siblings. It's an adorable portrait at first glance, but much like his other pieces, they become chilling when you look deeper.

The children are crying. For what, I'm not sure—there's nothing chasing them. No storm or even a cloud above them. The girl's face is red, and the boy's face is pained, glistening with tears. But neither have a clear reason to be upset.

It looks so familiar, and yet, I'm almost certain I've never seen something like it before.

"Ames?" Henry asks quietly.

I blink. Tip my head to the side. "Whatever you want," I say. "I don't think it'll matter."

He just nods. I'm more aware of his lingering gaze now, but still, I don't look away from the piece.

I hate art. I decided that long ago.

But something about Henry's work is very haunting. Enthralling. And I don't like the way I'm drawn to it even more than I used to be. The way I'm tempted to ask the story behind each piece. I *want* to know what went into this painting. I want to know where he drew the inspiration, what coursed through his mind while creating it.

"Do you recognize it?" He asks.

I blink, shocked. "No. Why would I?"

He shrugs. "Just curious. You've seen the photo it's based on before."

"Huh?" I shake my head. "I don't think I have."

"I showed it to you. It's a photo of Lizzy and I."

Now that I'm actively trying to remember, my brain goes blank. That's why it was familiar, I guess, but I don't recall the original image. I also don't remember it being a *sad* photo.

"You weren't crying in that one, though," I guess.

Henry exhales. "No, we weren't."

"So why did you make this sad?"

"I don't know," he says. "It just happened. But I haven't named it yet."

"You could put it out as a sort of competition," I say, looking up at him. "Let people suggest a name."

He shakes his head. "I don't like that."

"Why?"

"I don't want people naming something I created."

I shrug. "It would be good for publicity."

"No," he says with that tone of finality again. "Something else."

Sighing, I glance back at the painting and focus on the little boy's—*Henry's*—face. Despite it being sticky with tears, his expression is almost curious. Full of awe and something a little deeper. More terrifying.

"*Childlike Wonder.*" I look up at him again. "Something like that. Something ironic."

He crosses his arms. "Actually, yeah. I really like that."

"So we've got it?"

"I think we do."

Yes. One more thing checked off the list.

Henry snaps a photo of the painting and uploads it to whatever site he's on. I almost ask him to forward it to me so Meg can drop hints, too, but that sounds like a good way to get more attention than we want. I still believe that whoever is behind this *knows* Henry. Maybe a competitor that he's unaware of, someone who's popularity he's taken over with his own. The possibilities are, unfortunately, endless.

"It's done," Henry says a few seconds later. He holds his phone up and shows me the post, along with a mildly wordy caption that I don't care to read. "I'll call my dad tonight and tell him to leave the cameras on, and that I'll be gone for...how long is this?"

"A week," I say, then quickly add, "But you don't have to stay the whole time. It's sort of a birthday thing, too, so I'm sure Margot—"

"I'll be fine," he says, hitting send on the message he's been typing. I'm awaiting more questions, given that I've told him basically *nothing,* but Henry doesn't even look up from his screen. He dials a number on his phone and holds it to his ear. "Liz?" He says after a few seconds of silence. "Yeah. I'm gonna be gone for a bit. Can you—no, it's not something from Dad. Can you—Liz, let me talk. Can you feed and water Betty?" A pause. "Great. Thanks. Yes, I'll leave your payment on the kitchen table. Uh-huh. Okay, bye." He hangs up and looks at me. "Alright. My arrangements are set."

I gape. "It's that easy?"

"Sometimes."

How is that even possible? When was the last time I've gotten to do *anything* with that little effort? It takes an army for me to go shopping longer than an hour, and all he has to worry about in a week-long span is keeping his cat alive.

"Alright," I say, tucking my hair behind my ears. "Well, just... yeah. Pack warm clothes, like I said."

He nods, and it's suddenly insane to me that we're doing this.

My ex-boyfriend. I'm taking my ex-boyfriend to my family cabin and lying about it. And the worst part is, I don't feel any remorse. I'm honestly *relieved* that he's coming. I don't really care to think about why.

Henry and I make our way out to the living room, and I grab my purse off the rack. I put my heels back on—he's a *no shoes in the house* person—and he slides my coat onto my arms. I don't miss the way his fingers brush the back of my neck, the way his breath seems to catch in sync with mine, but I assume it's unintentional.

"Bright and early," I tell him, hiking my purse up onto my shoulder. "I like blueberry donuts. Also anything with sprinkles."

"I know. I'll bring you a black coffee to wake you up."

I narrow my eyes. "You wouldn't dare."

"We'll see." He grins, then opens the door. "Sleep well, Ames."

I throw a wave over my shoulder. "Have nightmares, Arlington."

24

———

HENRY

"You lied to *dad*?!"

Okay. Not a great way to start this conversation, though I couldn't think of a better one.

Liz is sitting on my couch, downing her third virgin mojito in twenty minutes. She came over a few minutes after Amelie left to show me that she made a pitcher full, then asked what I was packing a suitcase for. I was tempted to lie—to say the first thing that popped into my head, which happened to be *Finland.*

But there's no use, not when I really need to talk to someone about all this, so I finally just told her. She's one of those people that you can tell anything to...and then instantly regret it when the lecture comes.

Which is where I am right now.

"Just a little," I say, folding up a shirt. "But it's not that bad."

She huffs and drains her glass. "Yes, it is!"

"I couldn't tell him the *truth*, Liz. You know how he felt about Amelie."

"I know. I'm only saying, it's going to be bad when he finds out."

That's true. I told my dad I'm going out of town for a convention, because what else was I going to say? That I'm going to spend time with the girls he hates, as well as her entire *family*? No. If I had done that, he'd force me to get dirt on her. I would have no choice but to give him the upper hand.

And I don't want that. At all.

"Hen, I don't know why you did that." Lizzy shakes her head. "And he *will* find out."

"He won't," I say pointedly. "You won't tell him."

"Of course I won't. But don't...don't you ever feel like he knows more than he lets on?"

"All the time," I admit. I've always thought that. He's too intent about certain things to *not* be hiding something, though I assume it's because of his past.

According to Mom, Dad was a different man when he started his business. He was happier, more enthusiastic about small things. I'd paint something new, and he'd make it the biggest deal, saying that one day, it'll be displayed in his museum. When I was finally old enough to make it a career, I was thrilled.

But the whole thing slowly tapered off.

Business got bad for a while. Art thievery raised an insane amount in months. The worst it's been since the nineties, according to the reports. I remember reading stories about it when I was young—the most prominent thieves in the area, named *The Bandits*, ran this city. They were never caught, but they've also never been forgotten. Not by my family, anyways.

"Well, what outcome are you expecting?" Liz asks.

I look over. "What?"

"What are you wanting out of this trip?"

I swallow. "I don't want anything out of it. I'm going to help Amelie, and she's going to find my piece, and we'll be rid of each other."

"Hm," she says, clearly not believing me. "Henry, do you remember your prom, when you got home after dropping Amelie off at her house? Do you remember that?"

"No, but I'm sure you're going to remind me of it."

"I am." She sits a little straighter. "That night, you were ecstatic. Insane. A little giddy, if I might, but really—"

"I don't see what this has to do with anything."

Liz sighs. "You're talking about her with that same tone of voice. That same look on your face. Even while acting like you don't care about her."

My face turns hot. "No, I'm not."

"You are. You still love her, Hen, regardless of your want otherwise. You're doing all this because you miss her."

I don't know what to say. She's *wrong*. I don't miss Amelie. I don't still love her. I'm doing this because she needs help, and she's helping me, so it's a fair return. There's no need for her to be anxious over something I can easily fix. That doesn't mean I still love her. That's basic human decency.

"This is all just an observation," Liz says. "I don't think it's a bad thing."

"It's a *false* thing," I clarify. "I'm doing this in return for her help, Liz. Nothing else. I don't...I *can't* still love her. She set out to make my life miserable." *And she's doing a great job at it.*

Liz snorts, and I have yet to find what's funny. "You went to her for help, Henry! You can't act like she's all that bad. And she's not. I miss her dearly. But you need to man up and say what you're thinking."

"Liz," I warn. "Let it go."

"Tell me."

"No."

"Say it!"

"Say *what*?"

"What you think of her."

"I think a lot of her. I can't *stop* thinking about her, and it's aggravating." I exhale sharply, embarrassed as the words leave my mouth. "Good enough?"

"Sure! Now you've admitted it. That's all you need."

What I need is some memory erasure procedure, though I don't think those exist yet.

"It's going to be a disaster," I say, shoving more clothes into my suitcase. "We're going to kill each other."

"Or you'll fall back in love."

"Liz, I swear—"

"Do you need me to cover for you here?" She flashes a smile. "I can."

"I don't think it'll come to that," I say. "If something goes wrong, I'll take care of it when I get back."

She nods and pours herself another mojito. That's the fifth. "You know what you're doing, Henry."

"I don't." I give a strangled sounding laugh. "I have no clue what I'm doing."

"You'll figure it out, then." She hums. "Anyways, can I see your new piece? I was going to look, but I didn't want to overstep."

"You're always fine to break into my studio."

I stand and fling my suitcase shut so Betty doesn't lay on my clothes. Before I even turn toward the door, Liz shoots to her feet with a gasp. "Wait! What are you going to do about the piece? Do I need to put it in my apartment?"

I shake my head. "I told Dad to have the cameras on while I'm gone."

"And the likelihood of him listening is…?"

"Slim," I admit. "But he acted more compliant than usual, so I'm hoping that's a good sign."

It's either that, or he was trying to pacify me, which isn't an impossibility.

Lizzy shrugs and walks out of my room, clearly deeming the conversation over. I unlock my studio door and let her go ahead of me. She stops short in front of the canvas, staring at it with blank eyes and a downturned mouth.

"It's us," she says.

I nod. "That one photo, just…different."

She tilts her head. "I have that on my fridge."

"Why?"

"Because I was cute. What did you name it?"

I swallow, reluctant to tell her after our conversation. But Liz knows everything. She'll know just by the sound of my voice if I don't mention it.

"*Childlike Wonder*," I say quietly. "Ames named it."

She turns and raises her brows. "Oh, you are *gone*."

It certainly does look that way, which is why my next question is going to make Liz's assumptions ten times worse. "Moving on. What do you know about jewelry?"

Her brows raise. "Jewelry? You want to shop for *jewelry*?"

I nod.

Liz lets out an ear-splitting cackle before grabbing my arm and dragging me outside.

25

AMELIE

I break my alarm clock when it goes off the next morning.

It isn't intentional, of course, but I've never been an early riser. Five o'clock is an inhumane time to be awake, and Henry is going to regret saying yes to this when he has to deal with my grumpiness all day.

Groaning, I pick up the plastic casing that I shattered and throw it in my bedside trash can. It was a cheap one; to be honest, I'm surprised it's survived this long. I'm normally a little rough with turning the thing off. This morning, I just *happened* to grab the metal tumbler on my nightstand to silence it.

"What did you do?" Jensen stumbles into my room wearing a blanket cape. "It's five in the morning."

"Henry's getting here at six," I say, grabbing my brush off my desk. "I thought I told you."

"You didn't," he mumbles, dropping into my chair. "But this is fine. Now I can tell you what happened yesterday evening."

I stop dragging the brush through my hair. Jensen got home late last night, and I spilled all of *my* stories before he had a chance to tell me his. It's likely that I wouldn't have registered anything anyways—I was a little preoccupied with packing and worrying.

"We have an offer," Jen says when I keep silent. "This weekend. There's an older piece out locally, I guess, and someone got in contact with Meg last night."

My stomach flips, and instantly, I'm afraid it's the decoy. We aren't supposed to get offers for that!

"Is there a name on it?" I ask tersely.

Jen nods. "*Lover of Mine.*"

I release a breath and braid my hair back. Good. Not the decoy, and not one of Henry's, at least that I'm aware of. "You guys think you can handle it?"

"I do," he says, fully confident. "This one doesn't seem as demanding as our previous."

"How much?"

"Ten grand."

"We could use that," I mutter, flipping my hair over my shoulder. "And please get away from my desk. I need to get ready."

He sighs and stands. "I'm going back to sleep. Be careful today, Ames. I don't fully trust the guy."

"I'll be alright," I say. "He *did* save me the other night, Jen. I think he can help me evade a couple of questions from Margot."

He chuckles. "If you think you're getting fewer questions with a man—*him,* no less—then you're dead wrong."

He's correct. But I simply hope the questions are much more bearable than they would be otherwise.

Jensen goes back to sleep, and instead of going back to the couch, he crashes in my bed. I don't mind it because he sleeps heavily. There's no way I'll wake him while getting ready, especially not this early.

I blast an old Gwen Stefani album through my headphones and get dressed. A two-hour car ride calls for comfort, so I wear a matching pink set of sweatpants and a hoodie. It's not *obnoxiously* pink, not that there's any such thing. I put on some fleece-lined boots and tie a ribbon in my hair.

Makeup is useless, because I'm going to sleep the entire drive, but I still dab some concealer under my eyes. It's likely that Margot will be there in a blazer and heels, with perfect hair and a full face of makeup, but I try not to let that bother me. I try to be thankful that I'm seeing her again, even though that's the last thing I feel.

Last night, on the way home from Henry's apartment, I got Margot a birthday gift, and I haven't stopped second guessing it since I swiped my card. I'm not even expecting anything from her, but I panicked and bought her a new handbag. She loves hand-bags—or, she *used* to, anyways. I don't really know what she likes anymore. It's a brown leather one, with gold detailing and three different straps you can switch out.

I like it. *I'd* wear it, and I'm a harsh critic. So hopefully she feels the same.

At a quarter till six, I put my bags by the door. My stomach is growling a concerning amount, so I grab an unripe banana and eat half. While I wait for Henry to show, I decide to straighten up. I fold the blankets Jen kicked onto the floor and wash the few dishes in the sink. When I'm drying the last coffee mug, I hear a knock on the door.

"Coming," I call, frantically drying my hands on a dishrag. I cross the room and fling the door open to find Henry with the goods in tow: a brown paper bag and an unmarked to-go cup.

"Good morning," Henry says, handing me the coffee. "Drink this."

I take it, relishing in the warmth against my palms. The steam wafting off the cup carries the scent of the drink, and I gasp when I realize what it is. "You went to Parlon's!"

"So you won't be crabby." He hands me the paper bag and picks up one of my suitcases. I grab the other with my free hand and hike my purse a little further up my arm. "Are we good to go?"

"We are," I nod, locking the deadbolt behind me. "You ready for the time of your life?"

"Absolutely," he says, and I genuinely cannot sense any sarcasm in his tone. I know it's there—I'm not stupid. He's just hiding it well. "Fair warning, though. I'm counting on your enter-tainment to keep me awake behind the wheel."

I push the elevator button. "Do you often fall asleep while driving?"

"No, but it's six in the morning, and it's dark outside. It's not as though I *want* to be awake."

"You'll be fine. I'll perform my playlists for you, and it'll be the best experience of your life."

He chuckles and steps into the elevator with me. When the doors close, I notice him looking me over, and I get the urge to hide or something. It's not like he's checking me out or anything, but he *is* evaluating what's in front of him. Honestly, I'm not sure which of the two I'd prefer.

"I may be underdressed," he says finally, and I laugh.

Henry is not, and has never been, underdressed. He's wearing a very plain outfit that manages to make him look somewhat classy—jeans, white long-sleeved shirt, with a black vest. It's almost *formal* compared to my outfit.

"Nonsense," I tell him. "This is my casual attire."

"But it's...so much pink."

"You say that like a negative."

"Not at all." His eyes go higher, near the area of my ears. I glare at him when he reaches up and flicks the ribbon at the end of my braid. "And you even wore the bow."

"I always wear the bow. Don't get it twisted and think I wear it for you."

"I'd never be so foolish," he says, and once we hit the ground floor, I smile behind his back.

Henry's car is somehow already freezing, even though it couldn't have been stopped for long. He loads my bags in the trunk as I get in the passenger seat. This car is *nice*. The seats are leather, and it has those built-in warmers. He's got a corded connection to his radio, so I take the liberty of plugging my phone in and pulling up my playlists, just as I promised.

After what seems like *hours,* Henry gets in the car and starts the engine. I shiver when cold air blasts through the vents. It can't be any more than twenty degrees outside.

"Ready?" Henry asks, putting the cabin's address in his GPS.

I give a nod. "All ready."

"Good." He pulls out of the parking lot, and I quietly drink my coffee.

This is weird. It's *so weird*. I'm sitting in my ex-boyfriend's car, sipping on the drink he bought me, and watching his hands on the steering wheel as he drives us to my parent's cabin, where we'll pretend to be a couple again. This isn't normal. It isn't even smart!

I feel the need to bash my head against the window until my brain starts dealing with things rationally.

"You going to play your music?" He asks, looking over at me for a split second. "Or was that an empty threat?"

"I don't make empty threats," I say. "And anyways, yes. I'm just deciding which song to bless you with first."

"You know I like all that stuff you used to play. The boy bands and whatever."

I gape. "You don't even remember the *names*?"

"There were too many."

I sigh and click shuffle on a random playlist. *Man! I Feel Like A Woman!* starts playing at full volume, loud enough to make both of us jump. I reach forward and turn the volume down, shocked at the way it made my heart speed. "How loud do you listen to things in here?!"

"I don't even remember the last time I had the radio on," Henry says with a huff. "I normally just drive in silence."

That's right. I forgot about that.

"So you're still psychotic."

He bites back a smile. "I like to be alone with my thoughts."

"That's exactly what I just said."

"How would I know what I feel if I don't take time to figure it out?"

"I don't know," I say honestly. I prefer the opposite route, as in, *not thinking about it*. I'm well-versed enough in my own mind, but there are certain boxes that I won't open. One of them is about to be torn apart, though, given that we're driving toward it at 70 miles-per-hour.

Home.

The people, not the place. We didn't *live* at the cabin, not year-round, but we made a lot of memories there. I can trace a lot of things back to it. Back to summers spent swimming in the lake, winters ice skating on the frozen top. I didn't want to live there, though. It would've taken the magic from it.

Margot, on the other hand, had the exact opposite idea. She moved there after art school, not far from the cabin. Her travel today could literally be done on foot, if there weren't probably inches of snow surrounding the place.

I chew on my lip as my thoughts spin. This isn't going to be a pleasant visit. It's going to be tense. Strained. I really don't think it needed to be lumped into a birthday party, but what do I know? I'm the one who hasn't spoken to her twin sister in four years. I'm the one who doesn't care to fix things.

The song on the radio ends, and for some reason, another doesn't start. The intense, sudden silence is enough to drag me out of my thoughts, but not in a good way. It's uncomfortable, at least to me. Henry doesn't seem to notice, but I'm on the verge of ripping my hair out.

I find my phone that somehow ended up on the floor and hit play, hardly paying attention to the song that starts. I lift my coffee out of the cup holder and hiss when the lid pops off, making some of the liquid slosh over the edge. It lands on my thigh, leaving a dark spot the size of a cracker on my pants. How horrible!

"You okay?" Henry asks. "The—"

"I got it," I say, popping the glove box open. I know what he was going to say: *There're napkins in the glove box.* I know this because there are always napkins in the glovebox. Henry has never *not* had napkins in his glove box. He's like a packrat, but it comes in handy.

I grab a few and mindlessly swipe at my leg. If I were smart, I would've brought a water bottle, and then I'd actually be able to work the stain out. All I'm doing now is pressing the coffee further into the fabric. I blow out a frustrated breath as the napkin starts to shred, doing more harm than good, but I'm stubborn enough to keep scrubbing.

Henry reaches over and wordlessly grabs the coffee from me

before settling it back into the cup holder. It's systematic, something that requires no thought, and it ticks me off to no end.

Maybe I'm just moody because these pants are ruined.

Exhaling, I grab a final napkin for the side of my cup, but something catches my eye. Something that looks strangely like a polaroid, hidden away, peeking out from under the car's registration.

I wouldn't have noticed it if I hadn't drawn those hearts on the corner.

I slam the glove box closed with embarrassing vigor, wanting to ask Henry a million questions. Why does he still have that photo of us? I remember it vividly, though now, I'm really wishing I didn't. It was taken after my eighteenth birthday party, the one that would've ended in shambles if it hadn't been for him.

Marg was gone. Her friends had taken her on a road trip for the weekend, and she swore she'd be back for our birthday, but they got a flat tire. They ended up staying the night in a lux hotel, and there was no reason for concern.

For *me*, though, I had nothing to do. So my parents and Henry and Liz threw me my own party.

To put a long story short, my dad dropped my cake off our second story balcony. I'm still not sure how he managed it, given that the party was inside, but Henry snuck away while I was trying to think up a solution. He went to the grocery and bought the last cake they had in their display case, found candles and edible glitter, and somehow made a cake that said *HAPPY RETIREMENT* look very birthday-like.

It saved the whole day for me. The picture was captured as I laughed up at him, right after I'd smeared icing on his nose.

But there's no need to think about that right now.

"Ames?" Henry says randomly, drawing my attention back to him.

I sit back in my seat and sigh. "Hm?"

"Do you need me to stop somewhere?"

"No," I say, wiping off the side of my coffee cup as my stomach rolls. We're going to have to talk about things, I'm realizing. We'll have to talk about Margot, my family, and my job, but I *refuse* to talk about us. Not when I've got a hundred other things gunning for my attention. Henry isn't top priority—he hasn't been for a long time. "I'm going to sleep."

Henry looks over at me, just as I'm digging my eye mask out of my purse. He gives a contented laugh before turning his eyes back to the road. "Sleep well, then."

I hum to myself as *Linger* by The Cranberries starts to play. "Don't wreck."

26

———

HENRY

Amelie doesn't wake up until we reach a gas station, where she spends half my life's savings on candy.

"I just think," she says, now curled up in my passenger's seat, "that there's a certain sense of responsibility that comes with watching Audrey Hepburn movies. I've always felt this way. You can't sit through *Roman Holiday* and walk away unchanged, y'know?"

I grin and turn onto our exit. Amelie was closed off at the beginning of this drive, but I'm starting to think she was just annoyed about the coffee spill. As soon as she woke up, she immediately sped into her usual routine of rants, which has now circled back around to Audrey Hepburn movies. I've heard this one a few times before, and something about the familiarity is soothing. It gives me the false idea that things haven't changed.

"Hellooooo," she sings, waving a hand around my face. Not in front of my eyes, thank goodness—at least she's smart enough not to get us in the ditch. "Have you heard a word I've said?"

"I'm listening. I'm trying to make sure this truck doesn't ram us."

"If he were to do so, that isn't your problem. You can sue him."

"Not if I'm dead."

She shrugs. "How far are we?"

I look over at her. "Don't you know?"

"I haven't been here in years," she says. "So no, I have no idea. I always slept on the drives. Which I *will* end up doing again, by the way."

"Thank you for the heads up." I take a sip of my coffee, which is now cold and watery. "But before you do that, please give me a run-down on what I should know. Any topics to dodge? I remember the old ones—golf, Margot's ear…"

"The ear is still a sore subject," she says, wincing. "But mostly, there's nothing. We talk about whatever. Just, like, I don't know. If it gets tense randomly, you'll know. Like, if you say the word *cabbage,* and we literally go dead silent, then assume that it's a bad subject. Obviously."

"So you don't even know the sore topics?"

She shrugs. "Not always. I mean, Margot and I haven't spoken in ages. Anything could be a bad subject. I might say something about a nose job, and she might start crying."

"Why haven't you guys spoken?" I ask, curious. I can't imagine not talking to Liz for a week, let alone years. She's obnoxious and nosey but she's my best friend. I don't think Amelie and Margot ever had that relationship, though, based on what she told me in the past.

Amelie starts picking at her nails, so I quickly add on, "If that's not off-limits."

She gives a quiet laugh. "It's fine. Margot doesn't like what I do, and I haven't much liked her since graduation. When I moved away from home, it just…stopped. Everything broke off when Mom stopped handing me the phone to talk to her."

She sinks lower into her seat and turns toward the window. It's clear that there's a lot more there, but I know she won't tell me right now. I have the urge to try and comfort her, given how uncomfortable she looks at the admission, but I don't think that's my place anymore. Nor do I think she'd let me.

Did she break off *everything* four years ago? Did it all change for her then?

"I think it'll be okay," Amelie says. "*I'll* be okay. But I didn't want to come with nothing to say. Nothing to show. She doesn't want to hear about my work, and what else have I done?"

"That's why you lied about having a boyfriend?" I ask cautiously. "Because of her?"

She shrugs. "I wasn't the one that lied in the first place, but I think it's why I doubled down on it. Mom seemed overjoyed at the mere idea, and everything was already said, and I just..." She exhales. "I don't want to be a liar. And yes, I understand that this makes me one. But I couldn't back out."

"Well, that's why I swooped in," I say, matter-of-factly. "So you didn't have to."

"A real gentleman." Amelie grins and curls her legs to her chest. She's had the seat warmers on full blast this entire time, and it baffles me that she hasn't broken into a sweat.

"Thank you for helping me out," she says suddenly, her voice quiet. "This is an insane thing to do, but thank you for being willing."

I nod. Swallow. "It's not a problem."

"But why *are* you helping me?" She lays her head on her knees, shifts a little more toward me. "I've been wondering since you offered. I've given you no reason to."

"That's not true," I say, unable to think of anything else. "Amelie, I'll always help you."

She snorts. "I guess that makes me a bad person, then."

I frown. "Why?"

"Because you had to blackmail me to get *my* help."

My heart, for some reason, twists at those words. I shake my head and grip the wheel tighter, resisting the urge to say things I know I'll regret. "I'm sorry, Ames. I never really meant it."

Her mouth falls open, and she turns her head toward the window. She doesn't talk again, not until we stop at another gas station for her to get an icee.

27

AMELIE

"Ames."

"No," I mumble, reaching out to smack whoever is talking. I'm vaguely aware that it's Henry, because it's his voice and I'm touching his pretty face, but I'm partially convinced it's a dream.

"Amelie, you're groping my nose."

I huff and open my eyes, then immediately squeeze them shut. *Why* is it so bright? Why does the sun hate me? A little dramatic, I'm aware, but I don't care.

"We're here," Henry says. "Are you getting out, or am I going to leave you out here all alone?"

"The second one." I blindly fish my sunglasses out of my purse and put them on, keeping my eyes closed until I have ample protection. The first thing I see when I look around is our cabin, then the snow that surrounds it. Everything is dusted with white. "What time is it?"

"Quarter 'til eight." He extends his hand and helps me out of the car, then goes to the trunk and pulls our suitcases out. Before I can even grab my purse, I hear a voice behind me.

"Pumpkin, you're early!"

I turn around and laugh as soon as I see my dad. He's bundled up in a parka, which sounds lovely right now. That would've been a better option than sweatpants, but hindsight is twenty-twenty. "We thought you'd be later," he says.

"I did too," I say, returning the tight hug he wraps me in. "Henry speeds on the interstate."

"I do not," Henry clarifies, closing the trunk of the car. He dusts the snow off his hands and holds one out to my dad, waiting on a shake.

Dad clasps their hands together with zero hesitation. "Been a while since I've seen ya, son."

Henry looks a little intimidated. I'm sure he thinks I've cursed his name to the wind, or that I asked each member of my family to cast a separate spell on him or something, but that's not true.

I said it was over and didn't offer up room for questions because I didn't have answers. My family knows just as much as I do.

"I'm glad to be back," Henry says fondly.

Dad gives him a tight smile. "Melinda is inside. She'll be just as welcoming, long as she's had her coffee."

"Ah." Henry hums. "I forgot that *all* the Benoit women are hostile without caffeine."

"I know that's directed at me, and it's a lie," I say, though he's telling the truth. "And anyways, let's get these bags inside. I want to see Mom."

"Marg is here, too." Dad nods. "Got in last night."

My breath hangs in my chest for just a second, but I force my lungs to start working semi-normally. "Okay. Great."

He gives a bright, strangely oblivious smile before grabbing my suitcases. Henry takes his own, so all I have to do is carry my purse.

We stumble onto the porch, trying not to slip on the snow while simultaneously working to keep it off our clothes. I get ahead of Henry and Dad and open the front door, then kick my boots off on the front step. They set all the suitcases in the entry-way, and when I look around the place, something tightens in my throat.

Everything is exactly the same. A football game is on TV, blankets are strewn across every couch, and the air smells like coffee and sugar. Mom must've already started baking, and I mentally remind myself to snoop around for cookies later.

"This place is amazing," Henry says, sounding almost awestruck.

Only now do I truly register that he's never been here. I knew it in logical terms, yes, but to *understand* feels weirder than it should. I think I subconsciously assume that, wherever I was, he was too. Because that was always the case.

"Yeah," is all I come up with.

My bland reply goes unnoticed, because within seconds, I hear a squeal to my left. When I turn toward the noise, Mom is approaching me with her arms wide open. She's wearing a bright pink sweater that matches perfectly with my attire. I practically catch her as she hugs me, letting loose the breath I've been holding since I stepped inside this house. "I'm glad you made it safely," she says, squeezing me too tight. "The roads were slick! Did you notice?"

"I didn't," I admit, slipping away from her. I move closer to Henry and grab his arm, more than a little distracted by the feel of it. *Disappointed, but not surprised.* "He drove the whole time. I slept."

The second Mom looks at him, her entire face softens. She envelops him in a hug, and he doesn't seem shocked at all. The smile on his face actually looks genuine as he hugs her back. "We can't believe Amelie brought you! It's been so long since—"

"Let's not." I cut her off with a smile. "We can save the uncomfortable topics for later, hm? I'm sure dinner will be a grand time."

Mom rolls her eyes and grins. "Ames. Always one to set the mood."

I laugh, but the sound dies once I hear shoes click on the hardwood.

Speaking of uncomfortable topics.

"Amelie?" I hear from above me.

I glance up to see Margot standing at the top of the stairs, her expression unreadable. I can't tell if she's pleased or horrified to see me. I'm sure I'll figure it out soon enough, but *not* knowing kills me.

Margot looks exactly like me, only taller, thinner, and admittedly prettier. Her hair is cut shorter than mine, but it's the same rich brown color. Our eyes are an identical cool shade of gray. The only difference between our faces is my crooked nose—I broke it when I was seven, and it's been a little twisted ever since. Hers is perfectly straight.

"Hey, Margot," I say awkwardly. My stomach ties itself in knots when I realize how stiff my voice sounds. "When did you get here?"

It's a stupid question—Dad told me when she got here, but I don't know what to lead with. *Hi? You look great? I'm sorry I haven't called you in four years?*

"Last night." Margot descends the stairs, and Henry suddenly puts a hand on my back. It's meant to be reassuring, I think. A show of comfort.

I sink further into him, despite my efforts to *not* do that.

Margot seems to materialize in front of me, and I immediately wonder if I'm supposed to hug her. It would be the single most awkward hug in human existence, so I decide to spare us both and keep my arms at my sides. "You look great," I tell her.

She gives a dry laugh. "I look exactly like you."

"That's what I'm saying."

Her smile deepens, but there's something sad in her eyes. I wonder if my expression mirrors hers, though it's unlikely. We have the same face, almost exactly, but the way we carry ourselves and our emotions couldn't be more different.

Margot was easy to read. Always. I could look at her and tell if something was wrong. If she failed a test at school or if she had a fight with her boyfriend. But she could never read me back. It frustrated her, and I was aware of that, but I never made an effort to share my tells. Maybe that was a mistake.

"Let's get your things put away," Mom says, clapping her hands together. "Margot, can you show Amelie to her room?"

I blink. "But I always stay in the same room."

"Yes, but we put a new bedspread in there."

Margot frowns. "That doesn't—"

"Margot," Mom repeats. "Show Amelie to her room. Dad will show Henry to his."

We don't argue because we're smart. So Marg grabs one of my suitcases, I grab the other, and we make our way up the stairs.

Our cabin is massive. The stairs go up three floors, and even though one is the attic, it's still ridiculously spacious. Most of the living room walls are windows, but we've never had to worry about someone peeking inside. It's like an unspoken thing—you don't creep on us, and we won't creep on you.

"Mom put us alone to talk," Margot says when we reach my door. She opens it, and I almost laugh when I see the bed. There *is* a new bedspread, though it's not much different from my old one. A blue quilt swapped for a purple duvet. "But I don't want to, and I know *you* don't want to."

She's right. I don't want to.

"Yeah," I say, shrugging. "So let's not."

"Fine." Margot drops my suitcase onto the floor. "You're back with Arlington?"

Guess we're talking, then.

I nod. "Kinda crazy, I guess."

"Very. I didn't think you guys would make up."

"Why do you say that?"

She sniffs. "You're not very forgiving."

"People change," I say flatly.

Her eyebrows raise, and the laugh that escapes her is almost painful. "You would know, huh?"

Well! Okay.

"I'm done here," I say, crossing my arms over my chest. "Please. I don't want—"

"That's fine."

Before I get the chance to finish, she walks out of my room.

28

AMELIE

I hide in my room for a while like a petty human being.

It wasn't a conscious choice I made, but I sat down on the end of my bed and simply never moved. Probably half an hour has passed, and honestly, I have no desire to go downstairs. But I can't leave Henry to his own devices. I may not like him, but I'm not that cruel.

Groaning, I stand from the mattress and unzip my suitcase. I change into a pair of jeans and a shirt with strawberries on it, then prepare myself to brave the stairs. The routine involves a few deep breaths, opening and closing the door twice, then finally forcing myself toward the balcony.

Dad and Henry, unsurprisingly, are seated on the couch watching football. Henry seems as entertained as I would be by the game, but Dad is shouting things like *THAT'S NOT WHERE THE TWENTY-YARD LINE IS, YOU MORON* and such.

"Whatcha guys doing?" I ask, starting down the stairs.

"Watching football," Henry says, raising his brows at me.

I laugh as I sit next to him on the couch. He throws an arm over my shoulder, and for some reason, I don't hesitate to nestle closer. "I can see that. Who's winning?"

"Kansas City," Dad mutters. "Of all days."

"It's a *rerun!*" Mom calls from the kitchen.

Dad sighs and lowers the volume. "I haven't seen it, though, Mel. It's current enough."

Henry laughs, and the low sound reverberates through my entire body. It makes me more aware of where I am, how close we are, and I note things that I hadn't yet paid attention to. He's playing with my hair, twisting the ends between his fingers. I'm toying with the hem of his shirt, picking at a loose thread that needs to be cut. I put my hand back at my side when I realize, feeling like I've been burned.

Mom walks into the living room and sits next to me. I lean away from Henry to lay my head on her shoulder, and she pats my leg. She smells like sugar, and I get the sudden urge to raid the pantry for cookies. They have to be *somewhere.*

"Have you been baking?" I ask her, but she doesn't respond. I start to reiterate my question until Margot sits on the loveseat across from us, and I realize what's happening.

They're closing in on Henry and I. This is an interrogation.

"I have to pee," I say, trying to stand, but I fail. Mom grabs the back of my shirt and tugs me back into my seat with a *tsk*ing noise.

"No," she says simply. "You can wait."

Well. Now that I've been restrained, I actually *do* have to pee.

"Fine," I mutter, leaning back into the cushions. "Go."

"How'd you guys meet?" Margot looks me dead in the eyes. "Again, I mean. I know you met in high school, but I want this story."

Only now am I realizing that we didn't *formulate* a story. How could that have slipped my mind? I've been a little preoccupied, I guess, but I didn't think my focus was so far gone. Why didn't I—

"We met at an art museum," Henry says, and my jaw threatens to drop to the floor. Surely he isn't so foolish as to tell the real story. "She was staring at my piece, and I thought, *No, that can't be Amelie. She'd never stare at my work with such disdain.* But it was, and I found out she despised it. So I re-introduced myself with as much class as I could."

"He asked me why I hated his work," I blurt, trying to add something to the conversation.

Henry laughs, so I decide it was a good enough comment. "I did. She told me that she could paint better, so I asked her to get coffee. I didn't expect her to say yes."

He throws a sweet glance in my direction, and I try to look sappy enough for my family to buy it. It works on Mom, no doubt —she's got her hands clutched to her chest, and her eyes have little hearts in them. My dad is buying it equally.

But Margot isn't.

"Back up," she says, crossing her arms. "You're a working artist, Henry?"

"I am." Henry nods.

"Oh, I've seen your name around!" Mom looks much too enthusiastic for what she's mentioning. "Glad to know that art school worked out for you."

"Thank you."

"*Wow.*" Margot's tone makes my cheeks heat with embarrassment. I know what she's about to say, and I want to smack her for it, mostly because it isn't for Henry's sake. It's to get a rise out of *me.* "Henry, do you know—"

"Yes, Margot," I say a little too stiffly. "He's aware."

Her mouth drops open as she turns to him. "And you don't care?"

Henry shakes his head. "I don't. It wouldn't be fair of me to hold it against her, and if I'm being truthful, I'm quite intrigued by it. Besides, she'd never take something of mine."

I laugh as if I haven't done exactly that. "I wouldn't dare! I'm not a menace. And anyways, if I happened to annoy him, he wouldn't take me shopping. So that's a problem."

Dad gives a deep gut laugh. "Glad to know your shopping problem will never change."

"It's therapeutic," I argue. "In fact, I'm thinking of going to the outlet mall sometime this week. I need a new winter coat."

"You have six," Mom reminds.

I frown. "But not a pink one."

Henry whistles. "Just what have you dragged me into?"

"Nothing you can't handle," I say, leaning against him for show. I wrap my hand around his arm and he squeezes my thigh, right above my knee. His hand stays there, and it manages to make time feel slow as molasses. My traitorous skin seems to burn where his fingers are, despite the layer of fabric between us.

Dad starts yelling at the TV again, and Margot keeps staring at me like I've caused her personal discomfort, though I'm unsure why. I haven't done anything since arriving. Maybe that's why she's angry at me—because I didn't come downstairs to see everyone right away.

Suddenly, Henry's phone starts ringing in his pocket, making me jump. He quickly stands and answers it, looking frustrated at the screen. "Excuse me," he mutters, right before going to the bathroom.

The second he's out of earshot, Margot says, "When did this happen?"

"Hm?" I ask, even though I'm fully aware of what she means.

"When did you and Henry start dating again?"

"Oh," I mumble. "Uh, only a month or so. I've lost track of time."

She raises a brow. "Seriously?"

"Seriously *what*?"

"You guys just...picked back up."

I swallow. "Yeah. Like he said, we really just—"

"I don't believe it."

"You don't *have* to believe it."

"All I'm saying is—"

"Girls," Dad says, more so a plea than a warning. "The game is on. Halftime is over. You know I love hearing your voices, but I'd like to watch this game peacefu—*LEARN HOW TO MAKE A CALL, REF.*"

Mom sighs. "Marg, Amelie, it's—"

"No, it's fine," I say, entirely over this conversation. I stand and turn toward the kitchen. "I need to ask Henry something anyways."

Without waiting for a response, I go into the hall and lean against the wall opposite of the bathroom. I chew my lip raw while tapping my foot on the ground, fidgety for reasons I don't even understand.

Just as I taste blood, Henry opens the door. "What's wrong?" He asks instantly.

"Nothing," I say. "Is something wrong with you?"

He steps out and looks down the hall, as if to make sure we're alone. Thankfully, everyone has their eyes on the TV. "I just... thought my dad caught the guy. It was a false alarm."

I wrinkle my nose. "What do you mean?"

"There was some suspicious activity at my apartment building, I guess, but the decoy is still there. Nobody got the guy's name or face."

"Cameras?"

Henry just shakes his head, so I don't question him any further.

"I'm sorry," I say.

He gives a very unconvincing shrug. "It's fine. I'm not worried about it."

It's very obvious that he's worried, and he presumably won't *stop* worrying until we find the thing.

"Maybe it'll be gone soon, and your dad can trace him. I'll even get Meg and Jen on it when the time comes."

He tips his head. "Really?"

"Yeah, sure. They need something to do while I'm gone."

He laughs quietly. By the time I start to join in, Mom rounds the corner. "Oh!" She says, sounding almost startled. It's got a hint of falsity to it, so I assume she's trying to act like she hasn't been spying on us. "Silly me. I just need to switch the laundry over. Ames, did you know our washer stopped working? Your dad had to fix it last night."

"I did not know that," I say. "Is that an important detail?"

"Of course. I've never seen him so angry in his life."

"You wouldn't believe it, Ames," Dad calls from the living room. "There was water out into the kitchen!"

"That's terrible and very random, considering we haven't been here in months."

"That's what I said." He sighs, then swears at whoever threw the ball on TV.

Mom moves past Henry and I and goes to the laundry room, mumbling as she does so. Henry turns toward me, standing not a foot away, and looks directly in my eyes. The lighting in this hallway is enough to make the look on his face strangely intimate, and I suddenly feel the need to run.

Before I can act on that urge, Henry says, "I didn't realize how much I missed your family."

I hum. "Yeah?"

"Yeah. They like me a lot more than mine does."

He forces a laugh after that, like it's a joke, but I don't have it in me to join this time. Henry has never spoken highly of his family. He's never spoken *down* on them, but when the subject is brought up, it's never much of a positive. Save for the mentions of Lizzy.

"We can go back," I say, nodding to the living room. "You can keep acting like you care about football, and I'll keep enduring Margot's death glares."

He wrinkles his brow, looking almost confused. "I don't understand why she's so mad at this."

"She's not. She's mad at me," I say honestly. And *I'm* not trying to trash talk, either. It's just the truth.

"She's got no reason," he says, crossing his arms, and *again,* the thing with the biceps. It's sickening. "But it's fine. I won't let it deter me."

I blink. "From?"

"This," he says, and I wish that word didn't make my stomach flip.

"Come on, Arlington," I say, suddenly feeling a little suffocated in this hallway. "Football time."

With an exaggerated sigh, he follows me to the living room. I take a seat by Dad, and Henry sits directly to my right. By the time the fourth quarter starts, I'm laying against Henry's shoulder, trying to ignore the noise in my mind as I drift off.

29

HENRY

"We've got this tradition," Arnie tells me, all while knocking my rook off the chess board. "The first night we spend at our cabin, the girls make pigs in a blanket. I used to help, but Melinda told me I over-seasoned them."

"You did!" Melinda says exasperatedly. "Oh, they were awful, Henry. Just horrible."

"I'm not much of a cook myself, so I can't judge," I admit.

Melinda waves a hand at me as she pours some seasoning on the tray. It looks like everything bagel seasoning, which is interesting. I've never seen it put on anything *but* a bagel. Then again, I've never had pigs in a blanket, either. My mom detests finger foods. It's instilled in my mind to feel the same.

"I just don't see why we need this many," Amelie says, throwing the empty plastic wrapping into the trash. "There's five of us."

"Because it's what I bought, so we're making it." Melinda pops Amelie in the hip with the end of a dishrag. "We can store them and eat them all week. It's not like—*oh!*" She gasps, then turns to me. Arnie jumps at her suddenness, then keeps on studying the chess board. He's beating me horribly. We've been playing since he finished watching his football reruns, and I've won exactly one game. "Henry, do you have food allergies? I can't remember if you've told me before."

"You're such a *mom*," Margot says, setting the tray in the oven.

I shake my head. "Nope. I can—and will—eat mostly anything."

"My kind of person." Arnie gives me a nod before moving a piece. "Checkmate."

I sigh and clear the board. "Not a fan of this, I'll be honest."

He gives a deep, throaty laugh. "Three out of five?"

"Three out of five," I respond, setting the board up again.

Amelie laughs to herself, whether at us or something else, I'm not sure. She's been laughing more this afternoon than when we first arrived, though it's mostly around her parents. Her and Margot haven't spoken a word without their prompting, and I can't suppress my curiosity on what happened.

I know very little about Margot. While Amelie was best friends with *my* sister, I was more of a distant acquaintance with hers. Despite being at her house most days after school, we spoke maybe ten times, only on surface level things.

Why are you guys late? Henry, you parked crooked, are you the one that hit our mailbox? Did you flatten my bike tire?

For the record, I did hit that mailbox. But it was strangely placed.

The only thing I know for sure is that Margot hates that I'm back. She stared at me like I was a murderer when Amelie fell asleep on me during the football game, as if I've somehow manipulated my way back here.

I blame that nap on Amelie getting up early, by the way. It didn't have anything to do with me. Though she *does* seem to enjoy the feel of my arms a little more than I remember.

Arnie takes his turn, and I let out a sigh as I stare at the board. I'm seeing a blur of black and white, feeling unable to be fully present. That phone call with my dad won't leave my mind.

He told me my piece is still at my apartment. *Then* he asked me what convention I'm at, where I'm spending this time, and I made up some bogus name that doesn't exist. If I'm lucky, he won't look into it. But if he does...

Well, the bills come on Monday anyways. He's got enough to worry about.

"Hey, Ames," Arnie says, eyes trained on the chess board. "Did you get everything cleared up with work?"

She shrugs, wiping her hands off on a dishrag. "Sort of. I might have to run home early to check on a few things. If our plans permit, that is."

"That'll be fine, honey," Melinda tells her, squeezing her arm. "The only plans we've got set in stone are Marg's art showing and you guys' birthday party."

Amelie rolls her eyes playfully. "We're turning twenty-three, and you're still throwing us a party."

"With streamers and everything," Arnie says solemnly, giving her a wry smile.

Amelie laughs, the sound so natural that it makes my stomach stir. "As long as I get a tiara."

"Mom got us some," Margot says, wiping off the counter with a damp rag. "She already showed me."

"And a cake," Melinda says. "I'm going to redecorate it, though. It's just not as good as it could be!"

Amelie grins and grabs a can of soda from the fridge. "I suppose you got gifts, too."

"Don't be ridiculous," her mom responds. "You know I did."

"I did, too," Amelie says, eyeing Margot almost nervously. "Didn't know if we were doing that or not."

"I did," Margot says flatly.

Amelie gives a nod. "Okay. Great. Anyone else?"

I can tell it's a joke, but I still respond with, "I did."

Everyone turns to me, and their eyes weigh on me like anvils. "What?" Margot asks, sounding incredulous. "You brought gifts?"

I blink. "I mean, I'll admit that yours is quite basic, but—"

"Why?" Amelie asks.

I shrug. "Birthdays require gifts."

She shakes her head once. "Did I even tell you...?"

"I know when your birthday is, Amelie."

Her mouth drops open at that, as if it's some insane revelation. As if I haven't fought the urge to call her on that day every year, just to have some excuse for why I was thinking about her.

"Well, thanks, I guess," Margot mumbles before going back to her cleaning. I give a nod toward her, about to turn back to my chess game, but my eyes snag on Amelie. She's still staring at me, brows drawn together in confusion. I honestly assumed she'd expect something from me—not in a selfish way, but more in a routine manner. Something that happens simply because it *should.*

Eventually, she looks away, and she doesn't look back.

There's a blanket of silence until the oven timer goes off. Arnie and I basically speed run the end of our chess game, which doesn't matter in the slightest—he still beats me, and he gloats about it subtly throughout the meal, but I don't mind it. I think I'm the only person willing to play the game with him.

The five of us sit around the table with a massive tray of pigs in a blanket in front of us, and the meal seems to go quickly. We talk, but it's light, surface-level conversation. Margot asks Amelie passive-aggressive questions about work, and she deflects. Then vice-versa. I rattle off basic small talk, trying to stay on the safe side of things.

Arnie and Melinda are the only constants. They keep conversation with me like they're actually curious how I've been. I'm open about my career, they tell me about theirs, and Amelie even throws me a few pieces of the puzzle that I've found her to be.

She built her career at eighteen.

Jensen and Meg were never meant to be her partners, but they stumbled upon the opportunity and thought a cut of money was worth it.

She hates art.

I've guessed that last part for a while, but it becomes more apparent in this conversation. And I just want to know *why.*

I don't find out, of course. Not over this meal.

When we're all done, Amelie volunteers to do the dishes. Margot and her mom both offer to help, but she insists we go to the living room and talk. So we do—Melinda shows me her most recent crochet project, which is a blanket with cat ears. I've got no idea how it's practical.

She goes on a tangent about her *last* blanket that looked like a bee, and I listen. I do. But at some point, my eyes wander to Amelie, who's scrubbing the dishes like they've wronged her. She's got bubbles down the front of her shirt and I'm not even sure she cares.

Something about this environment has her more on edge than I've seen in a while.

"Excuse me for a second," I say when Melinda finishes her story. She nods and smiles knowingly, so I assume she can see right through me.

Slowly, I walk into the kitchen and approach Amelie. She doesn't even notice me until I stop next to her and say, "Hey."

To which she flings soap all over the front of *my* shirt.

"I'm sorry!" She winces at my chest. "You scared me. I was zoned out."

"I can see that," I say, a smile playing at the corners of my mouth. "Can I help you?"

She holds up her gloved, sudsy hands. "You wanna play house-wife? Be my guest."

I laugh. "Give me a towel. I'll dry them."

She doesn't hesitate to hand me the rag to her left. I start drying the chipped blue plates, setting them in a stack next to me when I'm done. For a brief moment, my brain wanders to how laughably domestic this is, but I push that thought as far away as I can.

"So," I start. "You thought I forgot your birthday, huh?"

Amelie shakes her head. "I didn't say you *forgot*. I just didn't know you remembered."

"I remember more than you want me to, Ames."

She straightens up. "What does that even mean?"

I shrug, aware that I'm close to talking myself into a corner. "I think you want me to act like I forgot everything between us."

Amelie sniffs. "Well, I mean, I did. So."

I laugh. "No, you didn't."

"And how would *you* know?"

"Because I know you better than that. You remember everything."

"Debatable," she says, but her voice is quieter than it was a moment ago. "And anyways, this is irrelevant right now. My mom is taking photos of us like a stalker."

I raise a brow and look into the living room. Sure enough, Melinda has her phone in the air with the flash on. Amelie snorts when she hides it away, trying to be sneaky even though that's the last thing she is.

"I saw that," Amelie says.

Melinda gapes. "I didn't do anything!"

I grin. "Forward me that photo."

Amelie looks up at me with a challenging expression. "If you want a photo of me, you can simply ask."

"Didn't think you'd comply."

Instead of responding, she hands me another bowl.

I finish drying the dishware and set it aside. Amelie drains the sink seconds later and removes her gloves, placing them neatly on the edge of the counter. She leans back against the marble countertop and crosses her arms, practically mirroring my stance.

"I can feel you staring at the top of my head," she says. "What do you want?"

I shake my head. "Nothing."

"So stop glaring at my scalp."

"Okay. Look up, and I'll glare at you."

Shockingly, she does. I expect some kind of retort, anything to try and get under my skin, but all she says is, "Thank you."

"For drying the dishes?"

She rolls her eyes. "Henry. You know what I mean."

I take my glasses off and clean the lenses against my shirt to busy my hands. "You don't have to keep thanking me. I wanted to do this."

"*Why*?" She asks, and though she's asked it at least twice now, I've never truly answered it. I told her it was a return for the help she's giving me, but she doesn't believe that. I can't even blame her because it's a flat-out lie.

I came because I wanted to. *That's* the truth.

I want to see her. I want to spend time with her, want to *know* her again. Because I never planned on losing this. I had no idea that when I kissed her against my car before I left for school, I'd never kiss her again. That wasn't my plan.

The plan was always her. I was supposed to come back to *her*.

But it's different now. Nothing is the same.

"I'm still figuring that out myself," I murmur, putting my glasses back on my face. My eyes stay on the ground, but I can feel Amelie's on me, trying to decipher what I mean.

After what feels like an excruciating amount of time, she must decide there's no point. Amelie walks out of the kitchen and joins her family in the living room without giving me a second glance. I follow slowly and take a seat next to her on the couch, and within seconds, Arnie has us roped into a game of poker.

Margot wins.

30

———

AMELIE

By the time I sneak off to bed, I'm exhausted.

Mentally, anyways. The five of us did nothing all day, and we will continue to do nothing for most of this trip. These things are always about relaxing; at least, they're *supposed* to be. It's a bit draining when you're considering leaving in the middle of the night, but that's just a 'me' thing.

I crawl into bed and bury myself under the mounds of blankets I gathered from the hall closet. I left enough for the others, but it is *cold* in this place. Especially in my silk pajamas. If I were smart, I'd have brought something else, but no. I did not do that.

I'm turning off my lamp and plugging in my phone when the device starts ringing. Meg's name flashes across the screen, and for some reason, it triggers every nerve in my body and tells them to freak out.

"Hello?" I say upon answering.

Meg exhales. "Hi. I'm sorry it's so late, but I just talked to Jen, and I've got a lot to tell you."

"You're good," I say through a yawn. "I'm sharp as a knife."

She snorts. "Okay. He told you about the job, right? Jensen did?"

"Yes," I say, then pause. Now that I'm actually thinking this through, it doesn't make a lot of sense. "Wait. He said they got in contact..."

"With me," she says, and I frown. "They found me online by a name I have on a listing site. Jensen said he told you this."

"He may have, but it was five in the morning, and I think I discredited it all," I admit. "Is there a problem, or...?"

"The problem...I guess there isn't a problem. It's just suspicious. Everything feels a little odd."

"How so?" I ask, even though I *know*. I get it. That heavy sense of suspicion has been weighing on me since Bondi's. I just want someone to confirm that I'm not overthinking.

"Well, for starters, I don't get contacted."

She's very right. We've never reached out to anyone through her online personas, and we've certainly never received an offer through one.

"Okay," I say slowly. "Anything else?"

"Yes. I dug deeper into the contact, and it stems from the same person who first teased that photo of Henry's *Ophelia*."

I sit up in bed. The mention of Bondi's reminds me of that ace I saw tucked into the corner of *Nautical Abyss,* but it feels like a poor time to bring that up. Maybe that problem has dissolved by now, or at least lessened. "The one that tricked us?"

"Yes."

Groaning, I kick the blankets off my legs and stumble over to my bag, yanking out my laptop. I brought it against my will because I knew I'd end up needing it. Despite this being a 'vacation' of sorts, it's never really on pause. Not if Jen and Meg are still working.

I sit on my rug and crack my knuckles. "Give me the name again."

"*Lover of Mine,*" Meg says, and I type it into the search engine.

About a million results appear on my screen, so I say, "Artist?"

"Gail Branson."

I tack that onto the search. A few photos of the exact same painting litter my screen, so I assume it's the correct one this time.

A young man and woman in an embrace. That's the piece. But

the room is dark, and a spotlight shines on them. Only them. There are people in the background, but the couple doesn't seem to notice or care. It's intimate. Calming, almost.

"Where's it based?"

"Another thing you're not going to believe," Meg says, sounding tired. "The piece is in their possession. They just want us to transport it."

I blink, set the phone down, and turn it on speaker so I can adequately raise my voice without deafening her. "HUH?"

"Told you it's weird."

"Okay, but are you going to do it?"

Silence for a beat. "It's ten grand."

"Is our cover worth ten grand to you?"

"Can I be honest with you, Ames?"

Oh, how I absolutely *hate* that. "Yes."

"I think our cover has been off for quite some time. I just don't think anyone has had the means to do anything about it."

I bite down on my thumbnail. She's right, and I've known it for a while. Our cover has been weak. We've gotten sloppy. How else would Henry have caught me *twice*?

It's not like I'm not careful. But to some extent, I've loosened up. I won't pretend like I don't enjoy an adrenaline rush. That thrill, that feeling of teetering on the edge, it's part of what keeps me in it.

"Go for it," I tell Meg. "I trust you guys. But if you get caught, I can't help you from here."

"We know the rules," she says, her voice tight.

'Rules' is a stiff way to put it, but we *do* have an agreement. If one of us gets caught, that's it. We don't sell out. That's why I like doing the work. The communication. I don't want Jen or Meg taking the fall for something I got them into. Yes, this job is their choice, but it was *my* beginning. They don't get to be in trouble without me.

That said, if they get caught on their own, I want to be left behind to deal with things. Someone's got to bail them out.

"Keep me updated," I say into the phone, hoping I wasn't quiet for long. "I'd say this is our last job for a few weeks, hm? We deserve a break."

She laughs. "I think you're right"

I grab the glass off my nightstand and take a long drink of water. "Just trust your intuition, Megs. If it feels like a trap, get out of there."

"We will." Meg takes a deep breath, then rolls over in bed, I think. Her phone speaker hits something like a blanket and muffles the sound. "How are things there?"

"Things here?" I hum. "Fine. Tense. Margot and I have had one conversation, and it wasn't great. The likelihood of us warming up by the end of this trip is slim."

"Hm." She sighs. "How's your fake boyfriend, then?"

"Also fine. Very fake-boyfriend-y."

"Has he kissed you yet?"

I balk. "Megan Lang!"

"What? C'mon, Ames. The man has probably kissed you before."

"But why would he do it in front of my parents? That's disgusting."

She sighs. "For *authenticity*."

"Do couples often make out in front of their parents and so-called in-laws?"

"I wouldn't know. My parents are dead."

Well! I'd forgotten about that little tidbit.

"No," I say, "he has not kissed me. We've only been here for fourteen hours. That would be jumping the gun a bit."

"Not really."

"What does that mean?"

She laughs, and it actually scares me. "Ames. He *wants* to kiss you."

My jaw threatens to drop off my face. "I will hang up, Meg. I'm serious."

"I'm only telling the truth. What boy in his right mind would stay with your family for a week if he didn't like you, at least a little? You two have history. He probably wanted to remind you of it."

She's gone mad. Genuinely. Time with Jensen has rotted her brain. When I get back home, moths will fly out of her ears, and I'll have to bring her back to life with my actual *correct* logic.

"You're out of your mind," I say, standing from the floor. "And anyways, he wouldn't do anything like that. We have this agreement."

"Which is?"

I open my mouth to rattle it off, only to realize that we *don't* have one. No guidelines. No precedent. There's an unspoken one in my mind, I guess, but that doesn't do me any good. Henry can't read my thoughts.

"Goodnight, Megs!" I squeak, wrapping a blanket around me like a cape. "Stay out of trouble."

She laughs knowingly. "Bye, Ames."

I hang up the phone with a relieved sigh.

What a ridiculous theory. I know exactly why Henry volunteered to join me—to keep tabs on my whereabouts. He wanted to make sure that I wasn't going to bail on our deal before locating his piece.

That's the *only* possibility.

Or maybe it's the only one I'm comfortable with.

31

———

HENRY

I don't sleep a wink.

This cabin is the most calming environment I've known in ages, and I can't even relax. First off, there was a feather pillow on my bed, which made me sneeze like a madman. But that wasn't the main problem, nor did it continue to be so. I set the pillow in the hall and tried my best to go to sleep. It shouldn't have been difficult—the house fell quiet within minutes of everyone retreating to their rooms, but I laid awake in the dark for hours.

Since I hate subjecting myself to torture, I paced around the room and prayed that it would put me to sleep, but all it did was wake my mind up further. So I chose to do something.

I sketched.

And I sketched *Amelie.*

The regret was instant. I didn't need to be reminded that I have every part of her face burned into my memory. That I can accurately depict the shape of her, but I'll never truly capture her air. The way she looks and breathes. My drawing is flat—it's a pencil sketch and nothing more.

But I know I could do *so* much more with my paints. And that's what kept me awake even longer.

I've never wanted to paint someone other than her.

That urge had finally left, or at least lessened. It wasn't constantly on my mind. It wasn't draining my inspiration as it once had, when I couldn't find a single other thing I wanted to depict.

And here it is again, showing up at a time where I cannot run from it. Not when she's in my presence like this.

It's morning now, barely even dawn, and I'm exhausted. I recall falling asleep somewhere around three, and the clock beside my head reads six. The only reason I'm *back* awake is because of some random noise downstairs. It's grating, and it shouldn't be bothering me right now, but I seem to be acutely aware of my surroundings.

I kick the covers off my body and walk quietly toward my door, wincing as the hinges creak. The room I'm staying in is cozy, though the porcelain doll in the corner is unsettling. Grown man or not, I'll be dead before dolls don't scare me.

The hardwood floor is freezing against my feet, but I walk over to the top of the stairs and peer into the living room. What I see isn't what I expected, though not a shock: Amelie is sitting on the couch with a stuffed animal tucked under her elbow, eyes dead as she flicks through the TV channels. I turn to go back to my room, intent on not disturbing her, but she looks up the second I start to move.

"Hi," she says, voice cracking. "What are you doing?"

"I didn't sleep." Our voices carry easily in this open space, but I still have the urge to go downstairs so I'm not being loud.

"I can tell," Amelie says, looking me over. I almost laugh, but decide against it when she says, "You look awful."

"Thank you."

She barely grins before yawning.

I start down the stairs and take a seat on the cushion opposite of her. She's staring at the TV again, eyes glued to a cartoon that I've never seen in my life. "I didn't sleep either," she says. "It was cold."

"You're always cold."

"Doesn't make it better." She grabs the remote and mutes her show, then looks over at me. Her eyes fall closed for a moment before she opens them again, staring at the wall behind my head. "I'm going to fall asleep, I think."

"Why are you even awake?"

She isn't just *awake*; she's been up for a while, at least longer than I'd suspected. Her hair is half-dried over her shoulders, so I assume she showered, and her face is bare. It's a privilege, I realize, to see her like this. Calm and relaxed in an environment where we aren't taking shots at each other.

Amelie yawns. "I'm not sure. My eyes just kept opening. And I didn't even go to sleep early, so that's...lovely." Another yawn, this one enough to send a tear streaming down her cheek. "It's fine. I'll take a nap this afternoon. I take lots of naps, and anyways—"

"Do you want to get breakfast?"

My question comes as a shock, I guess, because Amelie gapes at me like I've offered to shave her head. "Breakfast?"

"Yes. The meal you eat in the morning."

She doesn't relax. "Like...together? Just us?"

"I don't see anyone else awake."

A long pause. "Okay."

"Yeah?" I tip my head. "You seem reluctant."

"I am," she says, and I'd admire the honesty if it weren't aimed at me. "But I'm also bored and kinda hungry, and we don't have any frozen waffles."

Good enough reasoning for me. "Alright. Surely we can find somewhere to eat."

"I know a place. We used to go there a lot." Amelie peeks up the stairs, like she's worried someone is listening. "They might catch wind of this and invite themselves along."

I stand from the couch and hold out a hand for her. She raises her brows warily, but her mouth threatens to shift into a smile. "C'mon. I'll pay."

This gets her attention. She clasps her hand onto mine and pulls herself off the couch, walking right past me without further thought. I bite my tongue when I catch the notes of her perfume, shaking my head as I go to my room. I'm groggy and horribly tired, but not enough to gloss over what's going on.

Amelie agreed to be alone with me. She didn't have to; yesterday, it wasn't a choice. We had to be in my car. But *this* was a choice. She could've said no. And while that shouldn't matter, especially not to me, it does. It's a step in the right direction, though I'm not sure that what I'm considering 'right' is really so.

Still, I'm not going to squander this opportunity.

My phone is buzzing itself off the nightstand when I walk into my room. I pick it up, expecting a phone call, but that's not what I see. Notifications are flooding my screen. I presume they're in regard to the news about my most recent piece, so I skip past them. The one I click is all the way at the bottom, received at 12:08 last night. I'm shocked I didn't see it earlier, given my restlessness.

LIZZY

how's it going???

I find that to be a loaded question.

Fine, I think. Talk later.

LIZZY

OHHH so you're busy right now

Not exactly.

LIZZY

hmmmm i can take a dismissal! have fun with ames

i know you can't see me, but i want you to picture me winking as i say that.

Instead of furthering an unprompted, unwanted conversation, I toss my phone aside and get dressed.

32
———

AMELIE

I give Henry poor directions to my favorite breakfast place, second only to the patisserie back home. We make two wrong turns, since all trees look the same and I'm too prideful to use GPS, but we get there eventually. I develop a horrid appetite by the time we're seated, so I order my usual—the biggest stack of pancakes I've ever seen.

Henry gets a black coffee and an omelet. He thanks the waitress and hands the menus back to her when she brings out his mug, and I watch in horror as he drinks it. I understand that he likes black coffee, but that fact will never *not* get to me. Where's the flavor? It's dirt water!

"Why are you making that horrible face?" Henry asks through a smile.

I take a sip of *my* coffee—perfectly flavored with sugar and cream. "No reason."

"There has to be a reason."

"Nothing you'd be interested in."

"Ah." He nods solemnly. "Got it."

"I think you're just talking to hear your own voice."

A faint smile. "I thought you enjoyed nonsensical conversation."

"Only when *I'm* the one talking." I pause to stir my coffee. "You know, Arlington, I'm starting to realize that I don't know much about you."

He meets my eyes, shock clouding his expression. "How do you figure?"

"I don't know. Like, I know things *about* you, yeah, but what if they aren't true anymore? Do you still like baseball?"

He nods. "Yes, I'm alright with baseball."

"Tom Hanks movies?"

"Of course."

"*Lord of the Rings*?"

He shrugs. "I could do without it, but the sentiment is there."

I grin. "Okay. So that's all the same."

"I think I *am* the same," he says, shrugging. "Not much has changed. Though I feel like the opposite would be said about you. And that isn't a jab," he adds on, "before you mention it. I'm just saying."

I cross my arms and exhale. "So ask what you want."

Henry's brows shoot up, and I hold my breath. He's going to go in for the kill, I think. He'll ask the deepest, most personal questions he can think of just to see me squirm. Might even make a show of drawing information out of me.

"You said certain things are off limits," he reminds.

"You get one free question. Choose wisely."

He runs his tongue over his teeth, holding eye contact with me. I'm expecting a question about my job, or about what happened between us, or literally anything other than, "What's the deal with you and Margot?"

"*That's* what you're asking?"

Henry nods.

"I'm regretting giving you free reign over this," I mutter.

"I knew you would." He smiles, and my stomach dips at the sight. From hunger pains, obviously. Not because of the way his face brightens, or because his eyes are still glued on mine, or any of that other stuff. I'm simply starving.

"Margot and I stopped talking on our own four years ago," I

start, fixing my focus on the napkin holder. "At first, Mom would hand me the phone once a week and tell me to talk, but when I moved out, we didn't have that anymore, so we fell off. Shortly after that, it just..." I wave a hand through the air as my voice trails off. "You get it."

He nods, implying that he does, indeed, get it.

I sit further back and close my eyes as a small voice in my head screams at me. *That isn't the full truth. That isn't real.* And the voice is right; that isn't the whole story. But I'm not about to dive into the truth right now. Not at seven in the morning, when I have an opportunity to interrogate Henry.

"I assumed it would be something more dramatic," he admits, then frowns. "No, let me rephrase that. Not *dramatic*, just..."

"Worse?" I offer.

He shakes his head. "Layered."

I shrug. "It's never mattered much to me. I don't think about it."

Lie.

"Do you think this trip will change anything?" Henry asks.

I shrug again. "Not with how things are going so far. But it's fine, I guess. If it's meant to be fixed, it will be."

"It will," he agrees, and for some reason, that reassurance makes me tense up. I didn't intend to tell him all of this, and now that I have, I feel like I've said too much. It wasn't deliberate, but I'm not on my guard right now. His gaze is almost disarming—if I don't look away, I'm going to give up the codes to my safe.

"My turn," I blurt, clasping my hands in front of me. The quickest way out of this is to turn it around on him. "Now I get to ask questions."

"I didn't agree to that."

I cock my head. "You're going to turn me down?"

"No," he says smoothly.

"Okay. Good." I exhale. "Tell me about your family."

"That isn't a question, and you know about my family."

"Not really. I knew very little in the past, and I know even less now. Talk."

Henry sighs but doesn't bother arguing. "Fine. My dad—as

you've learned—owns The Gallery. It turned him into one of those stereotypical businessmen who lives in their office, surrounded by ink pens and deposit slips, and now, he's more of a business partner than a family member."

"What do you mean?"

"We don't talk outside of payment trades. Technically, I work on my own, but he insists on displaying my public work in *his* museum. I told him I wouldn't do it unless he gave me some form of return, so he pays Lizzy and I's rent. It was more of a petty request than an actual want, but I couldn't resist." A pause. "I've got a lot of work in there, some under aliases. It's too much to transfer, even if he'd let me." He takes a deep breath, glancing out the window before staring into his coffee. "I'm actually not sure I should've said that."

"It doesn't affect me," I say, but then I wonder if it does. How many pieces have I taken that were under an alias of his? How many will I take in the future? I can't do that. I already vowed to leave him alone. "What...what are the names?"

He looks at me, amused. "I'm not saying that."

"Oh, come *on*."

"You know too much, Ames." He grins. "More than most."

I try to ignore the way those words make me feel. Something is wrong with me this morning.

"My turn now," Henry says, and I scoff.

"I barely even got a turn!"

"I just gave you a fair bit of information."

True. "Fine. But I can turn this down."

"Alright." He leans forward. "What's your favorite color?"

I try—and fail—to hide my shock. "You want to know my favorite color?"

"Yes. Is it still green?"

Why is he asking me this? Is it to mess with me? There's probably some psychological thing in asking a deep question, then an impersonal one. Maybe it's meant to get my guard down even further.

"Pink," I say slowly, looking down at my blush-colored sweater. "I thought that was obvious."

"It was, but I didn't want to make the wrong assumption."

"A wise man," I mumble, stretching my legs out under the table. I go far enough that my legs knock into Henry's, but neither of us move away. "And yours?"

"Gray."

Of *course* his is the same, much like everything else about him. The way he acts and talks. His passions and cares. His snarky attitude, the way he can still make me freeze under his gaze—

"Like your eyes," Henry adds. "The same shade of gray as your eyes."

I clamp my mouth shut. "Pardon?"

He nods casually. "I've always loved your eyes."

My face goes hot. Henry is obviously enjoying this, because he's trying to hide the smile crawling across his face. But why do I care? He's an artist. He's always aware of colors and shapes and facial profiles and all that jazz. The second he saw me in the museum, he was probably sizing me up, evaluating me like a subject. Seeing what was different about me.

Her nose seems more crooked now, I'm sure he thought. *Her hair is tangled. WOW! I never noticed—her ears look like Dobby's.*

"Okay," I say, my throat feeling dry. "Thank you."

He laughs. "Don't act so stunned."

"Why shouldn't I?"

"Because you know I think you're beautiful. You've always been aware of that."

My mouth falls open, and I decide I need to leave this restaurant immediately. "You can't say things like that."

Henry hums and stretches his legs out further, enough that our shins are fully pressed together. This booth is *very* small, I realize, because we're both still sitting straight up. "Why not?"

Oh. That tone. This is a challenge.

I open my mouth to say something. I'm not really sure *what*, because my brain is genuinely not cooperating, but I never have to figure out an answer. A waitress appears with our breakfast and saves me from any further trouble.

I'm thankful for two reasons.

One, Henry can't keep confusing me if he isn't talking.

And two, I won't ask what I *want* to ask, which keeps the peace.

What are those aliases?

It shouldn't matter to me, but it does. And I'm going to get a concrete answer, no matter how much he tries to distract me with his words and glances.

33

———

HENRY

"Have you been listening to me?"

I slam my car door and look at Amelie. I *haven't* been listening to her, only because I've been analyzing our conversation over breakfast since we left the restaurant. It could've gone better—probably *would've,* if I hadn't said all those things about my dad, but it doesn't matter. Amelie would've found them out anyways.

At least, that's what I'm telling myself to feel less guilty about it.

"I'm sorry," I mumble, scratching my jaw. "What did you say?"

She sighs as she makes her way toward the front door. We came directly back to the cabin after eating, though Amelie debated shopping for at least twenty minutes. She decided against it after her sixth pancake. "I said, we need to set some rules for this whole thing."

I blink. "Rules?"

"Yeah. Guidelines."

"Guidelines," I repeat, and she nods. "What do you have in mind?"

She crosses her arms and chews on her lip. I study her face, trying to predict the outcome of this conversation before she even speaks, but all I do is distract myself at the sight of her. She's too much. This is *all* too much, so I should be thankful for her statement, but for some reason, it almost disappoints me.

"I think there are logical ones," Amelie starts. "No kissing, no being alone in a room with Margot—"

"What does she have to do with anything?"

"She doesn't, I guess, but if we're separated, she'll get the truth out of us."

That's probably true. I've quickly learned that when Margot wants to know something, she *will* find it out. Amelie is the same, but she's sly with her ways. Her sister, on the other hand, will forcibly remove the words from your mouth.

"Okay," I mumble, leaning against the side of the house. "What else?"

"No touching unless necessary, for sure."

I hum. "What does necessary mean? That's a vague rule."

"It's not *that* vague. Surely you can use some context clues."

"You want me to just...decide when to touch you. Without you breaking my limbs."

"Don't test me, Arlington," she warns, peering inside the house. There's no movement, and I'm not sure why we haven't gone inside yet, but I don't complain.

I clear my throat and shift slightly. "Just...clear it up for me."

Amelie sighs, not looking me in the eyes as she responds. "Like, if you casually put your hand on my back, or on my waist. That's normal. And last night, when you put your arm around me. That was fine too."

"No kissing?" I ask, only to antagonize her.

"Correct," she says firmly. "No kissing."

"It's not like we haven't kissed before."

She rolls her eyes. "Well, we're not going to do it again!"

"Come on, Ames. I wasn't that bad."

Her eyes widen, and I can't help but grin at her shock. Every time I say something like that, something a little more brazen than I normally do, she looks stunned out of her mind. It's enough to override the warning in my brain that says I shouldn't be teasing her this way.

"You're terribly unsavory today," Amelie says, giving me a tired once-over. "No kissing, unless it's on the cheek or something. That's something that couples do."

"Absolutely. Couples do that" *We used to do that.* "Anything else?"

"No talking about our past."

I gape at her for just a moment. "At all?"

"At all." She shakes her head, and from the solemn look on her face, I know that it's already settled. We won't be discussing *us*, despite the urge I have to do exactly that. "Do you have anything?"

I think for a moment. I have...very few qualms about this whole thing. If Amelie hadn't mentioned setting rules, it wouldn't have crossed my mind. I would've gone through this entire thing with a distant promise of her and I acting how we used to.

"No," I say. "Nothing."

"Great." Amelie unlocks the front door and steps inside the cabin. We take off our snowy boots in silence and leave them on the porch, and just as I remove my coat, I hear racket in the kitchen. Spoons clanging around in bowls, mugs being placed on the counter. I look up to find Melinda and Arnie in their pajamas, which happen to be identical matching sets.

"Morning, early birds," Arnie says, lifting a hand. "Where did you go?"

"Brenn's," Amelie says, crossing the room to sit next to him.

He laughs. "You get the pancakes?"

"A stack about a foot high," I say as I approach them. I take the barstool next to Amelie and pour myself a mug of coffee, despite just having two servings at Brenn's.

"When Amelie was little," Melinda says, leaning over the island toward us. "She would eat every last bite of those pancakes. We could only go once per trip, or else she'd get all jittery. The syrup there, Henry—it's pure sugar."

Amelie laughs fondly, but the sound dies when footsteps pick up behind us. I turn to find Margot walking down the stairs, fully dressed for the day like Amelie and me. I assumed she'd be in pajamas like her parents, but from the looks of it, she's been awake for a while.

"Morning, pumpkin," Arnie says to her. "Coffee?"

"No, thanks," she says, going to the fridge. "Where did you guys go so early this morning?"

"Brenn's," Amelie answers. "Henry and I went. I got the pancakes."

"I don't doubt that," Margot says, managing to make the innocent words sound sharp.

Whatever joy was on Amelie's face seems to disappear at her sister's comment.

"I would've brought you something back if I'd thought of it," Amelie says. "You're normally still asleep. Sorry."

"It's fine." Margot opens a container of yogurt and shoves a spoon into it. "I was awake, but I figured you guys wanted to be alone."

Neither of us acknowledge her.

"Did you sleep well, Marg?" Arnie asks, taking a sip of his coffee.

She nods. "Yep."

"Did you find the extra blankets?"

"Yes."

Amelie huffs. "Did you lose your voice in your sleep?"

"Ames..." Melinda sighs.

"Sorry," she mutters, standing from the barstool. She goes directly to the coffee pot and pours herself a mug. "I just think we should be talkative. Talking is a fun activity!"

"A favorite of yours," I say, giving her a sideways glance.

Melinda smiles at me. "She never outgrew the talking."

"Oh, I know." I grin. "She proved that when we ran into each other again."

"I didn't talk that much," Amelie mumbles from the fridge.

I laugh. "She wasn't even talking *to* me, if I recall. I think she just wanted to express her opinion to whoever would listen."

"Another hobby of hers," Arnie agrees.

I laugh again, hiding my smile with my mug. Amelie pokes her head out from behind the refrigerator door and looks at me, and when her face breaks into a smile, I feel it in my chest.

"It's true," she says. "I wasn't talking to Henry, but he was lucky enough to hear my ramblings." She sits back down beside me, this time armed with a pink porcelain mug.

"I've never been luckier," I say, and just because I can, I curl my hand around the back of her neck and press the softest kiss to her cheek. Her lips part out of shock, and she distractedly picks up her coffee mug, eyes staying trained on the kitchen sink.

Seeing her blush at my touch feels like much more of a victory than it should.

Before I can really revel in such a thing, my phone starts ringing from my pocket. I exhale and look at the screen, wishing I had let it go when I see my dad's name.

"Excuse me," I mutter, retreating to the hallway.

Very reluctantly, I hit the answer button and hold the phone up to my ear. "Hello?"

"I'm sending over footage," Dad says, no time for greetings. "According to the doorman, this man was lurking around the lobby for quite some time. Tried to talk his way into the elevator. He kept his face hidden from the cameras—how, I've got no idea —but Michael was able to vaguely describe him."

I release a breath as I stare at the link he sent. This could be it. This whole thing could be over, and then...I'd be out of this deal Amelie and I are twisted in. I'll have my work back, attend the auction this weekend, and that'll be it. Our partnership would be over.

Somehow, I don't like that plan. But I'm still tapping my foot in anticipation as I click on the video.

It takes a second for the quality to clear, but when it does, I see the back of a tall man in a dark jacket. He's talking to Michael, the doorman, but he doesn't look all that threatening.

And then I notice something different.

He's got a tattoo on the back of his hand, one that goes up under his sleeve.

The ink matches Jensen's. Amelie's partner. It's the same tattoo I noticed after the Bondi's incident.

"No," I say under my breath.

"What was that?" Dad asks.

"Nothing. Uhm, are you running the footage?"

"We can't get much from it, but we're trying. The tattoo gives us something to work with." He sighs heavily. "This is incredible, Hen. Don't you see? We're close."

He hasn't called me Hen since I was ten years old. It's a strange time to start.

"Yeah," I say. "Sure. Uh, I've got to go, but let me know if—"

"How's the convention?"

"*What*?" I croak.

"The convention. How's it going?"

I am never going to lie again.

"It's not...I—phone—bad—" I attempt a stiff, robotic voice, but it's a very poor attempt.

Dad sounds frustrated when he says, "I can't understand a word you're saying."

"Poor—connection—"

He gives another heavy sigh and hangs up the phone. It's likely that he doesn't buy the fake excuse, but he's too focused on the security footage to argue with me.

I set my phone on the counter and wring my hands together, chewing at my lip until it bleeds. It can't be. It *can't...*

But it must be. That's the only explanation.

I rub my eyes and exhale, trying to lessen the pressure behind my ribcage.

How do I tell Amelie what my dad found?

More importantly, how do I ignore the disappointment I feel at the thought of this being her work?

34

AMELIE

Margot and I have been at a standstill ever since Henry left to take that call.

Mom and Dad made a timely exit moments after, and Margot reluctantly sat next to me in Dad's empty seat. I basically drained my coffee and hoped that she'd say something, but it was useless. She ate her breakfast and stared at the back door.

Why can't we just be *normal*? Would one conversation that isn't strained kill us?

"Look, Margot," I start. "We have to talk."

"Why?" She pins me with gray eyes, a gaze that mirrors mine. "You don't want to. *I* don't want to. You know Mom will make it weird on Thursday, anyways. Let it go."

"I just—"

"Not now, Amelie." She stands up and tosses her spoon into the sink, and I wince when it rattles around. "I have to go to town."

"Okay," I say, kicking at the base of my stool. "The roads aren't great."

"It'll be fine." She grabs a key fob off the counter and goes out the back door, making sure to slam it closed. I huff dramatically and slump over in my seat, laying my head on the cool marble countertop.

This is exactly how I expected this trip to go.

We don't want to talk. We don't want to fix things. Mom was the one who decided it was time, and I *knew* that, but I almost hoped that Margot planted the seed. I thought she might lay things down first, and I'd be able to read the situation without making it worse.

This whole rift is so old, I honestly don't know if there's any point in trying to break it. It's stupid—*so* stupid, and the worst thing is, it started in high school. Four years of this, all because of what happened after we graduated. All because I used to love art.

I *adored* art.

I think the stories of my parents' heists planted a desire in my mind. Learning about the paintings they stole drove me to learn more about art. About why people were so intent on having these pieces. What it meant to them. I wasn't the best at painting—I was alright, but nowhere near as good as I wanted to be. But I planned to go to school for it. I wanted to learn and get better.

When it came time to apply to college, Henry and I talked about art schools. He encouraged me to go. Said I'd grow better if I took my time. I wasn't good with technicalities; I liked to rush my paintings. I wanted the end results. The process was fun, but it didn't mean as much to me.

So I applied. Eventually, near the end of our senior year, Henry and I were both accepted into the same school.

And so was Margot. She applied without telling anyone so it'd be a surprise.

And then my desire to go was quickly lost.

It's a poor reason to change a path. I know that now, but I didn't back then. The emotion that overwhelmed me felt like a pit. I saw no reason to try and climb out when I knew I couldn't.

Margot outshined me at *everything*. I didn't hate her for it, but I'd be lying if I said it didn't affect me. If it never changed the way I viewed her. I'd come home from school with a B on a test, and she'd have an A+. I'd get a callback for a play, and she'd get the lead. Even at school it was inescapable. Teachers would congratulate me on Margot's accomplishments, only to recognize that I was *Margot's sister* moments later.

For years, I wished we had different faces, just so I could be separated from her. So her victories and mine would not be seen as one.

I shouldn't have let it hurt me the way I did. She was just *living.* Doing her own thing. But I still couldn't help but think she was out for me. I admired everything she did, and yet, I wanted her to fail *just once* so I could come out on top.

It didn't matter in the long run, though. I turned down the offer to the school. Told my family and Henry that it wasn't going to work out, that it wasn't the right path for me. They all still believe that lie, I think. Not a single one of them ever questioned me on it. They just told me that I'd find something better for me. And I planned to.

I knew I'd find something that Margot would never dream of doing, and I'd finally have what I wanted. To be good at something without the fear of her being better.

Margot left for school. She chose a different one out of state, but that didn't sway me. I didn't want to take the same road as her. I didn't want to try for the same career as her, to be associated with her in any way.

And I'll admit it—I was bitter toward her. I felt overlooked. My parents were proud of her for what she'd chosen, but in my head, she'd taken something from me that I was meant to have. Slowly, my bitterness turned into resentment, and I just stopped talking to her. I didn't reach out, but she didn't, either. Our connection snapped with hardly any pressure, so I told myself it was meant to be that way and tried to move on.

I put my focus into anything I could find. I helped my parents around the hall. Tried to focus on supporting Henry from afar. Almost every night, he'd call, and he'd tell me how things were going for him. How his pieces were getting attention. How he'd be back in November and kiss me like no time had passed.

But then, on a random Saturday, his calls stopped coming.

And the next week, mine went unreturned.

And then it just stopped altogether.

We hadn't spoken since then until I saw him in the museum, and by *that* point...well, I've been in the same line of work since that year he didn't come back. There's no need for me to change my ways now, not when I've found something outside of him. Not when I used it to keep myself from breaking down at every turn.

I felt betrayed by Margot. Abandoned by Henry. Like I was a choice, the one that nobody wanted to pick. I felt overlooked by the only person who had never made me feel that way. Eventually, I realized that art had caused me more damage than good, and I wanted my love for it to vanish. But that wasn't possible. You don't just stop loving something because you tell yourself to. It isn't a choice.

So I simply decided to work with it in a different way.

My work wasn't revenge. I chose it for myself. At least, that's what I thought I was doing. Now, I realize that even *that* choice was influenced by the things around me. It might never have crossed my mind if I weren't so terrified of being in Margot's shadow. If I hadn't felt like Henry left me for something he loved more.

I don't regret it. Not at all.

But I won't pretend that my skewed relationship with Margot is completely my fault. Even though it stems from my insecurities, there are still two sides to it. There's still a nagging in the back of my head that reminds me how easily Margot let it go. How she never tried to contact me, either.

Still, I'd take the blame. I'd apologize and admit that I started this if it would just kill the tension.

But an apology would equal uprooting things that were left unsaid. And while I know that it *needs* to happen, I'm not looking forward to it. I'm not trying to further aggravate my sister; after all, she *is* aware of what I do, and I know that her secrecy isn't because of me. It's because of my parents. She loves them more than she loves herself, and so do I. If the cops found anything on me, they'd be close to my parents' work. I run through their concert hall. We have the same patterns and clients. It's too much.

But if Margot ever changed her mind, I wouldn't be shocked. I wouldn't even blame her, because if tables were turned, I can't say how I'd react.

Meg, ever the therapist, says that's why I don't like things I can't control. I couldn't control Henry's calls. I couldn't control the way I was second to Margot. But I *can* control nearly everything when I'm working. It's close to the wire—sometimes, the edge nicks me, but I'm still in charge.

Until Henry. He's caught me twice, and I feel like my control has fully slipped away.

No matter how hard I try, I can't think of anything I've ever hated as much as that.

As if on cue, Henry appears in the kitchen looking strangely tense. I'm waiting for him to sit down beside me and pour another cup of coffee, but he just stands, mouth open like he wants to say something.

"Hi," I say after a beat.

"Can I talk to you?" He asks, motioning to the hallway. "In private?"

That's not good. I don't like that in the slightest.

"Yeah," I say, slipping off the barstool. Anxiety pools in my stomach as I follow him to his room, and I can't help but shuffle through the possibilities of what's wrong in my mind. All I know is that his demeanor has changed since that phone call.

Henry closes the door behind us once I'm through. I sit on the end of the bed and wring my hands together, knuckles turning white in the silence.

"What's wrong?" I ask.

He crosses his arms. Exhales sharply. "Jensen has a tattoo on his hand, no?"

I frown. "Yeah, he does. He's got tattoos halfway up his arm. Why?"

He swallows, face pale in this light. "Amelie, my dad finally turned the cameras on. He got footage of someone with that tattoo in my building. The doorman said he was trying to talk his way into the elevator."

I sit back on my hands with a blank face. It's not Jensen. I *know* that it's not Jensen, but there's no way to convince Henry of that, let alone Roman.

Still, I try. "It wasn't Jensen. He—"

"It was the exact same tattoo, Amelie," he says, and he isn't raising his voice, but the irritation is obvious.

"I understand that," I say, my own voice straining. "But it wasn't him. He wouldn't have done anything, Henry. He *knows* you're off-limits to us now."

That last part wasn't meant to slip out, and I'm a little mortified that it did.

But Henry's focus doesn't waver. "You think it's fake?"

I shake my head. "I'm not saying that. I'm saying that maybe someone...has the exact same tattoo?"

That's impossible. The design is something Jensen drew himself, but that detail is void. I'm one-hundred percent sure that the man in that video is *not* Jensen.

"I don't know, Ames." He shakes his head. "I just don't know."

"Maybe it was planted," I blurt. "Not by your dad or anything, that's not what I'm suggesting. But someone is messing with us, Henry. I told you that at the start." I hesitate for a moment before asking, "Can I see the footage?"

Henry looks reluctant, but he pulls his phone out and hands it to me.

The man on the screen is chatting with the doorman—the same one I saw my first time there. He's turned fully away from the lens, so I don't even see the side of him until thirty seconds into the clip.

And when he shifts to the side, my stomach drops to my toes.

I see Jensen's tattoo.

Jensen's hair.

Jensen's build.

Jensen's leather jacket.

No. No. It isn't. It can't be.

"Don't let him look into it," I plead, handing Henry the phone back. "Not until I let them know. Please."

Henry rubs his eyes under his glasses. "I don't know if I can do that."

I slouch over, defeated, but I have no reason to be. He doesn't trust me. He *shouldn't* trust me, probably, so my disappointment is invalid. But I know that isn't Jensen.

We may be thieves, but we are *loyal* for heaven's sake.

"Give me a week or something," I say. "Surely I can get things straightened out."

"What am I supposed to tell my dad?" He crosses his arms over his chest. "I told him that I'm trying to figure this out. Asking him to put a hold on things doesn't help my case."

"Just a little bit of time," I ask quietly. I'm not above begging in a situation like this. It makes my skin crawl, but I'll survive. "Please, Henry. I've done what I can to help you. I'm *still* trying to help you. But you have to help me with this."

His face is blank. Completely and utterly unreadable. I can tell that he's weighing his options, deciding whether he'd rather deal with me or his dad's complaints. I'm not trying to make this difficult for him; I understand how selfish the request is. It's unfair. But I won't let this happen.

"I can't promise that," he says, voice monotone. "I'm sorry."

Instead of arguing anymore, I stand. "I understand. Just tell me when you decide, okay?"

Henry just nods. I leave his room and go to mine, dialing Meg's number before I even sit down at the desk.

"Meg," I say as soon as the ringing stops.

She doesn't seem to sense the rising panic in my voice. "What's up?"

"Nothing good," I say. "Roman has footage that shows Jensen at Henry's apartment building."

"*What*?"

"I know! It has his tattoo in there. But it's—it's not him, right, Megs? You guys wouldn't have done that. I know you wouldn't."

"We didn't," she says. "I'll vouch for him. We've been together the whole time you've been gone."

"Okay, we don't need to get on that topic." I sigh. "Have you guys snagged *Lover of Mine* yet?"

"Not until tomorrow."

"Please be careful," I say quietly. "Things are off. Just keep it more on the DL than normal, okay?"

"We do. You're the one that likes being frivolous."

Fair.

Shortly after, Meg hangs up with no further comments. I throw my phone onto the pile of clothes tumbling out of my suitcase and sit down on the floor, mind racing with solutions to a problem that shouldn't exist.

Henry has no reason to believe me. I know this.

But if this is the only time he ever trusts me again, I'll take it.

35

HENRY

Time seems to pass much quicker here than it does back home.

Days are a blur. Arnie and Melinda have us booked with more things than I can even count. Movies, poker games, baking, sledding; anything that pops into their minds. I think the busyness is a way to keep conflict away. It works, at least on a literal level— Amelie and Margot don't speak once over the entire weekend. Their communication lies solely in the passive-aggressive jabs they can get at each other.

Amelie *also* hasn't spoken to me outside of time with her family, and it's driving me mad. Leisurely conversation hasn't seemed like an option after our talk about Jensen. Or, whoever that man was on the footage. My dad hasn't made another mention of it, and I've tried not to think about it.

All I know is that I'm on thin ice with Amelie. I'm testing the waters by going to her bedroom, which isn't the wisest idea I've had, but I need to talk to her. I don't want her going through this day with two things to worry about. Margot's event is enough of a stressor for her; there's no need for me to be an add-on to her problems.

I knock on her door frame and wait impatiently in the hallway. I'm shifting uncomfortably on my feet, though I have no reason to be worrying like this. Either we talk and figure things out, or the day gets worse. I can't control it one way or the other.

The door swings open, and before I even get a sentence out, I have to take a step back.

I don't know why I'm caught off guard. Amelie is always breathtaking, but sometimes, I forget to brace myself.

She's wearing a dark blue dress, one that covers her arms and leaves a portion of her back bare. Her face is solemn, pulled into a frown, but there's still something so bright about her. I don't even realize I'm staring until she clears her throat, then takes a step backward.

"Hi," she says coolly. "Come in."

Hesitantly, I do. I stand with my hands tucked in my coat pockets, trying my hardest not to tap my foot against the floor just for something to do. "How are you?"

Amelie shrugs and drops into the chair in front of her vanity. "Fine. You look...fancy."

I blink and look at myself in the full-length mirror behind us. My attire is hardly different than normal—I'm wearing slacks and a button-down shirt, covered by the same trench coat I've noticed Amelie glare at in the past. I can't tell if her comment is a positive or negative thing. I don't know why I care.

"Thank you," I say. "So do you."

It's probably the biggest understatement I've ever said aloud.

"Thank you," she says in return. Her voice is weak, clipped, and it makes my chest tighten. Her eyes are lowered, focused on something that I don't even see. She's upset—I know that. But I also know that I can't fix anything, and it's making me feel like the most helpless person in the world.

"Do you want to talk about it, Ames?" I ask quietly.

Her head snaps up, and she meets my eyes through the mirror. "I don't..." She pauses. Picks up her hairbrush, just to drag it through the ends of her hair. "It's tomorrow, Henry. Our birthday is tomorrow, and we hate each other."

"I'm sorry," I say, wishing that it weren't my only answer.

Nobody has dared to mention the upcoming day. We're all very aware of what a sore topic it is, though the reasoning is still lost on me.

"It's stupid." Amelie sets the brush back down. "I shouldn't be here. I shouldn't have to pretend that I want to see her display, or that I want to spend time with her, or that I want to share a birthday with her. I shouldn't have to act like this isn't killing me. I don't even know *why* it's getting at me this way."

"You don't have to keep up an act," I tell her, crossing the room. Her shoulders tense when I get close, but I stand behind her and study her face in the mirror. "I know what you're feeling, Ames."

She shakes her head. "No. You don't get it."

"I'm not saying I 'get it'. I'm saying that I understand, and that I want to be there for you today if you'll let me."

Amelie exhales and slides a bracelet on her wrist. After a few seconds of flicking at the charms, she removes it, then looks at me over her shoulder. "What do you mean, *'If I'll let you'*?"

"You're angry with me, so I doubt that—"

"What?" Her eyes narrow, though ironically *not* from anger. It's more a look of confusion. "I'm not angry with you."

I gape at her. "Are you serious?"

"Why would I be kidding?"

I fight the urge to list off the reasons resting on the forefront of my mind.

Because we haven't talked in three days outside of fake conversation, and I feel like I'm betraying you by letting my dad look into that footage. I don't even think it was Jensen, yet I still argued on my dad's behalf, and now we're stuck in silence, and—

"Is this about the security stuff?" Amelie asks in disbelief. When I don't respond immediately, her eyes widen, and the corners of her mouth lift into a half smile. "Henry, really?"

"Yes," I mumble. "We've hardly spoken, so I just—"

"I'm not," she says, cutting me off. I'm guessing she doesn't want to hear my explanation, which doesn't make her argument that believable, but I keep quiet. "I'm okay. I just want out of this house. I've been around people for a very long time, and it's starting to mess with me."

I move away from her chair, but she stays seated, toying with a necklace clasp in front of her. Her face is downturned again, shoulders slumped forward, and I just want to *help*. I want to make her smile, though I'm unsure if I'm even capable of that anymore.

But I may have something.

"Give me a second," I say, stepping toward the door.

Amelie looks at me, confusion in her eyes. "What are you—"

"I'll be right back."

She doesn't argue as I step out into the hall.

Without a second thought, I go straight to my room and dig to the bottom of my suitcase. The small blue box has been tucked in the corner since I purchased it, exactly twelve hours before Amelie and I left the city. Liz dragged me to the nearest Tiffany's and practically threw my wallet on the counter, telling me to hurry up and pick something before the store closed.

I go back to Amelie's room and close the door behind me. She's still seated at her vanity, so I slowly approach her and set the box in front of her. "Here."

She stares at it like she's never seen a box before, keeping her hands clasped together on her lap. "What are you doing?"

"It's your gift."

"Today?"

"Yes."

She eyes me warily, like this is a joke. "Okay."

"Okay. Open it."

Amelie turns her attention to the box. Wordlessly, she lifts the top off, and she gasps when she sees the necklace inside. I let out a sigh of relief at what *seems* like a positive reaction.

I had no idea if she'd like it or not; I had to put my trust in Lizzy for this portion of things. She gave me three options to choose from, given that I know little to nothing about jewelry. I picked the only one that caught *my* eye, which is a pearl necklace with a silver clasp.

"I'm sorry I didn't wrap it," I say, fighting a smile at Amelie's wide eyes. "I didn't have time. Or wrapping paper."

"You're *kidding*." She looks up at me, her face flushed. "Henry, this—this is too much."

"It isn't."

"You didn't have to get me anything at all."

"I wanted to."

Slowly, fluidly, she stands from her chair and walks over to me. The box is in her hands, and I note that they're shaking the slightest bit. "I can't accept this," she whispers.

I pocket my hands. "You can."

"*Henry—*"

I cut her off. Hold her gaze as I take the box from her and remove the necklace. She keeps her eyes on mine as I work the clasp undone and loop the piece around her neck, fastening it at the hollow of her throat. Her breath catches as my knuckles drag against her collarbone, and her lashes flutter closed for a moment. She recovers quickly, forcing her expression back to neutral in a split second, but I don't miss the action.

Suddenly, as if it happened within mere seconds, I'm aware of how close we are. Of how I haven't been this close to her in ages.

I think back to the night I sketched her, when I outlined and shaded her face solely from memory, and I realize that I did it. I captured every line, every mark of her face, and I did it well. The bow of her lips. The curve of her nose. The beauty mark above her mouth, the one I've kissed hundreds of times. This woman is burned so deeply into my mind, I don't think I'm capable of forgetting her face.

"Henry," Amelie says again, her voice breathless enough to drag me out of whatever trance I'm in. "You shouldn't have done this."

My chest twists uncomfortably. "You won't convince me of that, Ames. I wanted—"

She steps forward and throws her arms around my neck, cutting me off by falling fully against me. It's enough of a shock that I have to remind myself to breathe before even daring to hold her. I pull her into me, resting my head on hers, and her body relaxes. She seems calm, peaceful, while I'm just trying to control the speed of my breathing.

"You're ridiculous," she mumbles into my shirt. "But thank you. Thank you so much."

I laugh. "You're welcome."

Amelie looks up at me, a faint smile resting on her lips. She keeps her arms locked around me, not making any move to step away. I'm still trying to breathe normally, but I'm failing, and it doesn't help that her eyes are lowering from mine.

Her smile suddenly disappears, and I can't draw my eyes away from her mouth.

No. I shouldn't.

Under no circumstances should I do this.

But I do.

I move my hand from her waist and hook a finger under her jaw, tilting her face up the slightest bit. She complies, keeping her gaze trained on mine, and I try reminding myself that I can't do this. This isn't an option. We specifically decided *against* this, yet the moment I hesitate, she tips her chin up further.

That's all it takes.

I slide my hand to the back of her neck as I lower my head. Our lips brush, and she stands up on her toes, but I don't kiss her. Instead, I drag my nose along her jaw, practically drowning in the feel of her. Amelie inhales sharply when I kiss the side of her neck, when my hands tighten around her waist. She grasps my shirt tighter, pulling me even closer, breathing as unevenly as I am.

Neither of us are unaffected by this. Neither of us are trying to hide it.

"What are you doing?" Amelie rasps, the words all air. "No one is here. This isn't..."

This isn't for show, my mind finishes.

Correct. It's not. And it leaves me with more questions than I've had in a long time.

I want to know if she's thought about it. If she ever dreamed we'd be back here, caught up in each other like this. When I saw her in the museum that first night, I did. I couldn't help myself. I wondered if there was some sliver of a chance that I'd see her like this again—wanting me. Wanting *us*.

Never did I expect it to be a reality.

I pull back slightly, enough that I can look her in the eyes. Her lids are heavy, face flushed. "Do you really think I'm pretending?" I whisper.

She swallows hard. Blinks twice. "You're teasing me, then."

"No." I shake my head. "I'm not, Amelie, I'm—"

Someone raps their knuckles on the closed door, and Amelie gasps.

"You ready, Ames?" Arnie calls from the hallway. "We're about to leave."

"I'll be right down!" Amelie takes a very generous step away from me and straightens her dress. "Just—just trying to find my shoes."

Arnie says something neither of us catch before leaving down the hall. Amelie wordlessly walks to her suitcase and digs out a pair of white heels. She slips them onto her feet, not sparing me a glance as she fluffs the ends of her hair.

"You know, I think they're really buying it," she says, sounding entirely unaffected.

Even though I know what she means, even though I don't want her answer, I still ask, "Buying what?"

"Us."

And right then, it's like I'm shaken awake from a dream.

36

AMELIE

I want to claw my skin off the entire way to the showing.

It's a small thing, Margot told us. Held in the town community center. She's proud of it, though—of the fact that someone recognized her work and wanted it displayed. I desperately wish I were happy for her.

She's been gone since the crack of dawn, according to Dad, and I've tried not to give it any thought. I've tried to focus on things other than this event, which honestly proved to be worse for me. I thought about the fact that our birthday is tomorrow and that I don't even want to talk to her. But I knew I'd come to the realization eventually. I was fine with it.

And then Henry decided to come to my room, and my judgment lapsed, and now I don't know what's going on.

I haven't so much as looked at him since he took his hands off me. We're in the back of my dad's minivan, sitting pressed against the doors like we're too scared to touch again. *I* am, anyway. Mistakes were made, and they can't happen again.

My parents are oblivious to the tension. They can't tell I'm angry; can't tell that Henry and I are acting strangely. They can't tell we're acting at *all*. Right now, the only focus is getting us here and getting back to the cabin before Dad's team starts playing.

I don't even notice we've arrived until Dad shuts the engine off. We're parked in front of a beat-down brick building, surrounded by no more than ten cars. I was expecting something packed out, but I'm not sure why. The population of this town hardly surpasses two-hundred people.

Mom takes the liberty of breaking the silence, turning around to stare at both Henry and me. "Is everyone ready?"

"Absolutely," I say before I can catch my tone.

Mom sighs. "Amelie, honey, it's—"

"I know, Mom. I'm happy for her."

Lie.

"It'll be fun," she says. "Promise."

"Just try to enjoy it," Dad says. "You'll find something in there to look at. We're just doing a walk-through, anyway, and then we'll be out. Marg will be home shortly after."

With a nod, I force myself out into the freezing air. Goose-bumps cover my skin the second the wind hits me. I'm wearing a coat, but it does little, given that my legs below my mid-thigh are completely bare. I grab my handbag and close the car door, and before I even start toward the building, Henry is at my side.

My stomach flips at the mere sight of him, but my heart rate kicks up when he offers me his hand, palm-up.

"Henry," I warn. "We—"

"Come on, kids," Dad calls, zipping his coat. "We don't have all day."

I roll my eyes and slap my hand onto Henry's, hating myself when I tangle our fingers together reflexively. It feels like every nerve ending in my body travels to where his rough skin is touching mine.

"Margot said she's somewhere off to the right," Dad says, opening the door. "Which piece does she have up, Mel?"

"*Agreeance,*" Mom says. "It's my favorite of hers."

I tuck my free hand into my coat, trying to warm myself as I look around this place. The inside is a stark contrast to the outside, as in, it isn't dilapidated. The walls are freshly painted, and the floors look new. I'd guess that any budget went toward the interior.

People flit around with their eyes glued to the walls, taking in the art hung around them. There are a few that catch my eye. Some that I know would sell if this were a larger populated area. One to my left is something that I, myself, wouldn't mind taking, solely because I *don't* like it.

"There she is," Mom says suddenly, tugging on my arm and dragging me toward the corner of the room. Margot is standing in front of a large canvas, shaking hands with an older man that looks almost entranced by her work. His kind eyes are settled on the painting behind her, even as he keeps talking. It's like he can't look away.

My face is neutral as I study her painting, but my thoughts are a whirlwind.

I don't understand it, not at first. It's a simple contrast of dark and light. Night and day. A dark shadow is at the base of the canvas, pushing back against the burst of light coming from the top. The two are muddled together at the center, mixed into a dark gray color, but otherwise, they're completely separated.

"Huh," I say under my breath.

"You like it?" Mom asks quietly, hopefully.

I nod. "It's interesting."

"I don't wholly understand the point of it," she admits in a low voice, "but I don't want to ask. The colors are nice, though."

"I think it's a literal show of agreeance," I say, recalling the name. "It's supposed to be two totally different things coming together."

She tilts her head and squints at the canvas. "Hm. Perhaps."

"That's exactly it, actually," Margot says, stepping forward.

My stomach rolls with something like dread as we approach her, and it only worsens when I see her face.

She looks happier than I've ever seen her.

"We're so proud of you, honey," Mom says, giving her a hug. "This is lovely."

"Thank you," she says, her eyes bright. "So you guys like it?"

They both nod. "I love it," Dad says. "It's incredible, pumpkin."

Margot gives them a smile, then turns toward me. I stiffen up, my back going totally rigid. "You? Do you like it?"

"Yeah," I say, nodding for good measure. "It's great, Marg."

She doesn't smile, doesn't say anything before turning back to our parents.

I blow out a breath and flex my hands at my sides, trying to shake the feeling in my gut. My skin is practically itching with nerves. I want to leave, badly. This place is anxiety inducing for reasons I don't fully understand. Or maybe it's not this environment; rather, it's the situation.

My discomfort must be more obvious than I'd like, because Henry picks up on it almost instantly. "We can walk around," he says so only I can hear him. "Do you want to—"

"Yes." I nod. "Let's do that."

He walks away without another word. I follow behind him at a slow pace, glancing around the room without truly focusing on anything. Henry does the exact opposite, though—he stops before multiple pieces, getting closer to examine each one. I'm watching him more closely than the art. At the way his face shapes into something new with each one he looks at.

"This one is remarkable," he says when we've reached the back of the building. We're tucked in a small alcove, alone except for the canvas in front of us. It's a simple work, no larger than a notebook. A field of flowers, laid out in pink and orange, with a promise of storms in the sky. "It's balanced well."

"The colors?"

"Yes," he says, sounding excited that I've even asked. "They complement each other well. I've attempted a few pieces like this, but they fail miserably each time. Nature isn't something I've learned to capture well."

Instantly, I think of his piece, *Fleur of Words*. That's nature, I want to say. It's a flower. But I don't, because I don't want him thinking that I've paid more attention to him than I've had to.

I nearly laugh at the thought. All I've done for the past few days is pay attention to Henry. I've gone back and forth from staring at him to trying *not* to stare at him, and I'm failing at the second part. He's taken up a good portion of my thoughts. It worries me more than anything else.

"What are you thinking?" He asks.

I shrug. "About the piece? It's alright."

He laughs quietly. "No, I know you're not paying attention to the piece. What's on your mind?"

I open my mouth. Close it instantly. I can't just tell him the truth—that I'm hardly even here, hardly even thinking. That I'm only focused on what happened an hour ago and I can't seem to shake the memory of it.

His hands on my neck. His lips on my jaw. The words he whispered—

"Nothing," I say, hoping there's enough conviction in my voice for him to believe it. "I'm fine."

He narrows his eyes, looking at me with a sense of disbelief. I hold my breath, waiting for an argument to come, but it never does. Instead, he says, "I'm sorry."

And somehow, that's worse.

"I'm so sorry for earlier, Ames." He shakes his head. "I shouldn't have—"

"No," I say, blinking rapidly. "It's fine, Henry. It wasn't...it wasn't all you."

He looks at me like he's shocked, but unfortunately, I'm telling the truth.

I wanted it. Wanted *him*. More than I've wanted anything in a long time.

Which is a very, very bad thing.

"It won't happen again." My voice is weak for what I'm trying to convey. "It just...it won't."

"It won't," he responds stiffly.

"Good." I look away. Toy with the necklace around my throat and try not to remember the way his skin felt against mine when he put it on me. "Great."

Henry clears his throat and removes his glasses. He cleans the untouched lenses with his shirt before looking over at me. "I'm proud of you, you know."

Those words alone are enough to make my jaw drop. "What?"

"For being here today." He puts his glasses back on his face. "I know you didn't want to."

I study his profile once he turns his gaze forward, those four words repeating over and over in my head.

I'm proud of you.

Hearing that—when I've done nothing more than begrudgingly show up—confuses me. Why would he say that? My first assumption is that I'm being made fun of, but I don't think that's the case, though I can't find another reason he'd be genuinely saying that.

"I meant that, Ames," he says quietly, seeing right through me. "Promise."

And for some reason, that's what makes the pieces fall together in my mind.

The pieces of why I changed. Why I altered what I wanted, the second that Margot wanted it too. Why I subconsciously still compete against her—*everyone*—in my mind.

Because I want someone to be proud of what I've chosen.

I think that's all I ever wanted. For someone to say it.

My parents may be proud of me, but they've never told me that. I used to assume they'd say it, given that I sort of followed in their footsteps, but that's not the case. And it's nothing against them. Maybe they didn't know I needed to hear it. Maybe I should've told them that I did.

Maybe I acted so self-sufficient that they thought I didn't want to hear the words.

But hearing them now, over *this,* is almost enough to send me spiraling.

I can't afford that, though. Not in front of him.

"Thanks," I mumble. "Thank you."

Henry nods, brows pulled together as he looks at me. Rather than asking what's wrong—probably because he knows I won't tell him anyways—he offers me his hand again. I take it and don't say a word as we walk back toward my parents. They ask us questions, but I let Henry answer them as I play his words over and over through my mind.

I need him out of my head.

But that's looking like less and less of an option the longer this goes on.

37

HENRY

The drive back to the cabin is silent.

Well, conversation-wise, at least. Not so much *noise*-wise, given that Arnie and Melinda find an oldies station that they simply *have* to sing to.

But Amelie doesn't say a word. She keeps her body turned toward the window and her eyes on the ditch. I answer the few questions that get tossed around, trying to give responses that satisfy her parents so she doesn't have to speak.

I want to know what's bothering her. I want to know what switch flipped, because it was almost instantaneous, and it seems to be causing a lot more trouble than I'd originally thought.

The four of us disperse when we're inside, each going to our respective rooms. I change into something comfier and more casual before stepping back into the living room, and when I do, the only person I lay eyes on is Margot.

I didn't expect her to be back so soon, but I can't even question her presence before Amelie's words pop into my mind.

No being alone in a room with Margot.

She's already seen me, though. It's probably pointless to leave.

Cautiously, I make my way into the living room, dropping into the seat across from her. She's still in her clothes from the showing, but she's got a book settled in her lap. Her eyes stay glued to the page, so I hope I'm free from questions. If I were smart, I would've brought my own form of distraction, because now I'm staring at a blanket on the couch.

"How was the rest of the exhibit?" Margot asks suddenly, hardly looking up from her page. "I didn't get to walk around."

"It was nice," I say coolly. "Your work was great."

"Thank you." She sets her book aside and, internally, I panic. A book being discarded means there's no chance of avoiding questions. It's real. This is an actual conversation now. "Why are you here, Henry?"

I blink. "Because I didn't want to stay in my room—"

"*Here*," she emphasizes. "With Amelie."

"Because she asked me to be."

That's a flat-out lie. I don't even think I was on her list of options.

Margot hums. "So you're really dating her?"

"Why is that in question?"

"Just curious." She shrugs. "That's a yes, then?"

"Yes," I say, loving the way that answer feels. "We're together. I wouldn't be here if we weren't."

"It was only a question. Not many people choose to date their ex again."

This is definitely why Amelie told me to stay away from Margot.

"Things just happen," I say, as if it's some profound thing and not the dumbest sentence I've ever said. "And I'm happy this did."

She does that humming thing again. I think it's her way of saying '*I don't believe a word you're saying*'.

"So this has nothing to do with...I don't know, trying to get dirt on her?"

My breath catches in my chest at the implication. At the fact that it's *exactly* what my dad asked me to do. "No," I say firmly. "I'd never do that."

"Really," she mumbles, dragging the word out. "That's strange. I wouldn't think you're okay with her job."

"We've discussed this already," I counter. "Though it's really none of your concern."

Margot frowns, like the sentence is distasteful. "And you're willing to love someone like her?"

My brows draw together. "Why are you belittling her?"

"I'm not. I'm asking you a question. You work in the same line as I do, Henry. You're an artist. That's something she hates."

"No, she doesn't," I say, aware that this argument is pointless. So what if Amelie does hate me? It wouldn't change anything. I'm arguing for little more than my pride at this point.

"Then *why*?" Margot sounds exasperated. "Why else would she be doing this?"

I run a hand over my face and exhale. "Maybe you should ask Amelie, rather than trying to make me talk down about her."

Margot's face is unreadable as she picks her book back up, seemingly irritated by my suggestion. I let her eyes dart around the page for all of ten seconds before I interrupt her. "I'm going to ask you something now."

She clicks her tongue. "Fine."

"Do you know what happened between Amelie and I?"

Her brows raise as she looks up at me, and I get the urge to take the question back. "No. I was at school, and when I got back, she was causing trouble in the city."

"She never said anything?"

"No. Why?"

I don't respond, but I don't have to. She picks up on it almost instantly.

"You don't even know, do you?" She sits up, crosses her legs. There's something like excitement in her eyes now, and I'd be appalled if it weren't making me nervous. "You've got no idea."

I swallow. "No. I have no idea."

"You guys haven't talked about it?"

"It hasn't come up," I blurt. I really get it now, why Amelie didn't want me alone with Margot. She's going to get information out of me just by confusing me. "It doesn't really matter, I guess. It was four years ago."

She snorts. "It was years ago, yeah. So what? It was enough to pry the two of you apart, and you were attached at the hip. It couldn't have just been anything. Do you really want to be together *not* knowing what happened?"

I crack my knuckles and realize that I'm about to make a very foolish decision.

"Our connection stopped. I don't know why." My throat tightens around the words. "I called her, and each one went unreturned. I wrote her, and—"

"You *wrote her*?" Margot sounds revolted.

"Yes. How else was I meant to get in touch with her?"

Her face wrinkles for a moment. "Huh. That's odd."

"That she never answered? I know."

"No, that you even wrote to her. If the connection falls off, it falls off." She stands and walks to the kitchen to pour a cup of coffee that I'm almost certain is cold. "It's a desperate thing to try and get it back."

I bristle. "Is that why you two haven't talked?"

She laughs dryly, and I know I'm about to get even deeper into this argument. "A phone works both ways. Amelie could've called me if she wanted."

I cross my arms, bite my tongue. I have zero right to argue over this. Amelie hasn't even told me the full story, and even if she had, it wouldn't be mine to handle. But the way Margot talks about her makes me tick.

Still. This isn't what I want to focus on right now.

"I'm sorry," I tell her. "It isn't my place to talk about this."

"You're right. It isn't." Margot takes a seat at the bar and grabs a magazine off the counter, opening it right to the middle. "I know you care about my sister, but you need to stay out of this. It's between the two of us. All of it."

I stay silent, mostly because Amelie descends the stairs as soon as Margot stops talking.

"Hi," she says, eyes going between her sister and I. "What's going on?"

"Oh, nothing." Margot's voice drips with sarcasm. "Nothing at all."

This room feels mildly combustible.

"Okay." Amelie drags the word out. She frowns in Margot's direction before turning toward me. "Come upstairs."

It's not a request, and I'm made aware of that when she grabs my hand and tugs me off the couch. She takes me to her room and closes the door behind us, sighing as she sits on her bed. Pillows and random articles of clothing cover the rest of the mattress, so I sit in her desk chair.

"Did she do what I said she would?" Amelie asks.

"Yes," I say, "and she should work for the FBI."

She blows out a breath. "I know. It's weird."

"I didn't say much of anything," I tell her, deciding to keep the slight argument to myself. "Mostly, I just talked in circles."

"She knows," Amelie says, grabbing a pillow and hugging it to her chest. "That we're pretending, I mean. I can tell that she does."

"She might *suspect*," I correct her, "but she doesn't know. We've given her no reason to think this is fake."

Amelie stays silent for a bit, picking at her polished nails as she stares at the wall. It's ridiculous, but really, I just want one of us to snap. To admit that Margot would have no way of suspecting a thing, because this hasn't felt fake to *us*.

It could be one-sided.

But after the way she reacted to me earlier, I'm not sure that's the case.

"Henry, I have to tell you something," Amelie says, voice lowered. "And you might hate me for it."

"I could never hate you." The words are too true. "What is it?"

She finally meets my eyes, her mouth pulled into a frown. "I lied to you. In high school, about the academy. Nothing fell through—I turned them down."

I have to actively drag that conversation out of my memory. Of all the things she could've been addressing, I didn't expect it to be this. "What do you mean?"

She swallows. Turns away from me. "Do you have that one person you can't beat? That you feel like you can't measure up to? Because for me, that's my sister. She was always better than me. She's *still* better than me. So when I got accepted..." She takes a breath. "Margot told me that she got in, too. She applied without telling anyone."

Oh. I guess this whole thing has been deep-rooted for longer than I realized.

"I turned them down because I didn't want to do the same thing as her. I didn't want to hear about how well things were going for her at every turn." She pauses. "No. Let me rephrase that. I would've been fine with hearing about her victories. I would've been happy for her. But I wanted to be good, too. I wanted to do something on my own, and I had no chance at that when I was constantly worried about what she was doing."

Amelie stops talking and looks at me. She's waiting for an answer, I think, but I'm calculating my words. I don't want to speak yet. She's just laid herself bare for me, and if I trip over my words or say the wrong thing, I'll never forgive myself.

Thankfully, I don't have to talk yet, because Amelie continues.

"It wasn't a direct thing," she says quietly. "I didn't choose this to hurt you, or her, or anyone else. It's just what I got into, and I'm good at it. I don't think I'll ever be this good at something else."

"Do you even enjoy it?" I ask. It may not be the correct response, but I'm curious. Based on her tone, her words, it doesn't sound that way. It sounds like an obligation.

Amelie nods. "I do. Though I enjoy it more when I'm in the city. It's weird to be away from it." She laughs dryly. "All of this...I don't know. Being back here makes me think of what I once wanted."

"You can have that, you know," I say, turning more toward her. "Nobody is keeping you from it."

"Don't." She shakes her head, sets her jaw. "Don't try to talk me out of it, Henry. That's not what I'm asking for."

"I'm not," I say incredulously. "That's not at all what I was saying."

Amelie opens her mouth, then snaps it shut before turning

away. It takes me a moment to realize why she sounds so defensive. Why she's giving me a warning, rather than flat-out arguing my statement.

She thinks I'm saying this for my sake. She's telling me that she won't change because she feels like I want her to.

"I don't want to change you, Ames," I say, and she meets my eyes when I say her name. "That's the last thing I've ever wanted. Your decisions are your own, and I've always respected that."

"I know you have." There's a challenging expression resting in her eyes, and it worries me for what's going to come next. "But what's changed?"

I shake my head. "I don't understand."

"What's changed with you? Because yes, you've always respected my decisions. But I think we both know that, four years ago, you wouldn't respect *this* about me."

I gape at her. "Amelie, I'm not lying."

"I know that," she presses. "That's why I'm asking. What has changed? Why are you okay with it *now*?"

There's not a single logical thought on the forefront of my mind, because despite how much I hate it, she's right. Four years ago, I would've been appalled. I would've been horrified at her openness with what she does. With both our attitudes back then, we wouldn't have lasted past the day that I found out.

But something *has* changed, because right now, it's the last thing I care about. It's not the thing I see when I look at her. I'm not focused on something that she chose four years ago out of what sounds like discouragement. And I guess I should be; I understand that it's technically wrong to 'overlook' something like this, but I'm *not* overlooking it. I'm aware of it. Have been for ages.

And it has not once succeeded in turning me away from her.

In fact, I'm more captivated by her than I've ever been.

These aren't simply old feelings being sparked again, and I know that. This is a different, newer sense of want. Of *need*. This is right now. It's real, and it could be a disastrous thing, but I don't care. If that's the case, then I want her to be my end.

Her infrequent, small admissions do nothing to quell my urge to learn more about her. I want to know everything she's willing to tell me. Every thought she's had in the past four years. I want to know how her mind works, how she thinks through each and every detail in her plans. How she's not gotten caught by anyone but me.

I want to tell her that she's allowed to take pride in her work. And the thing is, I know I'd mean it.

So why am I okay with it now? What has changed?

I have no idea.

My mind is running too rampantly to pinpoint the direction of my thoughts. I couldn't give her a straight answer if I tried, but I'm able to zero in on the one thing I *can't* say.

It's the fact that I still love her.

The fact that I never stopped, not really.

But I've lost her once, and I refuse to do it again. Not over this.

"I don't know," I say quietly. It's not the answer I *want* to give, but it's the only one I can get out. "I can't...I don't know."

She nods calmly, while I feel anything but. The look on her face says that she doesn't believe me, and she confirms that suspicion by asking, "Really?"

I hesitate, because I know my answer isn't enough for her yet. She wants a *real* answer, one where I explain my train of thought and why I feel this way. And I'm not going to do her the disservice of talking around it. We're already walking on eggshells—the more we gravitate toward the other, the more terrifying this becomes. It's so breakable, and I'll die before being the one to shatter it.

"I know why," I correct myself, "but I know it's not what you're looking for."

Amelie's brows draw together. "What does that mean?'

"It means that I know you, and you want a full answer. Not something like '*Because it's you*', or '*Because this is now and that was the past*'. That won't suffice for you, and that's okay."

Her face is painted with shock, like I've actually surprised her with this response. "Wow, Arlington. You get it now."

I give a dry, ingenuine laugh. "I know how you operate."

"Apparently so," she mutters, sitting up on her bed. The frown she's been wearing for days settles deeper around her mouth as she leans further into her pillows. She swaps the one on her lap out for a stuffed dog and closes her eyes, but I know she's not relaxed. She's tapping her fingers on her opposite wrist, and her foot is bouncing against her thigh.

"What happened to us, Ames?" I whisper, unable to keep the question to myself any longer. I know that it isn't the time to ask. I know that this is breaking the rules we set, that I've broken nearly every one thus far. But I have to know. "What was it?"

Her eyes open, and her entire body stiffens at my voice. "You're not serious."

"I am."

She sits up. Pins me with her eyes. "That's a cruel thing to ask, Henry. Especially when—"

"*I'm* cruel?" My voice is soft, but Amelie still flinches. "How? I didn't—"

"You *didn't*. That's the thing." She stands up straight, goes right to her door. "I don't need this. Not before tomorrow."

Guilt settles in my chest. "Amelie, wait. I didn't—"

"Not. Now."

She slams the door behind her as she steps out into the hallway.

I don't follow.

38

AMELIE

I'd really rather this day just end.

The moment I woke up, I was tempted to go right back to sleep. That wasn't much of a possibility though, given that Mom and Dad were in my room, singing happy birthday and placing a plastic tiara on my head.

I managed to escape breakfast by taking a shower. Unfortunately, I used all the hot water, so my paradise ended in half an hour. I hid in my room for an *additional* hour before being forced outside with the promise of cupcakes.

I wasn't told I'd have to *make* the cupcakes, but that's where I am now.

It's noontime, and Henry and Dad are in town. According to Mom, they're getting chicken wings for lunch. She put Margot and I to work baking our own cupcakes. I'm fully aware that it's her last attempt at getting us to talk before Henry and I leave to go back home, which happens to be tomorrow.

Just the thought of it makes my stomach pool with dread. I don't want to be in a car with him. I don't even want to *look* at him. Avoidance has been my solution all day, and it's worked wonderfully so far.

Though I can't truly push his words from yesterday out of my mind.

What happened to us, Ames?

He doesn't get to pretend he isn't at fault. I don't care that we're tangled up in this stupid partnership, that we're required to spend time together. He doesn't get to act like he did nothing to me.

But that can't be my focus. Today, I'm worried about keeping the peace with Margot. Our birthday celebration has been nonexistent, save for Mom and Dad's singing this morning, and honestly, I prefer it this way. It's easier to act like this is just another day, because it is.

"I hope you've had a happy birthday, girls," Mom says, scooping some batter into a cupcake paper. "I'm excited for you to open your gifts. I think you'll love them."

"I know we will," I say, and she bumps her hip into mine. "How long have you had them?"

"A lady never tells her secrets," she says, which I know means *a very long time*. Mom always has gifts long prior to the day, even for Christmas. "But I *do* want to know you girls' secrets. Have you talked yet?"

Margot and I exchange a sideways glance, and Mom catches it immediately. She sighs but doesn't say anything.

"I've tried," I mutter.

Margot scoffs. "Okay. Try and make me sound like the bad guy."

"I didn't mean it that way."

"We have talked," she argues. "I've told you what I think."

"That isn't *talking*."

"Well, that's what I'm willing to say."

"Girls," Mom repeats gently. "Let's not fight."

I bite my tongue and slather some icing on a cupcake. "We aren't fighting."

"Aren't we?" Margot sets the whisk in her hand aside. "Because I think we might need to."

"I see no reason why. We're allowed to disagree, Marg. It's fine."

She shakes her head. "But you wouldn't stop for me."

I finally look up at her. "*What* are you talking about?"

"Stealing. If I asked you to stop, you wouldn't. You're set in your ways, and you won't let anyone sway you."

"You wouldn't stop painting if I asked you," I say, suddenly feeling *very* ready to fight. "How's it any different? I've built something of it, just like you have with your art."

"You built something of crime. Don't act like you cured cancer."

My lungs constrict. This—whether she knows it or not—is her playing on my insecurities. I can't figure out if she's doing it on purpose. "Don't."

She ignores me. "Would you ever stop?"

I exhale. "I don't know, Margot."

"What about for him?"

"For who?" I ask stupidly.

She looks me directly in the eyes and says, "Your boyfriend. Henry."

I turn away and grab another cupcake. It's not like I didn't expect this question to some degree. I've waited and waited for Margot to make another jab at Henry and I, at his 'choice' to date me again. I'm only shocked that she waited until today to do it.

No, I want to scream at her. *Nobody will cause me to change. Nobody will dictate what I do ever again, especially not you.*

But I can't force the words out. Whether because there's some falsity to them, or because I know there'll be a rebuttal, I don't know.

Everything in my brain feels skewed right now. I can't have a thought that feels solid—they all feel half true, half false. I meant what I said when I told Henry that being here is messing with me. My emotions have never felt muddier.

After our words yesterday, after the argument that started just before I cut it off, I thought about Henry and I. About how different we are now.

He and I are opposites at this point in our lives. He creates what I steal, what I take and sell off. And even though I vowed to never take something of his again, I don't know if that really changes anything.

Because I am a problem in his way of life, no matter how you look at it. That's just the way things are.

"No," I say finally, not as confidently as I'd like. "He'd never ask me to."

"He will," Margot says, and I don't like the way it makes my heart drop. "He's going to ask. No one in their right mind would be okay with what you do."

"Margot," Mom scolds, her voice firmer than earlier. "Stop it. She cannot help that she has too much of me in her."

I give my mom a small smile. She's right, technically—she's the one who dragged Dad headfirst into her mess, though I don't think he put up too much of a fight. They were so in love, I'm not sure they would've cared if they got caught.

"I love Henry," Mom says suddenly. "Always have. He's such a sweetheart, and he's obsessed with you, Ames."

My mouth drops open a little. I try to control my expression, because logically, that shouldn't surprise me. If we were really dating, I'd probably be aware of it. But I can't stop myself from asking, "What makes you say that?"

She laughs. *Laughs.* "Honey, it's obvious—even more than it was when you two were in high school. That boy looks at you like you're art. He's mesmerized by you."

I swallow hard. Try to act normal. "Well, I guess that makes sense. I'm incredible."

Mom grins like she knows something I don't. With a sigh, she slides the last tray of cupcakes into the oven, then leans her back against the counter. She crosses her arms and studies Margot and I, eyes flicking back and forth between the two of us.

"Go get your gifts for each other," she says. "Now."

I do, obviously. I don't care how annoyed I am with my sister; when Mom says to do something, I do it.

I go to my room and grab the present I've had tucked in my closet all weekend. Margot is already in the kitchen by the time I go back downstairs, awkwardly holding her gift bag. I take it and give her mine, and the two of us don't say a word before opening them.

Hoards of tissue paper cover the actual gift. I set it all aside on the kitchen table as I dig to the bottom of the bag. There's a cardboard box inside, and a faint clinking noise anytime I make a movement. I remove it from the bag and hold onto it until I can open it with a knife, then glance up at my sister.

Margot, to my complete and utter surprise, is gazing at the handbag with the softest expression I've ever seen her wear.

"It's not much," I mumble, because it's the truth. It was the first thing I saw that I thought she might like.

"Thank you," she says, meeting my eyes. For the first time in a very long time, neither of us scowl or look away. "I love it. Really. It matches most of my clothes."

Most of her clothes are neutral, so I can see why this is the case.

I give her the faintest nod before grabbing a knife out of the block behind me and cutting the tape on my box. The clinking noise only gets louder as I rip the top, and my jaw drops open when I pull out the plastic carton inside.

Teacups.

Four teacups with saucers. They're floral—pink—with gold detailing around the rim and base.

"I love them," I say, my voice filled with more emotion than I've mustered all week. "They're perfect, Margot. Thank you. And I also just broke one of my teacups, so this is perfect timing."

She makes a noise that sounds like a laugh. "I figured."

I don't say anything after that, because this is the most civil we've been in ages. The silence isn't prolonged, though, because moments later, Dad's loud voice carries through the house.

"WE HAVE WINGS," he shouts, holding up the large plastic bag.

"Cupcakes just went in." Mom waves him over to the counter. "Bring 'em on over."

Normally I'd have my tongue hanging out of my mouth at the mention of chicken wings, but after what Mom said earlier, I can only look at Henry. At the way he's already staring at me when I glance at him.

His face isn't pleasant, though. He's upset, or angry, or sad, or *something*. I can't tell, but he isn't happy.

"We were just talking about you, Henry," Mom says, getting five plates out of the cabinet.

He chuckles, suddenly appearing behind me, and I don't realize how close he is at first. But then he slides his arms around my waist, hands flat against my stomach, and pulls me back against his chest. I hold my breath when he rests his chin on the top of my head and says, "Badmouthing me, I assume?"

I swear on everything in this life, I'm about to die.

"Obviously," I mutter, at the same time Mom says, "Nonsense!"

Dad laughs as he removes the to-go boxes from the bag. I should probably grab a box before he eats everything, but I don't exactly feel capable of moving right now.

Henry kisses my cheek before walking to the counter. I know my face is burning red, but I try to regulate my expression before even daring to look away from the ground. He hasn't so much as looked at me all day, and now *this*? He's playing at something. I've known it all along, and I let myself forget. I let my guard down.

Not anymore.

Once I'm confident in my legs' ability to move again, I grab a plate and about twenty hot wings. There's a chance I won't eat them all, but I need to distract myself from Henry, who is currently being more of a distraction than usual.

Dad turns *Happy Gilmore* on TV. Marg and I sit at the bar. Mom stands by the oven—she thinks leaving its side is bad luck for the turnout of the food—and Henry talks with her. Probably wise. I can't talk with a chicken wing shoved in my mouth anyways.

"So, you two are leaving in the morning?" Mom asks, removing her chicken off the bone with a fork. I've never understood this method. I may be somewhat dainty, but if you don't finish the meal with sauce up your nose, you're doing it wrong. "I can have Arnie scrape your windshield if you'll give us a time."

Henry shrugs and looks at me. I *do* indeed have sauce up my nose, and he looks amused at the sight. "When do you want to leave, Ames?"

"Don't care," I mumble, wiping my mouth with a napkin. "Whenever is fine, but Dad doesn't need to go outside. It's cold and his knees are bad."

"That's not nice," he says from the living room.

Mom sighs. "Yes, but it *is* true, Arnie."

He gives a little wave over the back of the couch, signaling for us to be quiet.

"I'd like these to hurry up!" Mom says, peeking into the oven. "They need to cool so we can ice them."

"We have at least two dozen on the counter," Margot tells her. "I think they'll have time to cool before we run out."

"Your dad will eat all the icing."

"Heard that," Dad says. "But that reminds me, Mel, we need to go to the car dealer this weekend. My vehicle is near shot. Might get a trade-in on the old thing."

Mom starts arguing, probably about how his vehicle will get absolutely nothing for a trade-in, but my mind is only focused on one of his words.

Dealer.

I still haven't told Meg about the card I saw on *Nautical Abyss*. It hasn't crossed my mind all week.

This is why I don't take breaks. I get used to doing nothing, and then something like this happens. I've been so focused on everything else, I forgot the one thing that might actually cause me trouble after this trip.

"Excuse me," I say, wiping my nasty fingers on a paper towel. "Nobody eat my food. I'll be right back."

"You okay?" Henry asks as I go for the stairs.

It actually gives me a moment to pause. To think. I'm *not* okay, but I don't say that. Instead, I remember that security photo of Jensen—his twin or whatever, you know—and that Henry hasn't said a word about it in days.

"Follow me," I tell him, going toward my room.

I don't look over my shoulder to see if he is, but I hear his footsteps as I walk down the hall.

39

HENRY

Amelie locks the door behind us, and it worries me slightly. "What's going on?"

"I just remembered something," she says, sitting at her desk. "Have you gotten any feedback on that security photo? The one from your apartment building?"

I shake my head. "No. Haven't gotten any word from my dad since he told me about it."

"Ask him."

I pull my phone out of my pocket and go to the closet.

Truthfully, I don't understand how he *wouldn't* have found anything yet. Surely there's a photo of this man somewhere. If it *is* Jensen, the tattoo should've been a problem by now, unless he took care to keep it hidden.

It's not like I'm gunning for him to be caught. In fact, I'm really hoping for the opposite, because I still don't believe it's him. I just want an answer.

My dad picks up on the first ring, right as I close Amelie's closet door behind me. "Henry!" He says. "So glad you've finally gotten cell service."

I wince. My whole *convention* lie slipped my mind. I doubt he still believes it, but at least he hasn't questioned me further.

"Yeah, me too. Anything new?"

"Nothing much," he says, "other than the fact that I've finally found a match to the security photo."

My stomach bottoms out, but I keep my voice nonchalant. "Oh?"

"It isn't an *exact* match," he amends, and relief tugs at my chest. "It mirrors the hand tattoo—not identically, because half his hand is pocketed, but it's the closest we've got."

"You don't have a name or face yet?"

"No. He was looking down at the ground for most of the clip. The footage is from a store security camera that I was able to get ahold of. He's holding hands with a girl for a portion, then shoves his hand in his pocket."

"You got footage from a store?" I ask. "That's random."

"Well, not really." He sighs. "The footage didn't get sent to me because of this search specifically. It got sent to me because *you* are in it."

He sends me a photo the moment he stops talking, and my mouth falls open.

It's from the night I went to Bondi's. When I spoke to Jensen and Meg on the street. His tattoo is barely visible, and his back is toward the camera, but my face is fully visible.

I can play this off. Small talk is a thing. I could've been telling him to tie his shoe, right? That happens.

"I don't recall speaking to him," I say coolly. "It was probably something quick. Maybe he dropped something, and I let him know."

"That would be plausible, if the footage didn't show you three standing there for four and a half minutes."

I give an exasperated sigh and hope it sounds annoyed rather than nervous. "I don't know what you want me to say. I don't remember this."

"You don't recall speaking to anyone on the sidewalk?"

"I talk to a lot of people." A lie. "I wouldn't remember someone specific."

"Do you remember this night, based on the clothes you were

wearing? It doesn't look like what you often wear. Much more casual. And I know you weren't at the museum, because I was."

This is where I start to panic.

I can't tell him the truth. He'll get the footage from Bondi's, and Amelie and I will be in serious trouble. I hadn't even thought about the cameras there, but I also hadn't anticipated the situation we got ourselves into.

"I was just on a walk," I say weakly.

He nearly snorts. "At ten at night? In *February*? It was snowing, Henry."

"It helps me get inspired."

That answer is horrible and untrue, and the likelihood of him believing it is slimmer than this conversation ending in my favor.

"I'm going to be honest, Henry," he says, voice cold. "I think you're lying. I think you remember exactly where you were this night."

"I *don't—*"

"I think you were meeting with Amelie Benoit."

Hearing him say her name makes my mind go blank.

"Why—why would you think that?" I ask. "That's ridiculous."

He doesn't take the bait. "Yes or no?"

I don't know what to do. Anything I say is going to dig my grave deeper, and at this point, I'm unsure of how to get myself out.

He knows. Somehow, he knows, and we go back *tomorrow*. There's no time to deal with any of this. So instead of responding, I end the call, save the photo he sent me, and block his phone number.

Not wise, not mature, and most definitely not the best option, but it's all I can think of.

With shaking hands, I exit the closet. Amelie is still sitting on her bed, typing furiously on her phone while staring at her laptop in front of her. Somehow, she looks totally focused on each individual task. I take a step closer and peek at the screen, nearly jumping back when I see one of my pieces.

Well, not *my* piece. Gail Branson's piece. A name I paint under when my dad needs more to display. But why is she looking at it? It's not popular; it hardly gets attention. If someone were going to snag one of the Gallery's pieces, I'd never think it to be this one.

"I don't know what's up with that," Amelie says, and it takes me a moment to realize she's on the phone with someone. "Is it like... obvious?"

"If it were obvious, I probably wouldn't be confused," the person on the other end of the phone says. Meg, I think. "But that can be dealt with later."

Amelie looks up at me and chews on her lip, clearly not worried about me eavesdropping. It would probably feel like a win if I weren't so focused on what my dad just said, and why my painting is on her laptop screen.

"Just be sure to keep the contact," Amelie says. "As long as you got it done, I don't care right now."

"I've got it copied," Meg returns. "It went smoothly, though, and that's all I can ask for. Until another problem shows up, I'm leaving it."

Amelie exhales. "I don't blame you, Megs. Just wanted to let you know. Nothing's open, right?"

"Right. Everything is closed now. No worries until you get back."

"I do carry those with me," Amelie says, looking back up at me. She pats the bed next to her, inviting me to sit, so I do. "I'll be back tomorrow. Just keep things under control 'til then."

"Will do. Giving Jensen your kindest regards."

"DON'T. I know he's slept in my bed."

Meg chuckles but doesn't deny the accusation. "Bye, Ames. Happy birthday. Stay out of trouble."

Amelie returns the sentiment, then hangs up the phone. She lets out a sigh and rubs her eyes, looking tired when she slumps forward. "What did you find out?"

"That piece is mine," I say, completely not registering what she's said to me. I'm staring at her computer screen instead. "Gail Branson. That's one of my aliases."

Her jaw drops. "Why didn't you *say* that when I asked?!"

"Because I think I'm under a contract to *not* say that." I shrug. "Why are you looking at it?"

Her face flushes. "Henry, I—we got an offer for that. Meg and Jen moved it the other day."

I look back at the screen, waiting for a pang of annoyance or anger or *something* to hit me, but it never does. "That's us, you know."

"What?"

"The painting." I nod toward the screen. "That's us."

She squints at the image. I can understand why she doesn't get it, but I'm telling the truth. It's based on an old photo of ours, one that her mom took the day of our school's homecoming. I remember it vividly.

This was before the actual event—we were at her house, about to leave. Amelie's foot nearly slipped out from under her on a loose rug, and I caught her around the waist before she fully fell. She was cackling when I finally got her upright, and instead of trying to walk again, she leaned into me. I settled my arms around her as she laid her head against my shoulder. I remember the feeling of her smiling against my skin; every time I saw this picture, that's all I felt.

I changed a lot, of course. The environment, the colors, things like that. But it's still us.

Maybe I should've displayed it under my name, but I wasn't due for another project yet, and I wanted to get it out there. So I foolishly let it go under an alias.

"I'm sorry, Henry," Amelie whispers, covering her mouth with her hand. "If I'd known, I would've told them no. I'm so, so sorry—"

"You would've told them no?"

A nod. "Yeah. I'm not..." She pauses, like this is painful for her to say. "We're not taking your work anymore."

"When did this get decided?"

"When you saved me at Bondi's," she says in a low voice. "That night, I made the decision."

I should be horrified at how easily I believe her words.

"I'm sorry, Henry," she says again, biting at her lip. "I'll get it back for you."

"That isn't necessary," I tell her. "It's fine. It was based on a real photo of ours, and I've still got that one."

She looks back toward the screen. Her eyes dart around the image for a few seconds before she says, "The homecoming one."

My chest constricts, solely because she remembered.

"Yeah," I murmur. "That one."

"I had that photo framed in my room. I loved it."

I bite back the smile that threatens to form on my face. "I had it in my wallet."

Amelie's face softens at that, her lips turning up into an apparent grin. She closes the laptop and sets it behind her. "Hey, did your dad have an answer?"

I drag my eyes away from her lips so I can think. "Yeah. He… found a match from the night we went to Bondi's. Outside a shop. Jensen's face wasn't in it—just the tattoo."

"Oh, that's good," she says, and then she notices the wary look on my face. "Why aren't you acting like that's good?"

I look at the ground. "Because I ran into Jensen and Meg that night. So *my* face was in it."

"Oh," she mumbles. "So your dad thinks something is up."

"He accused me of meeting with you."

A divot appears between her brows, and she stares at the wall in front of us, contemplating. "I'll figure something out."

"It's not your problem to deal with."

"No, it kind of is." She gives a dry laugh. "But I'm not worrying about it until tomorrow. Let's enjoy our last day of peace, okay? I'm going to eat now."

She stands, and I follow. Neither of us say anything until we're back downstairs, where Amelie *loudly* explains that she had a phone call to make and needed my input.

40
____

AMELIE

I told Henry that I'm not worrying about anything, and that was a lie.

It's three in the morning, and I haven't slept a wink. I haven't felt this riled up since being here, and honestly, the adrenaline is nice. It's familiar. I'd probably be grateful for it, if I *wanted* to be awake right now.

But I don't. So I'm in the attic right now, digging through boxes to find Mom and Dad's old journals just for something to do.

I don't really know why it was my first idea. These notebooks have been stashed up here for ages—I've only dug through here once, and that was how I found out the truth about my parents' past. Reading them now sounds like a small bit of comfort, so I'm hoping they'll be easy to find.

However, it would be a lot easier if my parents weren't hoarders.

There are boxes on boxes in this attic. Our house in the city doesn't have as much space, so we just store everything here. It smells like cardboard and dust and pine, and the chances that I'll sneeze are *extremely* high. I'm attempting to not do that, given that everyone else is asleep. Dad will come up here with a bat and I'll have a bruise on my forehead tomorrow.

I tug a blanket off a pile of boxes and start rifling through them. I'm vaguely aware that I could get bitten by a spider or rat up here, but I don't really care. My brain is wide awake, and I've already watched *Pride and Prejudice* twice tonight. There is literally nowhere else to go.

As I'm trying to move a shoe box full of ornaments, I manage to trip over a crate of Margot's old paints and slam into the floor at full force. My knees sting as I get back into a sitting position, and I frantically check over the ornaments to make sure none are cracked. Only one is chipped, but I tuck that one to the bottom. To be fair, there should've been a lid on the box.

I stay on the ground as I claw through another pile of things. Most of our storage is taped-up shoeboxes, so I set them aside, not at all worried about getting them open. The sealed ones are likely photos or mementos—I can't see my parents hiding their old journals.

I drag a normal shoebox into my lap and flip the lid off, and instantly, my throat tightens with an emotion I can't quite identify.

I should've recognized it from the outside.

I shouldn't have opened this.

Photos. All the photos I had of Henry and I. I could've *sworn* I burned these or something, but maybe I never made it that far. Maybe I set the box outside my door, and Mom brought them here so I wouldn't have to see them again.

The picture on top is the very one that Henry and I were talking about yesterday. The one he based *Lover of Mine* on. It feels so much like a sick joke that I actually start to laugh.

Suddenly, I'm angrier at him than anyone else.

I don't understand it. I don't understand how he can act like he did nothing to me. Like it was *my* fault. Him having the gall to ask what happened is ridiculous enough on its own, but the fact that he sounded genuine is even worse.

I hate that I'm still thinking about it. That it's all I've thought about for a good while.

"What are you doing?" I hear from the doorway, and I scramble to my feet at the sound.

Henry is standing near the doorframe, studying me with a frown and a wrinkle between his brows. I'm guessing that he heard me slam into the ground, but the snag on my pants is my very last priority right now.

"I fell," I say flatly. "What do you want?"

"I just—I came to check on you." His face is flushed, and I know it's not the truth. I don't think he's even been asleep. He's wearing pajamas—a gray shirt with plaid paints—but his face isn't remotely clouded with sleep like one would expect. He looks almost as bothered as I feel. "Are you—"

"Fine, yes. You can go now." I turn back to the photo box on the ground and kick it aside, praying that he doesn't see it. He looks a lot more concerned with my state than anything in this attic, and I need him to stay that way.

I don't need him to know how angry I am. I'm tired of him affecting me.

"Amelie," Henry says, voice rough, and I close my eyes. "I want to talk to you."

"*No—*"

"Yes."

I clench my jaw and turn around to see that he's already moved closer. He's no further than a foot away now, and under the dim light of the flickering bulb, I can see how quickly his chest is rising and falling. "*Please*, Amelie."

I don't know what possesses me to do so, but instead of responding, I reach down into Margot's old box of paints. My hands are trembling as I grab a bottle of indigo blue, squeeze some into my palm, and smear it down the side of Henry's neck.

He doesn't exactly look thrilled.

"Why," he asks, eyes closed.

I give the slightest shrug. "For fun."

"Amelie, I'm serious—"

"Me too." I hand him the bottle and grab another for myself. Bright red, which I'm aware is going to stain, but I don't have it in me to care. "Fight back."

He looks down at the tube in his hand, then at me, then at the tube once more. Slowly, hesitantly, he flips the cap off. I hold my breath as he squeezes some onto his hand. "This is your most pointless idea yet."

I ignore him. "You want to talk. We can talk."

"I'd prefer a genuine conversation."

"This is close enough." I don't know why I'm pushing this. I'm so intent on *not* getting into a full-blown argument with him tonight, which will probably happen if we try to talk through things, but this solution is hardly better. "Come on. It's not that big of a deal. Just—"

He smears paint down the side of my cheek, looking thoroughly annoyed at the situation.

Good. Me too.

"You like this shirt, don't you?" He mumbles, dragging paint over my collarbone. The color runs right over the strap of my tank top, pushing the fabric off my shoulder.

"Yes," I say hoarsely, fixing my shirt. "Yes, it's my favorite."

Satisfaction flashes across his face for a moment. He holds my gaze as he says, "I'll buy you another. Now let's talk."

I scoff and drag paint over his nose. He exhales, and I feel his breath against my palm. "You don't get to just *decide* when we talk, Henry. You don't make that decision." I go to trail paint over his jaw, but he grabs my wrist and holds it to my side. So I keep talking. "If I had it my way, this would've been dealt with years ago. I didn't get to talk about it. I didn't get to scream at you and tell you how I felt."

"Scream at me, then." His voice is slightly louder than normal. "Yell at me. Be as angry as you want, but do *not* ignore me. Don't give me your silence. That's never what I want from you. But *this*, Amelie—" He motions to his face, at the paint I've smeared over his skin. "—isn't doing anything. Tell me what's wrong."

My lips part, and I feel my heart in my throat. "Okay."

"Okay." He nods. "Tell me why you're so angry."

"Tell you *why*?" I bark a laugh, drop the tube of paint in my hand. "Is it really so much of a secret, Henry? You left me. The only person that I never thought I'd lose forgot about me, and he didn't even seem sorry about it."

"No," he whispers. "*No,* Amelie. I didn't—"

"And now you're back." I cut him off, because if I'm talking, I can ignore the stinging in my eyes. "You're back, and you're using me, and as soon as my help means nothing to you, you'll leave again. And I'm *tired,* Henry. I'm so tired of you looking at me like I mean something to you. So stop it. Stop with the games and the lies. The second we're home, the second I get your piece, this is over."

"No." His voice is firm again. "Listen to me, Amelie."

I shake my head. "I said *stop*—"

"*Listen to me.*"

I snap my mouth shut, solely at the emotion that floods his voice.

"I didn't leave you. I didn't forget about you."

"You ignored my calls."

"*You* ignored mine!"

My face turns hot. He's lying. After all of this, after everything we've done, he lies to me.

"I called you," he says again, and I squeeze my eyes shut. "And there wasn't a time that you answered. I wrote you *letters*—"

"You what?"

"I wrote to you!" His face is red now, flushed with emotion. "You never wrote me back. *You* are the one who ended things, Amelie. *You* are the one who left *me.*"

"Stop," I whisper.

"It's the truth. You ended things. You ignored me."

"You're a liar."

"*Why* would I lie to you?" He isn't yelling. His voice is filled with frustration, anger, but he still isn't yelling. "I *loved* you, Amelie. Do you understand what it did to me, waiting every day for your response? Do you know how I felt when it never came?"

"Yes!" I'm shouting now, not at all worried about my family asleep downstairs. "Because I felt the same thing. You broke me. You hurt me then, and you're hurting me now."

Henry's chest is heaving. He takes a few steps back and nearly falls into a cardboard box, just like I did. I turn away and press my fingers into my eyes, disgusted with the fact that I'm crying. I should've let my tears out alone. I shouldn't have to relive this in front of him.

"Leave," I say through a shuddering breath. "*Leave*, Henry—"

"My letters," he whispers.

I laugh dryly. "Yeah, I know. You already tried—"

"Amelie." His voice is heady. Confusing. I open my eyes and turn back to him, only to find him knelt on the ground in front of the cardboard box.

He's holding a stack of envelopes. All with the addresses marked out in black ink.

"What is that?" I whisper, my stomach turning. "Henry, what—"

"These are my letters."

41

HENRY

My letters.

The letters that I wrote to Amelie. The ones she's claiming to have never seen. They're sitting in her parent's dusty attic, staring back and laughing in my face. "Amelie, these are *my letters*."

"No," she rasps. "I don't believe you."

Frustration washes over me, more at the situation than at Amelie's disbelief. I don't know what more I can do to convince her when the proof is right in front of us.

I know these envelopes. I know that I addressed each of these directly to her house and waited months for a reply. I know that it's *my* handwriting covered by scribbled ink, blacked out in an attempt to...

To *what*? Why would someone do this?

"Here." I pick one up and hold it out to her. "Open it."

She stares at it like it's poisonous. "No."

"Take it," I urge, my voice rising the slightest bit. "Please."

With a shuddered breath, Amelie takes it and rips open the top. Carefully, she removes the sheet of paper, holding it up so she can read it under the bulb. Her eyes trail quickly over the page, and the further down they go, the more she chews on her bottom lip. I watch the tears build against her lashes, watch her fingers tighten on the page until it wrinkles.

By the time she reaches the end, full tears are rolling down her face.

"I wrote these to you," I whisper, motioning to the box in front of me. "All of them. And you—you *accused* me—"

"I didn't know about them," she argues, rubbing her eyes. "I've never—Henry, I've *never* seen those before. But why did you stop calling if you sent these?"

I exhale. "I didn't. I called you every day until I finally assumed you were trying to give me a hint. You never—"

"Stop. Just—stop." Amelie's skin is fully flushed now. "You could've tried my family's phones if you were so desperate. When I didn't answer, they might've."

I laugh dryly. "What good would that have done? For all I knew, my luck would've been worse with them." I have the urge to point out that she didn't try *my* family, either. Liz would have answered her in seconds, and she had to have known that.

"This...no." Amelie starts pacing, gnawing on her thumbnail in the process. "This doesn't explain anything. I'm not lying, and you *claim* to not be lying, so what's the reason? Why did our calls just stop? *Why*—" She kneels down in front of the box and knocks into it with her elbow. "—didn't I get these?"

I stare at the envelopes. "I don't know about the calls, but I'm going to assume that someone in your family didn't want you to receive these."

She closes her eyes as the words leave my mouth, and guilt washes over me. It's an accusation that I can't take back, but what other explanation is there? Why else would they be hidden with both our names blacked out? It's not as though this was accidental, or even meant to be a temporary thing. Each one is sealed. Each one is defaced.

Amelie exhales a shaky breath, and I watch another tear skate down her cheek. It rolls down her neck and soaks into the paint-covered strap of her shirt. She doesn't seem to care that she's crying, but I do. The sight of her in tears over something that should never have even happened is enough to gut me.

Despite myself, I lift my hand and brush my fingers under her eyes, trying to dry her tears. She doesn't allow me to, though; she moves her head away from me, ridding her skin from my touch, and it makes my throat tighten. I drop my arm and turn away from her, and when she covers her face with her hands, I can finally identify the feeling in my chest.

Anger.

I've never felt such a clear, sharp sense of indignation before.

Someone ruined Amelie and I. Purposefully tore us apart. Every day of these past four years, I've wondered what I did wrong. I've wondered what I could've done differently. I've blamed myself, regardless of how much I tried to blame Amelie.

But it wasn't us. None of it was our fault.

I lift another envelope out of the box, but before I can even tear the edge, Amelie takes it from me. Within a second, she's got the letter in her lap, chest heaving as she skims its contents. I don't even remember what these letters hold, and if I'm honest, I don't care to know. Part of me is tempted to tell her to stop reading them, to ignore anything I said, but I can't. It's her right to see what's inside.

"I should've tried harder." I close my eyes, hardly shocked by the throbbing behind my temples. "I should've found you when I came back, or—"

"You still wanted me?"

I open my eyes. Confusion washes over me as I realize that she's truly asking. She's lived these past years thinking that I didn't want her. Thinking that I forgot her and took the first chance I had to leave.

"Yes," I breathe. "I'm sorry that was ever in question."

Amelie takes a deep breath and pushes her hair behind her ears. Her eyes are red and swollen, lips bloody from how much she's torn at the skin. She gets to her feet and tosses the envelope back into the box before leaving the attic, not sparing me another glance as she does.

42

———

AMELIE

"Amelie. Up."

I'm going to disembowel whoever is talking to me.

I haven't figured out who it is yet because my vision isn't working. My eyes are probably swollen shut from how much I cried before bed, and on top of that, I hardly slept after everything that happened.

Just the thought of last night makes my headache come back.

"Leave before I hit you," I murmur, rolling over so my face is buried in my pillow.

The intruder sighs and pulls my blankets off me, and I practically hiss. "Come on."

Oh. It's Margot. That's her military officer voice. If I decline again, she'll drag me out of bed by my toes.

"I'm not in the mood," I mumble. "I'm tired."

"Don't care. We're going to Brenn's."

Oddly enough, that's the part of this that piques my interest. "Why?"

"Because I want breakfast."

"What time is it?"

"Seven, I think." She shrugs. "You're leaving today, right? We need to go early."

"It'll be fine." I wrap my sheet around my shoulders like a cape. "We can just—"

"We're going now," Margot says calmly. "Come on. I'd like to talk to you."

I roll my eyes. "You can't just spring this on me at six—"

"Seven," she repeats. "You'll survive. Let's go."

I don't find it likely, but since there's basically no chance of her backing down, I get out of bed.

I stumble to the bathroom and brush my teeth, nearly jolting when I catch sight of myself in the mirror. My eyes are puffy, and my face is still red. Even my lips look like they went through a meat grinder.

Margot is sitting in my window seat when I get back to my room. She stays completely silent as I lower myself into my desk chair, and I stare at her, gauging how 'ready' I need to get. She looks more put together than I will—her hair is done, and she's even wearing eyeliner. That won't be the case for me; I don't attempt the Dark Arts before ten in the morning.

I put on a minimal amount of makeup and the same red lip as always, hoping it'll cover up the dried blood and dead skin. I throw on a pair of jeans and a sweater, then shove my feet into some fleece-lined boots.

Margot is wearing a blazer. I do not own a blazer.

"Let's go," I say, grabbing my purse. "Before Mom and Dad wake up."

"That was my goal." Margot steps out of my room before I can. I trip over a high heel as I follow, and I hear her sigh from down the hall.

Margot drives and I control the music. This has always been our routine, mainly because I detest driving. I've driven us once, and it was a...negative experience. Margot was loopy from the dentist, and Mom and Dad couldn't get us home, so it had to be me. Let's just say that she might've been better behind the wheel on drugs than I was sober.

I order my usual stack of pancakes when we sit at the booth. Marg gets French toast and eggs on the side, then orders two coffees with sugar and cream for us. We sit in an awkward bit of silence for a few minutes until Margot says, "I'm sorry."

Which was honestly the last thing I expected to leave her mouth.

I stir a pack of sugar into my coffee as I plan my words. "How hard was that for you to say?"

"Amelie."

"Alright, I'm sorry." I set the spoon aside on a napkin. "But what makes you say that? Is it because I'm leaving?"

She shakes her head. "No. I just...I've never understood, Amelie. You could've gone to the academy with Henry. Maybe you'd even be working alongside him now. You could've had what you wanted."

"I eventually wanted something different," I argue.

"But *why*? What spurred that decision?"

I wring my hands together under the table. I don't want her to know the real reason, but I guess I have to tell her at some point. My options have run out. Talking around this can only serve me for so long.

"You're too perfect," I say casually, taking a sip of the too-hot coffee to give myself a moment to think. "You're better than me, and you know it."

"What are you *talking* about?"

"You were better at everything, Margot. Anything we did together, you'd best me. When I found out you applied for art school, I just couldn't do it anymore." I glance out the window. "I knew I'd always be trying to measure up to you. Trying to beat you, even in slight, knowing that I couldn't."

Her face is blank, and I presume that mine is, too. "I don't understand."

"I wanted to be *good*, Margot, and I finally found something. I knew you'd never attempt it, so you couldn't beat me."

"Well, you are good at it," she says, almost flatly. "*Too* good at it."

I scoff. "You wouldn't know."

Margot crosses her arms on the table, not responding to that statement. Her gaze lands on the *NO CELL PHONES* sign to our right, though I know she isn't paying attention to anything in here. She's taking time to think.

"That's why you stopped talking to me?" Margot asks.

I keep quiet because I don't want to say *yes*. I don't want to say that she unknowingly made me feel so horrible about myself that I wanted nothing to do with her. Despite the fact that I made it her fault, it wasn't, not really.

"People love you," she says when I don't respond.

I blink at her. "What?"

"People love you. They don't like me."

I tip my head. "That isn't true. You have friends."

"I'm not talking about friends." Margot folds a napkin into a tiny square to busy her hands. "You know the reason I tried so hard at everything?"

She looks at me, awaiting a response. I just shake my head.

"I tried because that's all I had. Good grades and medals were it for me, Amelie. But *you* actually had people that ached to be around you. You made people feel wanted, and I had a slight prayer of graduating with honors. Only one of those really mattered."

Hearing this is almost like hearing a foreign language. It doesn't add up. I never saw it this way; never considered that this was an option. I always saw Margot as someone people wanted to be around. People looked at *her*. People talked about *her*.

"I know what you're thinking," she says, "and you're wrong."

Well then.

She notes my fallen expression and continues talking. "People didn't want to be around me. People either worshiped me academically or tore me down behind my back. It was never what you thought. And I'm not trying to play the victim. I'm saying this so you know that I was no different."

I sigh. "Why didn't you tell me any of this?"

"Why didn't you tell *me*?" She asks, and for the first time in a very long time, her voice holds something other than stiffness or hostility.

She sounds hurt.

"I didn't think you'd care," I say quietly, and her frown deepens. "And I don't mean that as anything toward you. I just mean that it seemed minimal to me. It wasn't your problem."

She exhales. "We should've just talked more."

I nod slowly. "I think that would've fixed a lot."

Margot grabs a pack of sugar and stirs it into her coffee, taking a sip to find it still bitter. She adds another, then looks up at me with narrowed eyes. "I don't like this topic anymore."

"Me either," I agree, feeling mildly squeamish. This topic is horribly alien to us. We can't be fully stitched up over a cup of coffee. "Talk about something else."

She shakes her head. "You first. Tell me all this Henry stuff. I heard some racket in the attic last night, and it sounded like you guys."

My stomach twists into knots again. I'm hoping that this isn't going to happen every time I hear his name, because it's already getting old. I need to relax. "What did you hear? Talking?"

"Muffled noise." She shrugs. "I went up this morning to find it strangely pristine, but there was paint on the floor."

She eyes me, but I'm just trying to figure out how on earth *that* attic could look pristine. Henry straightened up after I left, I guess. A shame he didn't clean up the paint as well.

"That's my fault," I mumble, hoping my face isn't as red as it feels. "Knocked it over and forgot to clean it up."

She hums. "Must be why there's paint on your collarbone."

I gape. "Okay, well—"

"I'm not saying anything." She raises her hands innocently. "Do what you want."

"It wasn't like *that*." It was maybe the furthest thing from whatever she's thinking. "He came upstairs because I tripped, and he heard it. That was it. Not a worry for you." I take a breath and contemplate my next words, wondering if it's foolish to say what I want. "I did find something else, though."

She looks up. "Oh?"

"Yeah. Letters."

"Letters?"

"From Henry." I nod. "A whole box of them. There were, like, at least twenty, maybe more. Someone blacked out his address on each one."

Margot's jaw drops a little. "So you two finally talked, then?"

"About...?"

"What happened after high school. He told me that you two never discussed it."

I blink in disbelief. "When did that happen?"

"We briefly talked the other day. It was unimportant. But what did you find out?"

I swallow. "Well, apparently, he wrote me letters for a little while after our contact stopped. I never got a single one because someone intercepted them. I guess...I guess it had to have been Mom and Dad."

Just saying it aloud makes me feel wicked, but it's genuinely the only thing I can think of. Margot was at school, as far as I know, and despite our feud, I can't see her caring enough to do anything like this.

"I'm going to ask them this morning," I add, then shake my head. "I'm livid, Margot. That's *years* that he and I lost."

She sinks back into the booth. "What about the calls?"

"He says he never got any of mine, and I never answered any of his." I shrug. "It's weird, but...I believe him."

The admission is more to myself than Margot, but it makes my skin crawl all the same. I *do* believe him, I think. That's what's so terrifying to me. The desperation he showed wasn't fake. Neither was the anger—not at *me*, but at what happened.

I've always known that he doesn't play games. This isn't any different.

"His parents, maybe," Margot says, dragging me back to our conversation. "On the calls."

I raise a brow. "You think they were in cahoots with ours? Because I don't think they've ever spoken."

"No, not at all. But Mom and Dad can barely work their own phones, so I can't see them blocking calls from yours."

I take another sip of my coffee, just to realize that I've drained the cup. I don't remember drinking *any,* but I've been a little preoccupied. "If it's true, I'm mad at them. Really. I don't understand it. Henry never did a wrong thing to anyone, and they've seemed to adore him this whole time. Are they putting on?"

"I mean, if you really think about it..." Margot's voice trails off, and she zones out on a fork.

"No." I snap my fingers. "Focus. What?"

She shrugs. "Mom and Dad were art thieves, and Henry's dad owns an art museum. Something could be there."

"*Like*?!"

"I don't know! A subtle hatred or something."

I'm still not convinced our parents have even met. "You'd think they would've said something once I took their clients, though."

"No. It would've put you closer to figuring out what they did."

"I probably wouldn't have thought about it. I'm not that deductive."

Margot laughs at the obvious lie. I overanalyze most things, and now, I'm extremely irritated that I didn't look further into this. I shouldn't have just accepted all of it. I should've looked for answers, rather than being bitter and praying on Henry's downfall for four years. Present Day Amelie would have driven to the academy, screamed at him, and ripped his lashes out of his pretty eyes.

But you know. Hindsight and all that.

"It's just a lot," I murmur, scratching at my neck. "I have no idea what's going to happen when I get back, and now I have to deal with *this*—"

"What do you mean?" Margot asks, sounding genuinely curious. "What's going on when you get back? Is it something with work?"

"It's—" I start, then instantly shut my mouth. I forget that she doesn't know everything. She's got no idea that this whole thing started with Henry blackmailing me. She doesn't know about Roman. She doesn't know anything because I haven't *told* her anything. "It's nothing," I say. "Just in general."

She sighs. "Doesn't this job give you anxiety?"

"I prefer the term *adrenaline rush*."

"Most people just bungee jump."

"I'm bored, not suicidal."

She laughs, then sets her mug aside. Hers is empty, too, and I'm starting to wonder where our waitress is. "I really am sorry, Amelie," she says quietly. "For all of it."

"I'm sorry, too," I tell her.

We don't speak again until it's time to pay the bill.

43
─────

HENRY

I've been packing my suitcase for half an hour, still not brave enough to go into the living area.

I'm not sure why I'm hesitant. Maybe because of the letters, or because I don't know how Amelie is going to react to seeing me. I don't even know how *I'll* react to seeing her. We're about to be stuck in a vehicle for two hours, and I can hardly think about her without feeling crazy.

So I take my time gathering my things. It gives me some dose of comfort, knowing that nothing will be set in motion until I step out into the hallway. As long as I stay behind this door, things won't change. I can pretend that last night didn't happen the way it did. I can believe that everything is going to be fine.

It isn't close to the truth, but I let myself believe it anyway.

When the clock strikes 8:30, I hear the front door open and close. I release a breath and zip up my bag, forcing myself into the hallway.

Amelie is taking her coat off when I reach the living room, and I'm shocked to find Margot alongside her, doing the same. The two look strangely friendly this morning, in that, neither look as homicidal as usual.

Until Amelie's eyes land on me. Then it's a different story.

I can't even decipher the emotion that rests in her stare. It's somewhere between sadness and anger, but those can co-exist, so I give up trying to pick out which one. She looks away without saying anything, so I keep my mouth shut, too.

I've never dreaded anything more than I'm dreading the ride back home.

"Mom? Dad?" Amelie calls up the stairs, banging her fist on the banister twice. "Downstairs, please."

Her tone is so stoic that it takes me a minute to figure out what's going on. I don't connect the dots, not until she glances at me over her shoulder and shakes her head once.

She's going to ask them about the letters.

"One second, pumpkin," Arnie calls back, clearly not picking up on the hostility in Amelie's voice. Maybe it's not as obvious as I think—maybe I'm just used to being on the receiving end of it.

Amelie's parents come down the stairs and stop directly in front of her. They're both smiling until they look at her face. I can't even see her expression, but I know it's negative, given that the reaction was instantaneous.

"Sit down," Amelie says quietly, motioning to the couch. "We need to talk."

Arnie seems confused out of his mind, but Melinda looks terrified.

Both of them sit down and eye Amelie curiously. I stand near the corner of the rug, trying to stay out of this, but I still want to hear. I still want to *know*. I think I have that right; it's not as though this doesn't involve me.

"I found the letters in the attic," Amelie says, wasting no time at all. "You guys hid them there, right? Four years ago, before I could read any of them. *Why?*"

Melinda frowns, but Arnie laughs. "Pumpkin, why would you—"

"*Please* don't lie to me," she says. "It had to have been you guys. I just want to know why, because I don't appreciate what time was taken from me." She takes a deep breath. "Please. Just tell me."

Melinda glances at Arnie, and there's something pleading in her gaze. He doesn't seem to read it well, because he says, "Yes. We put them there."

His wife sighs and drops her head into her hands.

"Why?" Amelie asks again. Her voice is quiet, almost childlike. "I don't understand. What did Henry do to you?"

"Nothing," Melinda says, looking at me. "You did nothing, honey. But your father did."

My father.

Of course.

"What do you mean?" I ask, stepping forward. "What did he do?"

Amelie sits down on the edge of the coffee table, and I join. Obviously, I knew that someone in her family hid the letters, but I never thought it had to do with my dad. I really assumed that I did something to provoke it. Maybe they thought I chose school over Amelie, or they didn't trust me with her any longer.

But my *dad*?

I mean, I get it. But not really.

"You're going to find out a lot of things through this conversation, Henry," Arnie says, leaning back into the couch cushions. He's more nonchalant about this than Melinda is. "Many things that you could get us in trouble over."

"I won't," I say, a little prematurely, but I'm so curious that I'd really agree to anything right now.

Melinda exhales and looks at me. "I don't know how much Amelie has told you, but back in the day, Arnold and I were art thieves, too. We ran with most of Amelie's clients; she got lots of them from us."

"I got some on my own," Amelie mumbles, looking simultaneously proud and self-conscious at the admission. "But anyways. Keep talking."

"Well, we had a rival," her mom continues. "Back in...lord, Arnie, what was that? The nineties?"

"At least," Arnie responds. "Year of ninety-three, I think."

She nods, clasping her hands together. "Right. See, Henry, that rival...that was Roman."

I blink, not fully understanding. How could my dad be their rival? Back then, his museum was still at its beginning. Or so he's said; it's not as though I saw it myself. But lying over this doesn't make any sense.

Unless Amelie's parents specifically targeted his museum, and he made it his goal to put them away. That would make sense as to why he's always hated Amelie.

"So, what, this was like a cat-and-mouse thing?" Amelie asks, voicing my thoughts. "You took from him, and he retaliated?"

Melinda shakes her head once. "No, honey. Roman was a thief too."

And suddenly, nothing makes sense.

"You're not serious," Amelie says, at the same time I say, "That doesn't add up."

"It was a back-and-forth deal," Arnie says, sounding mildly exasperated. I'd guess that delving back into his past wasn't on his agenda for the day. "We met the man over a poker game. It's one of the most ridiculous stories I've got."

"I'll tell it, then." Melinda rolls her eyes. "Yes, we met Roman at a poker game. That was the only reason he knew our names or faces. This was back when casinos were fun, mind you. Anyways, Arnie and I had a job later that night. Roman happened to have a job at the *same* museum, stealing a painting displayed directly across from ours.

"Him and I simply made eye contact. Didn't say a word. He went on with his work, and us with ours. Now, your father and I had a very bad habit of transporting our pieces the next day. We'd leave our van parked out back with the piece stashed in it; that way, it could look like it was being transported *to* the museum if anything went wrong. But the next day, when we went to move this piece, it was gone."

"How do you know it was him?" I ask.

"He took it from you?" Amelie asks simultaneously.

Melinda blinks. "Okay. Amelie first. Yes, he took it. Quite easily, I assume."

"What were his patterns?" She presses. "Calling card?"

"Calling card..." Melinda mumbles. "I can hardly remember it. Arnie?"

"His calling card was...*cards*," he says. "He left playing cards around, right? Aces, I think."

Melinda nods vigorously. "That's it. Which brings us to Henry's question: *that's* how we knew it was him. Or, assumed, anyways. The cards told too much. Our signature was much less obvious, though we didn't start that until years later."

"What's your signature?" I ask quietly.

"Bandit masks," Amelie mumbles, looking at her parents. "That's it, right? You were the Bandits. You never called it by name in your journals, but that must've been you. I'm willing to bet you and Roman's little chase got the rates up."

"They gave us a *name*?" Melinda looks shocked as she turns to Arnie. "Well, would you look at that? I never would've guessed."

Amelie mutters something under her breath, but I stay silent. I'm trying to keep this information in my mind while simultaneously trying to figure out why it matters. That was over thirty years ago—what did it have to do with Amelie and I?

Perhaps my father didn't want his secret spilled, because at that point, he was trying to be the good guy.

"I don't understand how you've managed to act like saints all week, as if you didn't do this." Amelie says flatly. "I get that you don't like Roman, but that didn't give you any right to break Henry and I apart. It was *your* past. Not ours." She shakes her head. Cracks her knuckles. "I loved him. Don't you realize what that did to me?"

"It just couldn't happen, Amelie," Melinda whispers, having the decency to look ashamed. "Roman would've—"

"Roman would've done *nothing* to me." Amelie cuts her off. "I wouldn't have let him."

Melinda snaps her mouth shut and turns to Arnie. He sighs,

but finally sits forward and chimes in. "We did it to protect you," he says. "We never meant for it to hurt you, pumpkin. You were so resilient. We thought it would be another thing to roll off your back. It was never with ill intent."

"I believe you," Amelie says quietly. "I do. But I can't forgive you in an instant, and you know that."

The two of them nod in unison, like they expected the response from her. I take the rare moment of silence to ask my one and only question.

"Did you stop our calls, too? From Amelie's phone?"

At this, Melinda's face twists into confusion. "You can stop calls?"

Amelie makes a noise that sounds like a strangled laugh, and I take that as an answer.

The letters were her parents' doing, but the calls were someone else's. That *someone* just happened to have the same idea at the same time.

It's not exactly hard to guess who.

"We have to go now," Amelie says, standing abruptly from the coffee table. I stand as well, and her parents do the same. "I've got things to handle."

Melinda nods, her mouth still pulled into a slight frown. The expression wavers slightly when Amelie steps forward and hugs her. "I'm sorry, baby," Melinda whispers, squeezing her arm once before she steps away. "I really am. And I'm sorry to you, too, Henry."

I just nod, because it's not okay, but also, it doesn't seem like they were fully at fault.

Amelie and I wordlessly get our suitcases and work on getting out of the house. We say a final round of goodbyes on the porch and stumble out to the car, staying quiet until the engine roars to life. Arnie *did* scrape my windshield this morning—I wish I had thanked him for it, but I wasn't aware. Amelie instantly turns on music and keeps her eyes pointed out the windshield, chewing on her lips as I put the car in drive.

"You alright?" I ask her, my voice low.

She gives a nod, eyes slowly pulling away from the road but never coming to me. "Yeah. I'm good."

I can see the gears turning in her mind, sifting through every aspect of this mess, but only one thought pops into mine.

I hope my dad knows exactly what he's gotten himself into.

44

———

AMELIE

Henry and I are back to the city before either of us dare to speak.

The silence was lovely while it lasted, though somewhat destructive. I've twisted the ring on my finger so many times that I've nearly calloused my thumb against the jewel. Mom got Margot and I matching amethyst rings for our birthday, and it's absolutely lovely. It doesn't deserve this abuse, but it works as a distraction.

All I've thought about since we left the cabin is the fact that Roman is The Dealer. I *saw* an ace in *Nautical Abyss,* and it was in place of Henry's *Ophelia.* Roman being behind it all is the only explanation, and whether I like it or not, Henry has the right to know that.

"I have to tell you something," I blurt, leaning forward to turn the radio down.

Henry looks back and forth from me to the radio, clearly aware that this is a serious matter. And it is—that fact is only heightened because I interrupted Avril Lavigne.

"This worries me," he says.

"Maybe it should," I admit, "but it needs to be said."

He doesn't say anything to that, so I just keep talking. "So, you remember Bondi's. When we went for the *Ophelia* but ended up with *Nautical Abyss*?"

"Yes. Remember it well."

"Okay. Well, the next day, when we..." I wave a hand around, rather than saying '*When I sold off your work*', "I caught sight of a playing card. An ace. It was tucked into the edge of the canvas."

He blows out a breath. "And that was my dad's signature."

"Yes," I say quietly. "I think...Henry, I think he did it to bait me. He must've assumed I knew about his signature. I think he's behind all of this, and he probably knows we're working together."

His hands tighten on the wheel. "I should never have done this. I shouldn't have involved you, or tried to outsmart him, or—"

"He didn't give you much of a choice," I remind, cutting him off. "And I'm not saying it's the case one way or another. I'm only saying...it adds up."

Sort of. None of this *really* adds up on a logical scale, but on the side of details...

I don't believe in coincidences.

"Would it shock you?" Henry asks, looking over at me. I meet his eyes for a split second before he faces forward again. "Would you be surprised?"

I want to say no, but I don't.

"I'll figure it out," he continues, muttering the words under his breath. "I think I need to talk to him alone. Maybe he'll admit to it if it's just me—he doesn't think I can do anything about it anyways, and I really can't. But he claims to need my work for the auction. If he *has* it, then why is he doing this?"

"I don't know," I say, even though I have my guesses. "Are you going to pull your work from the museum after all this?"

The question seems to stump him. He taps his fingers on the wheel and chews at his cheeks. It's a few seconds before he says, "It depends wholly on how he reacts. What his reasoning is for this whole thing. I know he's going to lie to me—I'm not so naïve as to expect the truth. But I refuse for this to be something he can lord over my family." He exhales and shakes his head. "I don't even understand what he has to gain from this."

"The opportunity to catch me," I say quietly, wringing my hands in my lap. "That's it."

And it's the truth, I think. That's all he can possibly get out of this. My parents couldn't care less about this git anymore, so it isn't that. Besides, these problems are mine and Henry's. Not theirs.

It's never been about them. It's been about *me* this whole time.

Henry looks at me with a solemn face, one I haven't seen him wear since before we came to the cabin. He's thinking through my theory. Trying to figure out how plausible it is. And, if I know him at all like I think I do, he's still beating himself up for involving me. For getting me right where his dad wants me.

But that doesn't matter to me. I can easily deal with *that* part of things.

"What are you going to do when we get back?" Henry asks, breaking the silence.

I genuinely haven't thought about that at all.

I always knew we'd split up when we got back. We'd find his *Ophelia* and move on. Do our separate things and live our separate lives. I'd practically banked on that detail before this past week. But now, I seem to have lost the plan I had stashed in the back of my mind. Going back and finishing off my work with Henry doesn't feel as simple now.

"Tell Jen and Meg everything, I guess," I say casually. "I don't know. I guess that's all I can do. They'll be kind of thrilled with this new information."

"I'm sure," Henry says, with no sarcasm in his voice. "It'll probably give them a sense of relief."

I shrug. "Probably. I doubt they've given it much thought since I left."

"Do they leave it all up to you?"

"The details, yeah. But I like it that way. If something goes wrong, it's on me. There's rarely an argument about fault."

"You *prefer* that?"

"To arguing? Absolutely. I don't want there to be a rift. Though there normally is, given that Jensen and Meg can't keep their heads out of their rears for a week straight."

He laughs at that. I close my eyes against the sound, wishing that I felt a fraction as relaxed as he's pretending to be. I can't shake the feeling of dread in my stomach.

Henry accusing his dad of something that I planted in his mind is a terrifying idea. I don't know anything about Roman personally, which means I have no idea how he reacts to things like this. What if it goes poorly? What if something bad happens?

I want to be there to fix things, but I don't get to do that.

On top of those worries, there's Henry. His general existence has sent me into a spiral for the past week. I've tried my best to ignore what happened last night, to focus on the problems in front of me, but it's difficult. Almost impossible.

I want to talk about it. Now that we know the truth, I want to know what's going through his mind. What he's feeling. I want to know what I'm going to do about *my* feelings, in the event that he doesn't reciprocate them anymore.

It wouldn't be a shock. Not after the things I said to him in the attic, the things I've done against him.

I'm not an easy person to be around. Nothing I do is done quietly. My presence is loud, and at times, suffocating. I've never tried to hide that, and Henry never made me feel like I had to.

But Henry isn't like that. He's quiet. Tempered, but in a good way. He rarely acts without thought, and he knows the consequences of his actions. Being in his presence, I've found, is even more comforting than it once was.

Or, it usually is. Not so much when I'm wanting to crawl out of my skin.

I roll my head toward him, eyes roaming his face. He's still looking at the road, but he gives me a sideways glance every few seconds, like he wants me to know he's paying attention. But I don't say anything. I look at him, simply because I don't want to look away.

"Come to my apartment tonight," he says softly, suddenly. "Once we have all of this settled, then—"

"Why?" I cut him off, even though I know he was about to tell me.

He just shrugs, not picking up on my discomfort. "We have to talk, Ames. It's time to figure things out. We don't have an excuse to put it off anymore."

I bite down on my lip until I taste blood. I don't want to admit how badly that scares me, because it's ridiculous. We'll sort things out. And if we don't...at least this time, I have some form of closure.

Though I can't promise that I'll never want to scalp him again.

"I want to see you, Amelie," he adds on, glancing over at me.

I look out the window. "I don't know. That seems bad for business, no? Fraternizing with the enemy."

"You aren't the enemy," he admits in a low tone. "And you never were to me. Not in the way I wanted."

I keep my eyes on the skyline and ignore the quickening beat of my heart. "Fine," I say, regretting my words as they form. "Ten o'clock?"

He hums. "That's late. You got a gig?"

I grin against my better judgment. "Meg and Jensen require full attention for a few hours."

"Alright. Ten on the dot. I'll be at your door."

A small part of me hopes that time never comes.

45

___

AMELIE

On the elevator ride up to my apartment, I became increasingly aware of the fact that I have almost too much to tell Meg and Jen. I have no idea how they're going to react to any of it, and on top of that, Henry is talking to Roman soon. I wish I could know what's going on. I wish I were there, but also, I'm thankful that I'm nowhere *near* that man.

When I unlock my front door, I'm met with a very loud gasp. I wasn't expecting much of a reaction from anyone, and the noise is a shock enough to send me stumbling into the door handle.

"Ames!" Meg says, a whisk in one hand, mixing bowl in the other. I've never even seen her lift a spatula, and now, she appears to be baking. "You're back already?"

I sigh and throw my purse onto the counter. "Yeah. Kept it a secret for shock value. Did you miss me lots?"

"Sure, yes. Just sit down. We have a *lot* to talk about." Meg yanks out her ponytail and sits on the armchair. I flop down onto the couch and lay fully horizontal, not even caring that Jensen will need somewhere to sit, too. As if on cue, he steps out of the back bedroom as soon as I stretch my legs out. He drags out a chair from the kitchen and moves it next to Meg, dropping into it with a sigh.

"Okay, first off," I start. "What was up with *Lover of Mine*?"

Meg wordlessly stands and goes to the closet, returning seconds later with a box full of cash. Stacks and stacks of it. Each is held together with a worn rubber band, and I frown when I peek inside. "Just...look at it," she urges.

I glance at it for exactly one second. "It's fake."

"I *told* you!" Jensen sighs, runs a hand down his face. "I said—"

"Shut up," I tell him, setting the box aside. I should probably be livid that there's ten thousand dollars' worth of fake money in front of me, but I don't even care right now. "It's fine. We'll deal with it later."

Meg just nods, looking more than aggravated. Yesterday on the phone, she told me that Jensen suspected the cash they received for the job was fake, but neither of them were sure. It's not as though we can really do anything about it, but still, I try to make a habit of checking one bill before leaving. Of course, the *one* time I wasn't there, it's counterfeit.

It's a good enough segue for me to branch into *my* topic, though, because I have very little doubt that Roman is behind this bit of things, too.

"Alright," I start, laying back down. "Now that that's out of the way, let me tell you...everything."

And I do, in great detail. I tell them about my parents' and Roman's past rivalry. That he used to be an art thief himself. I explain that he *must* be The Dealer, and that he likely took the *Ophelia* and *Nautical Abyss.* That this whole thing was a round-about way to bait me and get me caught. I try to remind them that I'm not one-hundred percent sure of any of this, but they don't pay it any mind. They hop on my train of thought almost instantly.

I stray away from the topic of Henry, but I do explain the letters and calls, because I know they'd ask if I didn't. Especially Meg, who has become nosier than I'd ever have guessed, even after knowing her for this long.

When I finally stop talking, the first response I get is from her. "So, we're getting played by an old man. What do we do about that?"

"I don't know yet," I say honestly. "I have an idea, but..."

But I need to run it by Henry.

For once in my life, I want permission for something, only because this plan may cause more harm than it's worth. If Henry will give me the go-ahead, I have an idea for how to take down Roman at this auction *and* get Henry's stolen work back.

It's rusty. Extremely messy. But I think it can work.

"Ames," Jensen says warily. "That look on your face..."

"The plan would take place at the auction, and I'd need your guys' help."

They both groan. "That sounds like a trainwreck."

"Yes." I nod. "It probably is."

"Are you going to give us any further information?" Meg asks.

I shrug. "Not now, because I don't have it all yet.

The idea in my mind is very fickle. It involves the three of us, Henry *and* Lizzy, and a monkey.

I do wish I were kidding.

"Jenny," Meg says abruptly, turning toward him. "Go see if Ames has any mail. I forgot to check this morning."

He stares blankly at her. "Why would I—"

"Now, please."

He's up and out the door before she turns back toward me.

I raise a brow. "I take it you've got him wrapped around your finger again?"

Meg grins at me. "He was never *un*-wrapped."

True.

"Now, tell me the details. Henry details. I need to know if I was right about everything."

I sigh and try to ignore the way my stomach flips at the mention of his name. That has *got* to stop happening. "I can't even give you details, Meg. I don't know what happened."

"Did he kiss you?"

I keep my voice even when I say, "No."

"Did you *want* him to?"

Yes. "No."

"Hm." She doesn't believe me at all. "So you guys aren't back together, then."

"No." I need to learn a new word.

Meg just nods. "So what now?"

"I have no idea. It's just...sort of unreal. I don't understand anything. I don't understand the letters, and I don't understand what I'm feeling."

"But you want to be with him," she says, though it's not a question. It's a statement.

"I think so," I whisper, the admission burning my throat. I haven't let myself even think those words yet, and here I am, saying them aloud at the simplest prompt. "But it isn't plausible. Henry will tire of me eventually, and I...I can't handle that again."

She shakes her head. "I don't think he will."

"But he *should,*" I say exasperatedly. "Of all people, he should."

"You don't get to decide what he *should* feel for you, Ames. I don't think *he* even had much of a say in it."

I pull a throw blanket into my lap and sigh. "This is another thing that I can't control. I don't want to feel for him again. It throws a horrible dent in things."

"It wasn't part of your plan," she agrees, "and that's why it scares you. But that doesn't make it bad."

I don't respond to that, and I don't have to. Seconds after Meg shuts her mouth, the front door swings open with a ridiculous amount of force. Jensen is standing in the hallway, practically fuming. At least as much as he can.

"There's no mail," he says, "and Olive tried to set me up with her granddaughter *again.*"

"Just warn her that you're no Betty Crocker," Meg says. "You burnt the cake."

"The cake!" Jen swears and bolts for the oven.

Now that Meg mentions it, there *is* a faint scent of smoke in the air.

Jensen drags the cake pan out of the oven and sets it atop the stove. He frowns and studies the thing, trying to figure out where it's burnt, but he can't. And I can't either. The cake is perfectly golden, as if him yanking it out in a panic made it cook perfectly.

"You dirty liar." He peeks inside the oven, then pulls out a small scrap of burnt paper with his mitted hands. "Did you do this?"

"Who? Little 'ol me?"

"*Megan*—"

"Does this mean I win?" She asks, leaning playfully over the arm of the chair. "I think so."

Jensen's face clears immediately, all his annoyance melting away. "No. My apologies."

Meg is practically giggling as he removes his oven mitts.

I have no idea what any of that is about, but I don't care. By the time they've got the cake frosted and sliced, I've fallen asleep on the couch to my circling thoughts.

46

―――――

HENRY

I've never been less excited for something in my life.

After dropping Amelie off at her apartment, dread settled around me like a fog. I drove home as slow as humanly possible without causing problems. The only positive thing I can pinpoint about being home is that Liz lives across the hall. Maybe she can give me a heads-up as to what's going on.

I'm a ball of nerves when I knock on her door. She steps out, donned in a fuzzy purple unicorn onesie, and gasps.

"HEN! You didn't tell me you were coming back!" She rams into me with a hug, her bony elbows jamming into my arms. "Can you *please* tell me why Dad is losing it?"

Off to a great start, I see.

"I'll work on that later," I mumble, going across the hall. I unlock my door and step inside, greeted by Betty, who rubs all along the hem of my pant legs. "Has he been around?"

"No." She drops onto my couch and scoops Betty into her lap. "But he's been ringing me like crazy. I answered one singular call and got told off, so I'm over it. He asked where you were, what you were doing, why I didn't tell him, and about a thousand other things."

"Can I borrow your phone to call him? I blocked him."

She blinks. "You *did*?"

"The other day, yeah."

She seethes and hands over her phone. "Yikes."

"No kidding," I mutter. I send a text that says *Henry is home*, because he's much more apt to answer if he thinks he's talking to Liz.

It only takes a few seconds for his response to come through.

DAD

In the lobby. Be up in a moment.

"He's downstairs," I say through an exhale. "He'll be here soon."

Liz nods and grabs a package of cookies from my cabinet. "I'll be here for moral support."

"I don't think he's going to want you in the room."

"Don't care," she says, and I leave it at that.

It's only a moment before Dad walks into my apartment. I left it unlocked on purpose, but I still expected him to knock, at least as a warning.

"Henry, Elizabeth," he says, nodding to the both of us.

I'm in no mood for formalities.

"You used to be an art thief."

Dad's eyes lock onto mine, and he looks confused. I know it's a ploy—it must be, but still, it unnerves me.

"What are you talking about?" His voice isn't panicked. It's frustrated. "Why would you say that?"

"It's the truth, isn't it?"

Not giving him my reasoning is a bad idea, but I don't have a choice. I refuse to make mention of Amelie's parents. I'll be vague until I can't, which unfortunately may be sooner rather than later.

"I don't understand," he says flatly.

I take a breath. "You have my *Ophelia*. You've had it the whole time."

His brow wrinkles. "You're lying, right? I finally got the image reports back from your apartment. It's someone named Jensen Velasco." He pulls his phone out and turns it toward me, revealing a photo of Amelie's friend. With the way my dad is sneering, you'd think he discovered a mugshot, but that isn't the case. The photo is casual, candid, like something you'd see on social media. "That's the man."

"That's not true," I say with full confidence. "You're lying."

"Henry, don't test me. It's the same man. I've got multiple image match-ups. You'd know this if you hadn't blocked me."

"You're lying." I shake my head. "You've *been* lying—"

"*I've* been lying?" He smiles, and I know I've messed up, but I'm not quite sure how. "Son, do you really think I believed you were at a convention? I'm not stupid. I know you were with Amelie. I know she's burrowed deep in your mind, and that she has been for years, whether you'll admit it or not."

This is going to ruins much quicker than I'd planned.

"So that's why you cut our calls," I say, tired of holding back. "That's why you broke our connection. *You* did that, and still, you don't know why I'm angry."

"I know that you'll never believe a negative word about her again," he says, grasping onto the subject change. I'm annoyed enough to let it work. "So why are we arguing? What is it that she's got you believing?"

"Nothing that I don't believe on my own." I take a breath. "You have my *Ophelia*, and you sold *Lover of Mine*. Don't bother trying to lie to me."

Dad gives a deep, condescending laugh. "How would you know that if she hadn't told you? *Lover of Mine* wasn't on the open market; I looked for it when I noticed it was gone. You're believing her lies, Henry, and you don't even realize it. She could probably convince you that *you're* the one at fault."

I shake my head. "I don't believe you."

"And that's your weakness."

"Disbelieving someone who cares very little about me?"

"No." He gives a sad sort of smile. "Trusting someone who cares even less."

I swallow. All of this, it's part of his plan. It must be. He's trying to plant worry in my mind about Amelie. About *all* of this. He knows that I trust her, and he knows that she's figured it out.

I just wish he'd give it up. I don't understand why it has to drag on this way.

"I've given you everything," Dad says, his voice laced with venom. "I've put all my money into you. Into your work and into the museum. And you don't care. Your work is displayed because of me, and still, you'd rather believe the girl who's had her claws in you since—"

"*Don't,*" I say firmly. "This isn't about her."

Dad raises his eyebrows, looking amused. "So that's what happened the other night, hm?"

I pinch the bridge of my nose. "What are you *talking* about?"

"When you punched those men at Bondi's. Did they make a remark toward her? Or was that on your own free will?"

My mouth falls open. "What did you just say?"

He smiles. Truly smiles. "You really didn't think I'd find out?"

"*How* did you—"

"Henry," he says, almost condescendingly. "I *own* Bondi's."

And all at once, everything clicks into place.

The loose details. The pieces of information that didn't quite make sense, they add up now.

He's done pretending.

"So it's true," I breathe. "Everything. All of it. You were a thief. You're *still* a thief."

"Don't accuse me of things that you clearly don't care about," he says, pointing a crooked finger in my face. "If you can excuse your girl's career, you can excuse my doing the same thing."

I take a step forward. "*She* hasn't lied to me. Not about what she does or who she is. She didn't send me on some wild goose chase because—" I stop. Look at the ground. "Why are you even doing this?"

"For money," Liz pipes up from the kitchen, and I jolt. I forgot she was even here. "Mommy dearest told me about the bills."

Dad's jaw tightens. "Elizabeth."

"She said you're in the hole, *bad.* The bail from forty years ago is coming back to hurt you, I guess." She shrugs nonchalantly. "The tax evasion isn't helping, either. Maybe if you were ever home, she wouldn't let these things slip to me, but…"

"*Elizabeth*," he scolds, and Liz smiles like she's won the lottery.

I feel a little foolish for not connecting these dots.

I've always known business was in decline. That's never been a secret. But his bail…it was money that we've never truly made up for. I'd be willing to bet that a good chunk of Dad's wallet has also gone to getting his crimes covered up. Once, out of curiosity, I tried to look up his arrest reports online, but I never found them. The only thing that appears under his name is the museum.

"We're done here," I say again, my voice weaker than I'd prefer. "This can be over. Just give me my work back, and—"

"No." He cuts me off. "I don't think I will. We'll speak after the auction, Henry, and at that time, I will turn you out on your own."

I swallow, trying very hard to focus only on that last part. That's *fine*. That's what he doesn't understand. Being on my own is not a threat in the slightest, but I don't want this to hurt Lizzy or my mom in any way.

"Me," I emphasize. "You will turn *me* out on my own. This will not come back on Liz or Mom."

"You have my word on that," he says, as if it means anything at all.

I exhale and shove my hand into my pocket. "When is the auction?"

"This Sunday. Eight o'clock. If you're there…" He shakes his head. "Don't be."

"You asked me to bring Amelie. Is that void?"

"Yes. I'll deal with her myself."

"I have to be there," I continue, arguing just for the sake of it. "It's an artist exhibit."

"I'll make an exception." Dad shakes his head and walks out of my apartment, slamming the door behind him.

I stand in the middle of the floor, frozen in disbelief.

What am I supposed to do now?

"That was awkward to sit in on," Lizzy says, pulling herself up onto my countertop. "What was all *that*?"

I ignore her question. "Was that all true? About the money and taxes?"

She nods. "Yeah. Mom's doing terribly, Hen. The last time you saw her was a good day."

I chew on my lip. "How long does he have?"

"Until something big happens?" She shrugs. "Personally, I'd say a couple months, give or take. But based on the way Mom was crying, it could be tomorrow."

My heart twists at the thought of my mom crying over his mistakes.

"I've got to get my work back," I mumble, sitting at my kitchen table. "If only just so *he* doesn't have it any longer. I don't care what it takes."

"You'll get them. You'll think of a way. Just be careful."

"I will," I say, though that probably isn't the truth. I haven't been careful in a while.

Liz slips off the counter and puts the cookies back in my pantry. "Oh, before I go. I'll send you the link to my old Prada bag. Betty peed on mine, so I'll be expecting another. Also she's out of treats."

I force a laugh. "Bye, Lizzy."

"Fill me in on the trip later," she says, throwing me a look over her shoulder as she leaves.

Once the door clicks shut, I drop my face into my hands and sigh. What is there to do? If I know my father at all—and I'm afraid that I do—he'll have the auction hall locked down, with specific instructions *not* to let me in.

Or it'll be easy. *Too* easy. There's no reality where this goes smoothly.

Sighing, I lug my bags into my room and vow to unpack later. Knowing that Amelie will be here in a few hours to discuss this makes it a little more bearable. Maybe she'll have some ideas on how to solve this whole thing. If anyone can work through this insanity, it's her.

Finally, after a few minutes of standing completely still, I bite the bullet and go to my studio. The thought of even looking inside is harrowing, but I have to know if he's taken all of my work, or if it's only fun when it's a game for him.

I unlock the door, and I'm shocked.

Childlike Wonder is on my easel.

Suspiciously untouched, except for an ace of hearts tucked against the grain.

47

AMELIE

I've just started on a new dress when Henry knocks on my door.

I usually vow to not work on garments past eight p.m. Half the time, when I start something late in the night, I end up cutting the patterns weirdly or stitching the hem crookedly. But I've missed my sewing machine, so I don't care. A botched hem isn't the end of the world as we know it, so after waking up, I yanked out a roll of yellow fabric and started cutting the panels.

Still, though, I set it all aside when I hear the knock. It's ten on the dot, just as Henry promised. Jen and Meg are out together, and I'm thankful. I really don't feel like answering questions about this arrangement.

I slip my purse on my shoulder and open the door. Henry smiles at the sight of me, but I don't smile back. "How'd it go?" I ask, rather than waiting.

His smile wavers. "Wrong question."

A dry laugh escapes me. "I figured."

"He's keeping my pieces," he tells me as we walk to the elevator. "Unless I can convince him otherwise, that's the outcome."

"Oh." Somehow, I expected Henry to just...get them back. Today. It was a naïve assumption, but I've always pictured Roman as a man with very little fight in him. Clearly that isn't the case. "We were right, then?"

"Pretty sure," he says with a shrug.

I step onto the elevator. "I've been thinking of ways to get him in trouble, if that interests you. He'd be gone, you'd get your pieces, and you can display wherever you want. It's a win-win."

Henry sighs. "I don't think I can go about it like that."

"We don't want him caught?"

"Not...like that," he admits, offering no further explanation. "Truthfully, Ames, I just want my pieces back, and I never want to see him again."

I bite down on my lip. How can we do that? Getting Henry's work back without outing Roman seems like an impossibility.

The elevator door opens before I find a solution. Henry leads me out to his vehicle, and I thank my lucky stars that Mimi and Olive are in bed already. I couldn't explain this if I wanted to.

Henry's car is still warm, so I hop in and practically snuggle into the leather seats. Once he's settled in, I ask, "Are you going to tell me what we're doing?"

He starts the engine. "No."

"No?"

"Not yet."

I suddenly feel like I'm being kidnapped.

"It's nothing crazy, Amelie," he says, as if he can read my mind.

I huff. "It better not be."

"You have my word."

"Fine." It does not feel fine. "Back to the auction thing, then."

He exhales and pulls his car out of the parking spot. "He's not even letting me attend the event. I'm basically out of ammunition."

I tap my fingers against my thigh, keeping my eyes out the window. "I'm going to suggest something, and you're presumably going to decline."

"I'm not," he says, a laugh trapped behind his words. "I'm open to anything."

"Okay. You let me get your pieces back."

The words, I say them hesitantly. I've never offered anything like this to anyone. Risking *myself* to help someone? Risking my friends, and our cover, and our time? It's not something I take lightly.

I think Henry is aware of that, because he seems to contemplate the words carefully before responding.

"I don't know," he says. "I don't want it to be on you."

"I do this regularly," I remind, expecting that to jar him.

He just shakes his head. "Still."

"If I could get him caught, would you want that?"

I'm giving him a choice, because I very well could. I think, at least. But Roman being caught if Henry doesn't want it sounds horrible to me.

"I don't know," he says finally. "I don't know what that would do for my mom."

I nod. "That's fine. But if you change your mind, I have the resources for it."

He looks over at me. "You scare me a little, you know?"

I grin as I sink further into my seat. He scares me, too, whether he knows it or not. I'm terrified of what he makes me feel. What he makes me want. I wonder if he means it that way too. Maybe he's scared of what he feels for me.

I don't find it to be likely, but I guess it's possible.

"Yeah," I say, instead of saying all that. "Yeah, I know."

Before I know it, I'm in Henry's apartment building, waiting for him to unlock his front door.

I didn't really expect him to bring me here, but I guess there's nowhere else to be. It's not as though either of us really need to be parading around the city right now, not with the accusations we've thrown at Roman.

The door swings open, and I'm expecting to be greeted by Betty. Instead, there's a girl sitting on his counter in a purple onesie, holding a bowl of pasta and a can of diet coke.

"*Lizzy?*"

Her head snaps toward me, and her eyes widen. "Amelie?! OH MY GOSH I'M GOING TO CRY."

"Lizzy!" I repeat, this time more enthusiastic. "How are you?"

Liz basically vaults over the kitchen table and runs up to me, wrapping me in the most suffocating hug I've had in years. "I'm great *now*! I've missed you. Oh, my gosh, when Henry brought you up, I was like, '*Please let me see her*!', and he was all, '*No, that's not going to happen*'. We didn't actually say any of that, but I knew what his answer would be, so I never asked." She releases me and shakes her head. "How are you here?"

I turn toward Henry. "She doesn't know?"

"I feel as though she has to have the gist by now."

Liz grins. "I do. I just want you to say it."

Henry leans back against the countertop and crosses his arms. He does that a lot. I think he knows it distracts me. "We're working together."

"*AND?!*"

"There's no *and*," he says. I note that his entire stance shifts into something stiffer. "We're just trying to get my work back."

Lizzy's disappointment is obvious, but she tries to hide it. "Well, good. I've missed you dearly, Amelie. I've had no one to share my jewelry with—well, I've got Flo, but she just doesn't care as much as you. The lack of excitement is *gutting*."

"It's been equally as horrid for me," I say with full sincerity.

Liz gives my arm a squeeze and grabs her can off the table, downing the rest of its contents. She mirrors Henry's stance, and I think it's unintentional, but it's enough to make me laugh. "I'm glad you've figured things out. Have you guys...discussed..." She lets her voice trail off, as if she's worried to voice the problem.

Henry looks down at her. "Just ask, Liz."

"Oh, thank God. *Why* did you guys break up? What happened? I've been dying to know this for four years. This is like the royal wedding, but better."

"It was our parents," Henry responds dryly. "Both of ours. Amelie's took my letters, and, as you heard earlier, Dad stopped the calls."

She gapes. "*That's* what that was about?"

"Were you not listening?"

"No, I was really just there to antagonize him." She sighs, then turns back to me. "Well, you can help us out, right? You can really get Henry's work back."

Henry shakes his head. "*Liz—*"

"No, really!" She covers his mouth with her hand. "Look, Amelie, I don't want you to feel pressured. But since you're already *trying...*" She shrugs. "If you could simply lend us an evening, I think we could get it done much faster."

"We already discussed that," Henry says, maneuvering around Lizzy's arm. "That could go really poorly."

"Yeah, but do you want Dad to win?"

"I suppose not," he says, sounding resigned.

"Then let's start thinking!" Liz slams her fist down on the countertop. "How could this work? Amelie, you're skilled. Can't you do something with grappling hooks and web shooters?"

I snort. "I'm not well-versed in web shooters, but I think I could work something out." I look over at Henry. "I just need you to say the word."

He licks his lips and looks away. "I know you could do it. I just don't want you in hot water because of me."

"I don't think we could get in hotter water. If we think logically about this, your dad probably has as much dirt on me as I have on him, solely from my last name. He's just been too scared to use it." I exhale. "I'm going to help you, Henry. And I'd really like you to *want* me to, but if you don't...I'm sorry. But I'm going to help you anyway."

It's almost selfish, in a way, how badly I need to do this for him. Despite my reluctance to help him just weeks ago, I don't feel like I can get away from this without solving it. I want to be the one to finish this.

It stopped being just about Henry, though that's a lot of it. But finding out that this whole thing goes back to my *parents*...it changes things.

"You said you wouldn't steal anymore of my art," Henry says, almost playfully.

"Stealing it back is a little different."

"Do it," he says. "If anyone can get away with it, it's you."

My eyebrows raise. "That sounds like a compliment."

"It is."

A faint smile crosses my lips. It's enough to snag Henry's attention on my mouth, and *that's* enough to make me wish that Liz was in a different room.

She's not, though, and she makes her presence known by clearing her throat. "Well, anyways, I'm going home. I have an article due tomorrow and I want to kill my boss."

"Oh, speaking of." I grab her wrist as she walks past me. "I read your article on Louboutins, and it was amazing. You're so right for all of it."

She gasps and grabs my other wrist. "Thank you! My boss was *so* mad at me for that. He thought I was degrading them, but I wasn't! THEY'RE JUST SHOES."

"Liz, we have things to do, and it's nearing eleven." Henry nods toward the door. "See you tomorrow, hm? Mom isn't coming to the auction, but I assume you are."

"Unfortunately," Liz sighs. She gives me a quick squeeze and a peck on the cheek, then leaves the apartment. Her bowl and can are still on the table, and Betty is pawing at the dishware.

"She is a *mess*," Henry says through a laugh.

"I love her," I say solemnly. "I can't believe she doesn't hate me."

"Why would she? She loves you, too. The moment I said your name, she told me to get over myself and admit that I missed you."

My stomach dips, but I try to ignore it and keep the conversation on track. "I just assumed that she would."

"She sees you as someone who enjoys terrorizing my father, which means you're on our side. In a world of people who worship him, that's an incredible thing."

I start toying with a cat collar I found on the counter. "I was never against you, Henry," I say, and though I've told him this before, I want to say it again. "I never targeted you. I take what I'm told."

"I know."

"You also know that I'll never take your work again. I think I've said that at least three times."

"You have, yeah." He's grinning now, like this is funny.

"What? What are you laughing at?"

"You just..." He looks away, then shakes his head. "Nothing."

"*What*?"

"No, really, it's nothing."

"You can't just—"

"I have something for you."

I snap my mouth shut as Henry walks over to his coffee table. He lifts the vase off the center, and I blink. Is he giving me the vase? It's pretty and all, but it doesn't match my décor whatsoever. Surely he would know this; he's seen my apartment a few times. Though maybe—

There's a *pop* as he pries a small black square off the bottom, completely cutting off my train of thought. Henry holds it in his palm, staring at it for a few seconds before holding it out to me. "The memory card. Take it."

I stare at the card like it's a snake. It's ridiculous to think this piece of plastic started this whole thing. I'd honestly forgotten about it, though I can't understand how. A few weeks ago, it was all I worried about, and now, it's the last thing on my mind.

Hesitantly, I take it out of his hand. "I forgot about this," I say aloud. "But you can just keep it."

Henry looks at me curiously. "What?"

"Keep it. I don't want it."

He frowns and takes the chip from me. After staring at it for a few moments, he puts it in his pocket and grabs his coat off the hook. "Okay. Let's go."

I blink. "Where are we—"

"You'll know it when you see it."

I don't put up a further argument. There's no use, anyways. Whether I'm ready to admit it to myself or not, I'd follow him wherever.

Might as well start with something like this.

48
____

AMELIE

Henry stops the car in front of a beach.

A *beach*.

At eleven o'clock at night. As if it isn't freezing outside.

All I have to warm me is the jacket that I stole from him. He's folded himself in his sweater, and I feel slightly guilty for taking it, but it's well within my rights. I think there's something in the Constitution about taking the coat of a person who makes you stand in forty degree weather. It should be legal. *Encouraged*, even.

"This is ridiculous," I say plainly, slipping my shoes off so I don't fill them with sand. "Our toes are going to snap off."

"I don't think that's going to happen." Henry removes his shoes and offers me his hand, and I take it, albeit reluctantly. This isn't normal behavior. This beach is literally empty aside from us. If this *were* something that people do, surely there'd be at least one other person here.

Henry starts walking toward the shoreline, and since he still has a grip on my hand, I follow. I'm trying to be at least mildly optimistic, but I get moody when I'm cold. Hence the reason I took his coat when we arrived.

"Do you recognize it?" He asks once we're stopped directly in front of the ocean. Our feet are covered by the foaming waves, and the hem of my pants is damp, but I find that I don't care. The water in contrast to the cold air isn't as bad as I'd expected it to be.

I hold my breath. "Not...really?"

He nods and looks down at the ground.

"But it's dark," I continue, somehow feeling guilty over this. "Maybe I'd recognize it during the day."

He laughs. "You don't have to feel bad."

"But *you* remember it," I say.

He just shrugs and turns on his heel, pulling me along behind him as he keeps walking down the beach. I continue to look around as I walk mindlessly, looking for some tell as to why I should recognize this place, but nothing sticks out. It's *sand* and *water*. You could put me on seven different beaches and I wouldn't be able to tell you one from the other.

We're walking toward a pier, I realize, when my eyes adjust more to the dark. A run-down one, set out over the water. The moonlight is glistening off the waves, and Henry doesn't stop until we're about a hundred yards away. He stares at this, too, like I should recognize it.

I know we aren't here to *just* stare. There's a reason we're here, but I don't know it.

"You brought me here to talk," I say, when I feel like the silence is going to kill me. "So talk."

Henry drops my hand and slips his into his pocket, and I try not to focus on the lack of his warmth. Slowly, he pulls the memory card out of his pocket, and before I can even ask what he's doing, he takes a step forward and throws it.

Right into the rolling tide.

I look up at him. "Is that what—"

"Why do you hate my paintings so much?" He asks, keeping his eyes on the ground.

I gape, taken aback. "What?"

"I just want to know. I don't care that you hate them. I just... want to know what changed."

I bite my lip and stare at the waves because I don't have an answer. I decided to hate Henry's paintings, yes, but as for my reasoning? I don't have one. Not that goes beyond something petty.

I can't even say that I've truly hated his work, because I haven't. *Fleur of Words* is my favorite piece in the museum, and I always knew it could be his. I always felt that it was, and I still loved it. It was something that I looked at every time I went.

"I don't," I say finally, and I'm shocked to feel confident in that answer.

He looks over at me with a heavy gaze. "You said you did."

I shake my head once. "I think I hated the emotions they elicit from me. I hated that you could still make me feel, even after I said I wouldn't let you do that again. Your paintings are beautiful, Henry. I'm drawn to them."

He opens his mouth to respond, then turns away without saying a word, so I keep talking.

"Your piece, *Fleur of Words*? It's my favorite thing you've made. And it's not just because my name is in it. It's the tangle of words together. The absolute chaos that you made look beautiful. I didn't even know it was yours until a few weeks ago. I refused to look at the nameplate because I *thought* it was you."

"You're in all my pieces in some way, Amelie." His eyes pin me in place. "Your name, it's there. It's what I based the piece around. And the ocean in *Nautical Abyss*—" He motions to the water in front of us. "—is this. I came here and painted the base of the piece one evening."

I stay silent, staring directly at the wooden structure in the distance.

And then it clicks.

"You kissed me here," I say quietly.

Now that I've remembered, it's obvious.

It was a summer night, right before dark. Henry suggested we go down to the pier and watch the sun set, so we did. But we didn't go home immediately after; we stayed and talked until the moon was the only thing to light our path. My parents were positively livid when I made it home.

But he kissed me for the first time here.

It's one of those things I tried to forget, though I never fully succeeded.

Henry nods to confirm my answer. "You're in everything for me, Amelie. Everything."

My heart speeds up at those words.

You're in everything for me.

I frown and turn toward him to tell him that we can't do this. Not again. But before I even get my first word out, he's shaking his head, taking a step closer to me.

"No," he says. "Amelie, I have to tell you."

"I don't—"

"*Please*," he begs, voice dropping lower. "Let me."

I swallow. Trace the lines of his face with my gaze instead of looking away. "Okay," I whisper. "Tell me."

He holds my eyes as he speaks, looking more intent than I've seen him in ages. "I want you," he says softly. "And before you say anything about how that answer isn't good enough, let me finish talking."

My mouth is already open to argue, and he grins slightly when I close it. "Alright. Sorry."

"Thank you." He laughs quietly before continuing. "The other day, you asked me what's changed. And I didn't say it at the time, because I wanted to make sure I could say exactly what I wanted. But I know it now." He takes a breath. "*We* have changed. We're different people, Amelie. Different from each other, and different from who we were four years ago. Your choices are—and always will be—your own. So will mine. But my choice is you, and it's *always* going to be you."

I swallow hard, ignoring the blatant stinging in my eyes.

"Memories of you aren't enough for me. I want to know you now. All these things that you've learned about yourself, I want to know them, too. And I won't judge you. I won't resent you. All of it, it's a part of you, just like my work is a part of me.

"I wish I could change how things ended." He pauses. "No. I wish things never *had* ended. I'll never forgive myself for not trying harder to get back to you, but I can't fix that. I can't change the past, so let me say this now: whatever you choose to do, whoever you choose to be, I will always want you." He takes both of my hands in his, and I step forward. "I cannot escape you, Amelie, and I don't want to."

If I couldn't feel his skin on mine, I would fully convince myself that I'm hallucinating right now.

What am I even supposed to say? My mind feels like it's been wiped blank. His words always manage to catch me off guard, and this is no exception, but it does feel much more important.

Just take a breath. Think for a moment.

"We can't do this again."

Okay, no. That wasn't the plan.

"We can," Henry replies, not at all deterred by my obvious blubbering. I think it's actually making him enjoy this more. "You know we can."

Can. Not could.

I exhale sharply. "You don't know that for sure."

"I do." He nods and squeezes my hands. "You've been on my mind for four years, Amelie. It's only worsened with the time I've spent around you lately. You haven't left my thoughts. Not once. I don't think you ever will."

I stay silent for a beat, unsure of what to say. I have *so* many options, and not a single one of them actually comes out of my mouth. Instead, I decide on saying, "I'm not what you think. Not anymore."

He doesn't look away. "Yes, you are."

"I already said I won't change for you."

"And I said that I'd never ask you to."

I exhale, mildly exasperated. "You shouldn't have to compromise yourself for me."

"I'm not compromising anything," he says solemnly. "I want *you.* Just you. I've tried to make that clear, though I must not have done a good enough job."

I keep my mouth shut, because I think I've finally run out of arguments.

"I've done all that I can," he says, voice lowered. "If you want me to walk away, I will. But you have to *tell* me."

"I don't want that," I whisper. "I don't want that at all."

His eyes flick back and forth between mine. "No?"

"No." I shake my head. "I don't want you to walk away."

"Then what do you want?"

"You."

I don't know where I find the word, but I know it's true.

I do want him. I've wanted him for much longer than I care to admit.

Henry takes a deep breath and steps forward, enough to close the gap between us. He slides his hands around to the back of my neck and lowers his face to mine, making my breath catch.

"You *have* me, Amelie," he murmurs against my lips. "You always will."

I close my eyes. Shift closer to him. Before I can breathe, before I can say a word, he's kissing me.

And I don't know how I'll live without this again.

His fingers dig into the nape of my neck, and he kisses me roughly, desperately, like he's worried I'll disappear. Like he needs me to breathe. I take handfuls of his shirt, trying to move closer to him, even though that's not really possible at this point. I'm flush against him, enough to feel the rise and fall of his ragged breathing, enough to know that it matches my own.

It's overwhelming that this is real. That he's holding me, kissing me like I'm his. I'm worried I'm going to get addicted to this, to *him,* only to have it taken away from me again.

But that doesn't stop me from reveling in this. From dragging my fingers through his hair, over his shoulders and arms. I rest my palm under his collarbone, right over his hammering heart, and I can't help but grin at the fact that I still affect him the way he affects me. We're both in this. We both *feel* this.

This isn't going away, I tell myself, exhaling as he trails his hands down my sides. *Not if we don't let it.*

Henry breaks away from me for a second. Mumbles something I don't catch, something that must not be important. His mouth is back on mine again, and this time, it's slow. Gentle. His hands are tight around my waist, holding me where I am, and his fingers slip just underneath the hem of my shirt. I shiver at the warmth. At his hot hands pressing against my icy skin.

"You're freezing," he whispers into the air between us.

I tangle my fingers through his hair. His eyes close for a second, and I smile at him even though he doesn't see me. "I missed you," I breathe. "I didn't realize just how much."

He grins before pulling me into his arms. I close my eyes and relax against him, burying my face in his sweater. "We should go," he says, the words muffled by my hair.

I nod, trying to suppress a shiver that's actually from the cold. My toes lost feeling quite a while ago, and my fingers aren't far behind. "Yeah. We probably should."

He releases me and takes my hand again, walking back the way we came. He doesn't let go until we're back to his car and he opens my door. I slide into the passenger seat and instantly curl into a ball, my knees pressed to my chin. As soon as Henry starts the car, I turn the seat warmers on full heat.

"Well," Henry starts, rubbing his palms together. "I'd call it a successful outing."

I cover my mouth and laugh. "I'd say so."

He grins and pulls away from the edge of the road. I don't bother to turn on music for once—I sort of like this silence. The sound of my breathing, the tapping of his fingers against the wheel, it's intimate. Peaceful.

But I ruin it with my questions, of course. That's just how I am.

"What were you going to say back at your apartment?" I ask, toying with my shoelaces. "When you kept saying it was nothing."

"Right before we left, you mean?"

"Yes."

Henry hums as he makes a turn. "You worry so much about people hating you that you don't realize they love you."

I gape at him. "What?"

"You seem to assume people will hate you for your work. Earlier, with Lizzy, that's what you said. But that isn't the case."

"How do you figure?"

"You're a good person," he says simply. "You're kind, and self-less, despite what you say. You love people, and you show them. I mean—you're already helping me with something that I dragged you into, even though you shouldn't. You shouldn't want to help me, but you *do*."

"That's because you deserve something good," I say softly. "And to you, that's your work. I want to get that back for you."

He shakes his head. "You're my something good, Ames."

I flush and turn away, staring at the lights out my window. Henry laughs, and a few seconds later, his hand finds mine again. The things he says...half the time, I don't know how to respond.

This is one of those times, so I don't speak again. But I do kiss him thoroughly before going to my apartment.

49

HENRY

I end up at Amelie's place early the next morning. She called me moments after I woke up, asking me to come and figure things out before the auction tonight. I said yes, of course, though I'm not sure it would've mattered either way.

It sort of looks like her team has a hold on things without my help.

The four of us—me, Amelie, Jensen, and Meg—are sitting around their kitchen table, Meg with her nose in her laptop, and Amelie with a stack of papers in front of her. Jensen, in complete contrast to their singular tasks, has a corkboard's worth of scribbled notes and blurry photos. They look mostly useless.

Amelie sighs. "Okay. Dearest Megan—"

"I hate when you call me that."

"—managed to get us a floor plan of the auction hall last night. Obviously, I'm assuming that this whole thing will take place on the stage, so that leaves us a few doors to get inside of." Amelie hands Jensen and I a printed copy of the map. To me, it looks like a bunch of scribbled lines, but I can tell that it makes perfect sense to her. She's vandalizing the thing with a red marker. "West exit could work. The paintings are stored in a back room a couple yards from the stage."

"My dad will only be on stage for half of the auction," I tell her. "Only for the work that involves his museum. We'll have to get them while he's *off* stage."

"Will that be a problem?" Jensen asks.

Amelie shakes her head. "No. I've gone around him before. It'll be fine."

That, she has.

"I'm having trouble with the cameras," Meg says, looking at Amelie. "I can't do it from here. I have the data, but this place is secure."

"You'll get it done," Amelie says, more a demand than encouragement.

Meg nods. "It'll be done."

"Good." Amelie exhales and draws a big circle on the map before looking up at me. "You're not going?"

I blink, confused. "Is that a question or a statement?"

"Question."

"Oh. Well, my dad told me not to, but I don't particularly care." I drag my hand down my face. "Do you want me there?"

"Yes. And I have an idea, but it's a very bad one." A pause, like she's preparing us for the worst. "What if we just...walk in? Through the front door? No sneaking around tonight."

"That *is* a terrible idea," Jensen cuts in. "That's where the cameras are, right? The entrance?"

"I'm not trying to be slick," Amelie says, sipping on the coffee I brought her. "I'm fine if Roman knows we're there. Let him know we've bested him."

He stares daggers at her. "And you think that's wise?"

"Ah!" She pokes his nose, and he doesn't budge. "Never said that. But let this be a final send-off of sorts. For him and I, anyways. I don't see him messing with us anymore after this, and if we pull it off, we get the final word."

I'm grinning at the sheer amount of confidence in her voice, but I'm the only one. Everyone else looks mildly perturbed by her lack of worry.

"Fine," Jensen says, crossing his arms, "but I'm going, too."

"That's not a good idea," I mumble, pulling my phone out of my pocket. "My dad may or may not have...suspicious looking footage of you in my apartment building."

"I'm *sorry*?"

I get the picture of him and the doorman on my screen. "Can you look at this?" I ask Meg, who is not paying a remote bit of attention to me. Or, so I think; instead of responding, she just holds her hand out. I set my phone in her palm, and within seconds, she's connected it to her laptop through a USB cord, probably running it through some search engine.

"She'll get that taken care of, too," Amelie says, turning back to Jensen. "But you cannot go inside that building. You'll be outside, ready to help me load them."

Jensen sighs and scratches his jaw. "You said this is a final send-off. If that's the case, let me help with it. Who cares, right?"

Amelie bites the inside of her cheek. "What do you think, Henry?"

"I think it could go poorly," I admit, "but I think *a lot* of this could go poorly. With any luck, he won't be a problem after tonight."

She looks at me for a second, like I'm jumping the gun by joining her side rather than my dad's, but it isn't like that. I made this decision a long, long time ago, and it's finally time for it to be carried out. It's a strange, unconventional way of me getting out of his grasp, but it's happening regardless. The result is necessary, no matter what path we take.

"Okay, then. Final question for you." Amelie looks up at me. "How good is Lizzy at making a scene? She used to be grand, and that talent rarely leaves."

I can't stop myself from laughing. "The best."

"Perfect." She uncaps the pen between her teeth and writes something on the corner of the paper. "Megs, you got that?"

She doesn't say a word. Her eyes are narrowed on my phone screen.

"Meg." Amelie waves a hand in front of her eyes. "Do you—"

"This is fake," she says, looking up at me. "Edited. The image is manipulated."

Amelie gapes at her and snatches the phone away. I'm shocked to feel such an obvious sense of relief rush over me. I never believed it was real, not for a second, but I had nothing to go off of other than hope.

"That's good," I say. "Right? It won't hold up."

"It wouldn't anyways, but yeah. It's obvious."

"It's not," Amelie corrects her.

Meg shrugs. "It is to me. His hand is blurred against the desk, and his foot is crooked."

Amelie passes me the phone, and I stare hard at the photo, but I don't see anything she's talking about. The image is already blurry enough, given that it was meant to look like security footage, and the small scale on my phone isn't helping. But I believe her; I have no reason not to.

"So," Amelie continues. "Meg. Did you catch what we said?"

Meg blinks. "The parts that made no sense? Yes, I've got it."

"Wonderful. Jensen, you come in the back door. From the alley, where Meg'll be parked."

He nods. "Got it."

Amelie huffs and caps her pen again, tossing it to the center of the table. "Is this good? Are we doing this?"

"Can't verify that it's good," Meg says, "but yeah, we're doing it."

Amelie looks at me. "Be here at seven thirty?"

"No later," I confirm.

"Should we go early?" Jensen asks her. "Meg and I?"

She nods. "That's probably smart. I don't want to arrive too early, given the circumstances. Less time for Roman to find something wrong."

I'm vaguely aware that this is aiding and abetting, but honestly, I don't care. There are worse things I could be doing with my afternoon.

Besides, my dad started it. Not us.

"Sounds like a plan," Jensen mutters, standing from the table. He walks over to the fridge and removes two cans of cola, sitting one directly in front of Amelie. She grins and pops the top, but he doesn't open his. Instead, he stares directly at me like I've just kicked a puppy.

"So this is a thing now?" He asks, motioning between Amelie and I. "As in, this isn't ending after tonight. Am I understanding correctly?"

Amelie glances at me, then back at Jensen. "Yes, you're understanding correctly."

He blinks and waves vaguely at the disaster of a corkboard in the corner. "You're *fine* with this?"

"I am," I say solemnly.

His eyes say that he doesn't believe me, and I don't blame him. This whole thing started out with me blackmailing Amelie with proof of her job, which is a complete turnaround from where I'm at now. But it's true. All of it.

Amelie is it for me. Even *while* being an inconvenience with her work, she got under my skin in the most addicting way, and I'd be lying if I said this wasn't a little thrilling. If I said it wasn't a part of her I've grown to be obsessed with.

Jensen sighs and leans forward on his arms. He takes a long drink of water before laying eyes on Amelie once again. "Alright. Fine. I won't be plotting his demise any longer."

She laughs, but I'm not sure he's kidding. "Jen, really. Meg's hostility has rubbed off on you. And anyways, I have no time for this. I have to find a dress to wear tonight."

"You can't wear one of the seventy-two that you already have?" Meg asks.

Amelie scoffs. "*No.* And I've got no time to make one, either. I didn't think this through as thoroughly as I should've."

"So just...go buy one," Jensen suggests.

She shakes her head. "Can't. I've been banned from the dress shop on this street."

I open my mouth to ask why on earth she's been banned from a boutique, but she holds up a hand. "Don't."

"Noted." I stand from my chair and step away from the table, pulling my phone back out of my pocket. "Give me just a minute."

None of them protest as I step into the hallway and dial my sister's number. She answers on the first ring, so I assume she's either avoiding her work or simply bored out of her mind.

"Hi hi!" Liz says into the phone. Her tone is happy, so she's probably *not* at work. "What do you want?"

"I need a favor. Well, technically, it's an indirect favor."

"*Ooh*, okay. For whom?"

I lean against the wall. "How do you feel about dress shopping with—?"

Before I can even say Amelie's name, Liz squeals and says she'll meet me on the corner in ten.

50

AMELIE

"I'm picturing something red for you. I, personally, am opting for black, but that's because it's what I'm used to. These events are quite boring, and everyone wears neutrals to match their graying skin."

I grin as Liz grabs my hand and drags me into an elevator, pressing a button that nears the top floor.

This was the last thing I expected to be doing today.

Two minutes after I complained about *not* having a dress, Henry told me to follow him outside. Said he had a surprise for me. I had no idea that the surprise was Lizzy, who apparently wants to dress me like her own personal Barbie doll, but I couldn't be happier.

We aren't going shopping, though; not in the literal sense of the word. Instead, Liz led me to her workplace—which I've deemed *High Fashion Headquarters*, because I don't know what it's really called—and said we'd have better luck here.

I was expecting a bin of rejected dresses. Maybe a closet, best case scenario.

But when the elevator doors open, my jaw drops.

I'm greeted with rows and rows and *rows* of dress racks. Full shelves of shoes and handbags. Multiple jewelry displays, separated into gold, silver, and jeweled.

This is exactly what the inside of my mind looks like. Likely from overwatching *The Devil Wears Prada.*

"You work here?" Is all I manage as I gape at my surroundings.

Liz nods and steps into the room—or, no. The *floor.* I think these shelves occupy the entire level of this building. "My boss gives me hives, but yes. I guess it has its perks. When I'm bored, I come up here and scour things, though most of the pieces aren't my style on their own. But normally, I can make them work. Accessories and all that."

I can see why she'd say that. Liz's outfits are always impeccable, but they're nothing basic. She's the only person I've seen that isn't wearing a pencil skirt and a button-down that fastens at the throat. Her black slacks, lacy white tank, and brown leather jacket stick out, and I think she likes that.

"Do you want red?" Liz asks, stopping in front of a rack. The ones in this row are *all* red; some skirts are puffy, some fitted. Some look like the hem won't go past my hip bone.

"I like red," I say, still looking around the room. There's a pair of heels in the corner that I can't keep my eyes off of.

Liz hums. "Fitted?"

"Absolutely not. I need to be mobile."

"Good point." She grabs a couple of dresses off the rack and tosses them over her arm before moving further down. "Any specific fabric?"

I shake my head and toy with some of the skirts. "Long as I can breathe in it, I'm fine."

She laughs. "That's doable. The last event I went to, my dress was two sizes too small. I wanted to die for three hours straight. Though that could've been because my dad was the one hosting."

I wince. "You go to a lot of these?"

"I try to get out of them," she admits, going to the rack of black dresses. "It works sometimes. This is the only one I have the desire to go to, solely because of...you know." She waves her hand in my direction. "Any chance I have to see my dad fall is one I don't want to miss."

Her tone of voice is so even, so solemn, that it actually stuns me a bit. I know that she means it. I know she wants Roman to fail, because there's no hesitation in her words. It's still shocking to me; how ready she and Henry are for their dad to lose. I know that he hasn't been good to them—to *anybody*, it sounds—but it's hard to imagine wanting my own parents in turmoil.

Liz takes a step away from me and attempts to hold her arms up, trying to display the gowns she's gathered. "You ready to try them on?"

I nod. "Where do we...?"

"Oh, there's a curtain up here. These are used for last-minute photoshoots and promo, so we've got everything."

I exhale. "So I need to keep this dress totally unblemished."

"It would be preferable, but if you can't, my boss won't notice one missing." She pauses. Grins. "You know what? Keep it. I love to spite him."

A smile crawls across my face. "You really don't like that man, do you?"

"Don't get me started. You'll never hear the end of it." She sighs and starts toward the corner of the room, where three large dressing curtains take up the space. Liz walks into the one on the far left and hangs her dresses on a hook, then places mine in the next one over. "Okay. If you need help, yell at me. I'll wait out here until you're done."

"Don't you need to try yours on, too?"

"Well, yes, but I'm here to be your runner. If you need a different size or something, I'll go get it." Liz shoos me away with her hands. "Go! We don't have long!"

I comply and slip behind the middle curtain, snapping it shut and grabbing at one of the dresses. Liz picked out four, but one of them catches my eye immediately.

It's a stunning, off-the-shoulder gown with a loose skirt and a straight hem. The bodice looks sturdy enough to move around in, which I *hope* is the case. I'm already completely in love with the dress, and I'm totally going to wear it, regardless of its capabilities.

I shed my clothes and step into the dress, tugging it carefully over my hips and onto my shoulders. Liz has an eye for this stuff, because it fits like a glove. I *can* breathe in it, and the zipper goes up with ease. I make sure it's truly fastened before I step out from behind the curtain, and when Liz sees me, she gasps.

"THAT ONE!" She cries, clasping her hands together. "You have to wear that one, Amelie. Please. I'll literally pay you."

I laugh and look down at myself. "With that reaction, how can I not?"

"You *must*," she agrees, circling me like a vulture. "Oh, you're gorgeous! It fits you perfectly. My brother is going to have a stroke."

I laugh again at her comment, but she cuts me off by asking, "What's up with that, by the way? Can I ask? I'm going to anyways, but I want to make sure."

My eyes drop to the ground, and I toy with the fabric on my arm. Lizzy got the vague details yesterday, and I'm not sure how much more to say. Maybe that was all Henry wanted her to know, though I sort of doubt that's the case. Liz just *knows* stuff. If I don't tell her, she'll find out by this evening.

"We told you yesterday that we're just working together," I say, my last attempt at keeping it under wraps.

She snorts. "You know I don't believe that."

"Fine. It's..." I take a breath, trying to find my words, but I come up blank. "I don't know, Liz"

"Well, *I* know, so let me enlighten you." She slips behind her curtain before continuing. "He's enamored with you. Like, genuinely. It's worse than it used to be. As soon as he started talking about you, I wanted to smack him for even *acting* like he was indifferent."

I raise my brows. "You're kidding."

"Not in the slightest. So what's really up?"

I rest my hands on my hips, hoping that I'm not about to say something stupid aloud. "I think we're trying things again. I *think*,"

I reiterate, though I'm pretty sure that's the case. "I don't know. I'm willing, and I think he is, too."

"He is," she confirms. Her words are followed by swishing fabric and a heavy sigh. "Trust me."

I bite my lip against a smile. "What about you?"

"Me?"

"Do you have someone?"

It's silent for a beat. Her curtain snaps open, and she steps out in a gorgeous dark purple gown. I didn't even notice a colored dress in her stash, but I'm convinced the thing was made for her. It's completely fitted, all the way down to her ankles; the top is a scoop neck, and the back is low enough to send her dad into cardiac arrest. It's perfect.

"You look beautiful," I tell her. "That color is amazing on you."

"Thank you," she says, staring at herself in the mirror. "I didn't choose this one, but it was left in there, and it's my size, so *clearly* it was fate. But the back...is it bad?"

I shake my head. "No, I think it works. But this doesn't get you out of answering that question."

Liz smiles, barely. "Nope. I've got no one."

"No interest, either?"

She pauses. Decides on a shake of her head. "Not that, either."

I can't decide whether or not I believe her.

"*LIZZY!*"

Someone shouts from behind us, and I go ramrod straight. We're about to get caught pilfering dresses. Liz whips around, looking like she's scared of the same thing, but her face softens when she notices the girl stumbling toward us. "Florence!"

The girl—Florence—barrels forward, wrapping Liz into a hug. "I didn't know you were here today."

"I'm just here to snag a couple outfits. Do *not* tell Hewitt," she says pointedly. "He owes me for the Fendi shipment, anyways. He'll survive."

"As if I'd dare." Florence clasps her hands together. "You look ravishing, babydoll. You too," she says, smiling right at me. It makes her eyes practically glitter against her dark skin. Much like

I'd seen earlier, she's wearing a gray pencil skirt with a white button down that does, in fact, close at her throat. Rather than wearing neutral shoes, though, she's wearing hot pink pumps. I wouldn't expect them to look good with the outfit, but she manages to pull it off.

"They're my rebellion," she explains, noticing my gaze on her shoes. "We have a dress code, but I feel comfortable getting away with this."

"I've taught you well," Liz says solemnly. I'd bet anything that she rarely—if ever—abides by said rules. "Go for a scarf next week. Really spice it up, Flo!"

Florence grins, then sighs. "We'll see. I've got to go, though. I came to grab the new Valentino shoes we got in."

"By the makeup counter, I think," Liz says, motioning vaguely to her right.

Florence seems to understand that cue. She gives Liz a kiss on the cheek and waves to me before disappearing behind the maze of racks.

Liz turns back toward the mirror. "That's Florence, though I'm sure you got that. She's my assistant."

I blink. "You have an assistant?"

"Technically. Really, though, she's just my friend. I don't make her do much besides fax things. I don't know how, and I really don't care to learn." She shrugs. "Hewitt—my boss—has picked up on my general hate for delegating, so he normally has her running errands for himself."

"I'm still hung up on the assistant thing, honestly."

She laughs. "I'm an editor on the magazine, as well as a main writer, so he got me an assistant in case I ever felt overwhelmed."

The fact that she's only twenty makes it all the more impressive. "How long have you been at this?"

"Almost two years," she says. "I figured things out pretty easily. A lot of people here hate me because of how quickly I got where I am, but I didn't do anything differently. I literally just do what I'm told. I'm not passionate enough about this job to try and do something groundbreaking." She sighs and spins around, checking out the back of her dress in the mirror once more. "So, these? Are we good?"

"I think we are," I say, giving myself a final once-over. "We look good."

"We look *way* better than good. I'd go so far as to use the word beguiling."

I grin. "Let's change out of these *beguiling* dresses before your boss kills us."

Liz snorts and disappears behind her curtain. "Hewitt can't tell a stiletto from a kitten heel on a good day. I don't think he has it in him to murder someone."

I snap my curtain shut and slip out of my dress. "Speaking of... how badly do you want to spite him? I saw a pair of heels that I'm dying to try on."

A laugh sounds to my left. "I like the way you think."

51

———

HENRY

After Liz got ahold of Amelie, I went back to my apartment and tried to bask in the calm before the storm. It resulted in very little relaxation and lots of anxious pacing, for most of which Betty clawed at the hem of my pants.

Now, it's exactly fifteen minutes until the auction begins. I'm one block away from the event hall, checking the time every three seconds while I wait for Amelie to show. She called an hour ago and told me she'd meet me here, and I don't like it. I wanted to walk here together, if only to calm my nerves. I know Amelie can hold her own; that's not the problem. But the circumstances of today have me on edge. What if she runs into my dad? What if it's one of his workers? Can they get her in trouble?

I don't know, but it was no use arguing. She and Liz spent the entire afternoon getting ready at Liz's place, so Amelie never even went home. I didn't realize that it could take seven hours to get ready, but who am I to judge? I wear the same black suit to these events every single time.

I exhale and check my watch again. 7:49. I don't want to be late. Causing more of a scene than necessary is really something I'd like to avoid, but the longer we wait, the more difficult that becomes. Walking into this thing even a minute late is enough to get eyes on us. I just can't afford—

"You look nervous," a voice says from behind me. "You're tapping your foot like a wind-up toy."

I grin and turn around, taking a sharp breath when my eyes land on her.

Staying focused on the task at hand is going to be a chore, to say the least.

"Hi," Amelie says, sounding almost shy. She's wringing her hands in front of her, twisting at the bracelet on her wrist.

"Hi," I say quietly, pocketing my own hands so I don't reach out and touch her. I let my eyes run over her pinned up hair, her silky red dress. Her lipstick—as always, I've noticed, when she's wearing something red—matches the shade of fabric perfectly. The necklace I gifted her hangs around her neck, and I can't help but grin at the sight of it. "You're breathtaking," I tell her. "But I'm sure you know that already."

Amelie laughs, and the sound fills me with warmth. She steps forward and straightens my tie, and I hold my breath, solely at our proximity. "I do," she says, looking me over again. She doesn't seem to mind the general blandness of my attire; her eyes are glued to me, as are mine to her. "But you're giving me a run for my money."

Grinning, I run my palm down her arm, and she grabs my hand before I can move it. I want to pull her closer. To take the pins out of her hair and run my fingers through it. But we're on a street corner, and we have other things to attend to, so that'll have to wait.

"Are we ready?" She asks, tightening her grip on my hand.

I nod, starting down the sidewalk. "I guess so. Is everything ready on your end?"

"Yes. Jensen just called me; they've been here for a while."

"Good." I let out another sigh, and again, she squeezes my hand. I have no doubt that she's picking up on my discomfort. This situation isn't good. It isn't even *moderately* good; it's just bad, all around. The only positive I'll get out of this is being free from my dad, and that isn't even a guarantee. It's a vague end goal.

"It'll be okay," Amelie says softly, looking up at me. "I promise."

I don't respond, because my initial response is to argue.

It's not that I don't trust *her*. It's more that I trust my dad to make this night chaos.

But I don't have time to worry. Within minutes, we're standing at the entrance to the auction hall. Amelie manages to move closer to me, somehow; she loops her arm through mine and leans lightly against my shoulder. If I were smart, I'd take a step away from her so I can focus, but I can't bring myself to do that.

The security guard standing near the door gives each of us a nod as we pass him. I hold my breath as we enter, as if he'd somehow know what we're here for, but he doesn't give us a second glance. Just nods at the next person as they file in behind us.

I've got to calm down.

"This place is beautiful," Amelie says, looking around as we walk through the lobby. She's right—I love this place. It's always been a favorite of mine when my dad holds events. He doesn't own it, but he's rented it out more times than I can count. He and the owner are old friends.

The room is lit with scattered candelabras on the walls, as well as a dim chandelier that does absolutely nothing. Every inch of the ceiling is covered with paintings, and the style is a play on the Sistine Chapel's. It's much worse, execution wise, but no one could replicate such a thing. I'd be scared to even try.

"Should we go in?" I ask Amelie. "What's your plan?"

"I don't know," she admits. "But I say yes. I think it'd be a lot more subtle that way. We take a table, act like we care, and then I'll sneak out. Is that stupid?"

I shake my head. "Just do it discreetly."

"I will." She starts walking toward the doors, hand still in mine. Right before we step into the bidding area, a man gives us a paddle with the number 19 on it. Amelie thanks him before taking a seat at a table in the very back. I slide into the chair next to her, thankful that there are only two other people at this table. They're both preoccupied, busy with their drinks, so I'm hoping they'll keep to themselves.

As soon as I scan the room, I see my dad on the front row. He's talking with a few other men, wearing the stiff, fake smile I've come to notice from a mile away.

I exhale and focus on the candle on the table instead of the tightness in my chest.

"How does this thing go?" Amelie whispers to me. "The order of it?"

"If it's anything like others I've attended—and I'm sure it will be—the museum owners will be introduced, and the artists will get brief shoutouts. Then the bidding will start. My dad's segment is rumored to be second, so..."

"I'll go during the first, then," she says with a shrug. "It'll be funnier if he has no paintings to bid off, instead of stealing them from buyers."

I grin, and the pain in my chest seems to melt away. It calms me a little, to admit to myself that I need her here. I didn't expect to be so nervous about this, but her voice is the only thing keeping me somewhat grounded.

"Drinks?"

A waitress materializes in front of us, holding a tray of various drinks. I don't know what any of them are, save for the wine and champagne, but Amelie is scouring the choices.

"Champagne, please," she says sweetly, chin rested on her hands. "You, Henry?"

"No, thank you," I say, giving the woman a tense smile.

She nods to me, then hands Amelie a flute. After telling us to find her if we need anything else, she goes to the next table.

"I've never had champagne," she says, looking at the fizzy liquid. "It looks...odd."

"It makes Liz sneeze."

"Really?" She looks stunned. "I've never heard of that."

"I hadn't either. Though I'm not convinced it's a common thing."

Amelie hums and lifts the glass to her lips. After a few sips of the drink, she sets it down, looking mildly disappointed.

"Well?" I ask.

She opens her mouth to respond, but before she can, she lets out the daintiest sneeze I've ever heard. I laugh quietly as she frowns. "Ew," she says simply. "That wasn't pleasant."

"I believe it's the carbonation," a man at our table says. His back is facing us, and he hasn't paid us any mind this whole time, so him acknowledging *this* is a bit random. "Have you—have you ever had a soda that made you sneeze? Same concept."

"I have," Amelie says, sort of wistfully. "Long ago."

"I did, just today." The man sighs and turns to face us. When he does, both Amelie's and my face drop.

"*Dave*?" She laughs. I'm glad she addressed him by name because I didn't remember it. I simply deemed him '*Man from the patisserie*'. "What are you doing here?"

"I'm an art lover, what can I say?" Dave says, and it becomes glaringly obvious that he's drunk, even though there are only three drained glasses at this table. He must be a lightweight. "Got a little extra to spend. Might as well scope out some décor, no?"

Amelie sighs. "You *tease!*"

"I don't!" He laughs heartily. "Don't bid against me, though, Amelie. It would truly hurt me."

"I wouldn't dream of it," she says solemnly. "In fact, the second you grab your paddle, I'll chuck mine across the room."

Dave laughs again, then hiccups. "You flatter."

"I jest," she corrects, then takes another sip of champagne. She makes the same wrinkled face before setting the glass back down. "I really don't like that."

Dave responds to her, saying something about a drink she should try instead, but I don't catch the details. I'm distracted by my phone buzzing in my pocket, one notification after the other. I pull it out and find a string of texts from my sister.

LIZZY

okay i'm here (ew). where are you

WAIT I JUST SAW YOUR HEAD CAN I PLEASE
SIT WITH YOU

PLEASE

"Can Liz sit over here?" I ask Amelie. "Or will that throw a bump in things?"

She shakes her head. "It's fine. Tell her to come over."

I nod and send the text back.

Yes. Bring two waters. Amelie fell under the champagne trap.

LIZZY

poor girl. she'll be sneezing all evening

As if on cue, Amelie sneezes.

Liz arrives moments later with three glasses in only one hand. I have no idea how she does that, but Amelie doesn't seem fazed by it in the slightest. She accepts a glass and pats the seat next to her, signaling for Liz to sit there. My sister drops into the seat with a sigh, sloshing water into her lap but not caring.

"Why hasn't this started yet?" She asks, her expression annoyed.

I check the time on my watch and realize that I have the same question. It's five past eight, which isn't much, but these things are punctual. Time is not a suggestion. Last year, Liz and I watched the clock to the second, and the lights turned on at eight on the dot.

I really hope nothing is going on in the back.

"I'm sure it's nothing," I say, more to myself than anyone else. "Dad is likely fixing his combover."

Liz rolls her eyes. "That thing will kill me, I'm sure of it."

Amelie laughs, probably about to interject a jab of her own, but the lights finally brighten the room. I check my watch again—8:07. It's about time.

"It's starting?" Amelie asks quietly.

Lizzy nods. "Should be."

It does. A few older men walk up on stage and begin talking, introducing people I recognize only by name. Rounds of applause are raised, artists are named—me included—and my dad's name is mentioned last.

He rises to the stage at that moment, and every nerve in my body is screaming that this is going to go poorly.

Amelie looks too relaxed.

"Good evening," he says into the microphone, a grating voice booming over the speakers. "Who's ready to lose some money?"

Everyone in the room gives a hollow laugh.

"Good, good," he mutters. "Well, I won't say much. Nobody wants to hear me talk. My section is later in the night, so I'll be on the front row, shooting dirty looks at Greg." Another round of laughter, followed by glances at the man beside him. "Let's get it started. You take it, Greg."

The man takes the microphone and starts talking. My dad, along with the few other men on stage, walk back down to the seating area. He nearly trips on the bottom step, and I hear Lizzy snort very indiscreetly. It's loud enough to gain a few looks our way, but she tries to play it off by coughing into her elbow.

"Sorry," she mutters, taking a long drink of water. "Allergies."

It's enough of an explanation for the people around us, but not for my dad, who somehow heard the entire thing.

He's staring right at us.

Right at Amelie.

"I'll take that as my cue," she mutters, standing slowly from the table. She's holding eye contact with him, keeping her face completely neutral. He makes no move to turn away until one of the other men usher him into his seat. "Wish me luck."

"Please be careful," I say quietly.

She puts a hand on my shoulder. Kisses my cheek. "I'll try."

And she walks away, out the back door with her dress trailing behind her.

52

AMELIE

Jensen meets me by the men's bathroom. He looks absolutely crazed—wide eyes, shaking hands. I don't know why this specific job is stressing him out so much, but it seems to be his *least* favorite to date. I guess I understand why; one wrong move and this whole thing topples to the ground.

"Come on," he says, grabbing me by the elbow. "The door is already open."

I frown. "They left it unlocked? That's odd."

"No, Ames. I broke the lock."

"Oh, that's nice."

I mindlessly follow him while checking over my shoulder every few seconds. There are a few security guards flitting around, and I have absolutely no intention of catching their eye. Truthfully, I should've chosen a more downplayed dress, but I simply couldn't. This one was practically begging to come home with me.

"Has everything gone smoothly so far?" Jensen asks, moving my hand to the crook of his arm. "Any problems?"

I shake my head. "No problems. Roman knows we're here, but I don't think he'll do anything about it. He seems preoccupied right now."

"How do you know that he knows we're here?"

I don't answer immediately, which prompts Jensen to sigh. "You provoked him."

"I did not! We just made eye contact."

"Oh, joy." He turns us down an empty, darkened hall, stopping right in front of the first door. Faint shuffling comes from inside, and my heart speeds. The noise from the bidding area seems to increase, fits of laughter and applause clashing at the same time. There's a curtain further down the hall, which means we're directly behind the stage.

I don't love that.

"Let's get this over with," I mumble, pushing the door open.

Inside is my genuine worst nightmare.

There are *stacks* of canvases—at least fifty, maybe more. On top of that, there are workers on the opposite end of the room, pushing one of the paintings on a dolly. I duck behind the door and let out a breath before looking back inside.

This is fine. We only came here for two pieces. Surely, we can find them quickly enough.

"Start digging," I whisper to Jen, hiding behind a marble column. The men in the room seem very preoccupied, which is good. Their attention will be far from us. "We're looking for the *Ophelia* and *Lover of Mine*."

"That would be easy, if there weren't a thousand canvases in here," Jensen grumbles, crouching beside me.

"We need to find them before this segment ends." I pick up a few canvases by the edge and glance over them, finding nothing we need. "Start looking."

He wants to argue. That much is obvious, but to his credit, he keeps his mouth shut. Instead, he starts sifting through the row of canvases closest to him.

I'm sure there's some rhyme or reason to the set-up of this room, but I haven't figured it out yet. It wouldn't be totally random, right? There's got to be an order. Maybe by artist, or museum.

Wait. That's actually smart.

Quietly, I go back to my hiding place and spy on the men across the room. They're loading multiple pieces onto a dolly. I can't find anything that answers my question, but I *do* notice that they're all from the same pile. They're putting them in order, one after the other.

I'm about to do something *so* incredibly foolish, and I don't think it's going to work.

"Excuse me," I say, stepping out from behind the pillar.

Both men jump and look at me, clearly confused as to why I'm here and not at the auction. I put on my prettiest smile and try to look confident, though I really feel like knocking them out. It would be easier that way.

"Can we help you?" One of them asks, his voice gruff.

"Yes, actually. I'm working for Roman Arlington. I need to know which of these are from The Gallery so I can load them."

The other man—I deem him The Tall One—raises a brow. "You?"

"Yes." I raise my own brows in return. They're prettier than his; much more tailored. "Is there a problem?"

"Only confused as to why he sent...*you* over," Shorty says, looking me up and down. "No offense, but you don't look like you can lift a canvas."

I blink. "You think that lifting cloth and a few pieces of wood is hard?"

"Some of these pieces are nearly eighty inches wide. That's a pretty heavy load."

"Yes. Well." I sigh. "I'm really in a hurry, if you wouldn't mind showing—"

"The one's you're standing right next to," The Tall One tells me. "Those are for The Gallery."

"Perfect." Thank goodness they're finished with their antics. "Thank you. If you could spare—"

"Pick it up."

I scoff. "Pardon?"

"Pick up one of the pieces."

Ugh. "I don't have time for this. Roman has me on a schedule, and I'm not going to jeopardize my job to prove a point."

The Tall One takes a step forward. "Come on. You'll have to put them on a dolly anyways. Pick it up, put it on the thing. We just want to see you at work."

And I just want to see your head detached from your body, is what I want to say, but I don't.

I stifle a sigh and walk over to The Gallery's stock. It's hard to tell the difference between pieces since they're stacked together, but I'm lucky enough to see the corner of Henry's *Ophelia.* It's the second canvas from the front.

I step forward and move the front piece aside, more so dragging it than lifting. I feel guilty, given that the bottom will probably be scraped up, but it has to be done. I'm not weak, but I'm certainly not strong, and though Meg would kill me for saying so, I *really* would prefer a man to do my heavy lifting. It's not that I can't, it's that I don't want to. Less strain on my manicure.

"Alright, boys," I mumble. "If that's what you want."

"It is," The Tall One says, sounding overtly amused. Is this what men do all day? Ask women to do things for their entertainment? I really hope something heavy falls on his foot.

Rolling my eyes, I try to find a good grip on the canvas. It's nearly impossible to find somewhere that my hand won't slip. If I get a splinter, I *will* beat the life out of these idiots.

Just as I grab onto the corner, I see movement behind the men, and my entire body relaxes.

Jensen.

It's about time.

He mouths at me to keep quiet, so I do. I pretend to be extremely intrigued with the piece in front of me and make a show of looking for the perfect hand placement. One of the men sighs, like this is taking too long, so I do it even slower.

"You two are needed," Jensen says finally, standing stiffly in place.

Dumb and Dumber whip around on him. "Who are you?"

"Event coordinator," he says, and I stifle a laugh. The *last* thing Jensen could be is an event coordinator. "They need you two up front."

"For what?"

"Probably because you're harassing this woman who's trying to do her work, and your pieces aren't where they need to be." His stoic voice makes this all the better. "They've got some questions."

Shorty looks terrified, at least from the back. He's flexing his hands at his sides, shaking his head so hard it looks like it might topple off. I think Jensen's unapproachable air is really selling this thing. "It's only been—"

"I'd go if I were you."

They don't wait another second before exiting the room, leaving Jensen and I alone.

"Took you long enough." I put my hands on my hips and sigh. "Now, help me with this. I've found the *Ophelia,* and I just need—"

"*Nautical Abyss,* right?" He motions over to where he was standing earlier. "I found it."

My stomach flips, and I gape at him.

I'd nearly forgotten about the switch up at Bondi's.

"*Lover of Mine* is what I was going to say, but that's good too."

"Let's get these out of here first," he suggests. "Two for three isn't bad."

I chew on my lip, no doubt smearing my lipstick. He's right—retrieving two paintings isn't bad at all, but it also isn't good enough. "No. We're doing it right. Three for three."

He sighs. "Amelie—"

"Jensen."

"Those men have *jobs,*" he says, pointing out the open door. "They're going to come back, and then what?"

"I don't know, but we won't have to worry about that if we hurry."

His eyes are drilling a hole through my forehead. "Please listen to me, just this once. I don't have a good feeling about this."

I sigh and yank my phone out of my bodice, where I've had it nicely tucked against my ribs. "Just keep looking for *Lover of Mine.*"

I'm waiting for an argument, but one never comes. He nods and continues to leaf through the pieces in front of us.

I, on the other hand, pull up Henry's phone number with unsteady hands. The time on my screen lets me know that nearly twenty minutes have passed, and that gives me a horrible feeling.

you said lizzy can cause a scene?

His reply is instant.

ARLINGTON

Give me a minute.

I shove my phone back down my dress and keep searching for the canvas. Whatever Liz is about to do, I need it to stop the auction. As much as I hate to admit it, Jensen is right. Those men are going to be back here unless something bigger gets their attention, and problems don't just materialize. Not unless—

My thoughts freeze at the sound of a guttural scream.

"*What is that*?" Jensen hisses, grabbing onto my elbow like he's ready to drag me away from here.

I tug my arm loose and listen closely. After a moment, I realize that it *is* Lizzy's voice. She's wailing loudly, and I hear feedback from a microphone, like it's been dropped. Feet are shuffling wildly around the place, and I know she's done it.

She's bought us time.

"Perfect," I say. "It's perfect. Now *hurry,* Jen. We don't have long."

Jensen, ever the optimist, groans and keeps looking for the painting.

53

HENRY

I don't understand how Liz can turn on tears in two seconds.

She's wailing right now, and it's earsplitting. Everyone has rushed to her side. A few women are patting her face, trying to figure out why she's crying and failing. I don't know what her excuse will be. Perhaps that she's descending into madness?

"He doesn't care!" She cries, mascara gathering with her tears. "He's *never* cared about me!"

"Who, doll?" The ladies pry, still trying to wipe her face. She's moving around so spastically that they can hardly do it without poking her in the eye.

"My father!" Lizzy shouts. She releases a heavy sigh and points a finger toward the stage, right at our dad. "*Him!*"

Oh, she's good.

"Roman?" The ladies say in unison, turning to look at him. "What did he do?"

"He didn't want me to come. When I did, he stuck me at this table in the back. He's hated my face since I was a child. Says I look too much like my mother." She basically sobs her way through the sentence. "He can't even stand to *look* at me!"

I try to stifle my laughter as I stand, aware that I'm about to get myself in trouble. "Father!" I shout across the room, in the same direction Liz's hand is pointed. "Come quick! Lizzy is distraught!"

My dad turns his eyes slowly toward me, anger in his gaze. I know I'll pay for this later. I know this is foolish, but when Amelie's message appeared on my screen, I stopped caring about what I'll face after this.

Dad makes his way off the stage and into an aisle. Liz is still going strong with the tears, her sighs getting longer, her wailing more infrequent. I've never seen someone so perfectly play a damsel in distress. I don't think she's taken a normal breath in three minutes. Part of me wonders if this is fake, or if perhaps something actually triggered it, because this is ridiculous.

"What's the matter?" Dad says, hands pressed to his temples as he surveys the damage. He all but rolls his eyes when Lizzy blows her nose into the tablecloth, but the ladies surrounding her chair eye *him* with disgust instead of her. "Elizabeth, what happened?"

"You told me my nose—you said it was ugly!" She starts shuddering again. "That's why you didn't want me here. But I came anyway, and now I'm stuck in the back! All because I'm *hideous!*"

Dad's eyes widen. "That—that isn't true!"

"I'm going to get Liz some tissues," I say, weaving my way through the crowd that gathered around us. "Keep her company, Dad."

"I don't have time!" He calls back, failing to sound sympathetic. There's no way he can leave, because a decent portion of people have flocked him. He'd have to elbow his way out.

I give him a wave over my shoulder and make my way to the door.

The problem is, I have no idea where Amelie went, and I don't want to draw attention by asking where the pieces are being stored. I assume it's somewhere behind the stage, given the setup of this building, but finding the door is the hard part.

I pull my phone out and send a text to Amelie, not really expecting an answer, but figuring that it's wiser than asking someone.

How do I get to you? Where are you?

I'm halfway across the lobby when she replies.

AMES

go to the far right. don't stop until you see the funky little trash can, then go in that door. i'll be standing outside the correct one when i hear your footsteps

I look around for the trash bin. The only one I see is gray with strange claw feet, so I assume that's what she's referring to. There's security down the hallway, so I get to the door before he gets a glimpse of me. If this is the correct place, then he's just a *little* too close to what's about to happen.

Amelie must agree, because she doesn't poke her head into the hall until I'm only a foot away. She motions frantically inside the room, so I follow behind her, not shocked by what I see. The room is basically a massive storage closet, and they've already found my pieces. Jensen is trying to get *Lover of Mine* onto a dolly. Amelie is watching him, brow wrinkled like she could do it better.

"This'll go a lot quicker with two of us," Jensen grumbles in my direction. "Give me a hand."

I wordlessly cross the room and grab the other end of the canvas. These pieces are larger than most casual décor, and I'm now regretting the decision. I know this would be easier if they were smaller.

Jensen and I lift the piece on his count, and we get it settled almost instantly. Good. That's one down. I don't see any of my others, though I'm not sure if they're here. My dad made it seem like he was ready to sell every last one, but he must not have taken as many as I expected.

"This one next," Jensen says, motioning to my *Ophelia*.

I nod and grab a corner, settling it next to the other. Once we get the third and final piece balanced, Amelie walks over to us. Her motions are somewhat frantic, like she's worried about our time frame, and I understand. Regardless of Lizzy's 'incident', we still don't have a huge window. Her crying is no longer audible back here, which means she's cooling it down.

"I'll take these out," Jensen says, pushing the dolly slightly forward. The pieces aren't all that heavy on wheels, but keeping them upright will be a challenge. "Meg is out back. There's a door down the hall."

"I'll go first and make sure it's clear," Amelie says, standing up. "Henry, stay here. Or go back out. I'm not sure which is wisest. I don't—"

"I'll stay here," I say. I'm almost certain that reentering the hall could end poorly.

Amelie nods and walks out the door. I hear her shoes click down the hall, and slowly, the sound disappears until I hear nothing more. Jensen waits until she's no longer to be heard, because as soon as it's quiet, he follows.

Once I'm alone, I'm not sure what there is to do.

Am I a sitting duck if I stay here? What if my dad comes back? I guess there isn't much he can do—my pieces are already gone. There's nothing else for him to take from me.

I pocket my hands to stop myself from digging through the rest of these pieces. I'd be wasting time and drawing attention to myself. My focus needs to be on the situation at hand. Anything else is foolish. I either need to get out of here, or make sure that everything is going according to plan. The second is mostly impossible, so—

The door hinges creak behind me, and my breathing stops.

"Henry."

I close my eyes and swallow hard.

No.

Not now.

"Please," I say quietly. "Don't."

"This game is over, son." My dad's voice rolls through the room. "Turn around."

I don't turn around because I'm not stupid.

"Turn around," a second voice says. "Come on."

My stomach churns when I place the tone of voice.

"Henry," she says, voice practically dripping with disdain.

I turn around to see a face that mirrors Amelie's exactly.

54

HENRY

Margot Benoit is standing by my father, looking at me like I should've expected this.

"Explain," I say, staring at Margot and my dad. "Right now."

They give each other a sideways glance as if they're communicating silently. I have no idea what's going on. Nothing that I'm seeing makes sense to me.

"Where's Amelie?" I ask when they don't respond. "What did you do to her?"

Margot's face falls, and she turns to my dad. "You said she wouldn't be here."

"She wasn't meant to be," he mumbles.

"*Dad.*" My voice is shaking. "You have to tell me what's going on. I can't just—"

"You must know why I did it," he says, sounding much too calm. "You know I didn't do this out of the blue."

"What do you mean by *this*?"

"All of it." He frowns. "Henry, when I found out Amelie was back, I had to do something. Her parents would've taken your work, or *she* would've—"

"Her parents wouldn't have," I say, giving him the last part, because it's technically true. Amelie did take one of my pieces, but in the end, Dad had a hand in that, too. "They don't care about this anymore. But how does that tie into anything? It doesn't explain why you took my pieces or why she—" I motion vaguely to Margot. "—is standing next to you."

"Yes, it does," he says flatly. "If I had them, there was no chance of anyone else taking them." He pinches the bridge of his nose. "I can't just keep *saving* you."

I'm shocked enough to forget about my second question. "In what ways have you saved me?"

"I support you. I pay for your housing, and—"

"No." I shake my head. "Absolutely not. I've told you multiple times that I'm grateful, but I don't want you to."

He tries again. "I display your work—"

"*No.* I want other offers, and you know that. But you turn them down."

"Because I can't afford to have you *gone!*" His voice is loud now, and I take what I hope is a discreet step backward. "I can't afford to have your work somewhere else, Henry. Do you know why? Have you truly not caught on?"

He pauses, waiting for my answer. For my contradiction. But I stay silent.

"Without the money you bring in," he says, "The Gallery closes."

I exhale. I knew this was coming in the near future. It isn't a shock, but him finally voicing it makes it real.

"So close it," I say flatly. "Sell the buildings and the stocks. There are *so* many solutions to your problem, rather than stealing my work and framing others. I don't even see how this benefits you. If you'd just let me finish my *Ophelia,* you still would've gotten the money."

"I wanted her caught," he says, shifting the conversation right back to Amelie. "Is that so wrong? I wanted to kill two birds with one stone. To get your paintings for the auction *and* get her behind bars."

A laugh of disbelief escapes me. I'm vaguely aware of Margot observing this entire conversation, seemingly unbothered, but I'm too worked up to care. "You're so paranoid. The Benoits beat you out *years* ago, and you're still scared of their daughter. The only reason I even got her help was because *you* wouldn't let me get any other."

"And look where it's gotten me." His voice is drained. "You're in love with her again, is that it? You trust a criminal over your family."

"No, but I trust her over you."

He snaps his mouth shut after that. Whatever he was about to say is apparently void now, and I'm thankful. I note light footsteps passing in the hall, but they don't seem to stop, so I start talking again.

"You have to give it up. Just let it go. Go finish out the auction with the other pieces, and I'll leave."

He shakes his head, just as stubborn as I am. "No. I'm selling your work, Henry. You bring in the most money. *You.* Nobody else drags in over a couple grand in tickets."

I shrug, and his face shifts into anger. "I don't know what you want me to do. You aren't selling my pieces."

"Oh, why?" He stands a little straighter. "They're right behind you. Actually, they might be onstage already, waiting to be bid on." The smile on his face looks more like a grimace. "This night ends with me winning, Henry."

I squeeze my eyes shut and exhale. "I just want you to admit it. Tell me the truth. You know I can't stand being lied to, so please, enlighten me. Just lay it out for me. I don't want to wonder."

He sighs. Clasps his hands together. "That's all you want?"

I nod stiffly and hope my face is normal.

"Fine." He starts pacing, like he can't contain his energy any longer. "I took your *Ophelia.* Set up a fake meeting to snag *Lover of Mine* and *Nautical Abyss.* Your little friends never suspected a thing."

"You lost money with the meetings," I say, wondering if he'll deny the counterfeit cash. "They don't do all of that for free."

"Fake," he says, shocking me with the admission. "Wasn't a problem. Another thing that was easy to sneak past your *friends.*"

He says the word with such venom that I don't bother with a retort.

"What about Amelie?" I ask quietly. "You never told me how you cut our contact."

He laughs, so intensely that it startles me. "*That*?! Henry, I put a call blocker on your phone. It was the simplest thing. Do you remember the time your mother and I brought your brushes to your dormitory? It was child's play. I never expected you to find out, but I also never expected you to care this much about her." He exhales like he's disappointed. "Do you truly believe what she tells you? Does she even care about you?"

I swallow. Exhale sharply, then peek right over his shoulder into the seemingly empty hallway. "I don't know. Amelie, do you care about me?"

Both his and Margot's faces pale at my words. Dad whips around just in time to see Amelie stride into the room, holding a phone at her side. "I do," she says, giving me an overexaggerated smile before turning to my dad. "Roman, I don't know why you question such things."

"But—you—you can't—" He stutters. "What are you *doing*?"

"I'm helping," she says, her voice lethally soft. "Henry, anyways. Not you."

She doesn't look at her sister. Not once.

Margot, on the other hand, looks like she might throw up.

"You're here, though," my dad says, eyes widening. "You're here. You've entered the assembly uninvited—"

"As my date," I counter. "And I was invited."

Dad shakes his head. "Doesn't matter."

"No, it really does." Amelie sighs. "And anyways, you don't have proof."

Her voice catches on the last word, like she isn't sure if that's the truth. I notice her eyes slide over to Margot, as if she's waiting for a contradiction. It never comes.

My dad exhales sharply. "That's not..."

"Well, no matter what it is or isn't, I do have something for you." Amelie doesn't seem to regard the slight tremor in her voice.

She spins on her heel and presses a button on her screen, and seconds later, a voice starts playing back at us.

Mine.

"You know I can't stand being lied to, so please, enlighten me." My voice is airy through the phone. *"Just lay it out for me. I don't want to wonder."*

Amelie grins at my dad. She puts a finger to her lips, signaling for him to stay quiet. "This is where it gets good."

"That's all you want?" Dad's voice is stiffer than I remember it being only moments ago. *"Fine. I took your* Ophelia. *Set up a fake meeting to snag* Lover of Mine *and* Nautical Abyss. *Your little friends never suspected a thing."*

Amelie pauses the recording and looks at my dad. What little color was left on his face is gone as he stares at her phone. "What are you going to do with that?" He asks, his voice weak. "You can't turn that in without getting yourself caught."

"I can," she says simply. "As I've said, I'm here as Henry's date. That's entirely legal, as far as I'm concerned."

"But—but you have my money." His tone shifts from dry to enthusiastic in seconds. "You must've—"

"I'm not stupid. I know counterfeit money when I see it."

His smile drops again, but Amelie's shifts into something brighter. She's practically glowing while tormenting my father. "You were completely fine with doling out fake cash—albeit poorly made—because you thought you'd outsmart me. But you couldn't. So now, we need to find a new solution. One where you admit that I win."

"No," he says simply.

Amelie nods. "Okay. Fine. I'll just send this recording to my team—"

"No." Dad's voice is firm, though I can hear it. I can hear how desperate he is. "No. Just—*fine.* You win."

"I know." Amelie's face breaks into a catlike grin. "And in this little deal, *I* will keep this recording to myself."

"You'll delete it," Dad counters.

She shakes her head. "I won't. But *you* will release all of

Henry's displayed pieces in return. You'll give him the contacts for the offers that I know you've kept from him."

"That's *it*?" My dad asks skeptically, eyes darting between the two of us.

"Unless Henry has more." Amelie looks at me. "Anything else?"

I bite the inside of my cheek, because despite all things, I haven't thought of much. I know that I want the best for Mom and Lizzy, but I can take care of myself. I *want* to take care of myself. I want to be left alone by him.

"Sell what you have to in order to get out of debt."

He blinks at me. "That's not—"

"It's not a part of this deal," I clarify. "It's not something I'm going to hold over you. It's a request." I look at the wall. "I don't care about you, but I do care about Mom and Lizzy. I want you to put your family ahead of yourself for once. And from now on, I'll take care of myself. I'll pay my rent and handle my own jobs. Just get the money, fix your family, and leave *me* out of it."

Dad just nods. He looks defeated now, and I think that should hurt me, but it doesn't. It makes me feel bad that I *don't* feel bad. But this is the man that took the joy out of things for me. That put money and status over his wife and kids. I don't hate him, but that doesn't mean I respect him. That doesn't mean I'm okay with this any longer.

"And Mom doesn't need to know about this," I say quietly. "Keep her out of it, and I will too."

Dad lifts his eyes and looks at me, then gives one stiff, frustrated nod. "Okay."

I nod in return, waiting for more words to come to mind. They don't. But the room doesn't stay silent for more than three seconds, because Amelie turns right to Margot with flaming eyes. "Now. You."

55

AMELIE

Margot stares at me like she thinks I'm going to drag her out of here by her ankles and start a fight in the hallway.

I might. Not sure yet.

"Amelie," she starts, "*please* don't—"

"What on God's green earth were you *thinking*?" My voice is rising, and I'm not oblivious to the fact. Henry and Roman take a generous step away from Margot and I, clearly aware that this isn't going to be as quiet of an argument as theirs. "What is this? Is it a joke? Is that why you wanted me at the cabin?"

"No." She sighs. "Amelie, please. Listen to me—"

"I want the truth, then," I say. "All of it."

"Not now," she mutters, glancing over her shoulder. "This is a bad place, and—"

"*Now.*"

She swallows. Looks awkwardly over her shoulder at Roman, who is staring out the door.

"Go," I tell him, getting his attention by snapping my fingers. "Get out."

He doesn't have to be told twice. Roman walks out of the room, hands in his hair like he might tug it out. I don't look away from the door until his footsteps have gone silent, and when they have, I turn back to Margot.

"I'm sorry," she whispers. "It wasn't supposed to happen like this."

"*Talk.*"

She exhales. "Roman saw me. A couple years ago, he saw me in the city and he thought I was you."

Something heavy settles in my chest, because that was the last thing I expected her to say. "What?"

"I didn't even recognize him at first because I'd never *seen* him. He told me who he was, and I connected the names, then told him who I was. We talked briefly, and I mentioned that I was in art school like Henry, and he—" She takes a breath, like this conversation is physically painful for her. "—he offered me a spot in his museum. I declined, because I was still in school and wouldn't be in the city much.

"Well, about a year ago," she continues, looking anywhere but me. "I went back to The Gallery and asked if his offer was still there. I wasn't getting any work, so I thought it was smart. But he said *no*. He said that spot had been filled. So...he gave me something else."

Margot swallows hard, looking almost ill at this admission. "I helped him steal a piece. One singular piece. That was it. I didn't do much of the hands-on work, but I figured things out. And I *hated* it. A lot. But he gave me a decent cut, and I needed it.

"He didn't contact me after that. By the next month, I had job interviews, and I wasn't worried about it. I'd forgotten about him until a month ago when he got back in contact with me." Her words are running together now, like she doesn't want to tell me this, but she can't make herself stop. "It was me. This time, I was doing the hands-on work, and I was swapping out the pieces you were looking for. I did it all, and I'm sorry. I'm so sorry, Amelie. I should've—I should've just told you."

I'm silent. Frozen. Because it all makes sense now.

Margot *never* kept my work quiet for our family's sake.

She did it for herself.

"But you hate me for what I do," I whisper, hating that my voice is shaking. "You've said—"

"I hate that you *want* it, and I don't."

"You weren't forced," I say, though I'm not trying to be accusatory. I'm not trying to be rude. I'm simply stating what seems to be a fact.

"I wasn't," she agrees. "Not at all. But once I was in it, I don't think I could've gotten out. Before you did all this, that is." She motions to the phone I'm still clutching at my side. "I don't reckon he'll be contacting me any time soon."

I shake my head, still not convinced that this is real. "But you *knew*. When we talked at Brenn's, you knew what you were saying was true." I pause. "Were you trying to warn me? Or trying to prove a point?"

"I didn't know you were going to be here," she says again, avoiding my question. "I thought he'd keep you away."

I close my eyes and take a moment to breathe, because my chest seems to constrict tighter with each breath. Never in my life did I expect Margot to team up with a man who so strongly hates my family. Who so strongly hates *me*. I understand we aren't on the best of terms—I understand that it's partially my fault.

But I didn't think she had it in her.

"I would've never done this to you," I whisper. "Not now, not ever."

"I know," she says quietly. "I'm so—"

"Stop apologizing. I don't want to hear it."

Her mouth snaps shut.

"I don't want to see you. Not for a very long time." I cross my arms over my chest. "Right now, I hope I never see you again."

She exhales shakily. "You can't be angry, Amelie. You don't—"

"I can't be *angry*?" My voice sounds hysterical, even to my own ears. "Margot, I am *livid*. This past week, you knew what he was doing to me. You were the one *doing* it, and you never cared. You put me down, then turned around and did the same thing."

She doesn't argue. Doesn't even try.

"What are you going to do?" She asks instead.

I stare at her. "What do you mean?"

"Are you going to turn me in?"

Reluctantly, even though everything in me is saying *yes,* I shake my head. "No. I'm not. But if you ever—and I do mean *ever*—pull this stunt again, I have no problem doing so. And don't think for a second that you can turn it around on me. I can almost promise that I'm better at hiding things than you."

Margot nods. She opens her mouth to speak, then snaps it shut and leaves the room without a word.

I note that my eyes are stinging, but I do little to stop it.

"Hey," Henry whispers, grabbing my hand. "You're okay, Amelie. You handled everything so well."

"Let's just go home," I say quietly. He's trying to read what's on my face, but I can't tell if he's succeeding tonight. "I'm tired."

He nods. "I have to find Liz first. I can't leave her here."

"I've already got her," I tell him. "She was in the hallway with mascara running into her *mouth.* I tossed her in the van and told her we'd take her home."

Henry smiles lightly at that, though I think he's trying to keep his face neutral for my sake. "Okay, then," he says, pressing a kiss to my hair. "Let's go home."

56

___

HENRY

Amelie and I practically throw ourselves into the back of the van as Meg speeds away from the auction hall. To my knowledge, her and Jensen were supposed to leave ages ago, but they refused to go unless all of us were okay. I'd be flattered if I hadn't been yelled at for closing the door too slowly.

My mind is racing as I settle myself on the bench seat beside Liz. Amelie lowers herself next to me, absentmindedly untwisting the fabric that gathered around her hips as we ran out here. She looks worn down—her eyes are dull, and her face hasn't shifted expressions since we left the storage room.

I have no idea if the auction is still going on. Whatever is happening in the bidding area right now is completely lost on me, but I'm petty enough to hope that it ended. That everyone got mad and withdrew. It's unlikely, but it would be a treat for my pride.

"Alright, kiddos," Meg says from the driver's seat. "What happened? Why do I have two freeloaders in here?"

"I'll go first," Amelie says with a sigh. "Roman and Margot did all of this."

"*Margot?*" Jensen and Meg say in unison.

Amelie nods. "Yeah. She was the one doing all the work, I guess. Swapping the pieces, listing them..."

"Why would she *do* that?" Meg asks exasperatedly.

"I don't know," Amelie says, clearly trying to shut down the topic. I can tell by her body language that the knowledge of everything is weighing on her, and I wish more than anything that I could do something about it. "But before that, Jen and I found the paintings and brought them out here." She motions to the paintings across from us, balanced lightly against the window. "Then I found Liz, and I dragged her out of there, because who would want to stay?"

"Not me," Liz says, then clasps a hand over her mouth for interrupting. "Sorry. Keep going."

Amelie does. "When I went back inside, I heard Roman's voice. I hid in the hall for a bit, and then I heard Roman telling everything to Henry, and *bam.* I recorded his confession on my phone."

She says it so casually that the van drops silent for ten seconds.

"I'm sorry, what?" Jensen says, turning so he can see her from the passenger seat. "You got it?"

"Yep. Backed up and everything."

"Are you turning it in?" Lizzy asks, her loud voice coming across as quiet now. "Are you getting him in trouble?"

Amelie shakes her head confidently. "No. I think we have a sort of agreement now."

"Care to say what that is?" Meg asks.

Amelie turns to me and studies my face. She's trying to see what I want; what I think is the best option. Telling her team wouldn't result in havoc—at least, I don't *think*—but I sort of like the idea of keeping it quiet.

Just between the two of us.

So I give her the slightest shake of my head. It isn't instruction. It isn't even a request; by the look on her face, I know she's thinking the exact same thing.

A secret, I imagine she's thinking. *Something just for us.*

"No," she says, leaning her head on my shoulder. She grabs my hand and twines our fingers together, expelling a heavy breath once she's comfortable. "I think I'll keep it to myself for now."

"Alright," Meg answers, not caring half as much as I thought she did. "Well, I have a better question. What are we doing with these pieces?" She hitches a thumb over her shoulder, gesturing to the three canvases taking up most of our space.

"Those'll go to my apartment," I say, leaning forward so I'm better heard. "I'll take them whenever."

"Are we stopping at your apartment?"

I start to say *yes,* then stop, because I don't know anything about this. Is it wise to drag these up to my penthouse so late at night? I mean, they are *my* pieces, but I could understand it looking suspicious.

"It's late," Amelie says, looking up at me. "You and Liz can just stay with us for the night. We'll transport them tomorrow."

Before I have a chance to respond, Liz gasps. "*Really*? We haven't done something like this in so long!"

"I know!" Amelie reaches over my lap to grab Liz's hand. I try to shrink back out of the way but end up failing. I'm simply stuck between them. "It'll be so fun. You can sleep in my bed if you like. I've got silk sheets."

"I don't sleep on anything *but*," Liz says solemnly. "Where will everyone else sleep, though? Is there only one bed?"

"Meg and Jensen usually share the couch..." Amelie's voice trails off, and she gives me a sheepish smile.

I nod. "I assume I'll be sleeping on the floor."

"I'll give you pillows," she promises. "Lots."

"That really doesn't help when you're sleeping on tile."

"I've got a rug, too. A fuzzy one."

"My apartment isn't even far. I can just walk."

"You *want* to stay, though." She tips her head at me, and I sigh. I think she's finally learned that I'll do anything if she looks at me like that. I didn't hide it as well as I'd planned to.

"Yes," I say. "I do."

"Then it's settled." Amelie leans into me once more, so I toss my arm over her shoulders, holding her to my chest. "You'll sleep on the floor."

"How exciting," I say flatly, and she laughs against my side.

No one says a word until the van is parked again. Meg pulls

into an alley, and once we're all out of the vehicle, I help Jensen cover it with old tarps. It looks sketchier than just about anything, and yet again, I wonder how these three manage to stay so undercover. They have more luck than anyone else I've encountered.

The five of us make our way through the back entrance and to the elevator. As soon as Amelie hits the button to her floor, Liz grabs onto her hand and sighs. "I'll need to borrow clothes from you, if that's alright. I simply cannot sleep in my day clothes—*especially* not this dress."

"You can choose any of my pajamas," Amelie replies, patting Liz's arm. "And you can use all my products and things. I have three different makeup removers and a counter full of lotions."

"*Really?*"

"Really," Jensen mutters. "You can't move without knocking something over."

I grin to myself as the elevator doors open. The oddity of this situation should throw me off, but it doesn't. Strangely enough, being here feels like it could become something normal. It feels better than any interaction I've had in my own home for years.

Jensen unlocks the apartment, and we file in behind him. Liz and Amelie instantly go to her room, emerging moments later with a few stacks of clothing in their arms each. I don't know why they're all necessary for a one-night stay, but they must have their reasons.

"Jenny," Amelie says, and Jensen's head snaps up. "Get Henry some clothes."

He stares at her blankly for a second, then walks into the same room that she just left. I follow, assuming that it's what I'm supposed to do, though I can't really be sure. He gives me no clue as to whether I'm supposed to be here or not.

Jensen goes right to the dresser and yanks open a drawer. He drags out a pair of sweatpants and a plain white shirt, then hands both to me. I thank him and wait for him to leave so I can change, but he doesn't.

He just sort of stares at me, like my being here is inconveniencing him personally. It shouldn't intimidate me; really, it shouldn't. But it does. Jensen is unnerving for reasons I have yet to figure out, though it may be because I've never once seen him smile.

"I don't like you," he says casually, confirming my already existing suspicions.

I give him a stiff nod, because I'm not sure how to respond.

"At all," he clarifies.

I clear my throat. "I gathered that."

Jensen nods and collects some clothes for himself. "But Amelie does. So welcome around, I guess."

"Thank...you?"

He mumbles something under his breath before walking out of the room.

I laugh to myself once he's gone, then close the door behind him. Right as I go to undo my tie, though, Amelie says, "Henry. Come to the living room, please."

I do.

And when I get there, she, Liz, and Meg are standing over the box of fraudulent money my dad gave them.

"We should do something with that, right?" She asks. "Logically."

Jensen steps out of the hall, having already changed into his clothes—the exact same thing he gave me—and nods. "Probably."

"What is there to do?" I ask.

Amelie chews on her lip. "I don't know. I don't want to keep it, and I'd never use it. Maybe we could toss it in the dumpster? But that might raise questions. It *looks* real. I just—"

"We could set it on fire."

Every eye turns to Lizzy when she offers up the suggestion. "What?" She shrugs. "That would get rid of it."

"We could," Amelie says slowly. "There *is* a firepit on the roof. I don't know if it's really allowed for use, but..."

Silence, and then Meg says, "I'll get the lighter fluid."

"I'll get the matches," Jensen mutters.

Lizzy claps. "I'll find some marshmallows."

57

AMELIE

The night didn't end as I expected it to, but I can't say I'm mad about it.

I'm sitting on a roof in my pajamas, wrapped in a blanket, having a bonfire kindled with stacks of cash. Liz has burned more marshmallows than she's eaten, and Meg keeps throwing them at a pigeon on the ledge.

This is not the most legal thing we've ever done, but it certainly isn't the most *illegal* either.

It's freezing up here, and my blanket is doing very little to warm me. The only chairs we could find were those metal fold-up ones, so I didn't expect us to be camped out here for long. It's been half an hour, though, and it doesn't look like anyone has any intention of leaving soon.

"Marshmallow?" Liz asks, holding the burnt blob at arm's length. "Anyone? They keep burning."

I grin. We didn't have anything to roast marshmallows on, so Liz dismantled one of my wire hangers in substitution. It's not as inefficient as I thought it would be, though I guarantee it isn't her preference. It's short and flimsy and quite sharp on the end. "No, thank you."

"Sure," Jensen says, leaning forward so he can take it from Liz.

She grins as he slips the marshmallow off the end, holding it awkwardly for a moment before taking a bite out of it. I'm waiting for his face to turn in disgust, given that the thing was literally charred, but his face remains straight.

Liz sighs and sticks another onto the hanger. "You know, I think this is a wonderful omen."

"For *what*?" Meg asks, shifting slightly in her seat. She's directly next to Jensen, who dragged her chair closer to his the second they sat down. She didn't elbow him. Didn't even threaten it. Something definitely happened between the two of them while I was gone, but I'll be on my deathbed before they offer up details. They like their secrets, and that's okay.

"For what's to come, obviously," Liz says. "Think of it as a metaphor. We're burning something bad—my dad's ugly, fake money—and we're gaining something good."

"Burnt marshmallows?" Henry asks.

Liz shakes her head. *"Treats."*

"No offense, but this isn't really a treat for anyone," Meg says, gesturing to the flaming marshmallow on the end of the hanger. Liz gasps and whips the thing around, which results in the tiny ball of fire being flung off the roof.

Onto the sidewalk. Where there are people walking.

"Oops," she says quietly, peering over the ledge. "It's...fine. By the looks of it, it landed on an awning."

"Is it still on *fire*?" Henry asks.

Liz shrugs. "Doesn't look it."

"Fair enough," I murmur, holding my palm out. "Give me one, please"

She complies. Within seconds, Liz hands me a completely torched marshmallow. I wince as I take it off the wire, and I practically hold my breath as I chew through the thick layer of char on the outside. This girl has every ounce of my adoration, but she cannot make a normally cooked marshmallow to save her life.

"You're making a bad face," Henry whispers to me.

I lick my lips. "I'm smiling."

"I think *grimacing* is a more accurate term."

I close my eyes and swallow the last of the bite. It manages to get stuck in my throat, but I persevere until my mouth is empty. "That was lovely."

"It was burnt," Liz says.

"It was," I agree. "And it kind of tasted like lighter fluid."

"That's...not good." She frowns and tosses the rest of the marshmallows into the smoldering fire. "Well, then. Shall we call it quits?"

Jensen leans forward. He stares into the fire pit and gives a bored shrug, clearly deeming the night over. With a sigh, he grabs the bucket of water we brought in case this went poorly and dumps it onto the fire, dousing any of the remaining flames. "Yep. Let's go back inside."

So we do. I stand and instantly shake my legs out. They're cold and numb and asleep, and I prefer to *not* walk on pins and needles with each step. I stomp a few hundred times before even walking toward the door, blanket wrapped around my shoulders like a cape.

We all disperse once we're inside the apartment. Liz goes to the bathroom, probably to examine my makeup counter. Meg and Jensen go directly to the couch, gathering all the blankets we discarded there and setting them aside. I pick them up and take them to my room, then snag a few extra pillows out of my closet.

I attempt to build some form of cot on the ground. It's a very loose term for what I've got set up—really, it's just a pile of blankets and a couple pillows, but it's all I had.

Though it does sort of look like something you'd find in a prison cell.

"*That's* my bed?" Henry says from the doorway.

I grin and turn around. "I'm sorry. I tried."

He crosses his arms. "I'll survive."

I look away from him, because even though Jensen gave him the rattiest, most worn clothes that he owns, Henry still manages to look good. I don't even know how that's possible.

To distract myself, I sit at the end of my bed and slip my feet under the comforter. My toes are still freezing, as is the rest of me, but I'm too lazy to grab a sweater from my closet. The duvet will have to do.

"How are you?" Henry asks quietly, coming to sit next to me.

"I smell like wood smoke, so not great," I say, and he laughs. "But other than that...I don't know. I really don't want to talk about it." I look at him, and he nods. "How are you?"

"Still stunned," he admits. "I should've expected it long before any of this, but even after he *told* me, I still hoped it wasn't true. It's just..." He sighs. "I don't know. It's better to know the truth, though."

"It's okay to be hurt," I tell him. "Even if you 'should've known', or you expected it, it's still okay to feel that way."

Henry looks at me, his brows drawn together. "You mean that." He says it like a statement, not a question, but I know that he's asking me.

I nod. "It's the truth. You can feel whatever you want, Henry, and it will be valid in this situation. You don't have to make sense of it all."

"I feel like I need to," he says. "For my mom and Liz."

"But that isn't your job," I tell him. "However they handle it is their thing, just like this is yours. You can't take care of them unless you sort through your own thoughts first."

Instead of responding, Henry cracks his knuckles and stares at the wall. He chews on his lip mindlessly, and I know he's thinking of what to do next, but not knowing where to start.

And then, I realize that somewhere along the way, I've learned how to read him again.

The revelation shocks me, because it wasn't a sudden thing. It wasn't even a choice I made. It was simply putting the pieces back together. Re-assembling the puzzle that was broken years ago.

Now, I remember that the corner of his mouth tugs down when he's aggravated. That he's fighting a smile when he looks at the ground, right between his shoes. I remember that he avoids eye contact when he's trying not to laugh, that he clenches his jaw when he's mulling over his words. I know that he glares at me when he's amused but wishes he weren't.

I know *him*.

He knows me.

And for once, I don't feel scared of it.

I *want* it. I want him to know everything about me.

Henry suddenly touches my arm, a soft brush of his skin over mine. He holds my eyes as he says, "I want to paint you."

I just stare at him for a moment, because the words almost don't register in my mind.

"A portrait," he clarifies, smiling faintly at the look on my face. "Would you let me do that?"

I swallow, my throat feeling tight. His words from what seems like *ages* ago burrow into my mind.

I've always painted the same things. The things I care about. The things I want to preserve forever.

"Yeah," I say, my voice monotone. There's got to be a better answer, but I don't know it. "You can."

Henry laughs, the sound light. Easy. But instead of laughing along, I lean forward and take his face in my hands. He goes silent as I kiss across his face, across the bridge of his nose. His jaw. His neck. His mouth, just once, and when I pull away from him, he sighs and takes me into his arms. I go slack against his chest, feeling lighter than I have in years. His presence, his words, his touch—they bring me back to myself. They make me feel whole.

I never wanted someone to define me. To make me feel anything so overwhelming. Being seen as a counterpart of someone was a great fear of mine. I started to believe that loving someone like this would ruin *me*, but I'm finding that that isn't the case.

I am not defined by him, and he is not defined by me. But I feel at home with him, and that isn't wrong. Feeling safe with him isn't something to be scared of.

Henry pulls away from me and holds me at arm's length. He studies my face, and I think he's about to say something, but I talk first.

I talk before my brain can fully catch up to my mouth.

"I love you," I tell him. "A lot."

Once the words are out in the open, I don't understand how I kept them inside for so long.

Henry's face is so shocked that I actually laugh. It's probably the most poorly timed laugh of my life, but I don't care to try and stop it. "What?" He whispers.

"I love you," I say again. "And now, I realize that no matter what happens, I will always grow to love you. I will always find my way to you, Henry. I promise."

He takes a shaky breath, and I grin at the blush that crawls across his skin. "I love you, Ames," he tells me. "More than I know what to do with."

"I can't believe I found you again," I say, toying with a thread on my comforter. "Though we could've gotten off to a better start this time, hm?"

He shakes his head once. "No."

"*No*?"

"No." His voice grows quieter, almost a whisper as he says, "I never told you, did I?"

I shake my head once when his eyes find mine. "Tell me what?"

"That I hated it at first." The statement makes my stomach drop, but the subtle smile on his lips tells me that I don't need to be worried. "I hated that I was the one to catch you in the museum. That *I* had the responsibility of knowing what you were doing. It ate away at me. Tormented me. Conned me out of *many* nights of sleep, but I realize it now—it was a reminder."

I frown. "A reminder for what?"

He grins, just barely. "That if anyone is going to ruin me, if anyone is going to consume me this way, I want it to be you."

I swallow, my eyes darting between his. "I want it to be you, too."

His smile grows brighter, and I realize that he's right.

We've ruined each other for anyone else. Any*thing* else. And we've done so willingly.

I have no doubt it's the best thing I've ever chosen.

Henry leans forward then, his hands going to either side of me, but before I can even react, the bedroom door swings open.

"*Okay*, geez. Sorry." Liz covers her eyes, and I laugh at the sight of her. She's wearing a headband with alien eyes, a jelly patch under each eye, and a hot pink lip mask. "I should've knocked, but I didn't think—"

"It's fine," I say, pushing my hair behind my ears. "You're fine."

"I mean, if you *need*, I can sleep in the living room, but—"

"No, Liz." Henry sighs and stands up, then gracefully throws a pillow at Liz's head. She ducks out of the way before it can make contact, but the movement manages to rid her of one eye patch. "I'll be right back."

"Toothbrushes are under the counter," I call, and he throws a wave over his shoulder before leaving the room.

"He's so shy," Liz says, rolling her eyes. "He got what tact I was supposed to have."

"Your lack of tact is my favorite thing about you, Liz." I grin as I burrow into my bed. Lizzy does the same, removing the headband and setting it nicely on the side table. She removes all the sticky things from her face and puts them in my waste bin, then looks at me.

"I'm tired," she says solemnly. "I thought I'd be talkative, but really, I don't see myself lasting another moment."

I sigh heavily. "Thank God. I'm exhausted."

"We'll just have to do this properly soon."

"We will." I pull the sheets a little higher over myself. "Sleep well, Liz."

"Night, Ames."

I'm almost fully asleep by the time Henry comes back in and presses a kiss to my forehead, then turns the lamp off, cloaking the room in darkness.

58

———

HENRY

When I wake up, I'm convinced there's an arrow shoved through my skull.

It takes me a moment to identify a few things—what day it is, where I am, and what the noise is in my ear canal. I know that I'm at Amelie's, because her dress from last night is slung over her desk chair. The events of yesterday hit me like a truck when I sit up, along with a decent amount of back pain from sleeping on the ground. Amelie's 'pillow bed' was a complete and total failure, but I'd rather sleep on it for the rest of my life than let her know that.

The tiresome noise, though, is my phone.

It's ringing loudly, though I can't pinpoint where from. Did I even take it out of my pocket last night? I was thankful to be away from the device for a bit. I knew my dad wouldn't be contacting me, mainly because he can't, but I know that something will come to be from last night. Something on the internet, or a news article that I don't need to see.

I slowly stand up off the ground and paw around the night-stand for my glasses. They're right near the edge, close to falling, so I grab them before I knock them off. Amelie must be up already because the only person in her bed is Liz. She's slowly waking, sitting up with the speed of an injured turtle. I sneak out of the room before she actually opens her eyes.

My clothes are right where I left them—folded neatly in one of the kitchen chairs. As I'd suspected, my phone is ringing itself out of my pocket. Lizzy and I must be the only ones here, because the living room is empty as well.

I grab my phone and answer the call without checking who it is. "Hey."

"Henry, my sweet boy. I'm so sorry."

Mom.

Her voice is a shock this early in the morning. "Are you okay?"

"I'm fine." Her voice cracks, like she's been crying, and it makes my stomach roll. "You?"

"I'm fine," I return, racking my brain for what she could be worried about.

"Your dad told me everything last night," she says, answering my question without me having to voice it. I have the urge to ask what version of the story he told her, but I know that isn't what she needs. "I'm sorry, Henry. I didn't know. You know if I had—"

"I know, Mom," I say softly. "I trust you."

"I should've done something."

"You couldn't have. Please don't worry yourself over this."

"I *could* have," she says, sounding determined. "I knew something was wrong, but I foolishly let it go, and..." She begins mumbling something that the phone doesn't catch. It takes a moment for her to speak clearly again, her voice turning perky. "Would you visit me today? I've missed you, honey. Elizabeth, too. Drag her along."

"Is—"

"No. He isn't here."

I release a breath. "This afternoon, then. We'll be there."

"Wonderful. Your sister has been keeping me updated on all your *adventures*, and now, I'd like your side. She told me...Amelie Benoit is back?"

"Yeah," I say, my mouth forming an involuntary grin. "She's back."

"That's lovely," she says solemnly. "I liked her, Henry. She was good for you."

"She was. Still is."

Mom laughs. "Your father is scared of that girl. Downright *terrified.*"

"Really?" I say, hoping my tone is curious enough to get her talking.

"Certainly," she replies, taking the bait. "Even more so now. He's worried sick over what happened last night. It gives me quite the laugh."

I can't help the shock that courses through me. If she knows what Amelie did, what Amelie *does,* then...

"He really told you everything."

"No," she admits. "He didn't. But for every dollar that man spends to get his way, I've got a set of eyes somewhere."

Her admission sparks a whole new set of questions, along with a slight bit of fear. No—*fear* isn't the right word. *Respect* is more accurate.

"Can I ask you something?" I say into the phone.

"Of course."

"Why don't you use it? The dirt you have on him?"

Mom's voice is smooth, lethally soft as she says, "I will, honey. Someday."

That answer is enough to have me running instances through my mind, trying to recall if I've ever picked up these clues. I've always seen my mom as an oblivious, innocent thing that knew nothing of what my dad did. She's a strong woman, but she seemed to cower down in his presence. Now, I realize it was an act.

My parent's marriage is a web of secrets, but it isn't as one-sided as I'd always thought.

Before I can say anything in response, the front door swings open behind me. I turn to see Amelie, Meg and Jensen carrying a drink carrier and a brown paper bag. They must've gone to the patisserie early this morning.

"BREAKFAST IS HE—" Amelie cuts herself off when she sees

the phone in my hand, then covers her mouth with her palm. "I'm sorry!" She whispers. "I didn't realize."

"Is that Amelie?" My mom says through the phone. "Let me speak with her."

I take the phone away from my ear and hold it out to Amelie. "It's my mom. She wants to talk to you."

As soon as she registers what I've said, her face softens. She takes the phone from me and hands me the drink carrier. "Hi, Mrs. Arlington."

Their conversation picks up almost immediately. I catch bits and pieces at first, but Amelie sneaks away to the bathroom as the others dole out the breakfast stock on the counter. They must've raided the place, honestly; there's no way five people will eat all of this in one sitting, but I'm not opposed to trying. I didn't eat last night before the event, and my only other option was the lighter fluid marshmallows.

"Good morning!" Liz strolls into the kitchen behind me, her voice much too loud for just waking up. She's wearing something that I assume came from Amelie's closet, given that it isn't her dress from last night. "Oh—who got breakfast?"

"We did," Jensen says, dropping into one of the kitchen chairs. "Amelie dealt with the coffee orders."

As if on cue, Amelie comes back into the room and hands me my phone. She's grinning like a cat, looking positively joyous as she says, "Your mom invited me to dinner."

"*Ooh!*" Liz is beaming. "Are you coming?"

"Might as well," Amelie says flippantly, digging through the bags on the counter. She removes two cups from the drink carrier and hands one to my sister. "I got you my order because I don't know what you like. It's good, though. Promise."

Lizzy takes the cup and tips it back. Her brows draw together as she swallows the drink, and she pauses for a moment before saying, "You're a goddess, really. This is amazing."

Amelie laughs and takes a drink of her own coffee. I, on the other hand, am simply trying to find my own. There are three other cups in the holder, and my brain isn't fully functional yet. I pop the lids off each cup and look for mine, rather than just asking which it is.

"That one," Amelie says, tapping the lid of the only one I haven't opened.

I hum. "Black coffee?"

She fake shivers. "Uh-huh."

"I'm shocked you aren't trying to convert me."

"When I *do* you won't suspect it."

I laugh and dig through one of the paper bags. "I'll always be wary of you, Ames."

She tries to hide her smile behind her cup, but fails drastically.

We stand around in silence, slowly draining our cups and picking at the pastries. It's quite a while before anyone says anything, and when someone finally does, it's almost startling.

"Alright," Amelie says when she's finished her coffee. "We've got a very full day ahead of us. Lots of things to do."

"We have to drag three pieces to Hank's apartment," Meg reminds her. "We've had worse days."

"Megan, *please*," Amelie sighs. "Let me have a win."

Meg laughs dryly. "Fine. We've got a full day ahead of us. Lots of things to do."

Amelie nods before turning to Lizzy and I. "You two, grab your things. I'm ready to get this over with."

The task is not quite as simple as *getting it over with.*

I tell Meg to pull the van around back so we don't block off the main entrance. Amelie and I go inside first to let the doorman know we'll be loading a few things onto the elevator, but instead of giving us the go-ahead, he tells us that it's been out of order since yesterday evening.

Which leaves Jensen and I to carry the paintings up twenty-one flights of stairs.

It could always be worse, I suppose, but I won't pretend it's fun.

It takes about half an hour for us to get all of my paintings into my apartment. The routine is quite simple: Jensen and I drag them up the stairs, Liz opens the door, and we set them in my studio. Then Amelie claps for us. Jensen sighs and shakes his head with each round of applause, which only makes her clap louder.

"Last one," he yells as we make our way to my door. Amelie swings it open as we drag *Lover of Mine* inside, both panting and mildly annoyed. We wordlessly carry it to my studio and set it in the corner, far away from my window. I'm aware that my piece wasn't stolen because of its visibility, but it's still engraved into my brain to be extra careful.

Once I'm satisfied with the state of my studio, I stumble back to the kitchen and fill a glass with water, then drink it in one go. Jensen sidles up next to me and does the same, grabbing a mug from my cabinet and filling it to the brim.

"Thank God that's done," I mumble, leaning back against the counter. Amelie hops up on the granite to sit beside me. She takes extra care to press her arm against mine, and I'm embarrassingly aware of it. "How are we celebrating?"

"Mojitos," Liz says, walking into my apartment at that exact moment. Meg trails behind her, holding a pitcher and a stack of plastic cups. The two of them drop into chairs at the table and start filling the cups.

Amelie blinks. "We're drinking at ten in the morning?"

"Of course not," Liz says, waving a hand. "It's non-alcoholic."

"Ah." Amelie takes a cup off the table. She takes a sip, then looks at Liz like she's shocked. "Have you considered becoming a bartender?"

"I have," Lizzy says. "Multiple times, actually. I love mixing things, but I'd rather die than come home smelling like a bar every day. I can't wash my hair that often."

"Oh, understandable," Meg says, sounding one-hundred percent sympathetic.

"You know," Jensen says, taking the seat next to Meg. "I would say that this is a send-off, but apparently we aren't parting ways. Which is *your* doing." He points at Amelie. "You've got this all tangled up."

"Which is fun!" She argues. "We all get along. It's good. You're allowed to have more than two friends, Jenny."

He sighs. "I'm aware. But I'm a simple man."

"You literally are not," Meg argues. "And anyways, this is fine. More people for Mimi and Olive to torment during poker."

"Those ladies are going to eat you alive," Amelie mumbles, looking at me.

I raise a brow. "The women who scout the lobby?"

"The very ones."

Laughing, I cross my arms. "That'll be fine."

Amelie smiles and presses a kiss to my shoulder, a touch that lasts only a moment before she gets distracted by Betty. The cat jumps onto the counter and immediately sits on Amelie's lap, garnering every bit of her attention.

"You know," Liz starts with a sigh, "I really do like this. I want to thank you, Henry."

"For?" I ask.

"Dragging Amelie back into our lives."

Amelie grins at Liz, almost like she agrees with her, but I shake my head. "That wasn't my doing."

"No, it was," Amelie says. "If you hadn't asked me for help, none of this would've happened." She pauses. "Well, you didn't *ask*, but you know."

Jensen snorts. "Yeah, man, you went about that poorly."

"Thank you for the input."

"But it *ended* well," Liz says. "Now, I have someone to share my things with again."

Amelie sighs contentedly. "It's my favorite part of all of this."

I laugh quietly. It's hard for me to rationalize any of this—the people sitting in front of me and how they got here. If I hadn't been so desperate to appease my father's wishes, I likely never would've spoken to Amelie again. If I *had*, it would've gone differently. Probably a lot smoother than this whole charade went.

But I like this outcome. A lot.

"You're right," I say, giving a shrug. "You're all welcome."

"*Pssh.*" Liz rolls her eyes. "Don't get cocky."

I shake my head. "I'm not. I'd never live it down with this crowd."

Amelie nudges me in the ribs. "We're a good crowd, Henry. You've never been in such fabulous company."

"I know it," I say.

She looks up at me, a faint smile resting on her lips, and I realize how much I mean those words. This is the strangest, most unconventional way I've ever come about meeting a group of people, and yet, I wouldn't swap this situation for another.

It brought me back to her.

And whether or not anything about this moment stays the same, I know we will.

EPILOGUE
AMELIE (SIX MONTHS LATER)

The alarms stop blaring as soon as I pry the canvas's edge off the wall.

A strange turn of events, really. From the few times I've tripped an alarm, I know that they don't just *go* off. Though it isn't usually my fault. Jensen would deny that, but it's the truth.

The piece I'm working with is hideous. Art is subjective, yes, but this one truly has no appeal. It's got every color of the rainbow, and they're all mixed in a contrasting manner. Splotches of red, green, and purple pool on one end; blue, yellow, and brown take up the other. It's disgusting. Tearing it off the wall is going to be *so* therapeutic.

After everything happened with Roman and Margot, I gained a newfound appreciation for the rush I get when working. A sense of revenge, though it isn't heavy. This is still what I love, and it's still for *me*, but it doesn't hurt to have an extra layer of respect for the job.

Even though it's been months, I still haven't spoken with Margot. Neither of us have broken our no-contact streak, and my parents no longer push us to talk. I didn't tell them what happened, so I guess she did. Quite frankly, I don't want to imagine how the conversation went.

So I simply don't.

With a sigh, I slip the file back under the canvas. Doing this by myself is much more annoying than I'd expected. I've done it alone before, but it's been a while. I didn't realize how much I actually relied on Jensen and his annoying man strength.

He and Meg left me to my own devices. They disappeared last night, basically out of nowhere, by leaving a note on the counter that read *GONE FISHING*. I haven't heard from them since. I presume they're having an impromptu Vegas wedding. They're probably at the altar right now, wearing denim outfits and cowboy boots. An Elvis impersonator will officiate. The ring bearer will wear a phantom mask. It's so perfect, I'm tearing up just thinking about it.

No, wait. I've got drywall in my eye.

"Why are you crying?" Henry asks, appearing behind me. He sounds rather amused for the question he's asking. "Is this piece too ugly for you to lay eyes on?"

"Yes," I say, rubbing my eye with embarrassing vigor. "It's horrible."

He laughs quietly and takes the file out of my hand, prying the last bit off the wall that I couldn't get. Carefully, he lowers the canvas to the ground, and when he's done, he stands in front of me.

"This is strange for me, as you can imagine," he says, passing me the file. He's wearing a faint look of enjoyment, one he's trying to hide, but it doesn't fool me. Nothing fools me with him anymore.

"I think you're having fun," I say. "Just a little."

He crosses his arms, and I swear on everything I possess, I will never get tired of that sight. "Even if I were, I'd never admit it."

He totally wouldn't, but I know him well enough to know that he *is*, in fact, enjoying himself. It might be because we're at The Gallery, taking a piece that's labeled with an *anonymous* artist tag. According to Henry, these unlabeled pieces are ones that Roman made himself as fillers for the empty spaces.

Which explains why it's so ugly.

I really don't understand who's buying these.

All in all, though, this whole thing isn't so out of sorts. I didn't force Henry into this, or even ask for his help.

He *volunteered.*

Apparently, I've been complaining about my inbox being too full for too long. I told him that I can't work without Meg and Jensen, but he told me to take up a job for The Gallery. So I did.

I broke in the south window, and Henry took care of the 'security' side of things.

It's a story for the books, in my humble opinion.

Things are going great for him—Henry, I mean. He pulled his pieces from The Gallery just weeks after the auction, and he got an offer for another museum in no time. Now, he's their main attraction, and he isn't always on the verge of running out of pieces. He works at his own pace and creates whatever he wants.

Which is likely why most of his works are centered around *me.*

I can't say that I don't love it.

"We should go," I say suddenly, pushing myself off the wall. "The alarms being off really kills the suspense, you know?"

"You don't need the added anxiety," Henry says, leaning over to pick up the canvas. I took a job for a smaller piece tonight, mainly because we don't have the van. That's probably what Meg and Jensen took to Vegas.

Neither of us speak as we walk toward the window I shattered. I follow behind Henry, unabashedly staring at the way his arms look while he's carrying the painting. It's *allowed.* Expected, even.

"I can feel you staring at me," he says knowingly.

I step in front of him and climb out the window before he does, then watch to make sure he doesn't cut himself on the glass. The break isn't clean, though I tried my hardest. "I don't know why you always act shocked."

"I'm not," he says, walking to the car. I start to follow, then gasp and bolt right back to the window. *How on earth could I forget?*

Holding my breath, I crouch down beside the pane and dig the cassette tape out of my pocket. With shaking hands, I balance it against the windowsill, hoping it'll stay there until morning.

The label on the front reads '*The Dealer*', and I hope that he's the one to find it.

It's not a calling card. I'm not stupid enough to leave one of those. It's just...a reminder. To let Roman know that I still have the upper hand.

Henry starts the car engine, so I sprint down the alley and hop in the front seat without hesitation. He's already got the canvas loaded, propped against our seats, covered with a blanket. Before Henry even reaches for the gearshift, he stares at me with a heavily concentrated expression.

I blink in confusion. "What?"

He lifts his hand and brushes it through my hair, frowning at whatever he sees. "You've got drywall in your hair."

I laugh as I grab his face and kiss his jaw, leaving a perfect, red lipstick stain on his skin. He catches sight of it in the rearview and grins. "Every single time."

"You'd hate if I stopped."

"I know." He puts the car in drive. "Don't."

I grab his hand, tangle his fingers with mine. "I never plan to."

He's the only promise I've ever been sure that I'll keep.

ACKNOWLEDGMENTS

There were so, *so* many times while writing Bad for Business where I second guessed myself. Where I looked in the mirror and said, *"Wow! This book really sucks."* (Okay, not literally. But very metaphorically.)

And still, despite that, we're here. My second book is completed, and I love her more than life! This book is everything to me. These characters spoke to me so strongly, and I adore everything about them. They are the best and worst parts of myself, the parts I'm not proud of and the parts that I wear on my sleeve everyday. I hope you enjoyed reading their story, and if you did, please consider leaving a review on Goodreads and Amazon! It makes us indie authors happier than just about anything (or maybe I'm easy to please).

Okay, let's move on from me. Firstly, I want to thank Rachel, who was probably the most influential person that I worked with on this book. She's the one who read my first draft and talked me off the ledge of deleting the entire document (because it was BAD, guys. So incredibly bad). Thank you for enduring that absolute dumpster fire and helping me shape this book into something that I love. For the hours of voice memos and facetimes spent working out the kinks in this book. Thank you for being the best editor/proofreader/bestie a girl could ask for. I'll never take what you do for me for granted.

Next, of course, my very dedicated (very iconic) group of beta readers! I appreciate you guys so much. Thank you to Meaghen, Sophia, Charli, and Jaime for reading this book early and yapping about it with me! I'm so grateful for your support and enthusiasm about Henry and Amelie, as well as the crazy comments you left on the doc. I reread them everyday for a giggle.

To Niamh, my best girl, who let me talk for hours about my characters as well as my upcoming works. Thank you for withstanding the voice memos and snippets I send you constantly! I love you and your mind so much. (Also—thank you for being the #1 Betty stan. It's hard work, but someone has to do it!)

To Hannah, my favorite cover designer and designated rant recipient. Thank you for letting me talk about this book even when I made zero sense. I'm so thankful for the time you put into the cover art (which is STUNNING, is it not?!) and for the support you give me everyday.

To my family, who let me complain about my editing process even though it really *wasn't* that serious. I love you guys to no end. Thank you for always supporting me and lifting me up. I also want to specifically thank my grandparents. You guys asked me how this book was coming nearly everyday, and I can finally say that it's done! I'm so grateful for the love you guys show me. Thank you for caring so much about the things that mean a lot to me.

Finally, I'd like to thank YOU, reader! Thank you for taking a chance on this goofy little romance book that weaseled its way into my mind a couple years ago. This story turned into something that I never expected, but I truly couldn't be happier with the outcome of it! I hope that these characters connected with you like they did with me.

PS. Unofficially, I'd like to thank Sabrina Carpenter for writing the OG Bad for Business. She really did me a solid with that one!

Ames,

Do you know how much stamps cost? I didn't, and I've never been more appalled to find out an answer. It isn't much, though I truly don't understand why it must be a purchase at all. It's a piece of paper with glue on the back.

Anyway, I miss you. I'm not sure if your phone is down or something, but I haven't heard from you in a week and it's a strange feeling. I don't think we've gone a day without speaking, let alone multiple. I feel like I'm missing something that's well within reach.

I've never realized how heavily I rely on you to keep me laughing. Do you know that nobody has commented on the lack of flavor in my coffee all week? It's almost saddening how freely I'm allowed to drink black coffee. I do hope you'll be doubling up on your insults toward the beverage when I'm back home.

I hope everything is okay. Call or write to me when you get the chance. I have a lot to tell you.

Yours, Henry

Ames,

I ran through a sprinkler today. It was perhaps the most unpleasant experience I've had thus far at this place, though it's in a very close race with when my roommate dropped a container of cottage cheese on the rug. That was not pleasant, either.

All in all, though, I guess it's nothing. All I've been able to focus on as of late is the lack of you in my life. It's been weeks. I'm quite sure the problem isn't still your phone, given that you haven't written, either, though I guess it's possible.

If I've done something, I'm sorry. I miss you, Amelie.

I used to think you were the only good thing I had, and I'm starting to realize I was right. It's not the same without you, but I know you're doing incredible things back home. I can't wait to hear all about them.

Write back when you can. Please.

Yours, Henry

Ames,

I hope this finds you well. I've wondered for days if there's even a reason to write this, but I've decided that there is.

It's been a month since we've spoken, and I miss your voice. I miss hearing about your day and hearing your laugh. I miss you, and if I've done something to warrant you ignoring me, tell me. Let me fix it. I can't stand this silence between us when all I want is to be close to you.

I'll be back soon. We can talk then.

I'm sorry.

Yours, Henry

Amelie,

I understand. I'm sorry it took me so long.

If this is what you want, I won't write to you any longer.

All I've ever wanted is the best for you. I won't keep you
from it. That's never been my intention.

But if you change your mind in the future, find me.

I'm waiting, Amelie. You know that I am. I think you know
that I always will be.

Yours. Forever.
-Henry

ABOUT THE AUTHOR

Anna Grace writes books as a way to connect with others and escape reality. Born and raised in Missouri, she lives with her family and pets, most of which are cats. When she's not writing, she can be found with a book in her hand, always ready to discuss a current read—often to unwilling recipients. You can keep in touch with Anna on Instagram (@authorannagrace).